THE DREAM
DAUGHTER

DIANE CHAMBERLAIN is the bestselling author
of numerous novels including *Necessary Lies*,
The Silent Sister and *Pretending to Dance*. Her storylines
are often a combination of romance, family drama,
intrigue and suspense. She lives in North Carolina
with her partner, photographer John Pagliuca,
and her shelties, Keeper and Cole.

Visit dianechamberlain.com

By Diane Chamberlain

The Dream Daughter
The Stolen Marriage
Pretending to Dance
The Silent Sister
Necessary Lies
The Good Father
The Midwife's Confession
The Lies We Told
Secrets She Left Behind
Before the Storm
The Secret Life of CeeCee Wilkes
The Bay at Midnight
Her Mother's Shadow
The Journey Home (anthology)
Kiss River
The Courage Tree
Keeper of the Light
Summer's Child
Breaking the Silence
The Escape Artist
Reflection
Brass Ring
Lovers and Strangers
Fire and Rain
Secrets at the Beach House
(previously published as *Private Relations*)
Secret Lives
The Shadow Wife/Cypress Point

The Dance Begins (ebook short story)
The Broken String (ebook short story)
The First Lie (ebook short story)

Diane Chamberlain

THE DREAM DAUGHTER

PAN BOOKS

First published 2018 by St Martin's Press, New York

First published in the UK 2018 by Macmillan

First published in the UK in paperback 2018 by Macmillan

This edition first published 2019 by Pan Books
an imprint of Pan Macmillan
20 New Wharf Road, London N1 9RR
Associated companies throughout the world
www.panmacmillan.com

ISBN 978-1-5098-0858-8

3 5 7 9 8 6 4 2

A CIP catalogue record for this book is available from the British Library.

Typeset by Jouve (UK), Milton Keynes
Printed and bound by CPI Group (UK) Ltd, Croydon, CR0 4YY

Visit **www.panmacmillan.com** to read more about all our books
and to buy them. You will also find features, author interviews and
news of any author events, and you can sign up for e-newsletters
so that you're always first to hear about our new releases.

To John, for believing I could pull this off

THE DREAM DAUGHTER

Prologue

Carly

No one wanted to work with the man in the wheelchair.

"There's something strange about that guy," one of my fellow students warned me in the hall outside the PT ward. "If they try to assign you to him, say no."

I remembered his warning now as I stood in the doorway between my supervisor, Betty Connor, and the ward's director, Dr. Davies. Still, I was curious about the man who sat in the wheelchair by the window, a cast on his lower leg and foot. Crutches rested against the windowsill next to his chair. He was about a decade older than me, maybe thirty or so. He looked unkempt, his blond hair on the short side but tousled. His facial features were slack, his eyes half closed. I could see the shadow of stubble on his cheeks and chin.

"How about that patient for Caroline?" Betty asked Dr. Davies. "Broken ankle, is it?"

Dr. Davies nodded, light from the ward's windows bouncing off his glasses. "Displaced fracture of the lateral malleolus," he said, "followed by surgery."

Betty turned to me. "You haven't yet worked with a broken ankle, have you?" she asked, and I shook my head with some reluctance. I'd been a student intern in a private rehabilitation facility for the last two months, but this was my first time in the hospital ward and although I was excited to get started, my fellow student's warning echoed in my ears. *Say no.* Still, the man in the wheelchair looked harmless enough.

"I think it would be a good case for her," Betty said to Dr. Davies.

"I think not," he said. He was holding several manila folders in his hands and he tapped the top one with his knuckles. "The fellow's name is Hunter Poole," he said. "He sustained the broken ankle falling off a three-story building, or so he says, but we think he intentionally jumped. He's alive only because some shrubbery broke his fall. He refuses to learn to use crutches. None of our PTs have been able to get him to talk, much less engage in any therapy. He's suffering from depression and—"

"Oh, I think I heard about him," Betty cut him off. "Didn't he say he was working on the roof and just slipped?"

"That's what he told the driver of the ambulance, but his explanation doesn't hold water." Dr. Davies tucked his free hand into his pants pocket. "It was nine o'clock at night, for starters, and there were no tools found on the roof or the ground, so you tell me if that sounds like he was working. We have him on suicide watch. Next stop for him is the psychiatric unit if he doesn't begin to come around today or tomorrow."

"Well, you're right that he wouldn't be a good patient for Caroline," Betty said. She looked at me. "You need to focus on building your skills right now," she said. "You don't need an unmotivated, clinically depressed suicide risk, for heaven's sake."

I nodded in agreement.

"There isn't anything you can do for someone who won't cooperate," Dr. Davies said. "I plan to try to work with him myself today. Everyone else has given up."

The man raised his head slowly in our direction as if he knew we were talking about him and I felt his gaze lock onto mine. His eyes widened, brows lifting. Suddenly, he broke into a smile.

"You!" he nearly shouted, his voice so loud that several people in the room turned to look at me. "You're a physical therapist, right?" he asked. "I want to work with you." It was unnerving, the intensity of his gaze. The sudden disarming smile.

Oh God, I thought. Just what I needed. A crazy man for a patient.

"Me?" I said, almost to myself.

"You!" he said again. Then in a calmer voice, "Yes, please. Please work with me."

"I didn't know he could smile," Dr. Davies said to us under his breath. He turned to me. "Are you willing?"

"Is he . . . dangerous?" I asked in a whisper. I was hungry to work, but not to be murdered in the middle of the PT ward.

"If you're asking if he's psychotic," Dr. Davies said, "we don't think so, though he's so closed off that it's been hard to evaluate him. You're the first person he's responded to. It would be wonderful if you could get him to open up."

"I don't know about this." Betty looked concerned.

"Hey," the man called across the room, his voice softer now. "I didn't mean to scare you." He actually chuckled. "I'll do whatever you say," he added. "I promise."

He sounded harmless enough. "I'll do it," I told Dr. Davies, holding my hand out for the man's chart.

Dr. Davies handed me the top folder. "Main priority is getting him to use the crutches." He spoke quietly. "See what you can do."

"All right," I said, and I crossed the room toward the possibly suicidal man who was now grinning at me in a way that made me nervous. What did this guy want with me?

The large room had an almost electric atmosphere, very different from the somber private facility. WKIX played rock and roll over the loudspeaker and the Temptations sang "My Girl" as I dragged a chair from against the wall and placed it in front of the man so I could sit facing him.

"I'm Caroline Grant," I said, lowering myself to the chair. "Most people call me Carly."

He nodded, almost as if my name was no surprise to him.

"Hunter Poole," he said.

"Why me?" I asked.

"You remind me of someone," he said. "Someone I knew briefly. Dark eyes and the exact same hair—long and blond, only she wore hers parted in the middle. It was nothing . . . romantic or intimate." He flashed that grin again. "Nothing like that, so don't freak out. Just . . . it feels good to see you." His accent was Northern. New Jersey or New York, maybe.

"I remind you of someone you liked, then."

"Yes." He chuckled again for no reason I could discern. *He* is *crazy,* I thought. And hopefully harmless.

"I didn't know you . . . I mean *her* . . . well," he said, "but I—"

"You realize I'm not this person," I said firmly.

"Yes, of course. I'm not crazy. Though I know everyone here thinks I am."

"No, they don't." I tried to sound reassuring. "They just think you're depressed."

He nodded. "I am that," he said, suddenly very solemn.

"They have medication that might make you feel better," I said. "It could help lift your spirits."

"They have nothing that can help me," he said, "and the side effects of the medications are too great now."

This man was not suicidal. I doubted a suicidal person would care a lick about side effects.

"What do you mean, the side effects are too great *now?*"

He shook his head. "I don't know. Don't pay attention to anything I say."

"Is it your injury that has you so down?"

He looked away from me and I thought I saw the shine of tears in his eyes. "I lost someone I loved," he said.

"Oh." I sat back, surprised that he'd confided in me. "I'm sorry," I said. "Is that why you tried to . . . to hurt yourself?"

He turned to face me again. "Can we not talk about it?" he asked, dry-eyed now, and I wondered if I'd imagined the tears. "It's too hard to explain the truth and I don't want to lie to you."

"Of course," I said, touched by that explanation.

"Tell me about you instead." He looked at my left hand. "You're engaged?"

I looked down at my ring. Joe promised me a bigger diamond someday, but I wanted this one. I wanted this one forever. We would both graduate next month, me from the University of North Carolina, Joe from NC State, and our wedding would be the week after. Joe would graduate as a second lieutenant in the army after being in ROTC for four years and we'd move to Fort Eustis, Virginia, where he'd be stationed. I hoped I could get a PT job up there.

"Yes," I said, "I'm marrying a wonderful man. But we're not talking about me. We need to talk about *you* and how we're going to get you well again."

He sighed. "I'm not very motivated," he admitted.

"I understand," I said. "But you said you like me. Or at least, you like the person I remind you of, right?"

He nodded. "Very much," he said.

"Then help me succeed," I said conspiratorially, wondering if that was a terrible ploy. I would never tell Betty Connor I'd used it. "You're my first patient in this rehabilitation ward," I said. "Make me look good to my supervisor, all right?"

He laughed and I saw a sparkle in his blue eyes. A few heads turned in our direction. *The new girl got the suicidal guy to laugh.*

"All right," he said. "It's a deal."

We got down to business then. I demonstrated how to

use the crutches without putting weight on his ankle, and after a rough start, he got the hang of it. He was cooperative, doing everything I guided him to do as he practiced hobbling around the room. I led him to the ward entrance and taught him how to open and close the door while balancing on the crutches and his good right foot. Despite the discomfort he had to be experiencing, he remained cooperative, almost upbeat, and I felt excited, not only because I was doing what I'd trained to do but because I seemed to have magically brought him out of his shell when no one else had been able to. He actually sang along with a few songs on the radio as he practiced with the crutches, causing some of the people in the room to look at him, chuckling, and I smiled to myself as I walked next to him. He was probably a real charmer when he wasn't grieving.

He was getting winded from our circuits around the room, and I decided to let him have a rest before I taught him how to negotiate the stairs. As I helped him back to his wheelchair, the voice of the WKIX DJ, Tommy Walker, came over the loudspeaker.

"And here it is, as promised!" Tommy said. "The brand-new Beatles song! It's called 'Ticket to Ride.' Be sure to tell everybody where you heard it first. WKIX!" Tommy had been talking about the new song all week as if WKIX was the only station in the world allowed to play it. My sister Patti was going crazy with anticipation and it seemed unfair that I would be able to hear the song before my Beatlemaniac sister. Patti was teaching her fourth-grade class right now and had to keep a professional air about her, which I couldn't begin to picture, because even though Patti was twenty-four to my twenty-one, she was like a teenager when it came to the Beatles. She planned to drive directly from her school to the record store on Henderson Street to snap up the new forty-five.

To my surprise, Hunter began singing along with the song as I took the crutches from him, leaning them against the windowsill again. He knew every word as well as the melody, which simply wasn't possible, since "Ticket to Ride" hadn't yet been played in the United States. He seemed oblivious to the fact that I was staring at him in awe as I took my seat across from him again.

"How can you possibly know this song?" I asked. "It's brand-new, just released today. No one's even *heard* it yet, much less had the time to memorize it."

He looked briefly perplexed. "I have no idea," he said. "Obviously I heard it somewhere. Maybe a different radio station?"

"That's impossible."

"Apparently not." He shrugged with a sheepish smile.

"You're not . . . you're not connected to the Beatles somehow, are you?"

He laughed. "I wish," he said.

"Have you been to England recently?" The song had probably been released in England first.

"Nope," he said.

"Are you a Beatles fan?"

"Isn't everyone?" he said, then added, "I own every one of their albums."

"But 'Ticket to Ride'?" I queried. "I just don't get it."

He shrugged again. "It's a great song and I guess I must have somehow heard it and subliminally picked up the lyrics."

"That's crazy," I said, but I was thinking about Patti. Wait until I told her about this guy!

I glanced toward the side of the room where there was a five-step staircase. "We should get back to work," I said, knowing my job was not to sit and talk about the Beatles with him. "Are you ready to try the stairs?"

"If you insist," he said. Turning around in the wheel-chair, he took the crutches from the windowsill and struggled to stand again.

"Have you been to a Beatles concert?" I asked as I walked next to him toward the stairs.

"I wish," he said again. "But alas, no."

"My sister took the train to New York to see them twice last year," I said. "August and September. And she's already saving up to go to their August concert this year."

"She should see them as much as she can," he said. "You never know when they're going to just pack it in and say 'enough is enough.'"

"She would die if they did that," I said.

I taught him how to ascend and descend the stairs using the crutches, but my mind wasn't on the task. Patti had recently stopped seeing a guy who was a boring stick-in-the-mud and now she was at loose ends. Would it be unethical to introduce her to Hunter? I didn't know. I tried to picture how I would broach the subject with her: "Hey Patti, I met this strange, really depressed guy with a broken ankle at work today and I think you'd make the perfect couple!" Joe would tell me not to meddle. *Patti will find her own guy when she's good and ready,* he'd say.

When we were done working together and Hunter was settled back in his wheelchair, he caught my hand. Looking into my eyes, his expression turned suddenly serious. "Thank you," he said. "This was a treat. You have no idea."

I was taken aback by the intensity in his eyes, the sincerity in his voice.

"You know," I said. "I'd really like you to meet my sister."

PART ONE

1

APRIL 1970
NATIONAL INSTITUTES OF HEALTH
BETHESDA, MARYLAND

As we sat in the stark basement waiting room in one of the National Institutes of Health buildings, I thought Patti was more anxious than I was. She cuddled one-year-old John Paul on her lap, her left foot jiggling. Sitting next to her, Hunter held her hand. The three of us had the room to ourselves and we seemed to have run out of small talk after the long drive from the Outer Banks.

A dark-haired woman appeared in the doorway. The name on her white coat read *S. Barron, RN.* "Caroline Sears?" she called. She had a Northern accent, I thought, much stronger than Hunter's. She'd barely pronounced the *r* in my last name.

"Yes," I said, getting to my feet. "Can my sister and brother-in-law come in with me?"

"That would be fine," she said. "Follow me."

I walked ahead of Hunter and Patti as we followed the woman down a long bare corridor to a room nearly at the end. Inside the small room were six chairs arranged in a semicircle. The only other furnishings in the room were tall metal file cabinets that filled one wall.

"Have a seat," the woman said.

I sat next to Patti and John Paul, who was beginning to fuss. He'd been an angel during the long car trip, but I think now we were all getting stir-crazy. Hunter took him from Patti's arms and began bouncing him gently on his knee.

"I'm Susan Barron," the woman said, settling into her own seat, a clipboard and file folder on her lap. Her gaze was on me. "I'm one of the designers of the study, though I won't be the person doing your examination," she said. "My role is to gather some information from you beforehand, all right?"

I nodded.

She opened the file on her lap and glanced at it. "You're twenty-six years old, correct?"

"Yes."

"We received the records from your obstetrician, a Dr. Michaels. You're about twenty-four or -five weeks along at this point?"

"That's right."

"And your pregnancy has been uneventful until your last exam?"

"Well, last two exams," I said, shifting on the seat. I was tired of sitting. My legs ached. "Dr. Michaels told me a month ago that my baby's heartbeat was irregular, but he didn't think much of it. This last examination, though, he was more concerned."

"Right," she said. "And I don't know how much information you were given, but our study is actually full. We have all the patients we need at this time. However, your brother-in-law here"—she looked at Hunter—"is a puller of strings, I see, and he was able to get you in."

I smiled past Patti at Hunter. He sat there looking modest, but she was right. Hunter was a puller of strings. A fixer. I didn't think there was anything that he couldn't make right. Except for Joe. He couldn't fix what happened to Joe.

"So you need to understand that this study is in its very preliminary stage as we explore the uses and limitations of fetal ultrasound," she continued. "The technology is years away from being used on any regular basis and the images we can obtain are somewhat primitive. However, our previous study, as well as several recent studies elsewhere, had very good results in terms of accuracy, but not in every case, and I need to be sure you understand the limitations."

I nodded.

"In other words," Susan continued, "let's say the ultrasound results appear to tell us there's something wrong with your baby's heart. They might be inaccurate. Conversely, they might give us the impression everything is fine when it isn't. I want to be sure you—"

"I understand," I said. Hunter had told me all of this. He'd explained the mechanism of the ultrasound. It was simply incredible to me that it was possible to visualize my baby while he—I felt certain it was a he, a miniature Joe—was still inside of me. Hunter said it wouldn't hurt at all. He'd read about it. He was the founder of his own company,

Poole Technology Consulting, in Research Triangle Park—RTP—where he worked with enormous computers. He had access to all sorts of technology and material the rest of us couldn't imagine.

"Your baby's father," Susan said, looking at the folder on her lap. "Your brother-in-law told us he died recently?"

"Vietnam," I said. "Right after Thanksgiving."

"How difficult for you," she said. "I'm sorry."

"He didn't even know about the baby," I said. "He was only in Vietnam a couple of weeks."

Patti rested a hand on my arm. It wasn't a gesture of comfort so much as a warning for me to stop talking. Once I started talking about Joe, it was hard for me to stop. It was so unfair. Joe had been a structural engineer and we thought he'd be safe, away from the action. "I didn't discover I was pregnant until a few weeks after I learned he was killed," I said.

"Will you have help with your baby?" Susan asked, attempting to change the subject. I didn't hear her at first, my mind back on the day the captain and second lieutenant showed up on my doorstep with the news that literally brought me to my knees.

"Yes," Patti said when I didn't answer.

"Yes," Hunter agreed. "She has us."

"I live with them now," I said, coming back to the present.

"And where is that?"

"Nags Head," I said. "The Outer Banks." After Joe died, I'd moved from Fort Bragg into our old family beach cottage where Patti and Hunter had been living for the past couple of years. I'd expected the move to be temporary—just a few weeks off from my physical therapist job in a Raleigh hospital. But when I found out I was pregnant and my obstetrician told me I needed to take it easy, Patti and Hunter said I could stay with them as long as I wanted. Hunter worked three days a week at his consulting firm in Raleigh and I knew Patti welcomed my company when he was gone.

"Where are the Outer Banks?" Susan asked, confirming her Northern accent. Anyone south of the Mason-Dixon line knew where the Outer Banks were.

"North Carolina," Hunter said before I could answer. "About six hours from here."

"You drove a long way for this," she said.

"I have to find out if my baby's okay." I folded my hands tightly together in my lap.

Susan nodded. "Fine," she said. She asked a few more questions about my general health, which had always been good. "And how about the rest of your family?" she asked. "Do you have other siblings?"

"Just Patti."

"And Patti?" Susan asked. "You're a biological sibling, right? Any health problems?"

"None," she said.

Susan turned back to me. "How about your parents? How is their health?"

"They died in a car accident when I was fourteen," I said.

"My." Susan made a note in the folder on her lap, then looked up at me. "You've had some difficult times."

I nodded, hoping this pregnancy wasn't going to be one of them.

"How about your late husband's parents? How is their health?"

"Good," I said, thinking of my robust, tennis-playing mother- and father-in-law. They lived in Texas and they didn't know about the baby. I'd been about to write them when Dr. Michaels told me something might be wrong. I was afraid to tell anyone after that until I knew the baby was okay.

Susan asked a few more questions about my pregnancy, which had been unremarkable, although the truth was, I'd been so distressed over losing Joe that I couldn't have separated my symptoms of grief from symptoms of pregnancy. I worried my grief had somehow led to a problem for my baby.

Finally, Susan got to her feet. "Follow me," she said to me. "You two?" She looked at Patti and Hunter. "You can wait here. Tight quarters in there."

I followed her into a tiny room with an examining table, a wooden chair, two rolling stools, and a large machine bearing what looked like a small television screen. Susan handed me a pale blue gown.

"You can leave your bra on, but everything else off," she said. "Put this on so it opens in the front. I'll be back in a moment."

I undressed as she'd instructed and climbed onto the examining table. My baby gave a little tumble inside me. He'd been an acrobat for weeks now. I rested a reassuring hand on my belly. *There's nothing wrong with you,* I spoke silently to him. *You are perfect.*

Susan returned to the room followed by a very young-looking man with thick black hair, horn-rimmed glasses, and a white coat.

"Good afternoon," he said to me. "I'm Dr. Halloway, one of the researchers, and I'll be doing your ultrasound. Nurse Barron explained everything to you?"

"I think so," I said. Susan had produced a stiff white sheet to spread across my lap and motioned for me to lie down.

"Is your husband here?" he asked.

"My husband died," I said as I lay back on the cool leather of the table. I wished he had checked my file first so I didn't have to say those terrible words again. I ran my fingers over the rings on my left hand.

"Oh," he said. "Sorry to hear that."

"Her sister and brother-in-law are her support," Susan said. "The brother-in-law—that Hunter Poole you spoke with?—they're both here."

"Ah, yes." He nodded. "You have an advocate in that pushy brother-in-law of yours, don't you?" he said dryly. I couldn't tell if he found Hunter's pushiness annoying or admirable.

"Yes," I said, grateful for Hunter and his advocacy.

Susan lowered the sheet to expose my big belly. It was hard to believe I had months yet to go in this pregnancy. Dr. Halloway squirted some cold gelatinous substance onto my stomach, then began running a smooth wand across my skin. Susan lowered the light in the room and indecipherable images appeared on the small screen. Both she and the doctor leaned forward, squinting at the picture. Their heads blocked my view, although every once in a while I had a clear view of the fuzzy moving image on the screen. If my baby was in that picture, I certainly couldn't see him. How the two of them could make head or tail of what they were looking at was beyond me.

For at least two minutes, neither of them said a word as Dr. Halloway moved the wand this way and that, pressing it into my skin. *What do you see?* I wanted to ask, but I lay there quietly. In the light from the screen, I could see Dr. Halloway's frown. He pointed to something on the screen, speaking to Susan in muttered words I couldn't decipher. She also pointed to something and muttered her own response. My heart pounded in my chest. In my throat.

"Can you tell anything?" I asked finally.

They didn't seem to hear me. Instead, they continued pointing and mumbling to each other.

After what seemed like a very long time, Dr. Halloway lifted the wand from my belly and Susan used a white towel to clean the jellylike substance from my skin.

"What did you see?" I raised myself to my elbows.

"Why don't you get dressed and I'll speak with you and your family about our findings," Dr. Halloway said. I turned my head from him to Susan and back again, trying to get either of them to look at me, but they seemed to be avoiding eye contact with me.

"But what are they?" I asked, beginning to panic. "Your findings? What did you see?"

"Get dressed and we'll talk," he said, the lighter tone he'd had before the exam gone from his voice. "I've taken some pictures and I'll show you then."

Dr. Halloway met with us back in that small room with the semicircle of chairs. I didn't know what had become of Susan. I sat between Patti and Hunter this time, and John Paul was nearly asleep in Patti's lap. I introduced the doctor, who focused his attention on Hunter instead of me when he began to speak.

"I'm afraid there's a serious problem with the baby's heart," he said, handing a couple of fuzzy black-and-white snapshots to Hunter.

"What do you mean?" I asked, trying to pull the doctor's attention back to me. I was the one carrying this baby.

Hunter passed the photographs to me and Patti leaned over to see them. "How can you possibly tell anything like that from these . . . weird pictures?" she asked.

"Well, in many cases, we can't be sure what we're seeing because our images are still somewhat challenging to decipher," Dr. Halloway said. "But in your case" —he finally looked at me directly—"what we can make out is quite clear. I believe even you will be able to see the problem." He pulled his chair closer to us, scraping it on the floor. He pointed to a gray smudge on the image. "Your baby has severe stenosis of the aortic valve," he said, "which, I'm afraid, will inevitably lead to hypoplastic left heart syndrome."

"How serious is it?" Patti asked, as I searched the blotchy black-and-white images for my baby. I couldn't find him. I couldn't understand how anyone, no matter how brilliant and well trained, could find my baby in those pictures, much less my baby's heart.

"I'm afraid it's fatal," Dr. Halloway said.

My head jerked up. *"No,"* I said. I felt Hunter's hand come to rest on my shoulder.

"Fatal!" Patti said.

"How can you possibly tell that from these pictures?" I argued, suddenly disliking this man intensely. "This is just a study. The nurse . . . whatever her name is . . . Susan . . . she said the machine—the ultrasound—could give false information. That it's just experimental and—"

"That's often true," Dr. Halloway said calmly. He was looking at Hunter again instead of me and I wanted to kick him to remind him this was *my* baby we were talking about. "But in this case," he continued, "we were able to get a remarkably clear picture of your baby's heart and I'm certain of my diagnosis. I'm very sorry."

For a long moment, none of us spoke. "When he's born, can he have surgery?" I asked finally.

"Your baby is a girl," he said, "and no. I'm afraid there's nothing that can be done for her."

A girl! That was nearly as much of a shock to me as the news about his . . . her . . . heart, and I instantly felt even more protective of my baby. I looked down at those stupid pictures on my lap. I wished we'd never come. I hated this doctor. Hated Susan Barron. At that moment, I was close to hating Hunter for insisting I come here.

"I can't lose this baby," I said. "He's—*she's*—all I have left of my husband."

"You have us, honey," Patti said, though her voice, thick

with tears, told me she knew perfectly well that she and Hunter were not enough to erase this loss.

"What are our options?" Hunter said, as if we were all pregnant.

"You can try carrying the baby to term," Dr. Halloway said. "She'll most likely survive the rest of the pregnancy, but with HLHS, she will die very shortly after birth. Or you can abort," he added. "You live in North Carolina. You can have a legal abortion there due to a fetal anomaly, though it's not an easy procedure at twenty-four—"

"No," I said. "I can't do that. What if you're wrong?"

"I understand it's hard to accept," he said. "But you're holding the evidence in your hand." He nodded toward the fuzzy picture of my baby. I held the picture by the edges and I averted my gaze from it. If I didn't look at it, I could pretend I still had Joe's healthy baby inside of me. If I didn't look, I could pretend this last hour had never happened.

2

Hunter

My gut was in knots on the trip back to North Carolina. I was driving, my hands tight as fists on the steering wheel of the Chevy Impala. The sky was beginning to darken and I was so rattled by the last few hours that I could barely see straight. I glanced in the rearview mirror where Patti, Carly, and John Paul had taken over the backseat. John Paul fell asleep the moment we got in the car and I was glad. I could hear Carly's quiet crying and Patti's whispered words of comfort. What could she possibly be saying? How did you comfort a woman who lost her husband only five months ago and who was now being told she was going to lose her baby as well? The baby who'd been her one source of happiness since Joe's death? Still, my persistent wife tried. I couldn't hear what she was saying, but I sensed the depth of emotion in her words. The love. The worry.

I'd never lost the feeling that Patti, Carly, and Joe had saved me. I'd encountered Carly in the rehab unit at the lowest point of my life, and she unwittingly turned everything around for me. I'd never known the sort of all-embracing love I'd found since marrying Patti. I had no siblings. I'd never known my father—never even knew his name—and my mother had been the brilliant, cerebral type who made sure I had a stellar education but few hugs and kisses. She was an astrophysicist so lost in her work that she had little time—or incentive—to dote on her only child, although I never doubted her love. Joe, a smart, determined sort of guy from a military family, had been the brother I'd never had. He and Carly had lived on base most of the time, but when he was around, we'd boat and fish and work on his '55 Chevy and play tennis, which he always won because of my gimpy ankle, and we'd laugh our butts off and ... man, I missed him. Losing him had wrecked both my heart and my sleep. I still wasn't sleeping well. Nightmares dogged me and sometimes I woke up in a fit of terror, not knowing where I was. After today, I wasn't sure I'd ever be able to sleep well again.

When I met Patti and Carly, they were living together in the Raleigh house they'd grown up in. Patti'd only been seventeen when their parents died and she'd fought in court to be emancipated so she could take care of Carly and keep her out of foster care. That described Patti to a T: a devoted, family-first sort of woman. She and Carly had been thick as thieves back then, since all they'd had was each other, and there was still an unbreakable bond between them. When I came along, though, the three of them—Patti, Carly, and Joe—welcomed me with open arms and we became a foursome, a deep intimacy between us that I'd never before experienced. For the first time, I felt as though I had a family.

Now Joe was gone and Carly had to cope with her baby's problems on top of it. *Damn*. What was happening to our lives felt mean, almost abusive. I hadn't been surprised about the baby's heart condition, though. I wished I had been. I hadn't even bothered to hope the doctor would tell us the baby was fine. I knew better.

And I knew what I had to do now. It seemed wrong. I could guarantee nothing. Still, I knew the role I needed to play in this miserable drama.

Right now, though, I wasn't going to make it through another hour of driving without a break.

"I need to stop for coffee," I said over my shoulder. We were a bit south of Richmond and I knew a place where we could get something to eat. "Maybe a hamburger," I added.

"All right," Patti said from the backseat, her voice small and tired.

I pulled off the highway and into the parking lot of the little Tastee Hut.

"I don't want to go in," Carly said. "I'll stay out here with John Paul."

"What should we bring you?" Patti asked.

"Nothing."

"You need something, Carly," I said. "Tea, maybe?" Carly was a tea drinker. Never coffee. "A burger? Fries?"

"Fries," she said, though I was sure she was saying it only to get me off her case. I doubted she would eat them.

I held Patti's hand as we walked across the poorly lit parking lot. She nearly dragged me to the door, and once inside she turned to me, her arms around my neck, her head on my shoulder as she cried. I rubbed her back, her strawberry-blond hair tangling in my fingers. "I know," I said, although she hadn't spoken. "I know. It's not fair."

"She can't take it," she said. "Why does she have to lose everything? What is wrong with God? She wants that baby so badly."

"I know," I said again. My words sounded helpless.

But I wasn't helpless, I thought, as I held my wife close. I wasn't helpless at all.

3

Carly

The following Sunday, I sat alone on the crest of the beach-grass-covered dunes behind our cottage, staring out to sea. It was the third of May and the weather was warm. I wore my maternity jeans and a light sweater that stretched over my growing belly. I had the beach to myself for as far as I could see in either direction. Nags Head's population barely topped four hundred people in the off-season. A mile and a half to my left, the Nags Head pier was a long, dark finger reaching far into the blue-gray ocean. To my right, sea and sand stretched all the way to the horizon. And behind me, the Unpainted Aristocracy, that string of ancient, original Outer Banks cottages, rose from the dunes. The cottages were a mile and a half of history. Ours was one of the northernmost homes, nearly across the beach road from the massive dunes of Jockey's Ridge. My maternal grandfather bought the house, one of the largest, for a song at the turn of the century. For most of my life, we'd used it only in the summertime, driving to the coast from our home in Raleigh the day after school let out. As kids, Patti and I would race through the closed-up house in excitement as we opened the windows and pushed up the wooden shutters to bring in the salt air and light up the heart pine walls and ceilings. When I was small, the house had only outdoor plumbing and no hot water. But when Patti and Hunter got married, they added indoor plumbing, a water heater, and baseboard heat. They did their best to seal the cracks in the old siding, but the house was still chilly when the wind blew in the winter, and no matter how well sealed the walls, sweeping the sand from the floors and windowsills was still a daily job. So worth it, though. That house was our treasure.

I used to like to sit here alone on the dunes to feel the peace of the sea and sand and sky. In the last few months, though, I'd been coming out here to grieve, and I was so, so tired of grieving. A few days had passed since that visit to the National Institutes of Health. I wished I'd never gone. I rested my hands on my belly through my jacket. *Joanna Elizabeth.* The name had come to me the day before. I would name her after Joe and my mother.

"Please, God," I whispered. "Let that doctor be wrong."

"Hey, Carly."

I turned to see Hunter walking down the path from the house toward me. I didn't answer him. I was still irrationally angry with him for making me go to NIH to hear news I didn't want to hear.

He sat down next to me and I kept my gaze on the water. I waited for him to ask me one more time how I was doing. I was quickly getting tired of that question.

"Carly . . . do you trust me?" he asked instead.

Not the question I'd expected. I turned to look at him, suddenly guilty for the anger I felt toward him. I loved this man. I loved him for the joy he gave my sister. For the way he'd treated Joe like a brother. For the love he showed my sweet little nephew. I loved how easy he was to lean on.

"Of course I trust you," I said.

"And do you think I'm sane?"

I frowned. "What are you talking about?" I asked.

"Do you?" he pushed. "Do you think I'm mentally sound?"

"You're the sanest person I know." I remembered meeting him in the rehab ward when everyone thought he was suicidal. What no one had known was that he'd recently lost both his wife, Rosie, in a bicycle accident and his mother to a heart attack. Of course he'd been depressed and uncommunicative, poor guy. Possibly he *had* been suicidal, momentarily, anyway. But I'd seen absolutely no hint of any psychological problem in him since that day five years ago.

"I want to tell you something about myself that no one knows," he said now. He plucked a piece of beach grass from the sand. "Not even Patti knows this," he said as he began tying the grass into a knot. "I *need* to tell you. But you have to promise me you won't talk to her or to anyone else about what I say."

"About what?" I couldn't imagine where he was going with this.

"Promise me," he said. "You'll keep this between us."

There had always been something of a mystery about Hunter, although Patti didn't see it. Patti saw only perfection in him. "Did you serve time in jail or something?" I asked.

He smiled, the sun small specks of gold in the blue of his eyes. "Nothing like that," he assured me.

"Is it something that could put Patti or John Paul in danger?" I asked. I wouldn't be able to keep that promise.

"No. No, they're safe. I would never put them in jeopardy."

"All right, then. What's this big secret?"

He took in a deep breath and looked hard into my eyes. "I was actually born in 1986," he said.

I frowned. I couldn't imagine why he'd joke with me when he knew how upset I was. "What are you talking about?" I asked. "You're thirty-seven years old. You were born in"—I did the math in my head—"1935. I saw your medical record in the rehabilitation unit, remember?"

He shook his head. "No," he said. "I was born in 1986."

I felt a chill. He looked entirely serious. "Please don't tease me. I can't handle your teasing right now."

"I'm not teasing," he said, his voice sober. "I know this is going to sound crazy, but please just listen. Hear me out."

"I'm listening." I felt annoyed.

"I was born in 1986," he said. "I got my doctorate from Princeton in 2017."

"You got your doctorate from Duke."

He shook his head. "I'm afraid that was a lie."

I drew away from him, unnerved. "You're scaring me, Hunter," I said. "I don't know why you're being so weird, but stop it, okay? Seriously. I don't need this right now."

"Actually, you do need this," he said soberly. "Otherwise, believe me, I would never tell you."

"Tell me *what*?" I snapped.

He looked away from me then, out to the sea. His eyes had lost their sparkle and red splotches formed on his neck. He was clearly nervous and I softened toward him. Touched his arm. "Tell me what?" I asked, quietly this time.

"I told you the truth about being married and losing Rosie," he said. "At the time of her death, I was working in a private astrophysics program near Washington, D.C., called Temporal Solutions."

"But you grew up in New Jersey," I said. "Is that still true?"

"Yes, but I moved to the Washington area—specifically, Alexandria, Virginia—when I was fifteen." He glanced at me. "Which was 2001."

"What do you mean, two thousand and one?"

"The *year* 2001. That's when I was fifteen."

"Hunter! Do you hear yourself? What is wrong with you? Please stop." My eyes prickled with frustration. I couldn't understand why he was doing this to me. Telling me nonsense. My brief burst of sympathy for him disappeared.

"I'm sorry, Carly," he said, "but I *have* to tell you this. Hear me out, all right? Just hear me out."

I folded my arms across my chest, annoyed, as I waited for him to continue.

He took in a breath. "I was involved in an experimental time-travel study," he said.

I stared at him as the words registered. Then I laughed, although the sound was false, I hadn't laughed in so long. "You act like you really believe what you're saying."

"I do believe it, because it's the truth. Will you let me finish?"

"Sure," I said, then added sarcastically, "I can use the entertainment."

"My mother was a physicist," he said. "The most brilliant person I've ever known. She was studying quantum physics and she—"

"What's quantum physics?"

He brushed his hand through the air dismissively. "It doesn't matter. What matters is that during her studies, she discovered it's possible to travel forward and backward in time."

"Ridiculous."

"She started a secret program under the cover of a sham business she called Temporal Solutions," he continued as if I hadn't spoken. "I didn't know what she was involved with until I was in college. She told me then because she wanted me to study physics as well so I could join her in the program. When she told me about it, I—"

"Hunter, enough. Please stop."

"There were only twelve people involved in the program at that time," he said, as if he hadn't heard me. "Twelve scientists my mother knew she could trust enough to enlist. By the time I got involved, five of them, including my mother, had already been sent backward and forward in time. And then—" He stopped, and I knew he saw the look of worry on my face. "I'm perfectly sane," he assured me.

"But what you're talking about isn't possible," I said.

"Yes, Carly, it is. To be honest, it's not even all that complicated once the mechanism is understood. But it takes courage to do it. Stepping into the unknown and all of that. I made my first trip into the past when I was twenty-five.

I went to 1900. It was a life-altering experience." He smiled as if at a memory, while I wondered if I should run back to the house and get Patti. Tell her what was happening to her husband. Instead, I sat rooted to the dune, unsure what I should do as he continued.

"Then when I was thirty-two—it was 2018," he said, "my mother wanted one of us to go to the sixties. She knew technology was going to take off during that era . . . *this* era, right now . . . and she saw savvy investing as a way to gain funding for the program. So whoever came to the sixties was not only supposed to record the experience but also invest in technology stocks, et cetera. I was reluctant to use the program in that mercenary a way. But then Rosie was killed. And my mother . . ." He hesitated for a moment. "She died," he said. "And I thought, what the hell? I might as well volunteer to be the guy who goes to 1965. It's what she wanted. But the problem was, there was a storm when I traveled and it threw off my calculations. Or maybe I was so depressed then that I screwed them up myself. I don't know." He gave a dismissive shrug. "I was supposed to land on the UNC campus. Instead I landed on the roof of that building and fell off. That's how I broke my ankle and ended up in rehab. That's how I . . ." He hesitated, then continued. "That's how I met you and then Patti and—you two saved my life." His voice cracked and he swallowed once, twice, before he continued. "Once I met Patti, I didn't want to go back," he said. "I'll never go back. I don't want the . . . the clutter of the future right now. There's so much more going on in 2018, Carly. You can't imagine what it's like. Hundreds of channels on TV.

Everybody has their own computer. Their own phone they carry around with them. There's a digital revolution happening, and the medical and scientific advancements are unbelievable. But none of that compares to having Patti in my life. And to the . . . the simplicity of this life." He swept his arm through the air to take in the sea and sky. "I love my life here."

Tears welled up in my eyes. I felt both sad and frightened sitting there with him. Something was radically wrong with him and he needed my help. Maybe I should humor him as I quietly got to my feet and walked slowly back to the house to call for an ambulance. The closest hospital was in Elizabeth City, an hour and a half away. Did they have a psychiatrist there? I didn't know, but I had to do something. I had to admit it to myself: Hunter had never been like other people. He always stood out in a crowd for a certain brilliance. A certain quirkiness, if truth be told. Had Patti and I been kidding ourselves for the past five years that he was perfectly normal, psychologically? Was he decompensating now? Maybe losing Joe, his best friend, and then learning the grim news about my baby . . . maybe all that had thrown him over the edge. He'd hidden his illness all these years and now it was back with a vengeance, and I was scared for him and for Patti and John Paul. And for myself. My entire world seemed to be crumbling around me.

"Honey." I leaned forward, covering his hand with mine. "I think we need to get you some help," I said. "Tomorrow, let's drive to Elizabeth City and—"

"I'm . . . not . . . crazy." He bit off the words, one by one.

"I'm telling you this because there are ways to help your baby in the future."

I leaned away, my concern for him suddenly turning to anger.

"That doctor said nothing can be done," I said. "Why would you tease me like this?"

"I'm not teasing you," he said. "He's right that nothing can be done in 1970, but something can be done in the twenty-first century."

I got to my feet and took a few steps away from him. I suddenly felt afraid of being alone out here with him. "I'm going in," I said. "I'm finished talking to you about this."

"Please don't say anything to Patti!" he called after me. "Whether you believe me or not, please don't say anything. You promised."

I wouldn't say anything to Patti, I thought, as I walked toward the house. At least not yet. I didn't want to hurt Hunter. I adored him and didn't know what I would have done without him in the months since Joe died, but I needed to get a better handle on what was wrong with him before I burdened Patti with it. He might be losing his mind, but I was sure he wasn't a danger to himself or the rest of us. I wondered if he'd taken a hallucinogenic drug. I'd never known him to use drugs or even drink more than a couple of beers or a glass of wine. But someone might have slipped him something. I would see how he was later tonight before I mentioned anything to my sister.

4

Patti and I made fried chicken for dinner that evening, the radio blaring in the kitchen as we cut up the chicken, chopped bits of ham hock for the butterbeans, and rolled out pastry for biscuits. We'd started cooking together after our parents died. We'd had no choice but to do it ourselves back then, and we always cooked with the radio on. Patti'd make it fun, dancing around the kitchen to Chuck Berry or the Everly Brothers. I was older when I realized she'd kept the mood light for my sake. Patti was always trying to keep the grief away.

Hunter had taken John Paul out to the beach to burn off some of the little boy's one-year-old energy, and as I rolled out the pastry, I kept a careful eye on them through the window. John Paul was walking pretty well in the house, but on the beach he resorted to a crawl much of the time. I watched Hunter grab him from the sand, toss him gently into the air and catch him, nuzzling his neck with kisses while John Paul screeched with joy. My eyes burned watching them. I wanted my own healthy little baby. My Joanna. And I wanted my brother-in-law to go back to being his sweet, sane self.

"Hey Jude" came on the radio, and Patti shook her head. "I still can't believe it," she said.

I knew what she was talking about without her being more specific. A couple of weeks ago, Paul McCartney had announced the breakup of the Beatles and Patti wasn't quite over it yet.

"I blame Yoko Ono," she said. "Seriously. That woman cast some sort of spell on John."

"Maybe they'll get back together," I said. "Maybe this is just a temporary thing."

"I wish," she said. Then she looked at me while I slipped a tray of biscuits into the oven. "Why don't you get off your feet, Carly?" she said, the worried-big-sister tone in her voice. "I can manage everything. Just sit at the table and talk to me."

"I'm fine," I said, though I felt anything but fine. I picked up a cucumber and peeler from the counter. I didn't want to sit. I wouldn't be able to keep an eye on Hunter and John Paul through the window if I sat down at the broad old wooden table. Hunter was sitting on the beach now, playing with John Paul and a pail and shovel. The dunes blocked most of my view, but the two of them looked fine. I couldn't believe I was actually having doubts about Hunter as a father. He was the best.

Patti followed my gaze outside as she pulled a stack of plates from the open shelving above the counter. "I worry it's hard for you to see John Paul," she said gently. "That it makes you feel sad about—" She motioned toward my belly.

I was a bit stunned. "Are you kidding?" I said, setting

the cucumber on the chopping board. "It *thrills* me to see John Paul. He's so healthy and happy, and I'm so glad you have him."

She turned toward me. Setting the plates on the countertop, she bit her lip as though trying to hold back the question she was thinking. "What are you going to do?" she asked finally, her blue eyes studying my face.

"I'm going to have her," I said simply. I worried I was condemning Joanna to terrible suffering by giving birth to her, but what if those doctors were wrong and she was actually fine? I still clung to that fervent hope. I wished I knew the right thing to do. All I did know was that, with the baby inside me, I still had a little bit of Joe with me. My throat tightened and I focused once again on chopping the cucumber. "I hope I'm making the right choice, sis," I said.

She put an arm around my waist and rested her cheek on my shoulder. "I love you," she said. "And whatever you decide, I'll be right there with you."

After dinner, Patti and Hunter took John Paul upstairs to get him ready for bed while I did the dishes. Hunter had seemed like his usual self over dinner, and I wondered if he even remembered his crazy talk from the beach. I was drying the last plate when he walked into the kitchen.

"I want you to look at something, Carly," he said quietly. "Put down the plate and hold out your hand."

I set the plate on the counter as he reached into his pants pocket and drew out two coins, dropping them into my palm. "Look at them," he said. "Look at the dates on them."

They were quarters and I turned them over so I could see the dates in the fading sunlight that sifted through the kitchen windows. One was 2014 and the other 2016. I looked up at him. "Where did you get these?" I asked.

"I saved them from when I . . . when I arrived here," he said. "And I have a stack of bills—a lot of money—a *lot*—from 2018, too. The money is in a safe-deposit box in Raleigh. Of course it can't be used in 1970."

I felt shaken. I wasn't sure how to explain what he was showing me. He could have had the coins minted someplace, I supposed, but why would he do that? Why would he go to that trouble? And that advance planning would shoot a hole—several holes—through my wishful thinking that he was suffering the effects of a drug that would soon wash out of his system.

"So," I said slowly, "if you had a lot of money when you fell off that roof in '65, where was it when the ambulance came to take you to the hospital?" I'd read his records back then. He'd arrived at the hospital with a change of clothes and a wallet in a mustard-yellow backpack and that was it.

He nodded as though he'd expected the question. "I hid it in the shrubs where I fell," he said. "I had it in a plastic bag and I didn't want to be found with it, so I dug a hole in the dirt with my hands and buried it. I got it back once I was well."

"This is . . . it's ridiculous, Hunter." I shook my head. "I'm sorry, but these coins notwithstanding . . . it's just not believable."

"I have a way to convince you," he said. "To truly convince you. What date is today?"

"May third," I said.

"All right." He nodded as though pleased by the date. "In a day or so—I can't remember the exact date, but it's soon, very soon—"

"*What's* very soon?"

"Something terrible is going to happen." He made a face as though he tasted something sour. "I hate doing it this way," he said. "I hate telling you about this ahead of time, but it may be the only way I can prove to you that what I'm saying is true."

I hung the dish towel from the oven door with a sigh. "What now?" I asked. "What is—supposedly—going to happen?"

"It's at Kent State University in Ohio," he said. "You know how the student war protests are intensifying there and they called in the National Guard?"

I nodded. The protests were intensifying everywhere, actually. At UNC, my alma mater, the students were on strike. I always felt torn, watching them on the TV news. The scenes of their angry protests were often followed by footage of our soldiers fighting in Vietnam, the war that took my husband from me. I found myself agreeing with the protesters more often than not these days, and then I'd fill with shame. I didn't ever want to feel as though Joe had died in vain, fighting a war we should never have gotten into.

"Are you listening to me?" Hunter frowned. "Did you hear what I said?"

"I . . . no," I admitted. "What did you say?"

"Kent State. It's sometime this week, I'm pretty sure. I

don't remember exactly when, but the National Guard will kill four students there."

"*What?* Hunter, I don't know what's going on with you, but you need to stop it." I lowered my voice. "Stop talking this way or I swear I'll tell Patti."

"It's going to happen," he said. "And they'll injure other students, too. I don't remember how many, but I do know four students die and another one is left paralyzed. It's a horrible piece of American history. If it doesn't happen, you can tell Patti I've gone off my rocker, all right? But it's going to happen."

"How can you possibly know that?"

"Because it's in the history books I had in school in the nineties," he said simply. "Then Neil Young will write a song about it. 'Ohio,' it's called. Only he pronounces it 'Oh-Hi-Oh,' and—"

"*Enough,*" I said, putting my hands over my ears. "I don't know what to think or believe or . . . If you supposedly know this is going to happen, why don't you stop it? You're going to just let those students get killed?"

"One of the questions we were researching at Temporal Solutions was if the past could be changed," he said. He sounded like a madman.

"And . . . ?"

"It can be, but it's a very dangerous thing to do, so my mother laid down the law," he said. "No tampering with the past." He was talking rapidly, the way he often did when he got excited. Even when I was first getting to know him in the rehab ward, he occasionally talked that way. I remembered wondering if he was manic then, and I was thinking the same thing now. "Martin Luther King, for example," he continued. "One of our scientists was this black guy and he worked out an experiment for himself. He planned to go back to 1968 and somehow stop the shooting that left King paralyzed. But—"

"Left him dead, you mean."

"No! That's exactly my point about how we have to be careful when we tamper with the past," he said. "King was shot in the neck and paralyzed from the neck down, but our guy—Dave was his name—he broke into the room where James Earl Ray was staying and knocked him off balance. Ray still fired, only this time it resulted in getting King killed instead of saving him."

"Oh my God," I said, before I remembered this had to be a made-up bunch of poppycock. "Hunter," I said, shaking my head. "I don't know why you're doing this. Making all this stuff up. But even if I believed you, even if it's all true, why are you telling me about it?"

"Because I want to send you to the year 2001," he said. "They can treat your baby then. Before it's born. It's called fetal surgery. I know they—"

"You want to *send* me to 2001?" I rolled my eyes. "On a plane or a ship or what? This is nonsense. I'm going up to my room to read," I said. "I can't listen to this anymore."

"I'll be going to RTP in the morning," he reminded me, and I remembered tomorrow was Monday, the start of his short workweek away from home. That worried me. If he really was going off the deep end, I didn't like the idea of him being alone. "You and I can talk more about this when I get back," he said.

"You'll call Patti a couple of times a day, like you usually do?" I asked.

He smiled. He knew I thought he was losing his mind. "Of course," he said. "And I'm fine, Carly," he added. "You'll see."

5

By the time I came downstairs in the morning, Hunter was already gone and Patti was making John Paul breakfast. I headed out to walk on the beach as I'd been doing nearly every morning since moving in with them. My obstetrician—back when he thought I had a normal, healthy pregnancy—told me the gentle exercise was good for my baby and I liked the time alone. Since getting the horrible news at NIH, I had to force myself just to get up in the morning, much less go for a walk. I had to keep going, though. I was hoping for a miracle—a perfectly healthy baby. I needed to keep doing my best for her.

It was warm enough this morning that I kicked off my sneakers, rolled up the hem of my jeans, and headed barefoot toward the water line. The sun was barely above the horizon, spilling wavy peach and orange light onto the water. I walked toward the pier, which was my usual route. I liked seeing the pier in the distance, the way it stretched far into the water. I liked knowing it was exactly a mile and a half from our house, making my walk three miles. And I liked how the sound of the sea, rhythmic and so familiar, gave me time to think, and sometimes to cry.

There was another reason I liked walking to the pier. Memories. My walk took me past the small cottage that used to belong to Joe's aunt and uncle. It was where I met him in 1959, a year after my parents' death, when I was fifteen years old. His aunt and uncle's cottage wasn't officially one of the old Unpainted Aristocracy. It was much newer, the siding barely weathered back then, but it was only a few houses away from our string of ancient cottages and it fit in well.

I was beachcombing by myself early on that particular morning, something I'd done every morning of every childhood summer for as long as I could remember. That summer, though, was my first without my parents. My first as an orphan. Patti and I rattled around the big musty house, stumbling over summertime memories of our parents in every room. Being out on the beach was something of an escape. My quarry as I walked was shark teeth and sea glass and I had huge collections of both. I had the beach to myself that morning when I spotted Joe a short distance ahead of me. He was fishing, alone, casting his line into the waves. I'd only recently started noticing boys in a new way—a way that made my stomach tighten, my mouth water. This particular boy had that effect on me even from a distance. He wore only blue bathing trunks, and while he certainly wasn't heavy, he was muscular for a teenaged boy. His legs and arms were tight and toned, although they were pink instead of tan. He was getting a burn and I knew he had to be a tourist. His reddish-blond hair was short, somewhere between curly and wavy. I couldn't have said back then why the sight of him made my stomach do a flip. All I knew was that, at that moment, the last thing on my mind was finding another piece of sea glass.

I didn't stop to think before walking right up to him.

"Hi!" I called out as I neared him. "Catching anything?"

"I'm about to give up," he said, reeling in a long strand of seaweed and nothing else.

I peered into his empty pail. "What are you using for bait?"

"I *was* using squid," he said. "But I'm out, so I guess I have to pack it in for the morning."

"I'm Carly," I said.

"Joe." He had mesmerizing translucent blue eyes. The skin on his arms and chest was freckled, and a spattering of freckles ran across his pink nose. "My aunt and uncle just bought that house"—he pointed toward the new cottage behind us—"and I'm here for the summer."

The entire summer? My heartbeat quickened. "Do you *want* to give up?" I asked.

"Huh?" He looked perplexed by my question. "What do you mean?"

"I mean, you said you had to give up fishing because you don't have any bait," I said. "But you don't have to stop."

"Fish without bait?" He laughed. "That's a new one."

"No, really." The tide was going out and I walked barefoot into the surf where it pulled back over the beach, leaving dozens of V-shaped rivulets of water behind. Dropping to my knees, I dug my fingers into the sand at the point of one of the Vs and pulled out a mole crab. I carried it back to him.

"This is a sand flea," I said, holding the unlucky two-inch crab out to him on the palm of my hand. "Pop it on your hook and see what bites."

He stared at me, a look of amusement on his face that made me suddenly weak in the knees. "Seriously?" he asked.

"Seriously."

He looked at the crab in my hand. "How do you put it on the hook?"

I pulled the seaweed from his line and demonstrated baiting the hook with the crab. I did it quickly, rather cockily, showing off. I was suddenly grateful to my father for teaching me this trick when I was six years old. I felt as though Daddy was peering over my shoulder at that moment, cheering me on.

"Do you have a pole?" he asked when I'd finished. "Want to fish with me?"

I hadn't fished in a couple of years, but I decided that was a very good day to begin again and I ran home to get my pole. Together that day, we reeled in half a dozen sea mullet and a seven-pound sheepshead. Joe's aunt and uncle invited Patti and me over for dinner and the sheepshead fed all five of us.

I spent the rest of that summer with Joe, fishing and swimming, playing miniature golf, rubbing lotion on his hideous blistering sunburn—he didn't have the right skin for the beach, which was a shame because he clearly loved it. We laughed a lot that summer and fell madly in love. We'd kiss for hours at night on the gigantic dunes of Jockey's Ridge. *Puppy love,* Patti called it, but she adored

Joe and trusted him to treat me well. I knew it wasn't puppy love. I knew I'd met The One. I was right.

Joe was an "Army brat," one of those kids who moved from place to place depending on where his father was stationed. He was an only child, and ever since he was small, he'd spent the summers with his aunt and uncle wherever they were living. He said they were the opposite of his strict parents. "I like the balance," he told me, and I thought that he was so mature to be able to appreciate both the discipline and the freedom in his life.

It was an idyllic summer, but as always happens, it came to an end. Joe went back to his parents in Texas and Patti and I went home to Raleigh, and everyone—except Joe and me—thought that would be the end of our romance. But we wrote to each other several times a week and saved our allowances for long, sweet phone calls on Sunday nights. He'd always start those calls the same way: *Hey, girl,* he'd drawl, his voice full of affection, and my heart would melt. Our relationship grew deep and serious even before the next summer began.

I knew Joe planned to follow in his father's footsteps and join the army. It was the life he knew and understood, and even though it was alien to me, I respected his passionate longing to be part of it. As for me, it was my mother's footsteps I'd always wanted to follow. She started out as a nurse but received extra training to be a physical therapist so she could work with polio patients. The University of North Carolina at Chapel Hill had a physical therapy major, and nearby NC State in Raleigh had the ROTC program and engineering degree Joe wanted. Our schools were less than an hour apart. For once, we didn't need the summer months to be able to see each other.

When we graduated, Joe was commissioned as a second lieutenant in the engineer corps of the army and we spent the first two years of our marriage in Fort Eustis, where I was able to get a job as a PT. Then he was transferred to Germany for a year and a half. We made a lot of friends in Germany, where people treated us—treated the soldiers— better than they had in the States. Joe had been spit at by a girl in the airport in New York and once had to be transported in a bus with cages on the window as protection from the rocks and apples and bags of urine war protestors threw at him and his fellow soldiers. The Germans, though . . . they appreciated us, and for that year and a half, our lives were perfect. That was when I stopped taking the birth control pill.

Patti and Hunter didn't support the war in Vietnam. They were careful when they talked to us about it, though, especially to Joe, not wanting to offend or hurt the close friendship between the four of us. We thought they were being brainwashed by all the antiwar hype at home, but maybe Joe and I were the ones who'd been brainwashed. All our news came from the *Stars and Stripes* newspaper or the Armed Forces radio or our military friends who thought we were winning the war, keeping South Vietnam free of communism.

When Joe received orders to go to Vietnam, I was frightened. We were living in Fort Bragg. The day before those orders came through, we'd seen a young soldier being interviewed on the news after spending two months as a prisoner of war in South Vietnam. He'd lost thirty pounds in those two months, he said. He had weird lesions on his skin. He told the interviewer he'd been forced to live in a cage, his legs chained together whenever he'd been let out. They fed him rice and not much of it. He didn't want to talk about the torture, but his eyes filled with tears at the question.

Joe had turned off the television before we could hear the end of the interview. If he was nervous about going, he didn't let on, though he grew quiet as the date to leave neared. He was a kindhearted man and I worried that the kind heart that I loved so much would be a liability in a war.

"You don't need to worry," he'd say, pulling me into his arms for a kiss. "I'll be behind the lines as an engineer the whole time."

The captain who showed up on my doorstep told me what happened. Joe had been supervising the rebuilding of a bridge in Pleiku—bridges were his specialty—and he needed to see the bridge in person. The Vietcong picked that very day, that very hour, to blow up the bridge, killing dozens of soldiers in the process. Later, I received a letter of condolence from one of Joe's friends and he wasn't as careful with his words as that captain had been. *They were all blown apart,* he wrote. *Body parts all over the fucking place.* It was an image I would never be able to get out of my mind.

After that, I was too angry at having Joe stolen from me to be able to discern the truth about the war myself. All I knew was that too many young men were dying and I could no longer clearly see the reason why.

By the time I heard about Joe, I was quite sure I was pregnant. I knew, too, that my letter telling him I thought we were going to have a baby wouldn't have reached him before he died. I wished it had. I wished he'd at least had that little bit of joy, knowing he was going to be a father.

Our little girl.

She was the only connection I had left to Joe.

I didn't tell Patti or Hunter that every time I made this walk to the pier, it was with Joe, even if only in my mind. Patti had gently suggested that every time I found myself obsessively thinking about him, being pulled under by the grief, I substitute the thought with one about the baby. I'd been angry when she said that, although I didn't let the anger show. She was only trying to help. She didn't understand that I needed my memories of Joe. I was so afraid of losing them.

And now, thoughts of the baby were hardly the thing to bring me comfort.

In the future, Hunter had said, there was a way to help my baby.

This morning, I thought of my sweet—and possibly crazy—brother-in-law making his long weekly drive to Raleigh, singing along with music on the radio as usual. He'd fiddle with the dial as he lost one station and found another. He always complained about the stretch of highway, twenty miles or so, where he could only get the Bible-thumping stations on the radio and no music.

Ticket to Ride.

I stopped walking, suddenly remembering the day I met Hunter when he'd stunned me by knowing both the melody and every single word of a song never before played in the United States. He'd wowed Patti, Joe, and me that way several more times over the years. We thought it was because he listened to the radio more than the rest of us. We thought he was just a quick study. But could he possibly have known those songs from another time and place?

"Don't be ridiculous," I said out loud as I began walking again.

It wasn't possible to travel in time. To leave the here and now. It simply wasn't possible.

That afternoon, I cuddled John Paul at the kitchen table as Patti peeled apples for a pie. We had the radio on and were listening to music when the announcer suddenly broke in.

"Four persons, including two women, were shot and killed on Kent State University's campus an hour ago," he said.

I didn't hear the rest of the report. I nearly dropped John Paul to the floor, a chill spiking through my body. I thought I was going to be sick.

"Watch him!" I said to Patti, and I hurried from the kitchen to the bathroom, where I was overwhelmed by dizziness. I dropped to the floor, my back pressed against the wall.

"Oh my God," I whispered to myself. "Oh my God."

6

Hunter

My business, Poole Technology Consulting, was housed in three rooms in a large, nondescript brick office building in the outskirts of RTP. The smallest room belonged to Gloria Shepherd, my sharp, well-paid, middle-aged secretary. She had a desk, a typewriter, a phone, and a filing cabinet. She also had one of the few answering machines in existence, which I'd managed to get from a friend who worked for a communications company. I'd installed a second machine at home, as well.

The middle-sized office was mine. Except for the size and an extra filing cabinet, it didn't look much different from Gloria's, although mine also had a radio. I needed music and I liked to keep up with the news, much of it not a surprise to me. The third room was quite large, fifteen by twelve feet, and empty except for another couple of filing cabinets. Gloria was always on my case about moving my desk into that room. "You're the *boss,* for Pete's sake," she'd say. "Why are you squeezing yourself into that little office when you have all that space?" I'd tell her I liked my cozy quarters. The truth was, I had plans for the big room. By 1980, I hoped to have several computers in there along with some bright young techie types to operate them. Not yet, though. The computers I wanted in that room had not yet been invented.

It was nearly two thirty and I'd been working on a database program for one of the fledgling RTP drug companies for a couple of hours. I'd worked out the programming in my head, and sheets of paper covered with my chicken scratch littered my desk. In a few minutes, I'd head over to the mainframe computer at Duke, where I leased time on Mondays and Tuesdays, and I'd test my work there. The truth was, my consulting business was a bit of a cover and had been from the start. I was first and foremost an investor. Along with the cash I'd carried with me from 2018, I'd brought a long list of companies and technologies I could invest in. My mother had given me the list, expecting me to travel to '65 and make millions to feed back into Temporal Solutions when I returned to 2018. Since I had no intention of ever returning to the future—at least not in the way she'd anticipated—I invested for myself. For my family. Occasionally I felt guilty about it: my knowledge gave the term "insider trading" new meaning. But I wasn't greedy. Patti and I didn't live in luxury. All I wanted was enough money so that my son—and my future children—could graduate from college debt-free.

I looked down at the papers scattered on my desk. I'd done a sloppy job for the drug company today. My concentration was way off. My impatience with Carly felt like a living thing under my skin. I was counting on the upcoming massacre at Kent State to wake her up. Surely then she'd know I was telling her the truth. But while I was nearly certain that deplorable event occurred this week, I couldn't remember the exact date and I felt antsy as I waited for the inevitable. I had that helpless feeling that was all too familiar to me when I knew something terrible was going to happen and couldn't do a thing about it. The war in Vietnam was the most painful example to me. From my rearview-mirror perspective, I could see what an abomination that war was. I tried to talk Joe out of staying in the service. I tried and tried, and failed miserably. I knew I would fail, and yet I couldn't help but try to save him. Such a damn loss.

I hadn't been able to do anything about Joe, but I *could* do something about Carly's baby. All I needed was her cooperation, and I knew I would get it. I only wished I knew *when* I would get it. She wasn't making it easy for me.

There were days I missed the comforts of 2018. I missed my laptop computer and cell phone and the internet more than anything. I missed being able to easily communicate with my friends and clients. I missed being able to look up information in seconds. But 1970 came with a sort of peace I'd never known before despite the turmoil of the war and the racial strife and the startling inequalities. I traded in my laptop and cell phone for a hammock and a book. I had a joy-filled, life-embracing little son. A sweet, wounded, tenderhearted sister-in-law. And above all, I had Patti. I would be forever grateful to Carly for introducing me to my wife. Patti was so different from Rosie. I'd loved Rosie, of course, but I couldn't even imagine her and Patti in the same room. While Rosie had been smart, sharp-witted, and wildly opinionated, Patti was gentle, insightful, and loving. I'd loved Rosie for her brain; I loved Patti for her heart. She made me laugh, and what could be better than that? She'd brought me out of my private pain. She was a planner, and everything she planned was fun: picnics and parties and concert after concert—that woman loved her rock and roll. Within days of meeting her, I couldn't imagine my life without her. I'd known her exactly a month when I asked her to marry me, knowing it meant I would never return to 2018. I had no desire to go back to my old life where I'd felt empty and alone, bereft of all positive emotion. I had the future I wanted now with Patti. I looked forward to being with her for the rest of my life.

Turning off my radio, I gathered the papers I'd been working on from the desk. Putting them in the proper order, I looked them over one last time before slipping them into my briefcase. I called over to Duke to be sure the mainframe was available. Sometimes it didn't matter if I had an appointment if some professor thought his or her project was more important than my work. The mainframe was free, so I picked up my briefcase and left my office, walking next door to Gloria's to tell her I was leaving.

"I'm heading to—" I said to Gloria, then stopped when I saw her face. She was hanging up her phone, her eyes wide with shock. "What's wrong?" I asked.

"Did you hear the news?" she asked.

I froze, my fingers tight on the handle of my briefcase. "What news?"

"That was my sister on the phone." Gloria numbly shook her head. "She said the National Guard just killed four students at Kent State. Isn't that the most grotesque thing you've ever heard? Four children, dead just because they were against the—"

"I have to go back to Nags Head," I interrupted her, already heading for the door.

"*What?*" Gloria frowned. "You have that appointment tomorrow and—"

"Cancel it for me," I said. "Cancel everything for this week." I raced out the door, out of the building. *This is it,* I thought. Carly would have to believe me now.

Instead of going to Duke, I drove to my Raleigh bank, where I'd long ago rented the largest safe-deposit box they offered. The bank clerk set me up in a small private room where I withdrew a packet of bills from the box, checking the dates on them before slipping them into my briefcase and lowering the lid on the box again. Then I got into my Impala and headed for Nags Head. Whether Carly knew it or not, she was going to 2001.

7

Carly

Patti and I sat in the living room that evening watching a special news report on the debacle that took place at Kent State. It was horrific to hear the details of the carnage and to see the fuzzy images on our small TV. Reception was always terrible on the Outer Banks, but tonight it seemed particularly bad. We could hear the commentator though, loud and clear. Two thousand students had been in the commons of the university, he said, participating in a banned rally. The National Guard told the students to disperse, but the kids responded by throwing rocks and shouting at the guardsmen, who fired tear gas at the crowd. The students didn't back down and the guardsmen let loose a volley of gunfire. "More than sixty shots in thirteen seconds," the newscaster said. Nine students were wounded in addition to the four who were dead. Patti cried as the photographs of the dead students flashed on the screen, but I was too numb to cry. I couldn't seem to react in any way at all. At least not on the outside. Inside, I was trembling with disbelief.

Hunter had called at four o'clock to say he was coming home tonight, and as I watched the report, I listened for the sound of his car crunching over our crushed oyster-shell driveway. On the phone, he told Patti he'd finished all his work early, but I knew his real reason for making the four-and-a-half-hour drive home tonight: me. He figured I'd believe him now. I guessed I did, though the realization that he'd been telling me the truth unnerved me. My head ached with the impossibility of it. Hunter, the guy I'd known and admired and loved as my brother-in-law for the past five years, was truly from the future? It was ludicrous, and yet it had to be the truth. I could think of no other way he could have known in advance what was going to happen at Kent State.

He arrived home at nine. He walked in the front door, set his briefcase and small suitcase on the floor, then pulled his sad wife into his arms. He held her, whispered words of comfort into her ear, but his gaze was on me where I stood twisting my hands together in the doorway to the kitchen.

"You heard about Kent State?" Patti asked, pulling away from him.

He nodded. Smoothed her wavy red-blond hair with his hands. "Such a tragedy," he said. "Are you all right?"

"It's just so . . . so *wrong*," she said, and he nodded.

"I know, babe."

From where I stood, I thought I could see the grief in his eyes. Four young people had their futures stolen from them and he had known it was going to happen and yet had been unable to do a thing about it. I couldn't imagine that burden.

"And how are you holding up, Carly?" He looked in my direction again as he picked up his suitcase.

"Okay," I said, trying to send him a message with my eyes. *We need to talk.*

"Come up to bed?" Patti asked him, and he nodded. They headed for the stairs. He walked behind Patti and I saw him mouth the words *I'll be back* to me. I nodded.

I made a cup of tea I doubted I would drink and carried it outside to the wraparound porch. Sitting down on one of the rockers, I set my cup on the small table next to me as I watched the moonlight illuminate the waves rushing toward shore. Ever since I moved into the old cottage after Joe's death, the porch had been my place of solace, especially at night, even in the icy chill of January and February. There was something about the never-ending vastness of the sea and sky that usually gave me comfort, reminding me that in the enormity of the universe, my problems, no matter how painful, were very, very small. Tonight, though, much as I struggled to feel that comfort as I watched the moonlight flicker like glitter on the sea, I felt only fear and confusion. How could it be true? How could Hunter—how could *anyone*—travel through time?

At least half an hour passed before he came out to the porch and sat down in the rocking chair next to mine.

"How are you holding up?" he asked again, and I knew he was talking about more than the news from Kent State.

"It must have been terrible for you," I said softly. "Not being able to do anything to save those students when you knew what was going to happen."

He was quiet a moment. I could barely see him in the

darkness. I could make out a flicker of moonlight in his eyes. On his cheek. That was it.

"Yes," he said. "Thank you for understanding that."

"If you have that rule . . . that 'don't tamper with history' rule . . . then wouldn't it be dangerous to try to help my baby?"

Again he was quiet. "I don't think so," he said finally. "Your baby hasn't been born yet."

I wished he sounded more certain about it. "Could you go back to 1969 and somehow stop Joe from going to Vietnam?"

"I *did* try to stop Joe, against my better judgment," he said. "I knew . . . I know . . . this war is a mistake . . . that will all come out later. But talking to Joe didn't work, as you might remember. He was so committed to doing what he felt was the right thing." He let out a long sigh. "Anyway, I can't change what happened in the past, but your baby is alive right now. Maybe we can save her."

"They'd operate on her while she's still inside me?"

"Yes," he said. "Fetal surgery."

"It would save her life?"

"I'm not positive of that," he cautioned. "But it would give her a chance. Right now, it sounds like she has none."

I winced, remembering the cool, clinical predictions of that doctor at NIH. It was a moment before I could speak again. I heard the squeak of Hunter's rocker against the old porch's floorboards.

"How do you do it?" I asked finally. "Travel to the future? Assuming I wanted to do it, what would I have to do?"

Hunter drew in a breath and I thought I heard a tremor

in it. "I'd use the computer at Duke to help me figure out exactly where and when you'd have to step off, and—"

"Step off? What are you talking about?"

I heard rather than saw him rub his hand over his chin. "It's been a long time since I've had to explain this to anyone, so bear with me," he said. "I'll give you the simplified version, all right?"

"All right."

"There are naturally occurring gateways into time," he said. "They exist all around us. There are an infinite number of them and each of them is linked to a specific time and place. We call them portals. You have to figure out the exact—within seconds—time you need to move into a specific portal to get to a particular time and place. You step off—literally—from something that's at least sixteen feet above the ground—a roof or a ledge of some sort—so that, for a few seconds, you're not earthbound. That's the important thing. To be in the air, untethered, at the right moment."

"Oh my God," I said, thinking there was no way I could ever do that. "That's insane."

"Also," he continued as if I hadn't spoken, "like I explained to you yesterday, the atmosphere should be still. If it's too stormy, for example, it can throw off the calculations, like it did when I arrived in '65. It can be a problem on the other end too, which you can sometimes predict if you're going back in time, since you can research the weather on that particular day, but going forward is harder." He spoke rapidly, almost to himself, overwhelming me with images of me leaping from a rooftop. "It's more challenging to travel forward than backward," he said. "But it's certainly possible, so we would make it work for you, and—"

"Wait a minute." I stopped him. "I'm not saying I'm doing this."

"I know, I know," he said. "I'm just telling you that I'll make it work—if you decide to go. I promise you that. If the calculations are done correctly—and I promise you I'll make sure they are—you'll have no problem. See my watch?" He held his arm toward me and I looked down at his wrist, where the numbers and hands of his gold watch glowed a pale green in the darkness. Three smaller dials were nestled inside the regular clock face and even they were illuminated. He'd worn that complicated-looking watch since the day I first met him.

"Yes," I said. "What about it?"

"It's actually a chronometer," he said, withdrawing his arm from in front of me. "It's extremely accurate, down to the second. It sets itself to the atomic clock that—"

"You're losing me," I said, overwhelmed by all he was laying on me. "What's the atomic clock?"

"Just the accurate time," he said. "You know when you call for the exact time on the phone? The time the automated voice gives you is from the atomic clock. The chronometer sets itself automatically to the atomic clock, which is critical, because if your time is off—or your location is off—you can end up someplace you don't want to be."

"It sounds like there are too many ways this could all go wrong."

"Not really," he said.

"How does it feel when you're . . . traveling?" I asked. "Is it like flying?"

"No, actually, not at all," he said. "For a few seconds you're unconscious, or at least it feels that way. You are . . . out of it. You lose or gain some time, possibly days, depending on a bunch of factors. When you come to, you'll be within a few yards of where you planned to land."

"I don't understand the . . . the portals. Do you create them or—"

"No. Like I said, they occur naturally, but they aren't stationary. They're moving all around us all the time, and each one is connected to a location and a particular time in the past or the future. So the trick is finding one that not only jibes with the stepping-off point, but with the place and time you want to land, as well."

"My God," I said. "How do you figure out where and when to . . . step off?"

"Computers," he said. "Don't worry." He must have heard the worry in my voice. "I'll get you there and back safely. I promise."

"How come people don't disappear all the time if the portals are everywhere?" I asked, trying to work through all he was telling me. "When they dive from a high dive, for example? How come they don't end up in another time?"

Hunter nodded. "When I hear about someone disappearing, someone who's never found, I do wonder." He fell quiet as though he was imagining such a disappearance. I rocked a little in my chair, looking out to the ocean. A bank of clouds passed overhead and stars popped out from behind it, one by one.

"So," I said slowly, "let's say I agreed to do this. Where would I land?" I could barely believe the question was leaving my lips.

"Princeton," he said with certainty. "I'll get you as close as I safely can to where I want you to go, which is my mother's house."

"Your *mother's* house?"

"Yes," he said, as simply as if his mother lived down the street from us. "You'll be a few miles away from her, so you'll have to walk or find a cab. You could hitch a ride, but be aware that people don't hitchhike in 2001 like they do today. It would seem strange. You'd have to say your car broke down or something . . ." His voice faded away and I thought he was deep in thought, trying to imagine me in Princeton, New Jersey, in the year 2001. Which was an insane idea.

"Why would you send me to 2001 instead of 2018, the year you came from?" I asked. "Wouldn't that . . . wouldn't fetal surgery be even more advanced in 2018?" I couldn't believe I was talking about 2018! I couldn't imagine a world nearly fifty years in the future.

He didn't answer right away. I watched a light bobbing out on the horizon. *Fishing boat*, I thought. It would probably be out there all night long.

"You'll have to trust me on this," Hunter said finally. "The year 2001 is the right time."

"So, I'd go to your mother's house . . . and then what?"

"I'd give you a letter of introduction." I heard hesitation in his voice. "She'll have a lot of questions about me," he said. "Just tell her I'm well and very happy, okay? Needless to say, don't tell her you know she's going to disa . . . to die in 2018."

I cringed. I didn't want to meet anyone whose death I could predict. This was so bizarre. I tried to picture his mother. I envisioned a gray-haired woman welcoming me with tea and cookies as she peppered me with questions about her son. "You realize I'm still not saying I'll do this," I said.

"You'll need documents to live in 2001," he continued as if I hadn't spoken, "and my mother will get them for you. She'll also help arrange the surgery. That'll happen in New York."

I frowned. "How can you possibly know that?" I asked.

"I just do."

"What documents would your mother get me?"

"ID. Driver's license. Health insurance. Maybe—"

"I have insurance."

He actually laughed. "Do you really think your insurance will pay for a procedure done in 2001?" he asked. "To be honest, I'm not sure insurance will pay anyway, because I think the surgery is experimental, but my mother—her name is Myra—she'll figure it out for you. I can promise you that. She'll take care of you. She'll get you a new birth certificate, too, in case you need one for some reason. And a more believable social security number. As well as an email address."

"What's an email address?"

"A way to communicate via computers. Myra will give you a computer called an iBook that you can carry around with you."

I felt a stab of fear. "I can't do this, Hunter," I said. "For a million reasons, I can't do it. It's too scary. Just for starters, I have no idea how to use a computer."

He laughed again. "That is the least of your problems," he said. "Don't worry about any of that stuff. It'll all fall into place. I'll give you a backpack to carry things in. I still have that backpack I brought with me from 2018, remember? You'll wear it when you step off. Whatever's attached to you will travel with you. And when you're there, you'll buy a type of baby carrier that you strap to yourself. It'll be a perfect way for you to bring the baby back with you."

Bring the baby back. My heart fluttered in my chest at those words. Joanna would be alive. "Why would I have to stay there until the baby's born?" I asked. "Couldn't I just have the surgery and come back?"

"There are no doctors here who could, you know, do follow-up," he said. "No one in 1970 knows anything about fetal surgery. So you'd have to stay there until she's born. Then bring her back with you."

I rested my hands on my belly. I felt my baby's vulnerability. Her complete dependence on me.

"Could she withstand the time travel?" I asked. "Once she's born, I mean?"

"Time travel's not physically painful or taxing or anything like that," he said. "When you land, you'll feel disoriented and groggy, but that will pass quickly. Some people are nauseated, but again, it doesn't last. Your head clears within a few minutes and you'll be okay."

"That sounds like it'd be hard on a newborn baby."

"I think she'll be fine," he said. "I'll give you a list of

portals to bring you back to 1970, so if the baby needs a little extra time in the hospital in 2001, you'll still be able to get home. All right?" He made it sound like I'd already agreed to this insane plan.

I didn't answer him. I tried to imagine leaving Nags Head. Being away for so long. Being alone without Patti and John Paul and Hunter when I already felt lost and adrift without Joe.

"Hunter," I said, thinking. "I'd be gone for months. Patti would—"

"I'll have to tell Patti the truth," he said with a sigh. "I hoped never to have to tell her. I never wanted either of you . . . I never wanted *anyone* to know the truth about me. But if you go, of course she needs to know or she'd have the police out searching for you. I won't tell her till after you've left, though, or she'd try to stop you, plus she'd call the men in the white coats to take me away."

"But . . ." My imagination was suddenly on fire. "If I'm in 2001," I said, "I could call up Patti or you . . . or even *myself*, and find out—"

"No!" he nearly barked, then softened his voice. "That's the cardinal rule of the program," he said. "Remember? 'No tampering.' Just keep those words in mind. You want to leave a very light footprint, wherever you go. No getting in touch with people from your past in the future. There's far too great a chance of getting seriously hurt, Carly. What if, for example, you learn Patti's dead? Or *you're* dead? Don't do it."

I shuddered at the thought of learning of my own death. "I wish there was a guarantee my baby would be healthy."

"So do I," he admitted.

"Did you know anyone who had fetal surgery?"

"No, but I know a fair amount about it because it fascinated me. I read case studies. That's how I know they can do it on the sort of heart issue your baby has."

"Can you go with me?" I asked. "I mean, I know it would be hard for you to be away from—"

"I wish I could," he said, "but here's something we discovered in our research: four trips is the limit. By the time I left in 2018, three of our researchers had disappeared on their fifth trips, so fifth trips were taken off the table. The 'fifth-trip rule,' my mother called it. I don't know if they ever figured out what—"

"What do you mean, they disappeared?" The muscles in my chest seized up.

"Exactly that. They left—it appeared that they had a successful stepping off, but they never returned. I've traveled three times now. So if I went with you, it would be my fourth time, and I'd have to stay in 2001 or risk . . . I don't know what. It's the great unknown."

He stopped talking altogether for a moment, but I didn't push him. It was clear he had more to say.

"I told you and Patti that my mother died of a heart attack," he said.

"She didn't?"

Again, that hesitation.

"Hunter?" I prodded.

"I guess you have a right to know." He let out a reluctant-sounding breath. "My mother was one of those three researchers who disappeared," he said.

"Oh, no."

"She thought she'd solved the fifth-trip problem, and, of course, she experimented on herself rather than ask me or one of her other travelers to do it. She didn't let any of us know the date or place she was going, though she said it would be a short trip, just for experimental purposes, but she never came back. We were helpless to try to find her." He drew in a long breath. "She took her computer with her, so I couldn't dig through it for clues. I pieced together papers she'd shredded, trying to study her calculations, all to no avail. I have no idea what happened to her."

I heard real loss in his voice. "I'm so sorry," I said.

"We tried everything we could think of to track her down, but just like the other fifth-trip travelers, she'd disappeared."

I shut my eyes and listened to the waves break against the sand. The word "disappear" rang in my ears. "This all sounds way too scary," I said.

"We haven't really discussed the scary part yet," he said, and I thought I heard a smile in his voice now. "Stepping off. It's terrified every person I know who's time-traveled, and at least as of 2018, we hadn't found a better way to do it. If they've figured out a better way since I've been . . . gone, I don't know it."

"I don't think I could do it," I said. "You said the place you step off from has to be sixteen feet high?"

"The roof of the house would work."

I tried to imagine being on the roof of the cottage, stepping off into the air. "I can't possibly do that," I said. "There's no—"

"The end of the pier!" He interrupted me, some excitement in his voice. "It's high enough. Psychologically, you'd feel better if there's water below you rather than solid ground, wouldn't you? Not that you'd ever hit the water."

A tiny bit better, I thought. Drowning seemed preferable to being splattered on the sand beneath the roof. I felt a chill and hugged my arms across my chest. "It's too crazy."

"You can leave when it's dark, maybe very early in the morning, so no one walking along the beach will see you," he said as though I hadn't expressed any doubt. "I'll go out there with you to the end of the pier. I'll be right there with you."

"Insane," I said. "Wouldn't people see me suddenly materialize in . . . wherever I end up? Princeton?"

"They'll think they're seeing things if they do."

"How would I get back?" I asked. "You said you'd have . . . portals or whatever they're called, but where would they be from? Where would I have to 'step off' from? They'd have to be over water, too."

"I'll work on that," he said. "You're going to be in New York at that time, so I'll have to do some research. I'll see what I can find over water that I'm certain will still be there in 2001. Okay?"

"I'm still not saying I'll do it," I reminded him.

"Assuming your baby is born near her due date and is healthy, I'll come up with a portal shortly after her birth." He sounded far away from me, working things out in his head. "Then I'll add on a new date every week or so. I'll give you a list of portals so you know where and when to step off. My mother will help you with money and places to live, but I took a thousand dollars from the stash I keep in the safe-deposit box to get you started."

"A thousand dollars!" I said. It was a crazy amount, as crazy as everything else about this conversation.

"That's nothing in 2001," he said. "Trust me."

"You already took out the money?"

"Yes."

"You really thought you could talk me into this?"

"Yes."

Neither of us spoke for a while. I watched the light of the fishing boat shimmer on the horizon. The boat had moved ever so slightly to the north. Above it, stars dotted the sky.

"I have one really important question about the future," I said.

"What's that?"

"Do the Beatles ever get back together?"

He laughed. Leaning over, he squeezed my hand and I felt his affection. "I'm afraid not, Carly," he said, letting go. He was quiet a moment, then sighed.

"What?" I prompted.

"Nothing," he said. I thought he sounded sad. "But here's something." His voice brightened. "I saw the Stones in concert in 2016."

"You're kidding! Weren't they . . . sixty-something years old?"

"In their seventies, actually. I think Mick Jagger was seventy-two."

I laughed, trying to picture sexy Mick at seventy-two. "Did they come on stage in wheelchairs?" I asked.

"Not hardly. They looked pretty beaten up, but they had a boatload of energy. Mick still danced around the way he does now, and the music was awesome."

"My God, Hunter." I laughed. "I can't picture that at all."

We both fell quiet, the levity of the moment dissolving into a reality I couldn't avoid. I didn't know what he was thinking about, but my mind was back on my baby. My Joanna. I imagined giving birth to her in 1970. Holding her tiny fragile body in my arms as I watched her struggle to breathe. To survive. I saw her lose the battle before my eyes. If there was a chance to save her, how could I turn it down?

"Hunter?" I said.

"Hmm?"

"I'll do it," I said. "I'll go."

He reached over, searching for my hand again in the darkness. When he found it, he squeezed my fingers.

"Yes," he said. "I know."

8

Hunter

RESEARCH TRIANGLE PARK

I'd gotten used to the primitive access I had to information in 1970. When other tech companies marveled at the advances I was making, I had to chuckle to myself. If only they knew what technological changes were coming down the pike. I *did* know, and that knowledge kept me well ahead of my competitors, so I rarely minded the technical limitations of 1970. Today, though, as I sat in my RTP office, radio blaring, I did mind. Very much.

I'd bought three excellent detailed maps: one of central New Jersey, one of Manhattan, and a navigational map of the Carolinas, along with a giant coffee-table book filled with photographs of New York. My mother developed the program to locate portals in the eighties, perfecting it over the years as new technology became available, and it was her program I used now, only I had to do most of the calculating on my slide rule instead of by computer. I'd use the mainframe at Duke to check and recheck my work.

When I left Nags Head early this morning, Carly had dark circles under her brown eyes, and I imagined she'd been up all night, stewing about all I'd told her. We were in the kitchen and Patti was with us, feeding John Paul, so we couldn't really talk. Patti was upset with me for returning to RTP again today. She hated me being on the road so long, always afraid that I'd fall asleep at the wheel or some drunk driver would take me out, which was what happened with her parents. Her anxiety had grown more intense since Joe died. She seemed to have some irrational fear that both she and Carly were destined to end up widows. Usually, I tried to minimize my commuting. Those four-hour-plus drives back and forth to RTP were a supreme drag. Today, though, I had no choice. I had work to do that I couldn't possibly accomplish in Nags Head.

I'd quickly figured out the longitude, latitude, and altitude for the southeastern corner of the Nags Head pier as well as the athletic field in Princeton where I wanted Carly to land. I remembered that athletic field well and could picture it easily. I'd run track and played soccer on that field during two of my years at Princeton. I knew it would be there in 2001. The mainframe computer at Duke, with the help of my mother's elegant formulas, would give me the exact time for Carly to step off. She would be safe.

So that was the easy part: Nags Head to Princeton. How to get her home again was the bigger challenge. I didn't know New York City well. I opened the Manhattan coffee-table book on my desk and studied the pictures, hunting for a good stepping-off spot that would be over water. There was plenty of water—Manhattan was an island, after all—but I had no way of knowing the altitude of the many piers or the accessible locations on the bridges. I turned the pages slowly, hunting for a launch location that would work. It was jarring to see a 1968 picture of Lower Manhattan. The Twin Towers of the World Trade Center were under construction, rising about halfway to their final height. I was surprised when I choked up as I looked at that picture. After a moment, I turned the page. Sometimes knowing the future truly sucked.

The next page had an awesome view looking south from the Empire State Building. If I were the person stepping off, I'd simply pick the Empire State Building and be done with it, but I knew Carly lacked that sort of courage. Who could blame her? I would have to find her water. That was all there was to it.

I turned a few more pages, and then I found it: the Gapstow Bridge in Central Park. The small, lovely stone bridge spanned a pond in the southeastern corner of the park, and the kind soul who'd captioned the photograph even informed me that the arch was twelve feet above the pond's surface. If I added in the stone sides of the bridge, I was certain the height rose to at least sixteen or seventeen feet. Carly would have to take a stool with her, something that would help her get up on that stone wall. It wasn't going to be easy with her backpack and a baby in a carrier, and all of that coupled with the jangling nerves she was sure to be feeling. The park was not completely safe at night, either, especially for a young woman alone. She would have to be careful.

I actually knew the Gapstow Bridge, however vaguely. Rosie and I had strolled across it on our last trip to New York only a few months before she died. We'd scored tickets to *Hamilton* and had spent the weekend in the city. I stared at the photograph of the bridge for a while, sad for my late wife. Sometimes I could get lost in circular thinking. If Rosie hadn't died, I wouldn't have Patti and John Paul. Yet if she hadn't died, I would still have her. That kind of thinking could make you crazy.

I used the detailed map of Manhattan to determine the coordinates of the Gapstow Bridge. Then I packed up my notepads and maps, turned off my radio in the middle of Three Dog Night singing "Mama Told Me Not to Come," said good-bye to Gloria, and headed for Duke and the mainframe to pin down those magical few seconds that would lift Carly safely across the decades.

I parked my car on the Duke campus, my visitor parking tag hanging from my rearview mirror. Then I began walking toward the computer science building. The day was overcast, the sky threatening, but the air was warm. There was a protest going on—I could hear a voice shouting through a megaphone—but it was a distance away from me. Three students—at least I assumed they were students—walked ahead of me on the sidewalk toward the computer science building. One of the girls had on a long-sleeved heather-gray T-shirt bearing the graphic of the cartoon Beatles from the *Yellow Submarine* movie. I thought of Carly's innocent question: Do the Beatles get back together? I hadn't been able to tell her about John and George. It would have broken her heart. She didn't need to hear one more sad thing. She would learn many things in 2001 that would break her already aching heart, but having a healthy baby would heal her. I was counting on that, maybe a bit too much.

I spent the next two hours on the computer in the enormous mainframe room. I sat at the terminal while the giant magnetic-tape drive whirred in the room's perimeter. I would have liked more than my allotted two hours, but I knew I was lucky to get any time at all on short notice. By the time I finished, I had Carly's launch date and time: She would have to step off the southernmost corner of the pier at 4:11 A.M. on May 8, just two days from now. She'd arrive on April 23, 2001. I also had four portals for her return to Nags Head with her baby. I'd have her land on the dunes at Jockey's Ridge where there was plenty of room if I miscalculated by a few feet in any direction. Coming up with the portals was tricky and exhausting work and I went over and over my calculations until I was confident they were perfect. The first one—the most optimistic one—was a week after what would be her due date. The next, a week and a half later. I couldn't get another matchup for two more weeks. Surely by then her baby would be able to travel, but I added a final portal two and a half weeks after that. Her baby would be nearly two months old by then. I looked at my numbers, going over them one more time. Satisfied, I sat back. We were good to go.

I was wiped out and bleary-eyed as I drove from Duke to the Raleigh apartment where I stayed when I was in the Triangle for work. On the radio, Melanie sang "Candles in the Rain," her song about Woodstock and peace, and without warning, I choked up. *Damn this world,* I thought.

Damn the war that took Joe and so many others. Damn all the wars to come. I was the only person alive who knew how bad things were going to get, and at that moment, I felt horribly alone with the knowledge.

At a stoplight, a young couple crossed the street in front of my car, a streetlight capturing them in a pool of silver. The guy had hair to the shoulders of his fringed vest. The girl's blond hair hung to her waist. They both wore jeans tight around their thighs, dramatically flared at the bottom. I remembered Carly bringing home a bag of maternity clothes only a couple of weeks ago, happy because she'd found bell-bottom maternity jeans. Carly wasn't a hippie, exactly. She was no airy-fairy flower child. After all, until Joe's death, she'd lived the life of a military wife. But she'd always had the *look* of a hippie even if she didn't wear peace-sign earrings and flowers in her hair. She had that long, straight blond hair, parted in the middle. She loved her bell bottoms and her fringe and her long dangly earrings and beaded necklaces. She would stand out in 2001. Those flared maternity jeans wouldn't do. I'd have to give her a 2001 fashion lesson to the best of my ability—if I didn't die of high blood pressure before then. The hours I'd just spent with the mainframe had shown me how precarious a trip I was sending her on.

Yet I had to send her, I thought as the light changed and I pressed the gas pedal. I was one hundred percent confident I could get her safely to 2001.

I wished I felt as certain that I could bring her back.

9

Carly

Tonight was the night.

Hunter was feigning calm as the four of us ate dinner in the kitchen. I knew him well enough to recognize the anxiety beneath his easygoing façade. He was quiet, choosing to cut up John Paul's chicken to mask the fact that he was barely eating anything himself, and there was a small patch of skin near his eyebrow that twitched every minute or so. I ate even less of the chicken casserole Patti had made than he did. Patti didn't seem to notice either of our out-of-character moods. She was chattering on, the way she always did, completely ignorant of the fact that her sister and husband were both nervous wrecks.

I kept glancing at the clock on the stove while Patti talked about "The Long and Winding Road," the Beatles song that had been released today.

"They say this is the very last one," she said as she filled her fork with another bite of the casserole. "It's so beautiful, it made me cry." She looked at Hunter. "Honey, could you pick up the forty-five next time you go to civilization?" she asked.

Hunter slipped a forkful of chicken into John Paul's gaping little mouth and I knew he hadn't even heard her question.

"Hunter?" She gave his shoulder a nudge. "Where are you?" she asked. "You're a million miles away."

"Oh, sorry." He turned to her with a smile. "Thinking about a project I'm working on, but I heard you. And yes, I'll pick it up next week."

"Thanks," she said, then she sighed. "I really wish I was back in Raleigh this week so I could have gone to that candlelight service for the Kent State victims at UNC."

"Me, too," I agreed, although my mind was on my own problems at that moment.

"I was trying to imagine how those parents must feel," Patti continued. "Imagine sending John Paul off to college where you think he'll be perfectly safe and then losing him that way." She shut her eyes in anguish. "Oh my God," she said. "I would die."

Hunter turned to look at her. "Don't torment yourself over things that will never happen, babe," he said, his voice patient and kind. He was always that way with Patti. He loved her, and whenever I saw that love between them, I felt both happy and wistful. I wanted Joe back.

I looked at the clock on the stove again. Six ten. In less than twelve hours, if I didn't completely lose my nerve, I'd step off the end of the Nags Head Pier. I fully expected to land in the inky water, and if that happened, Hunter promised to jump in after me and make sure I could safely swim to shore. And where would that leave me, then, if this all turned out to be an elaborate ruse? No worse off than I was now, I figured, carrying a baby who wouldn't survive outside my body.

Hunter had given me the mustard-yellow backpack that I recognized from five years ago when I helped him learn to use crutches in the rehab unit. I remembered someone telling me "that's all he had with him." I thought then that he might be homeless. He'd had a few clothes in the backpack along with a driver's license bearing an address that didn't exist. In the few days since Kent State—the few days since he'd convinced me he was truly from the future—those old facts about him began to come back to me and make sense. Now the mustard-colored backpack was mine. I had only one change of clothing in it, a nightgown, and some extra underwear. No driver's license. No identification of any sort. My small brown leather purse was also in the backpack, my wallet filled with the twenty fifty-dollar bills he'd given me, along with some smaller bills in case I needed them, all of them bearing dates from the late 1990s. I'd stared at the dates, part of me still disbelieving. Hunter's mother had invented a time-travel program? It sounded like a joke. On the outside pocket of the backpack, Hunter had put a slip of paper with his mother's address, along with a handwritten list of the return portals he'd worked out for me. The dates and times differed on the list, but the location was always the same: *exact center of the southern wall of the Gapstow Bridge in Central Park.*

Hunter was worried about my clothes. Sitting there at the dinner table, I was already dressed in what I planned to wear when I stepped off the pier: the only pair of maternity jeans I owned that were not flared at the bottom and a UNC sweatshirt over a too-tight white cotton blouse that I hadn't worn in years. The gauzy, loose peasant tops that I wore day in and day out wouldn't do, Hunter told me. He was suddenly an expert on fashion.

Spending the evening with Patti and Hunter would be unbearable, I thought, so once the dishes were done, I pleaded exhaustion and went up to my room. I lay on my double bed, fully clothed, and simply stared at the ceiling for hours. I'd moved beyond fear, I thought. I was now deep, deep into curiosity. I set the alarm clock on my nightstand for 3 A.M., although I was certain I wouldn't sleep. I didn't know what 4:11 was going to bring me. Perhaps nothing. And if that happened, I would be sorely disappointed.

I didn't sleep. I wondered what Joe would think about what I was about to do. He wouldn't let me do it, I was certain. He'd always been so protective of me. I missed that pampering, although . . . there were times he acted as if I weren't capable of doing something on my own without his help. *Well, I'm doing something on my own now,* I thought, *and it's a doozy.*

All night long, I watched the minutes and hours tick by. At three o'clock, I got up, splashed water on my face, brushed my teeth, and ran a comb through my hair. My hands trembled as I put my toothbrush, toothpaste, and comb into the backpack and zipped it shut. Then I walked quietly into the hallway. Outside the nursery, I rested my hand on the door. I had a sudden terrible feeling that I might never see John Paul again. Never see Patti again. For a few seconds, I considered changing my mind but I thought of my baby and the moment of indecision passed.

I padded softly down the stairs, avoiding the two steps that creaked. I found Hunter already in the kitchen, where he leaned against the counter, drinking coffee. He smiled at me.

"Ready for your great adventure?" he asked, his voice quiet.

I nodded. I tried to smile back at him but wasn't sure I succeeded.

"I moved the car out to the street so we won't wake Patti when I start it up." He set his mug down on the counter, then reached in his jeans pocket and pulled out his watch. "Hold out your left hand," he said.

I offered him my wrist. If he noticed the tremor in my hand, he didn't mention it.

"Here's your chronometer," he said, slipping the gold watch over my hand. "I took a couple of links off the band. Looks like a perfect fit."

I looked down at the chronometer. It was heavy. Definitely a man's watch. It looked peculiar on my slim wrist.

"You don't need to wind it," Hunter said. "Be careful with it, although in 2001 you can easily replace it if necessary. Precise watches are a dime a dozen then, though this one is a cut above the rest. You need the precision to safely step off, all right? When you come back from New York, give yourself lots of time to get in position on that bridge. You can be off by twenty or thirty seconds, but don't risk any more than that."

I nodded, too nervous to speak.

"You ready?" he asked.

I nodded again. He put his hand on my elbow and we walked together out of the kitchen and through the living room. We left through the front door, closing it quietly behind us, and walked in the darkness down the long oyster-shell driveway to the road. Behind us, the never-ending roar of the ocean was marked every few seconds by the crash of waves hitting the shore. We didn't speak as we got into the Impala, closing the car doors as softly as we could. He turned on the headlights and drove the mile and a half to the pier in a charged sort of silence. Parking on the side of the road by the pier entrance, he looked across the bench seat at me.

"Let's do it," he said, and I nodded and opened the door.

The pier lights sparkled against the night sky as we walked its length. The wood was quiet and forgiving beneath my sneakered feet, and I was aware of Hunter's faint limp as we walked, the result of his broken ankle that had brought us together in the rehab ward years ago. A few early-morning fishermen stood at the railings holding their poles, buckets nearby for their catch. They paid no attention to us. The scent of fish and bait was strong and not at all unpleasant to me. I'd grown up with that scent and I breathed it in.

I knew I was to step off from the far end of the pier and I squinted into the darkness, trying to see if there were any fishermen down that far. I didn't think so.

"What if someone sees us?" I asked as we walked. "Sees me? Stepping off."

Hunter laughed. "They'll think they're seeing things," he said. " 'Woman disappears in midair.' They'll think they need some sleep."

We didn't speak as we neared the end of the pier. The ocean was strangely quiet this far out, the sound of the waves far behind us. My heart was beginning to race. Hunter seemed to know.

"You doing okay?" he asked.

"I'm fine," I said, more to convince myself than him.

We reached the end of the pier with seven minutes to spare. I didn't know if I wanted less time or more. I needed to do this before I lost my nerve. I rested my hands on the rough wooden railing and stared out to sea. To my left, the moonlight lay across the water like a narrow silver carpet, and my throat tightened. My beautiful Nags Head. I was afraid if I left it, I might never see it again.

"It's a perfect night," Hunter said. "Clear. Still air. We're lucky."

"Yes," I agreed. I shivered beneath my sweatshirt, although the night was mild. I dared to lean forward. To peer over the railing into the water far below. It was mottled, black and green, and sprinkled with moonlight where it lapped against the pilings. For a moment, my head spun and I thought I might be sick. I gripped the railing tight, swallowing against the nausea.

"Do you have the list of return portals I gave you?" Hunter asked.

"Yes," I said again. I looked at the chronometer. Nine minutes after four. *Oh, God.*

I felt Hunter's hand rest softly on my back.

"If I land in the water," I said, "it'll ruin your chronometer."

He chuckled. "You're not going to land in the water," he said. "Come here." He turned me to face him, wrapping his arms around me. "We love you," he said against my ear. "Come back to us with a healthy baby, all right?"

He let go of me and I nodded, suddenly unable to speak. Never in my life had I felt so nervous. I remembered the fear I'd felt when Joe died. I didn't know how I'd be able to go on alone. But this fear was different. This was visceral. I felt it deep in the center of my body.

Hunter held out his hand to me. "Let's get you to 2001," he said.

I clutched his hand as I put one sneakered foot on the lowest slat of the railing.

"Atta girl," he said.

I was holding his hand so tightly it had to hurt him as I placed my foot on the upper slat, then stepped onto the flat, rough wooden top of the railing. I squatted there so I could still hold his hand. The muscles in my legs shook so furiously that I was afraid I would slip.

"You're doing great," Hunter said.

I swallowed hard, listening to the water lap against the pilings far below me.

I have to do this, I thought. *Have to. Have to.*

"Don't look down," Hunter said, and I realized I'd lowered my gaze to the water again. I jerked my head up, still clutching his hand, and focused on the dark horizon. "Okay, now," Hunter said, "when you stand up, you'll have to let go of my hand." He spoke slowly. Calmly. "I can see the face of the chronometer," he said. "I'll tell you when to straighten up and then you'll immediately step off, all right? Immediately."

I couldn't do it. The muscles in my thighs seized up. "I don't think I—"

"You're going to be fine, Carly," he cut me off. "I promise you."

I heard myself whimper.

"Think of Joanna," he said.

Closing my eyes, I thought of my baby. "I'm okay," I whispered, more to myself than to Hunter.

"All right," he said. "I'm going to count down for you. When I let go of your hand, stand up and step off. Ready?"

"Yes," I whispered.

He was quiet for a few seconds. I heard my rapid breathing. The sound of my heartbeat in my ears.

"Here we go," Hunter said. "Five, four, three, two, one. Stand up and step off."

He freed his hand from mine. My legs wobbled and jerked as I straightened them and then, before I could change my mind, I leaped forward into the dark salt air.

10

A damp, earthy smell filled my head.

My eyes fluttered open and it took a moment for my vision to clear. I lay on my side, very still, my cheek pressed against short prickly grass. My left palm rested on a damp, brick-colored road or some sort of sidewalk. Slowly, cautiously, I pushed myself up into a seated position and felt the straps of the backpack tug on my shoulders. The world did a quick spin around my head and I shut my eyes, wondering if I was going to be sick. Was I alone out here? I felt a frightening isolation.

"Hunter?" I whispered.

No answer.

I swallowed once. Twice. Breathed in and out. I was all right. Opening my eyes again, I looked around me as the spinning settled down.

Heavy gray clouds hung low in the sky. There were buildings. A massive structure on my right. A stadium? There were other buildings in the distance, and trees nearby, only beginning to sprout their springtime leaves. I was sitting half on grass, half on that brick-colored surface. A road? No, a *track*. I saw a few people running on it in the distance. I heard the slap of their sneakers.

"Hey, are you all right?"

I turned my head toward the voice, the motion too quick, too jerky, and the buildings and grass and track spun one more time. Shutting my eyes, I bowed my head low, swallowing down the nausea.

"Are you all right?" the voice said again.

Lifting my head, I looked up at a tall black girl dressed in white shorts and a blue sleeveless top.

"I think I . . ." My voice sounded weak. "I think I just fell."

The girl squatted down in front of me. Her thick black hair was plaited into dozens of long braids. "You've got to get off the track," she said. "You'll get run over."

I didn't think I could possibly stand up, but I managed to scoot over enough that all of my body was on the damp grass rather than the track.

"Are you hurt?" the girl asked. There was concern in her dark eyes.

"I don't think so," I said. I remembered holding Hunter's hand. It seemed like only a second had passed since I let go of him and stood up, wobbly and frightened, on the railing of the pier. I looked around me, wishing he had somehow come with me.

"You're pregnant?" The girl seemed to notice how my sweatshirt stretched across my belly.

I nodded.

"And you seem sort of confused," she added. "Did you hit your head when you fell? Maybe you should go to the hospital. Want me to call an ambulance for you?"

"Hey!" said a skinny brown-haired boy as he ran past us. He did an about-face, still running in place. "Is she okay?" he asked the girl as if I weren't there.

"Yeah, she's fine," the girl said, but the lines between her eyebrows told me she wasn't sure about that. I didn't want her to call an ambulance. I made myself sit up straighter, shaking my head to try to clear it.

"I'm just trying to get to Princeton," I said.

"You're *in* Princeton," the boy said, as he took off running again. "This is Princeton University," he called back over his shoulder.

Oh my God. It worked. I wanted to ask the girl, still crouched in front of me, what year it was, but then she'd definitely call an ambulance.

"That's great." I tried to smile, hoping to look perfectly normal and healthy in her eyes. "Could you tell me how to get to a certain address?" I slipped the backpack from my shoulders and fumbled with the zippered pocket, my fingers trembling. Reaching inside, I pulled out the piece of paper bearing Hunter's mother's address. I handed it to the girl and watched her frown deepen.

"I don't know where this is," she said.

A second boy had spotted us now. From the corner of my eye, I saw him slow his run as he headed toward us, his red hair frizzy around his head. A gold cross dangled from his pierced ear. "Hey, Kendra," he said to the girl. "What's going on?"

"She fell, but she thinks she's okay," the girl said, straightening up from her crouch. She shook out one long dark leg, then the other. I knew I should get to my feet to show them I was indeed fine, but I was afraid my own legs weren't ready to hold me and I didn't want to fall in front of them. "And she's tryin' to get to this address." The girl—Kendra—handed my precious slip of paper to the boy.

"That's, like, maybe five miles from here," the boy said, looking at the address. "Do you have a car?" he asked me.

I shook my head. I remembered Hunter telling me I'd land a few miles from his mother's house.

"Is she okay?" the boy asked Kendra. "She seems kind of . . ." He rocked his hand back and forth as if to indicate I wasn't thinking clearly. I needed to get up now. No more dawdling or I was going to end up in an emergency room.

"I'm all right," I said, getting first to my hands and knees, then struggling to stand up. I felt awkward and embarrassed. The earth seemed spongy beneath my feet and that weird nausea teased me again, but I didn't give in to it. "Can you point me in the direction of that address?" I asked the boy.

He pointed to my right. "You just go that way to get off the campus, and then—"

"She can't walk five miles!" Kendra said. "Look at her."

I tried to smile. "I'm fine, really," I said, though she was right. There was no way I'd be able to walk five miles right now.

"You from the South?" Kendra asked.

"North Carolina," I said.

"I could tell," she replied.

"Do you have any money?" the boy asked. "You could take a taxi."

"All right," I said. This would be my first taxi ride. "Is there a phone booth I can use to call one?"

Kendra unzipped a pocket on her shorts and pulled something out. At first I thought it was some sort of metal wallet. Then she flipped the top open and I saw it was a little phone. She pressed some buttons and asked someone—information, I guessed—for the number of a taxi company. After a few seconds she handed the phone to me.

"The cab company," she said.

I lifted the small phone to my ear. "Hello?" I raised my voice as I turned the little device in my hand, unsure what part of it I was supposed to speak into. I was aware of Kendra and the boy exchanging a look.

"Where are you going?" a harsh-sounding female voice asked.

"Oh! Um . . ." I reached for the slip of paper, still in the boy's hand, and read the address into the phone.

"Where should we pick you up?" the woman asked.

I looked at Kendra. "Where should they pick me up?"

"Tell them the Faculty Road entrance to the campus."

I repeated her instructions into the phone.

"We'll be there in ten minutes," the woman said.

"Thank you," I said, but she'd already hung up. I handed the phone back to Kendra and she flipped the lid shut and slipped it back into her pocket. "Can y'all point me in the direction of that entrance, please?"

" 'Y'all.' " The boy chuckled.

"Follow that road." Kendra pointed to my right. "It's not far."

"Thanks so much for your help," I said, looking from her to the boy as I started to walk. My legs felt rubbery, but I forced them forward. "By the way," I asked, looking at them over my shoulder, not caring now what they thought of me. "What's today's date?"

"April twenty-third," Kendra called.

"And the year?" I asked.

They glanced at each other.

"Two thousand one," the boy said.

"Thanks!" I waved as I turned away from them, a thrill of victory in my step. "Joanna," I said softly as I walked, "we're on our way."

11

From the backseat of the taxi, Princeton passed me by as if in a dream. Everything was a blur of muted colors on this overcast day, and I was consumed with touching my hands, my cheeks, my knees, trying to wrap my mind around the fact that my body had traveled thirty-one years into the future. I alternated between giddiness and nausea, not responding to the taxi driver as he tried to engage me in conversation. I was too wrapped up in what was happening to me.

The driver pulled to a stop in front of a small brown Craftsman-style bungalow, similar to some of the houses in my family's old Raleigh neighborhood. The paint was peeling on the tapered columns of the porch, and the yard looked neglected compared to the meticulously maintained landscaping of its neighbors. I checked the house number on my slip of paper. This was the right address. I paid the driver, and as I was taking my change, I saw a small blue car back down the driveway from the detached garage. Leaping out of the taxi, I ran toward the driveway, waving my arms, the yellow backpack flapping against my shoulder blades. The car came to an abrupt stop and the woman behind the wheel rolled down her window. The scent of cigarette smoke wafted toward me.

"Yes?" the woman inquired. She had short, sloppily cropped gray hair, a network of wrinkles around her eyes, and a cigarette between her fingers.

"Are you Myra?" I asked.

"Depends on who's asking," she said cagily.

"My name is Carly Sears and your son Hunter is my brother-in-law in"—I glanced behind me as though someone might be listening—"in 1970," I said quietly.

She stared at me as though she didn't understand, then broke into a laugh. "Well, holy shit!" She pounded a fist on the steering wheel, ashes flying onto the dashboard. "You have got to be kidding me." She raised her eyebrows as if waiting for me to tell her I was indeed joking.

"No, I'm not kidding," I said. "He's married to my sister. In 1970."

The woman turned the key in the ignition and the car fell quiet. "Let's go inside," she said, opening the car door and stepping out.

She walked ahead of me toward the house, crossing the damp lawn—which was in dire need of mowing. She wore jeans and a tan jacket, a soft-sided briefcase strapped to her shoulder. She was slender—skinny, actually—and she walked with a quick, businesslike step, stopping only to crush out her cigarette in the grass. I followed her up the porch steps and waited behind her while she unlocked the front door.

"Come in," she said, taking a step back to let me walk ahead of her.

I entered a small living room where there was a long, cushy-looking gold couch and a couple of straight-backed chairs. The requisite Craftsman-style bookcase that filled one wall stood empty and the whole room had a bare, chilly feel to it. There wasn't a single piece of art or décor on the walls. Around the room's perimeter large boxes were piled helter-skelter on top of one another. On one of the piles of boxes rested what looked like a miniature movie screen.

"Ignore the mess," Myra said, motioning toward the boxes. "I've already started packing for a move to Virginia this summer. I need my business to be closer to Washington." She glanced at my face, then lowered her gaze to my belly. "You're pregnant!" she said. "You traveled from 1970 pregnant?"

"Yes." I rested an anxious hand on my stomach. "Was that a dangerous thing to do?"

"No reason it should be," she said with a shrug. "It's just that it hasn't been done before, at least not that I know of. We'll have to record everything about your experience. Sit." She motioned toward the sofa. I slipped the backpack from my shoulders and sank into the cushions. Literally. The cushions were so soft they cradled me. I started to put the backpack on the floor, then thought better of it and held it—and its thousand dollars—on my lap. I didn't want to let it out of my sight for a second.

"Where the hell are you from, with that accent?" Myra sat down on the opposite end of the sofa and dug around inside her briefcase, producing a notebook and a pen.

"North Carolina."

"Hmm," she said, a curious frown on her face. She jotted something down on the notepad. She had long, bony fingers and short, neat nails. It was hard to believe she was Hunter's mother. She looked nothing like him, and she seemed too old. She had to be at least sixty.

"When did you arrive?" she asked.

I looked at my chronometer. Eleven forty-five. "About an hour ago, I think," I said. "I . . . stepped off . . . at four eleven A.M. on May eighth, 1970."

She looked surprised. "Was this your first time?"

"Yes."

"You must be thirsty as hell," she said.

I realized she was right. My mouth felt bone-dry. "I am," I admitted. My tongue clicked against the roof of my mouth as I spoke.

She set her notepad on the arm of the sofa and disap peared down the hall into another room—the kitchen, I supposed. When she returned a moment later, she placed a bottle of water and a bowl of grapes on the end table next to me. "I'll get you something more substantial shortly," she said, "but right now, I need to know more." She sat down again, notepad back on her knee. "My son is in 1970?"

Unzipping the backpack, I pulled out the envelope Hunter had asked me to give her. My so-called letter of introduction. I handed it to her and she tore one end of it open and pulled out the sheet of paper. I watched her read it silently, shaking her head with a grin. In a moment, she looked up at me. "Do you know what it says?" she asked.

"No."

Myra looked down at the letter again. " 'Hey, Mom,' " she

read, " 'I know I'm breaking the rules here, but in this case, I have to. I'm living in 1970, married, and have a son. Caroline, aka Carly, is my sister-in-law and she needs twenty-first-century medical help for the baby she's carrying. I stepped off for my last trip in 2018, fell in love, and have chosen to stay in 1970. No worries, all right? Please help Carly all you can. I miss you. Love, Hunter.' "

She looked at me. Were her blue eyes glistening? There *was* something of Hunter in those eyes, I thought. Something in the shape of them. Something in that pale blue. "He's staying in 1970," she said quietly, more to herself than to me.

"That must be . . . weird for you to read," I said. How must she feel, knowing that her son would someday leave her permanently? But then I remembered that he left shortly after she disappeared on her fifth trip. I felt another wave of nausea. I didn't like knowing this much about her. About her future.

"Actually, this pleases me," she said, holding the letter in the air. "I've often wondered if Hunter would join Temporal Solutions, and I see that he has. But he's a naughty boy." She grinned at the letter. "He knows better than to let me know the future. I suppose he had no choice in this case."

"He's really a wonderful person," I said. "He—"

"Shh," she said. "Don't tell me about him." She pulled a cigarette from the pack on the end table next to her. "You mind?" she asked me, already lighting the cigarette with a silver lighter, and I shook my head. "I'd like to know about him, of course," she said, blowing smoke from the side of her mouth, "but it goes against all the rules. I already know too much." She motioned toward the letter, which now rested between us on the sofa. Putting the cigarette to her lips again, she took a long inhalation. "So," she said, letting out the smoke, "what sort of help do you need for your baby that you couldn't get in 1970?"

Wow, she's tough, I thought. If I'd learned something so monumental about my child, I would want to know every detail about his life.

I shifted a little on the soft cushion to better face her. "Hunter thinks you can help me get fetal surgery," I said. "There's a problem—a very serious problem with my baby's heart—and if nothing is done, it's going to turn into something called hypoplastic left heart syndrome, which will be fatal. In 1970, nothing can be done, but Hunter said I could get fetal surgery in New York in 2001, so that's why I'm here." Myra studied my face without comment, and I continued. "I don't have a surgeon's name or anything," I said. "I don't even know why Hunter's so certain a surgeon can help me, but I have to try to save my baby. She's going to die if I don't." My voice cracked. I took a long drink from the bottle of water, my hand shaking. "I'm scared," I said as I set the bottle back on the table, and suddenly, without warning, I began to cry. My nerves had had it.

"All right, now." Myra sounded impatient, whisking her hand through the air. "Get it out and get it over with."

It took me a second to realize she was talking about my crying. I straightened my spine. Sat up tall. Wiped the skin beneath my eyes with my fingertips. "I'm all right," I said. She crushed out her partially smoked cigarette in the ashtray on the end table. "Okay now," she said. "We have a lot to figure out and I need to think everything through very carefully, every step of the way." I thought she seemed excited by the challenge I was giving her. She looked at her watch. "First, let me call my office and tell them I won't be in this afternoon," she said. "Then I'll get down to business getting you documentation. This isn't the first time I've had to do this for someone, but your case is certainly unique. The other times were for scientists involved in experiments. Not for a pregnant woman. A civilian. Where did you step off?"

"The end of a fishing pier."

She raised her eyebrows. "You're a brave woman, aren't you?" she said. It was a statement rather than a question and I thought I heard some admiration in it. I'd never thought of myself as all that brave.

"I'm a *desperate* woman," I said.

She glanced at the rings on my left hand. "Where's your husband?" she asked. "Does he know what you're up to?"

"My husband died in Vietnam," I said.

"Vietnam!" She slapped a hand on the arm of the sofa. "Shit. The worst mistake in modern American history. An unnecessary waste of so many young men and women."

Her insensitivity stung. I knew Hunter had told me practically the same thing, but there was something about the way Myra said it that got my hackles up. My eyes burned and I blinked back the tears. I wouldn't cry in front of this woman again.

"Well, let's get started on documentation for you." Myra reached into the soft-sided briefcase and pulled out a large, flat rectangular metal box. She rested it on her lap and opened the lid, exposing a typewriter keyboard.

"Is that a typewriter?" I asked.

"Laptop computer," Myra said, hitting a few of the keys.

I remembered Hunter telling me his mother would give me a computer . . . as if I'd have a clue what to do with it. I watched her type something, her brow furrowed in concentration, and I wondered what she was looking at. I sipped more of the water; I had no appetite for the grapes. I hadn't eaten anything since the few nibbles I'd had at dinner the night before. Still, I didn't feel as though I could get anything down.

I looked around the room as Myra typed. *You would never know a scientist lived here,* I thought. Someone bright enough to have created a time-travel program. I would have expected a sleek, modern house filled with sleek, modern furniture.

"How did you . . . come up with this?" I asked. "Time travel?"

She didn't look up from the computer. "Completely by accident," she said. "I was running some experiments and discovered an anomaly in my results. An aberration that made no sense and seemed to be pointing to an opening . . ." She typed a bit and I thought she was finished talking, but then she began again. "I didn't know what it was an opening *to,*" she said, glancing up at me, "but eventually I realized it was *time.* An opening in time. And over the course of a few years of obsessing over it and fiddling with it, I discovered how to calculate the portals and here we are."

"I didn't understand a word of that," I admitted.

"You don't need to," she said. "Come closer." She moved Hunter's letter from the sofa cushion between us to make room for me. I moved over, setting the backpack on the cushion I'd just vacated.

"Here's a map of North Carolina," Myra said, turning the computer so I could see a sort of television screen above the keyboard. "Show me where you stepped off."

I found Nags Head on the map and pointed to it.

"Strange name," Myra said. "Is that in the area they call the Outer Banks?"

I nodded. I felt suddenly homesick—painfully so—for Nags Head. For our cottage. For Patti and Hunter and John Paul. They were so, so far away from me in both place and time. It was like they were dead to me.

Myra hit some of the keys. "This is email." She showed me the screen. I had no idea what I was looking at. "I'm going to send a request to one of my staff to create documentation for you and also to procure an iBook for you."

I smiled, remembering Hunter using that word: iBook. "Hunter said you'd get me one of those, but I have no idea how to use it."

"You'll learn," she said, fingers flying over the keyboard.

"Hunter told me you've time-traveled," I said.

"Uh-huh," she said without looking up. "Four times, so I can't go again. Four is the limit."

"Yes, Hunter told me that," I said. "He called it the 'fifth-trip rule.'"

"Exactly. I've been as far as 3000," Myra said, shaking

her head. "You don't want to know what a mess the world is in in 3000."

"Hunter said that right now—2001—it's pretty peaceful."

Myra laughed. "Yes, for about fifteen minutes," she said.

"What do you mean?"

She shook her head. "Let's focus on what you need in the here and now," she said. She began typing a note to her coworker, or whatever he—or she—was. I tipped my head to be able to read the screen.

Traveler from 1970. Caroline Sears. Needs DL, SS#, insurance, CC attached to Temporal Solutions, and cash. Phone and iBook. Will send pic. Myra.

"What's a 'CC'?" I asked.

"Credit card," she said.

"Oh, I don't need one of those." I'd never had a credit card. "Hunter gave me a thousand dollars, and I'd feel guilty taking any more money that's not mine."

"Get over it," Myra said. "A thousand dollars won't go very far in 2001. We'll call your trip an experiment and that will justify using Temporal Solutions funds for you. Use them for living expenses and clothing. Medical costs. A hotel in New York. Whatever."

"Is . . . does Temporal Solutions do anything except time travel?" I asked.

"People think it's a time-management consulting firm, which cracks me up." Myra chuckled to herself. "They're right of course, but not the way they think."

"Wouldn't the military be interested in what you do?" I asked. "It seems like they could put it to good use."

"Oh, they'd be interested, all right," she said. "But I'm not interested in *them*. They'd abuse it, I have no doubt, so I keep everything highly secretive. If anyone gets too close, we have a code word we use to put everyone on alert. We instantly change our phone numbers and email addresses as well as our office location. We've done it three times in the fourteen years we've been in existence." She typed as she spoke. "Twice the FBI got a whiff of what we were up to," she said. "The third time, it was a private organization sniffing around. We fly under the radar." She stopped typing. Looked over at me. "So it would make my people very nervous if they knew about you," she said. "I'm going to keep you my little secret. I'll trust you because Hunter trusted you, but that's it."

I nodded. "I understand," I said.

"That accent of yours," she said. "You're going to stand out here, so expect people to ask." She went back to her typing. "I'll get you a North Carolina license rather than New Jersey," she said, "so you'll have to make up why you're up here. You have family here, or a friend. Whatever. Make it up."

She stood up abruptly, setting the computer on the coffee table. "Come with me," she said. "We need to snap your picture for the driver's license. Need a blank wall, and since I've already packed all our art, that's easy."

She led me to a bare wall in the dining room and had me stand against it. I was certain this would be the worst picture of my life. Straggly hair. An exhausted face full of confusion and uncertainty. She picked up a small camera from the otherwise bare buffet and held it to her eyes.

"Don't smile," she said. "Nobody smiles in a driver's license picture. They're too fed up after waiting in line at the DMV." She pressed a button. "Okay, good," she said, popping something I couldn't see out of the camera. "I'll email that to my partner."

"I don't understand how email works at all."

Myra snickered. "Your head's going to explode by the end of today," she said. "Don't worry so much. You'll learn all you need."

Back in the living room, we took our seats on the sofa again. She stuck something in the side of the computer and hit a few keys. "Okay," she said. "We're all set for the documentation." She closed the computer, then her gaze lit on my belly. "You'll be returning to 1970 with an infant," she said, and I could tell she was thinking out loud.

"I really hope so," I said. "Hunter said I'd need some way to carry her attached to me."

She nodded. "We'll research the best way. Some sort of sling, probably. How has Hunter arranged your return to 1970?"

"He figured out a number of portals for me to use." I reached into the pocket of the backpack and handed her the list of portals Hunter had given me. "They're all from a bridge over a pond in Central Park, because I can only step off over water."

"Why?" She made a face as though she couldn't possibly understand. "You're not going to hit the ground as long as the calculations were done correctly."

"It's just . . . too scary," I said.

She rolled her eyes. "Whatever," she said. Then she very nearly smiled as she looked at the paper. "I recognize Hunter's handwriting," she said. "Let me go over these a little later and verify his calculations." I thought I saw a bit of pride in her face that her son had followed in her footsteps, but she was a hard person to read and I wasn't sure.

She got to her feet and I took it as a signal that we'd come to an end of our conversation. I felt suddenly nervous. I remembered Hunter saying that I could stay with Myra, but I couldn't imagine coming right out and asking.

"Is there a hotel nearby?" I asked.

"You'll stay here with us until we figure out your next move," she said, lighting another cigarette.

"Us?" I asked. I didn't think she was married. I remembered Hunter saying he didn't know his father.

"Hunter and me," she said, and my eyes widened.

"Hunter lives here?"

"Well, of course," she said, blowing a stream of smoke over her shoulder. "He's only fifteen. He's at school right now and you are not, under any circumstances, to let him know why you're here or that you're time-traveling. Hunter doesn't know what I do and I don't plan to tell him until he's in college. We'll say you're the wife of someone I work with and that I'm helping you find a . . . what did you call it? Fetal surgeon? I'm helping you find a fetal surgeon and letting you stay here while we make those arrangements. We often have scientists staying with us. He won't think it's strange."

Well, *I* certainly thought it was strange. "Okay," I said.

The thought of actually seeing a teenaged Hunter shook my nerves. This was so bizarre.

"We need to get you some clothes, too." She glanced at my backpack. "Looks like you don't have much with you."

"Hunter said my clothes would stand out too much in 2001."

"True," she said. "Are you tired? The stepping off can exhaust you."

"I really am," I admitted.

"Come on," she said, heading for the staircase that opened into the room.

She led me up the stairs, cigarette smoke blowing into my face. We reached a hallway and I followed her into a small bedroom. The bed was bigger than mine at home, and as with every other room I'd seen in the house, there was nothing on the walls. Boxes were piled beneath the window. She told me where the bathroom was, then left me alone, and as I crawled, exhausted, under the covers, I wondered if I would wake up to discover this had all been a dream.

My chronometer read two thirty when I finally opened my eyes in the unfamiliar little room. I felt remarkably refreshed and hungry. I got out of bed and used the bathroom, where I caught a good look at myself in the mirror. I looked no different than I had the day before. My hair needed washing and the skin around my eyes was darker than the rest of my complexion, but that was about it.

I walked downstairs and found Myra at the small square

table in the kitchen, where she sat leaning over her laptop once again, cigarette in hand.

"Good, you're up," she said, without even looking at me. "I was hoping you'd be awake before I left."

"You're leaving?"

"I need to pick up your documents."

"Already?" I sat down across from her. "I don't understand how you get them," I said. "A social security number and everything."

"I have a trustworthy coworker who gets us documents for a price, shall we say," she said, closing the top of the computer. "Now as for clothing and such"—she stood up—"I despise shopping. Can you order online and we'll have things sent overnight?"

"Online?" I asked.

"On the computer." She sighed and I heard impatience in the sound. "I'll show you how to do it later." She lifted her tan jacket from the back of the chair and slipped it on. "In the meantime, help yourself to whatever you can find in the fridge."

"Thank you," I said. "Hunter said you would help, but I never expected all . . . everything you're doing for me. I was so afraid to do this. To time-travel. But I would do anything for my baby."

She stopped rushing for a moment, her hands still on the zipper of her jacket. "I understand," she said. "I know I come across hard-edged. I can't help it. I'm a scientist and my mind is always full of facts and figures. But when I was pregnant with Hunter, I nearly lost him. You would have seen a different side to me then. A maternal side came out of me that even I didn't know existed. So I do understand, even if I seem all business, and I'll help however I can. Once we get your insurance, I'll do some research to find you the best fetal surgeon."

I shut my eyes. "I'm so afraid he'll say there's nothing he can do."

"One step at a time," she said, "though I'm afraid your fear might be founded. I read up on fetal surgery while you slept. You said it's the baby's heart, right? Some condition leading to hypoplastic left heart syndrome?"

I nodded, frightened of what she would say.

"Fetal heart surgery for that condition seems to be experimental right now, but if the help you need exists, I'll find a way to get it for you."

I didn't think Hunter would have put me through this if he didn't think I could find the help I needed. "I can't believe how kind you're being," I said. "Thank you."

"Hunter might come home before I get here," she said, heading toward the hallway. "I'll text him that there's a guest in the house so you don't surprise him."

I had no idea what "text him" meant, but I nodded. Maybe it was another way of saying "email."

"What you should do while I'm gone is watch TV," she said. "Watch CNN. That's the news station. The TV's already set to it. You should learn what's going on in the world."

"All right," I said.

Once Myra left, I made myself a peanut butter and jelly sandwich and carried it into the living room. It took me a minute to realize that the large flat screen on top of the pile of boxes was the television. I'd never used a remote control for a TV before, but I figured out how to turn it on and was surprised that the huge picture was in color. I knew a few people who had color televisions but had never seen one before.

That CNN station apparently ran news all day long, which seemed crazy to me. I was used to getting my news in the early evening from Walter Cronkite. How could there possibly be enough news to fill a full day? Today the reporters or whatever they were talked mostly about some bombings in Israel, and they kept showing the same pictures over and over again. I supposed that was how they filled an entire day. In between that repetition, I learned that the president was a Republican named George Bush, and he seemed no more popular than Richard Nixon in 1970. A movie called *Bridget Jones's Diary* was the most popular movie of the past weekend. I also learned that the price of gas was a dollar sixty-three. It was thirty-four cents at home. How did people afford to own a car in 2001? I wondered.

Then they were back to the bombings in Israel, so I used the remote to change the channel and discovered to my shock that *As the World Turns* was still on the air. I stared at the TV in openmouthed wonder. Not only was Patti's and my favorite soap opera still running, but the same actors still played the characters Lisa and Bob and Nancy. They were older, of course—thirty-one years older than the last time I saw them—and watching them was the strangest experience. I felt comforted by them, as if I were seeing old friends.

I wished I could call Patti. I wanted to tell her I was all right. She had to be completely freaked out. I *could* call her if I could find a number for her. That thought sent a shudder through me. In 2001, Patti would be sixty years old. I could ask her if everything turned out okay with my baby. *No tampering*, Hunter had said. I wouldn't dare call her. *What if she's dead?* Hunter had said. He was right. I had to follow the rules.

When *As the World Turns* was over, I switched back to CNN again. I watched it for over an hour. The biggest difference between the news of 1970 and 2001, I thought, was no mention of Vietnam. Of course there wasn't, and yet it felt strange and disorienting to hear nothing about the war that had absorbed all our time and attention for the past few years. Had Joe and all the others who died been completely forgotten?

I was watching another soap opera, one I'd never seen before, when I heard the back door slam. I held my breath, and in a moment, a tall blond boy walked into the living room, green backpack slung over one shoulder, an apple in his hand. He grinned at me.

"Hey," he said. "I'm Hunter. Whatcha watchin'?"

12

Hunter

MAY 1970
NAGS HEAD

I walked in the back door after a long, emotionally agonizing run to find Patti pulling a pan of brownies from the oven.

"I need to check on Carly," she said. "It's not like her to sleep this late."

I drew in a breath. I'd avoided Patti so far this morning, eating breakfast on my own only an hour after sending Carly to 2001. Then I'd walked around the house thinking through how I would tell Patti what I'd done. When I finally heard her stirring upstairs, I chickened out and went for the run. Now it was nearly 10 A.M. and I could avoid her no longer.

I glanced through the open kitchen doorway to the living room, where John Paul was playing contentedly—for the moment—in his playpen. "I need to talk to you," I said.

Patti looked instantly worried. She set the pan on a trivet. "I don't like the sound of that," she said. Her gaze was riveted on me as she turned off the oven. "Are you all right?" she asked. "Are *we* all right?"

I couldn't believe she'd asked that. We'd always been all right. I wasn't so sure I'd be able to say that after today, though.

"It's nothing about you and me, so don't worry," I said. "It's about Carly."

"What about Carly?"

"Come sit, okay?" I patted the back of one of the chairs at the kitchen table and she moved across the room and lowered herself to the chair, her eyes never leaving mine. I sat down, pulling my chair close to her. I wanted to be able to touch her.

"You look so serious," she said. "Is something wrong with Carly?"

I'd practiced beginning this conversation a dozen different ways while I walked on the beach. In my imagination, none of those beginnings came to a good end.

"This is going to be really hard for you to believe, so I'm asking you to just bear with me, all right?" I asked.

She gave me an uncertain smile. "What are you talking about?"

"Carly's not upstairs."

"Yes she is." She started to get to her feet, but I grabbed her hand and held it down on the table.

"Wait," I said. "Let me explain, all right?" I licked my lips. "I happen to know that, in the future, there's a type of surgery they can perform on unborn babies," I said, speaking slowly. "And I knew how I could actually send Carly to that future . . . to 2001 . . . where she could get the surgery."

Patti stared at me and I wondered what was going through her mind. Did she think I'd gone crazy? I could see the thrumming of the artery in the fair skin of her throat.

"Is this a joke?" she asked.

"No, not a joke." I gripped her hand a bit tighter. "You always say I'm so brilliant. That I seem to know so much about so many different topics. But it's not that I'm brilliant, Patti. I seem to know a lot because I actually lived from 1986 to 2018 before I ever came here. Before I came to 1965, when I met you."

She jerked her hand out of mine and scraped her chair a few inches away from me. She thought I was losing my mind. I could see it in her frightened blue eyes. "What the *hell* are you talking about?" she asked.

"I told you my mother was a scientist, remember? Well, she discovered a method of time travel," I said. "She—"

Patti leaped to her feet. "I'm checking on Carly!" She flew out of the kitchen and I stayed at the table, my eyes closed as I waited. I could think of no way for this conversation to go well. A moment later, Patti was back, her face red and full of fear. Was she afraid of what was happening? Of me? Probably both. She stood in the doorway to the kitchen, clutching the jamb, as far from me as she could get without being in the next room. "Where is she?" she demanded.

I looked up at her, not budging from my seat. I was afraid if I went to her, I'd scare her more than she already was. "That's what I'm trying to tell you, honey," I said. "I know it sounds . . . insane. I know that, but I'm telling you the truth. Please sit down again."

"No!"

"I came here from the future as part of an experiment," I said. "I was never supposed to stay, but when I fell in love with you, I didn't want to go back." I hoped that would soften the anger and fear I saw in her face, but instead her eyes narrowed to stormy slits.

"Where . . . is . . . my . . . sister!" She bit off every word.

"I sent her to 2001," I said again. "Once I explained everything to her, she wanted to go. She wanted to get help for her baby. She's—"

"What have you done?" she asked in a near whisper. Tears ran down her cheeks and it was all I could do to stay in my seat. "Did you kill her?"

"Of course not!" I said, horrified she could even think that. "She's with my mother right now, in Princeton, New Jersey, in 2001," I said. "She's actually with me right now, only I'm just a kid. Fifteen. That's why, when I met her in the rehab unit, I recognized her and got excited. I knew her from 2001 and I—" Before I knew what was happening, Patti crossed the room and slapped me hard across the face.

"Stop it!" she shouted.

I lifted my hand to my stinging cheek, stunned. In the living room, John Paul began to wail.

"What have you done with my sister?" Patti was crying herself. I stood up and put my arms around her and I was relieved when she melted into my embrace.

"She's safe," I said against her temple. "I promise you, Patti, she's safe. I would never do anything to hurt her, or you, or John Paul."

She let me hold her for a peaceful moment before

pushing me away. "You're having some kind of horrible breakdown or something," she said, "and I swear, if you did something to Carly, I'll never forgive you." She headed across the room toward the wall phone. "I'm calling the police," she said.

"No!" I grabbed her by the shoulders. She struggled to get free but I held her fast. "Listen to me!" I pleaded. "Listen! I'll show you. I'll prove it to you."

She stopped fighting, but she was breathing hard, facing away from me. "How?" she asked. "Prove it how?"

I let go of her. "Here," I said. My hand shook as I reached into my jeans pocket and pulled out my wallet. Opening it, I took out the yellowed newspaper clipping. I'd been glad I hadn't needed to dig it out to convince Carly I was telling her the truth. It was too painful for me to look at, but now I knew I needed it. I unfolded the clipping and handed it to Patti, watching her face as she read it. I knew exactly what it said because I had written every word of it myself. It was cut-and-dried. I'd been in no place to pretty it up at the time.

Beneath the black-and-white photograph of a smiling woman with short, spiky dark hair, and plastic-rimmed glasses, it read:

ROSE EVERETT POOLE
March 20, 1988–December 15, 2017

Rose Everett Poole, 29, was killed in a bicycle accident on December 15, 2017. Rose had a masters degree in math education from Georgetown University and a doctorate in physics from Princeton

University. She is survived by her husband, Hunter, of Alexandria; her brother, Kenneth Everett of Annapolis, Maryland; and her parents, James and Laura Everett of Charlottesville, Virginia. A service to celebrate her life will be held at 12:00 P.M. Saturday, December 23, at the Unitarian Universalist Congregation of Fairfax in Oakton, Virginia. In lieu of flowers, contributions may be made to Rose's favorite cause, Saving Grace Dog Rescue.

I watched the color drain from Patti's face as she read. She sank back onto the chair, then lifted her gaze to mine. "This is real?" she whispered.

I nodded. Sat down again. She was trembling. We both were. I reached out to touch her, but she drew her arm away from me as though she was still afraid of me. As though, in the last few minutes, I'd become something less than human in her eyes. Some strange being. A monster

"Why didn't you ever tell me?" she asked. "I mean, I know how Rosie died and that you loved her and all of that. But you left out one very significant fact. That you and she lived in . . ." She looked at the date on the clipping. "In 2017? How is this even possible?"

"How much of a scientific explanation do you want?" I asked.

"I just want to know Carly is okay." Her voice caught on "Carly."

"She's okay," I assured her. "My mother's taking good care of her." I leaned forward and she didn't pull away when I took her hand. "Honey, I was there, like I said." I ran my thumb over her fingers. "Carly stayed at our house. My mother found a fetal surgeon to help her."

She looked out the window toward the beach. "Does the surgeon save her baby?" she asked.

I sighed, because here was where my reassurances had to end. "I don't know what happened after she left us," I said. "I know she went to New York to have the surgery. That much I do know. But I didn't know she was from the past. I had no idea about that until I met her in the rehab unit in 1965. It was a shock to see her then, but I was glad, too. I'd really liked her for those few days she was with us. She was a nice woman. After she had the surgery, I don't know what happened to her. I just know she went to New York to have it."

"She's there now? With you? In 2017?"

"No, in 2001."

She shook her head in confused annoyance. "How . . . how did she get there?" she asked. "How did you get *here*?"

I told her about my mother's Temporal Solutions program and how she taught me to calculate portals. I told her about stepping off. I explained it all, while her face filled with something between wonder and horror.

"Why didn't you tell me this about yourself before?" Patti asked again.

"I just wanted to be a regular guy living in the sixties," I said. "I was pretty instantly in love with you, Patti, and didn't want to scare you away. I wanted you to think I was normal. I wanted to *be* normal."

"You should have gone with her," she said. "You should have made sure she was okay."

"I couldn't," I said. "It's because of the 'fifth-trip rule.'

Trying to return to 1970 would have been my fifth trip and for some reason, the people who've attempted to travel a fifth time have—" The word "disappeared" sounded too frightening. "We lost track of them."

She pressed her fists to her temples. "This is crazy," she said.

I nodded. "I know it sounds that way."

"But Carly's safe?" she asked, lowering her hands to the table again. "You can promise me that?"

"Yes," I said, because I knew that at that moment in 2001, she *was* safe.

"When will she come back?"

I told her about the portals I'd calculated for her return, and Patti's eyes grew wide.

"She'll be there for *months*?"

"Yes. She needs to be there until the baby's born."

"Months by herself?" she said. "In a strange place without us? With no friends? My poor baby sister. You should have sent me with her. John Paul and me. I hate that she's alone."

"I thought of it," I admitted, "but I knew you didn't go with her."

She looked annoyed. "What do you mean, you knew I didn't go with her?"

"Because Carly showed up at our house alone."

Patti pressed her fists to her temples again, eyes squeezed shut. "This is making my head hurt," she said. "It's too bizarre." She gave her head a shake, opening her eyes again. "Hunter," she said, "if she doesn't come back safe and sound, in one piece, baby or no baby, I will never, ever forgive you."

I nodded without speaking, but I was thinking: *if Carly doesn't come back safe and sound, in one piece, I will never, ever forgive myself.*

13

Carly

I wondered what this adolescent Hunter saw in my face as I sat on the sofa looking up at him. My smile must have seemed positively goofy to him and I had to resist the urge to jump up and hug him.

"You must be Hunter," I said.

"Yeah," he said, pulling headphones off his head, leaving them looped around his neck. "And you're the lady my mom said is staying with us for a while."

"Right," I said. "I like that shirt." He was wearing a black shirt with NIRVANA printed across the chest in gold letters, and I guessed this young Hunter was dabbling in Buddhism.

"You like Nirvana?" He gave me a *you've got to be kidding me* look of surprise, and I realized Nirvana had a different meaning in 2001 than it did in 1970. It was probably a music group.

"I'm not really familiar with it . . . them," I admitted, wondering if that was a stupid statement. Was it like saying someone wasn't familiar with the Beatles in 1970? But he didn't seem surprised. "I just like the shirt," I said.

"They broke up, but I still like their music. Want to hear them?"

"Sure," I said, clicking off the TV with the remote.

Hunter sat down next to me on the sofa and put the headphones over his ears. They were attached to a small plastic box he pulled from his pants pocket and he pressed some buttons, then handed the headphones to me. I put them on and was instantly assaulted by some throbbing music. I pulled the earphones away from my ears. "It's a little loud," I said, and he laughed and turned down the volume. I nodded along with the music then, trying to look like I appreciated it. The musky scent of adolescent boy wafted toward me, unrecognizable from the Hunter I knew. Still, for the first time since my arrival in 2001 that morning, I felt safe. I felt grounded, somehow, sitting next to him.

After a minute, I took off the headphones and gave them back to him.

"Thanks," I said. "They're . . . interesting." I smiled.

"You've got a Southern accent," he said, getting to his feet.

"I know," I said. "And you've got a New Jersey accent."

He laughed, seeming to find that funny. "I gotta do homework," he said, putting the headset back over his own ears. "See ya later."

"Okay," I said, wishing he would stay longer.

I sat smiling to myself after he left the room. So this was why the grown-up Hunter reacted to me the way he did when he saw me in the rehab unit in 1965. He remembered me from today. And this was why he picked 2001 to send me to. He knew I was here then, in his house. The circular thinking made my head spin. It was mind-blowing. I hoped I would have a chance to talk to him again.

I turned on the TV once more and was watching CNN news about an experimental unmanned spy plane when Myra returned home. She stood in the doorway of the room for a moment, a canvas bag slung over her shoulder, and looked at the TV.

"Learning about the screwed-up state of the world?" she asked.

"A lot of it's going over my head," I admitted. "But I know you have a Republican president named George W. Bush."

Myra rolled her eyes. "Don't remind me," she said, sitting down at the other end of the sofa. The late afternoon sunlight coming through the front window caught every line in her face, and I suddenly realized that my showing up the way I did had most likely thrown her day into chaos.

"Thank you for helping me," I said.

She didn't acknowledge the sentiment. Instead, she reached inside the canvas bag. "Some goodies for you," she said, and I clicked off the TV to give her my attention. "Here's your driver's license." She pulled it from the bag and examined it. "It says you live in Raleigh, North Carolina. That's the capital, right?"

I nodded. "And it's actually the city where I grew up," I said.

She leaned over to hand it to me and I studied it. The laminated license had the picture Myra had taken of me—had it only been a few hours ago?—along with my height, which was off by an inch, and an unfamiliar Raleigh address.

"It's a fake address," Myra said. She handed me a second card, this one bearing my new social security number, and another card for Blue Cross Blue Shield insurance. "Top-of-the-line insurance," she said. "Only the best for my travelers. Now"—she gestured toward the cards she'd handed me—"memorize your address and your social security number," she said. "And your phone number. The things everyone knows by heart about themselves."

"I don't have a phone," I said.

"You do now," Myra said. Reaching into her bag again, she pulled out a small phone that looked much like hers, the word NOKIA printed above the buttons. "This phone will store numbers, make calls, and send texts."

"Thank you." I reached for the phone, but she held it away from me.

"I'm going to put my number in it right now so you'll always have it with you," she said, pressing some buttons on the phone. "And this is your number." She leaned forward to show me the small screen and told me how to view the numbers any time I needed them. "But memorize your own, like I said. It'd look odd if you don't know it by heart." She handed the phone to me, along with a plastic package containing cords. "You charge it every night," she said. "Otherwise, it's useless."

I loved the size of the phone. The light weight of it in

my hand. What a miraculous little thing! "Can you show me how to use it?" I asked.

"I'll ask Hunter to show you," she said. "I'll also ask him to show you the iBook basics." She pulled a large blue and white plastic case from the bag. The computer. She handed it to me. "This thing is gonna rock your world," she said.

So this was an iBook. I set it on my lap and ran my hands over the smooth plastic, shell-shaped top.

"You're never going to want to go back to 1970 once you start using that thing," Myra said.

I smiled, but she was wrong. I didn't care about computers or fancy phones I could carry in my pocket. All I wanted was to have a healthy baby and take her home to the people and the life that I loved.

She tilted her head and gave me a curious look. "Was it weird talking to Hunter?" she asked, but before I could answer, she held her hand up to stop me. "No," she said. "Don't tell me. I shouldn't have asked."

"All right," I said. I was happy, though, that she was going to ask Hunter to help me with the phone and iBook. I couldn't wait to talk to him again.

Myra had brought a couple of bags of Mexican food home with her, and she and Hunter and I sat at the small kitchen table to eat food I'd never laid eyes on before. It was all from a place called Taco Bell, and I had no idea what any of the paper-wrapped items were.

"I bought a bunch of everything, since I didn't know what you like," Myra said, littering the top of the table with the small packages. They were labeled "taco," which was something I'd heard of but never tasted, and "burrito" and "enchirito" and a few other alien-to-me items. "These are for you, Hunter." She handed him three of the packages.

"They're cold," Hunter complained, his hands on top of two of the packages.

"Nuke 'em," Myra said. She turned to me as Hunter got up from the table, opened a metal-and-glass cabinet above the stove, and stuck his paper-wrapped food inside.

Myra followed my gaze. "Microwave," she said under her breath to me. Then louder, "What would you like?" she asked. "Taco? Burrito? Or—"

"I've never had Mexican food before," I admitted, hoping that wasn't a giveaway to my 1970 status to Hunter. He was already back at the table with his food and I was wondering how the food could be warm and the paper around it not at least charred.

"You're kidding!" Hunter said. "You've never had Mexican food?"

"I guess Taco Bell hasn't reached North Carolina yet," Myra said smoothly. "I'm sure you have some food down there we don't have here, either."

"Like what?" Hunter asked, unwrapping the package labeled "burrito." He took a bite and spoke around it. "What do you have that we don't have?"

"Um . . ." I tried to think of quintessential Southern fare. "Grits," I said. "We eat a lot of grits. I bet you don't even know what that is."

"Sounds gross," Hunter said.

"Some kind of ground corn, right?" Myra guessed.

"Ground hominy, yes," I said. I opened the package marked "burrito" and followed Hunter's example, holding the wrapped tube and taking a bite. It was on the luke-warm side but I didn't dare try to operate that microwave machine. The burrito had a mealy texture but the flavor was delicious.

"If your homework's done, I'd like you to help Caroline learn how to use her iBook and phone after dinner," Myra said to Hunter. "She's never had either of them."

He looked reluctant. I'm sure there were a million things he would rather do, but he shrugged. "Okay," he said.

"Thanks, Hunter," I said. It was so hard for me to look at him without grinning. "Are you going to follow in your mother's footsteps?" I asked. "Do you think you'll work for her Temporal Solutions company someday?" Myra gave me a kick under the table, but I thought I'd been careful with my question and I was so curious to hear his answer.

"No way," he said as he opened a package labeled "enchir-ito." "I'm going to be a music producer."

"Oh," I said. "I bet that'll be exciting."

"It might help if you'd study music," Myra said.

He rolled his eyes. "You don't need to be a musician to be a producer, Mom," he said.

"I think maybe you do," Myra countered.

"Whatever," he said, dismissing her.

Myra looked across the table at me. "He's a genius at math and science, but they come so easily to him that he gets bored with them."

"I'm not a genius," he muttered, obviously annoyed with his mother. He was such a teenager. I was having a hard time not laughing as I witnessed this snotty side to my future brother-in-law.

Hunter had finished devouring the contents of three of the wrapped packages while I was still working on the burrito, bits of which were oozing out of the bottom onto the paper wrapper on the table.

"Would you like a fork and plate?" Myra asked. She looked amused.

"I think I can manage, thanks," I said.

Hunter stood up from the table without asking to be excused. He had pretty terrible manners. "When do you want to learn the stuff?" he asked me.

"Right after dinner?" I asked.

"Okay. Come to my room." He took a can of soda from the refrigerator and disappeared from the kitchen.

"So," Myra said quietly with a smile, and I realized it was the first smile I'd seen from her. "He doesn't become a music producer, huh?"

I returned the smile, and shook my head. "No, but I can tell you this, Myra. He turns out to be a wonderful man. A wonderful husband and father."

She looked away from me and I thought I saw a hint of sadness in her face. "You shouldn't be telling me this," she said.

"I'll say no more." I ate the last of the burrito while Myra quietly folded the empty wrappers, laying them one on top of the other on the table.

"I always worry about him, growing up without a father." She took my empty wrapper and added it to the pile.

"He never talks about his father," I said. "He said he never knew him."

"His father was a sperm donor," she said quietly. "And I

mean that literally. Number 1026 at the sperm bank. I never had any interest in a relationship, but I did want to be a mother, and when I turned forty-four, I knew I was running out of time."

"Wow," I whispered. "Does he know?"

"Of course he knows. I wouldn't keep something like that from him."

We both fell quiet as we heard Hunter's footsteps heading back to the kitchen. He looked at us from the doorway. "Are you coming or what?" he asked me.

"Yes, sir," I said, getting to my feet. I started to carry my glass of water to the sink, but Myra waved me out of the room.

"I'll take care of it," she said. "You go learn what you need to learn."

The walls of Hunter's room were plastered with posters of rock bands. I had no idea who any of them were, with the exception of the Beatles and the Rolling Stones . . . and now, of course, Nirvana.

"You're a Beatles fan," I said, as he took the iBook from me and sat down on the edge of his unmade bed with it. He glanced at the Beatles poster.

"Yeah," he said. "Like, I only discovered them a couple of years ago. They were so awesome. George is dying now, did you hear about that?"

"I . . . George is dying? He's only . . ." I struggled to do the math. "Fifty-something?"

"Well, he's pretty old, but still." Hunter opened the lid of the iBook and began clicking the keys. "At least it's not like it was with John Lennon."

Oh, no, I thought. What did that mean?

"Sit here and I'll show you how to do stuff," he said, nodding next to him on the bed.

I felt sobered as I took my seat next to him. There were things in 2001 I didn't want to know. I remembered Hunter—the adult Hunter—warning me against contacting anyone from my past because I might learn things too painful to hear. He'd been right. On a visceral level, I now truly understood the wisdom of that "no tampering" rule.

Hunter opened the top of the iBook and began showing me how to set up an email account. He was shocked to learn I didn't already have an email address. Shocked and a bit put out to realize all he was going to have to help me with. "You really don't know anything, do you?" he said, and I knew it was a rhetorical question.

"I just haven't needed email before," I said.

"People in the South are kind of behind, I guess," he said matter-of-factly. "No offense."

"No offense taken," I said. *You're going to be one of us in a couple of decades, Buster,* I thought. *Watch it.*

He helped me set up the email account and then began showing me how I could search for things on the internet. "What do you want to look for?" he asked.

"What *can* I look for? I mean, what sort of information is there?"

"Anything you want."

"John Lennon, then," I said, steeling myself for what I might learn.

"Here." He handed the iBook to me. "You need to learn to do it yourself. This is called Google." He pointed to a blank space on the screen. "Just type 'John Lennon' right there," he said.

I did as he told me and a long list appeared.

"Now just click on one of those sites. Any one of them."

I clicked hesitantly on the one that read "John Lennon Death." Instantly, the machine transported me to a close-up photograph of John and Yoko. Yoko's crazy hair was pulled back, and for the first time, I thought she looked beautiful. They both did, their faces softened by age. I scanned the paragraph below the picture quickly. He'd been killed. Shot by an assassin at the age of forty. My throat closed up.

"So that's how you do it," Hunter said, unmoved by the news on the page. John had been killed before Hunter was even born. "Now I'll show you how to use your phone."

I peppered him with questions as he helped me learn the intricacies of the phone and its email application. "You've got my mom in here already," he said. "Who else's number do you want to put in?"

"Oh, gosh," I said. "I don't know them by heart to put in right now."

"What about your husband's?"

"My husband passed away."

He frowned. "Mom said you were, like, married to somebody she works with. One of the scientists."

Uh-oh. "I was," I said, "but he died."

"Oh. Well, when you find your friends' numbers, now you know how to do it." He handed the phone to me and

I had the feeling he was dismissing me. I didn't want to leave his room. Leave him. He was the only familiar thing in this strange new world I'd entered. I knew he thought I was a little out of it. A bit off. I would have to be more careful. Would I seem out of it to other people I met? Would I seem that way when I spoke to the surgeon? But a pregnancy was a pregnancy in 1970 or 2001, I reminded myself as I got to my feet and left Hunter's room. I would be fine.

Later that evening, Myra helped me order clothing— maternity pants, tops, underwear, and a lightweight jacket—from Sears on the computer. We sat side by side on the comfortable sofa in her living room, the iBook open on my lap. We were using "my" computer rather than hers so I could get used to "surfing" on it. Myra would point to things and I would order them. All the clothes she picked out were casual, but pretty conservative-looking compared to what I was used to. I had to trust her to dress me appropriately, though.

"Everything will be FedExed to us here and you'll have them by Wednesday," she said. "Thursday at the latest."

"Amazing," I said. Things moved fast in 2001. I hoped I could get an appointment with the fetal surgeon as easily as I could order clothing, but Myra said there might be long waits to see that sort of specialist. I was already twenty-seven weeks pregnant. I wasn't sure how much longer I could wait.

"Hunter—the 1970 Hunter—said my hair is wrong for 2001," I said to Myra as she stood up from the sofa. I spoke quietly, though the 2001 Hunter was in his room. I could hear music blaring all the way down the stairs.

Myra appraised me. "It's definitely got that sixties vibe," she said. "Long and straight and parted in the middle like that. And it's true that most women don't wear that style now, but that's all right. No one's going to say, 'Oh, you must be from 1970.'" She laughed at the ludicrous thought and I smiled. "This is enough for tonight," she said, motioning for me to close the top of the iBook. "In the morning, I'll make some calls and find out what your next step should be."

"I can't thank you enough, Myra," I said, getting to my feet.

"No problem." She scooted me from the room with a wave of her hand. "We take care of our travelers."

14

I spent the following morning sitting on the sofa in the living room as I explored the internet, tentatively, terrified that I would hit the wrong key on the iBook and destroy it. Myra was at her office, trying to "make arrangements" for me. It was nearly noon when I heard her car pull into the driveway.

"You have an appointment for Monday," she said, as she walked in the front door, her briefcase over her shoulder.

I pressed my hands together, excited and anxious. "With a fetal surgeon?" I asked.

She nodded, sitting down at the opposite end of the sofa. "His name is Cole Perelle and he's in Manhattan at Amelia Wade Lincoln Women and Children's Hospital. Apparently he lives down the shore, and just comes into the city to perform surgery three days a week, so we're lucky he can take you."

"Where's 'down the shore'?"

"He lives in one of the beach towns in New Jersey and commutes to New York, and the reason you could get an appointment with him is that they're doing a study on cardiac fetal surgery. Hopefully you'll meet their requirements and can be accepted into the study."

"Oh God, I hope so," I said, shutting the lid on the iBook. I didn't know what I would do if they turned me down. Did Hunter know for certain that they would take me? Would he have sent me here otherwise?

"There's a snag, though," Myra said. "The woman I spoke with said you should bring your records with you."

"I don't have them," I said. "Hunter said they'd be useless because of the dates."

"He was right." She shook a cigarette from the package on the end table and lit it, inhaling deeply. "So I had an idea," she said, the smoke sailing from her mouth. "I called an old friend who's an OB and she can squeeze you in at noon on Friday. That way you'll have some current records."

"Does she know about . . . where I'm from?"

"I told her you're the daughter of a friend of mine from North Carolina." Myra sounded businesslike. Cool and detached. "You saw a physician down there but didn't feel confident about his findings, so you came up here where I could refer you to someone I trusted," she said. "You didn't bring your records with you—you wanted an unbiased, fresh look at what's going on. So when this Dr. Perelle asks why your records are only from this week, you can tell him the same tale."

I nodded, thinking that what Myra lacked in warmth, she made up for in resourcefulness. "Okay," I said.

"Between now and Friday, you should watch the news and read the *Times* online—I'll show you how to do that.

You need to turn yourself into a twenty-first-century woman so these professionals don't look at you askance."

"Can I go for a walk?" I asked. I missed my daily walks to the pier and back.

"Yes, but if anyone asks, remember you're now the daughter of my North Carolina friend, up here for medical care. That's the new story."

"Okay," I said again. I wondered how many stories I would have before this trip was over.

I followed her advice and watched CNN and read the *Times,* but when she was out, I turned the TV to the soaps and the shows where people simply talked to one another, like Oprah Winfrey's show and *The View.* Oprah was a smart black woman who shied away from nothing when it came to her interviews, even saying the word "vagina" on television, which blew my mind. I could tell the people in her audience loved her. And I was shocked to see Barbara Walters on *The View.* She was on the *Today* show back home—I kept thinking of 1970 as "back home" now—where she was much younger and her hair much darker.

I learned plenty about the world watching those shows. Homosexual people didn't have to hide who they were anymore and, in the Netherlands, they could even get married. The last president, Bill Clinton, had been impeached for having oral sex in the Oval Office, and there was some comparison made to Richard Nixon, so I had to look that up. I was no fan of Nixon—I hated that he was escalating the war in Vietnam—and I learned he would eventually have to resign in disgrace. It shook me up sometimes when I discovered things that would happen . . . that *had* happened. Occasionally it disoriented me to the point of nausea and I had to stop surfing the internet or watching TV for a while. That's when I took my long walks down the tree-lined streets in Myra's neighborhood. I passed a few people here and there, but no one asked me who I was. I saw plenty of bike riders, and they all wore helmets, which I learned from the internet was common. And then there were the people running, their pace slow and loping. Hunter told me they were "jogging." Even he jogged sometimes, he said.

I thought about Patti on my walks. I could only imagine how she'd reacted when she learned what I'd done. I wished I had a way to let her know I was all right and that I missed her. I hoped Hunter was able to reassure her that I was safe.

Sometimes I talked to Joe as I walked. Not out loud, of course, but he was always there in my mind. I told him what I was doing and—in my imagination—he thanked me for giving our daughter a chance at a healthy life. He'd have wanted this baby. This daughter. Of that I was absolutely certain. I thought back to his two weeks' leave before he left for Vietnam. We could have spent those two weeks anywhere. Done anything. But he wanted to spend them in the house at Nags Head with Patti and Hunter, so that's what we did. Hunter and I both took off from work and Patti had stopped teaching before John Paul's birth six months earlier, so all four of us were footloose for those couple of weeks. It was like being kids again, in a way. Although it was October, the weather was unseasonably balmy—warm enough for the guys to surf while Patti and I stayed with John Paul on the beach or cooked. Joe and I crabbed and fished like we did when we were teenagers. All four of us watched the Mets beat the Orioles in the World Series, turning the TV off only when the news broke in with coverage of the "Moratorium Against the Vietnam War" in Washington, which Joe didn't want to watch. We played Monopoly and Spit and The Game of Life. Joe read *The Godfather*, and when he finished it he started it again. I read one Daphne du Maurier book after another. We blasted the Stones and Beatles and Led Zeppelin and Janis Joplin on the record player. We danced in the living room in the daytime and cuddled up in blankets on the porch in the evenings.

Every day, Joe ran and ran and ran. He'd smear zinc oxide on his nose and head out to the road. His running was the only clue I had to his fear. He was afraid of losing his conditioning. He didn't want to arrive soft in Vietnam.

The last night, we built a bonfire on the beach. Since it was October, we had the beach to ourselves and the fire was a beautiful thing. The four of us wrapped up in blankets and we grilled hot dogs and toasted marshmallows. We talked about nothing of consequence, as if we'd made an unspoken pact to keep things light on our last night together.

As the fire was dying, Patti suddenly jumped to her feet. "Hey, look!" she said, pointing toward the ocean.

We all turned to see what had caught her attention. Bright, neon-blue waves rolled toward the shore in the moonlight. Bioluminescent plankton. I hadn't seen that breathtaking phenomenon since I was a teenager. That it was happening on this night, our last night all together, felt significant somehow, and we walked down to the water's edge, our blankets over our shoulders, and watched, mesmerized, as blue wave after blue wave rushed toward us through the darkness. When we'd been standing there for a while, Joe moved next to me. He wrapped his blanketed arm around my shoulders, pulling me close. "Hey, girl," he said softly in my ear. "Let's go make a baby."

And we did.

I wondered now if somehow he knew—or at least he worried—that he would die. Had he wanted a part of him to live on? I was determined that a part of him would.

Joanna kept me going that week as I waited for my appointment with Myra's obstetrician friend. She reminded me why I had made this crazy trip by wriggling and bouncing around inside me. Would a desperately sick baby be that active? The more I thought about those blotchy images from the experimental ultrasound at NIH, the more certain I felt that Dr. Halloway had been wrong and Joanna was fine. By Friday morning, as I ate breakfast with Myra and Hunter, I felt certain of it. I had a healthy baby. I expected Myra's obstetrician friend would tell me all was well with my pregnancy when I saw her that afternoon. Maybe then Myra could give me an earlier portal and I could go home to my beloved Nags Head and 1970.

The obstetrician's office was near Princeton University, not far from where I'd landed a mere four days earlier. My appointment was at noon, and I realized Myra's friend was most likely squeezing me in on her lunch hour. I thought we should go into the appointment fresh, without revealing to the doctor the diagnosis I'd received in 1970—or as Myra said to her friend, "down in North Carolina," as though I lived in some dusty little backwater. But Myra had obviously told her the bad news and the woman—her name was Anita Smythe—greeted me with a look of pained sympathy. She held her hand out to me.

"I'm Anita," she said with her gentle smile. "Let's see how you're doing."

We left Myra in the waiting room and I followed Anita through a doorway and down a long hall.

"You're the daughter of one of Myra's good friends?" she asked, although I could tell it was more of a statement than a question. "She told me about your diagnosis."

"To be honest with you," I said, "I'm hoping the diagnosis is wrong." I wanted to put that out there up front. I wanted to be sure she'd consider that possibility. "My baby is very, very active," I added.

"Of course," she said. "Let's get your vitals and then we'll do an ultrasound and see what we can see."

In the hallway, she weighed me, then took my blood pressure and then stuck a probe in my ear, which I realized was some sort of thermometer only after she told me my temperature was ninety-eight point four. She led me into an examining room that was bigger and brighter than the one at NIH, and the clean, modern look of the room gave me irrational hope. The machine had a streamlined space-age look to it, too. The screen was larger and flatter than the one at NIH, and it was attached to an illuminated keyboard. I was going to get good news in this room, I thought. I could feel it.

I didn't have to undress, either. I simply lay down on the examining table, lifted my shirt, and lowered my brand-new maternity pants below my belly. She squirted gel on my belly and began running the wand or whatever it was called slowly over my skin.

"Oh!" I said when the image appeared on the screen. I could see her! I could see Joanna. Yes, the picture was still fuzzy and gray, but I could easily make out the shape of her head. Her adorable, perfect profile. The fingers of one little hand were splayed in a wave. Instinctively, I lifted my own hand to wave back. The connection I'd felt to her from the start instantly became even more solid and real. "The picture is so much clearer," I said.

"Really?" Anita sounded surprised. "Myra said the other ultrasound was done in North Carolina?"

"Yes." I realized my mistake. I wasn't going to tell her it had been performed at the National Institutes of Health in Maryland, and I certainly wasn't going to say anything about 1970. "She looks perfect," I said.

Anita didn't answer as she pushed buttons and turned knobs on the machine, and the image of my baby turned into something I could no longer discern. "Have you had a fetal echocardiogram?" Anita asked.

"No," I said, wondering if such a thing even existed in 1970.

"I could refer you for one, but Myra said you're going to

be evaluated for a fetal heart study in the city, right? Fetal surgery? So they'll certainly be doing one there."

"What do you see?" I asked.

She pointed to the screen. "It appears that there's a severe blockage of the aortic valve, which I'm afraid will result in her having hypoplastic left heart syndrome."

I couldn't breathe. I was suddenly back in that claustrophobic office at NIH trying to make sense of an image that was a blur before my eyes.

"It's very serious," Anita continued, "but I'm sure you already heard that from your North Carolina doctor." She turned off the machine and handed me a wad of tissues to clean the gel. I wiped it off, but I was too depleted by her news to even sit up. I stared at the ceiling. That beautiful little head. The way she was waving with her tiny fingers. The way she kicked and tumbled around inside of me. How could she possibly be so sick?

"Are you all right?" Anita asked. "Would you like to rest a moment before you sit up?"

"I'm just sad," I said quietly as I tugged my pants over my stomach. Elbowing my way into a sitting position, I swung my legs over the side of the table. "I was hoping you wouldn't see what you saw. Is there any chance it just *looks* like . . . what you said? Could it actually be something less ominous?"

Once again she wore that unbearably sympathetic expression. "I'm sorry," she said. "You'll need an echocardiogram to know for sure, but I'd be very surprised if I'm wrong here. The fetal surgery is experimental, but it might save your baby's life. I hope you get that opportunity." With a hand on my elbow, she helped me off the examining table. "I'll look forward to hearing how it goes," she said.

"I'll go with you to the appointment with the fetal surgeon on Monday," Myra said as we drove away from Anita's office, my new medical record, such as it was, in a manila folder on my lap. "I'm worried that they'll want to evaluate your mental health before putting you in the study, and you might say or do something that'll land you in a psych hospital, so I should be there."

I was taken aback. "Do I seem that ... out of it?" I asked. I wanted to tell her I'd been following her advice, reading the *Times* and watching TV. But no matter how much I was learning about 2001, I knew I still had the heart and soul and spirit of a 1970s woman.

"You seem fairly normal." Myra glanced at me. "But every once in a while, you say something that shows a remarkable ignorance of the current day. The microwave the other night, for example. They've been around for a long time and it makes no sense that you wouldn't know how to operate one. I think Hunter sent you here unprepared."

"He had to send me quickly," I said, annoyed by her criticism of both Hunter and myself.

"You need to be careful," she said. "When you meet with the surgeon, you'd better go with the story that your husband is dead to explain why he's not with you. Figure out how he died. Car accident is probably best, so you don't get a ton of medical questions. I'll say I'm a family friend. Are you familiar with New York?"

"I've never been."

"Well, prepare to be overwhelmed. The hospital isn't far from all the action in the city. It's only about a mile from Central Park, too, which is where Hunter has you stepping off for your return portal, so that's perfect. While you're waiting for the baby, you can catch a Broadway show, visit MoMA, do the usual touristy things."

"MoMA?"

"Museum of Modern Art."

I shook my head. "Is that the sort of . . . ignorance that will make me look stupid?" I asked.

She snorted. "Well, if you're from North Carolina, I guess you'd have no reason to know about it, so don't sweat it. I'll be with you to clean up any faux pas."

"Thank you," I said.

She glanced at me again. "The woman I spoke with from the study said you'll need to stay close to the hospital once you have the surgery and before your baby's born," she said. "They'll be doing tests regularly. Ultrasounds and such and probably blood work. I don't know what else. She said as long as you're in the study they'll pick up a good part of the tab for you to stay at a nearby corporate residence."

I felt alarm. "Can't I stay with you and Hunter and go back and forth to New York?"

"She said they want you in the city."

I stared straight ahead, taking this in. "What's a corporate residence?" I asked, wondering if that was another thing everyone in the world knew except me.

"Rooms or apartments that are rented long-term, usually to businesspeople," Myra said, "but often a hospital will have an agreement with them at a reduced rate."

"So I wouldn't be coming back here at all?" My palms were beginning to sweat. Even though Myra was not the warmest, most encouraging woman, I didn't want to leave the safety of her. I didn't want to leave Hunter. The thought of being alone in a strange city . . . and a strange time . . . overwhelmed me.

"If they accept you into the study, no, you won't be coming back," she said, turning onto her street. "You'll stay there. But I'll keep in touch with you. I come into the city from time to time. A couple of my travelers live there, though one of them is on an extended trip to the late 1800s. And you can always call me. But we're getting ahead of ourselves," she said, pulling into her driveway. She stopped the car and looked over at me. "First," she said, "we have to get you into this study."

15

Hunter had already left for school by the time I went into the kitchen on the morning of my appointment in New York. I made oatmeal for myself in that crazy microwave oven and I was slicing bananas on top of the cereal when Myra walked into the kitchen speaking sharply into her phone.

I moved my bowl to the table as she poured her coffee, the phone clutched between her cheek and shoulder.

"You should have had that all figured out by now," she snapped into the phone.

I had no idea what she was talking about, but she set my nerves on edge with the tone of her voice. I poured hot water over the teabag in my cup and took my seat while she continued berating someone on the other end of her phone line.

Finally, she slammed her phone onto the counter and sat down across from me, coffee cup in her hand.

"I can't go with you today," she announced. "We have a problem with the calculations for one of our travelers and I have to work today or the current experiment will be called off after a year of planning. There are too many people depending on it for me to risk screwing it up."

I sat there, fingers white on the handle of my teacup, quietly freaking out.

"You'll be fine," she said. "You've been here what? Eight days now?"

"Seven," I said quietly.

"You're doing a lot better. You're not going to screw up. I'll drop you off at the train station." She lifted her cup to her lips and took a sip. "You'll take the train to Penn Station, then instead of hassling with the subway, just take a cab to Lincoln Hospital." Picking up the pack of cigarettes from the table, she shook one out and lifted it to her mouth. I waited wordlessly while she lit it and blew a stream of smoke to her right. "The cabs are right there outside Penn Station," she said. "It'll actually be good for you to be on your own, I think. You need to prove to yourself you can do it."

I nodded. "All right," I said, although I felt like a little kid whose mother was abandoning her. But if I could travel from 1970 to 2001, I told myself, I could certainly travel from Princeton to New York.

The hour-long train ride was easy and getting a cab outside Penn Station a snap, as Myra had said. New York, though, stunned me. I knew what to expect, certainly. How many movies had I seen set in New York City? I knew there would be skyscrapers and glaring lights, even in the daytime. I expected the crowded sidewalks. But I wasn't prepared for the noise that assaulted me despite closed taxi windows, or the gaudy advertising on the buildings. The utter sense of chaos. The insanity of the drivers. The street was wall-to-wall taxis and cars and trucks and there appeared to be no lanes that I could discern. I'd never been claustrophobic, but I felt my heart pound with the sense of being trapped. Although I was surrounded by hundreds of vehicles and thousands of people, I'd never felt so alone. I was in a strange place where I knew no one and no one knew me. Except for Joanna. Hand on my belly, I reminded myself my baby was with me. Joanna was the reason for everything.

My cab driver spoke broken English, and I could only hope he understood where I needed to go. I could have walked much faster than the cab was traveling, I thought, but soon the neighborhood changed dramatically and I knew we were getting closer to the hospital. The cluttered streets gave way to a more open feeling, and small trees bearing tiny new leaves rose up along the broad sidewalks. The tall buildings gave way to shorter—short being a relative term—buildings made of . . . limestone? Granite? Concrete? I didn't know, but the overall effect on the atmosphere was lighter and brighter and I felt as though I could breathe.

The driver pulled up in front of a modern, many-storied white-and-glass building. He said nothing, simply pointed to the meter. I paid him with some of my cash and got out of the taxi.

The lobby of the hospital was nearly as chaotic and crowded as the streets around Penn Station. It was filled with chatter and, ironically, the soft notes of piano music.

I looked around and spotted an elderly man dressed in a suit sitting at a grand piano, his thin fingers flying over the keys. The music—I didn't recognize the melody—echoed against the hard surfaces, but it took an edge off my nerves as I hunted for the elevator.

I rode the elevator, crammed with far too many people, to the tenth floor, then followed the signs to the Maternal and Fetal Care Center. A receptionist greeted me and I sat in a nearly empty waiting room for fifteen minutes before a woman showed up in the doorway, calling my name. She looked about my age and wore a white jacket, with *E. Rightmire, RN* and a few other initials embroidered above the pocket. She smiled.

"I'm Liz Rightmire," she said as I approached her, and she shook my hand. She had a pixie haircut, the color somewhere between red and purple, and now that I was closer, I noticed a thin gold hoop through a piercing in her left nostril. I'd seen pierced noses and eyebrows and even tongues in the music posters in Hunter's room, but I was slightly stunned to see this sort of piercing on a professional woman. "Follow me," she said, and we started walking together down a wide hallway.

"I think you've been advised that the study is full, right?" she said as we walked.

My heart seemed to drop. "No," I said. I was suddenly on the verge of tears.

"Well, don't worry," she said. "If you meet our criteria, we're not going to turn you away." She was a quick talker, the words full of hard edges and dropped *r*s, but there was a kindness in her voice that I clung to. "Your OB faxed us your most recent ultrasound and Dr. Perelle took a look at it. He wants us to do another one here, a little more detailed, plus you'll have a fetal echocardiogram and some blood work. But first, we'll make sure you're a good match for our research."

"All right." I was afraid to say too much, remembering what Myra had said about my possible faux pas. One thing I'd learned in the last seven days was that I didn't even know when I was making them.

Liz led me into a small room where four leather straight-backed chairs were the only furniture, and we sat down across from each other. I clutched my purse on my lap while she held a clipboard on hers, and I noticed with a jolt that her nails were painted blue. She asked me my name and birthdate—now March 5, 1974—and verified much of the information she must have already known from my brand-new, very slim medical record.

"You're from North Carolina, right?" she asked, and I nodded. "What brings you up here?"

"I have a family friend here . . . well, in New Jersey . . . who felt strongly that I could get better care up here if there was a problem with my baby."

"So you're staying with your friend?"

"Yes. In Princeton."

"Any support—family or friends—in the city?"

"No," I said. "My family's in North Carolina."

"Who's in your family?"

"My sister and brother-in-law and nephew," I said, and just saying those words made my heart ache. *Do not cry,* I told myself. I needed to look strong. Psychologically healthy.

"And it says here that you're widowed?"

"My husband died in a car accident in November."

She looked both concerned and sympathetic. "What a rough time for you," she said, her voice kind enough to nearly trigger the tears I was fighting to hold back.

"Yes," I said. "And the most important thing to me now is to do everything I can to give our baby a chance at a healthy life."

"Of course," she said, without looking up from the clipboard. "This is your first pregnancy, right?"

"Yes."

"Are you working? Can you take time off from your job?"

"I'm not working right now. I'm a physical therapist, but I took time off after my husband died, and once I realized I was pregnant, I decided not to go back right away."

Maybe it was my imagination, but I thought her opinion of me climbed a notch or two at the realization that I'd worked in the medical field, and I sat up a little straighter. I needed to remind myself I was an accomplished person. I'd felt so small and weak and fearful lately. Liz went on to ask me questions about my health, my family's health, my alcohol consumption—none since learning I was pregnant— my nonexistent drug use, any experience with depression, and on and on.

I must have passed her assessment, because she then sent me from place to place in the hospital, first for blood work, then for the ultrasound, and finally for the echocardiogram. The technicians running those tests gave absolutely nothing away in their steely blank faces, so I had no idea what to expect when I was finally called into the fetal surgeon's office.

Dr. Perelle stood up when I entered the spacious office and he walked around his desk to shake my hand and offer me a seat. He was fiftyish, his hair mostly gray, and he wore jeans and a long-sleeved blue shirt, open at the neck. No white coat. No stethoscope. His warm smile was infectious and I liked him instantly. I began to relax a bit after the harrowing morning of tests.

He took his seat behind his desk and looked at me with sympathetic blue-green eyes. "I believe you already know this," he said, "but your baby is critically ill."

My eyes filled at hearing the words spoken so clearly. I nodded, acknowledging the truth for the first time.

"Our tests show conclusively that the valve controlling the flow of blood from the left ventricle to the aorta is partly blocked. Without intervention, the left ventricle will become hypoplastic . . . in a nutshell, no longer able to do its job, and—"

"And that's fatal," I said.

He nodded. "As I said, 'without intervention,' yes."

I bit my lip. "I was hoping somehow . . ." My voice faded into the air.

"Of course you were," he said, "and I'm sorry that the news isn't better. The good news, though, is that you qualify for our study."

I let out my breath. "Thank God," I said, more to myself than to him.

"It'll have to be very soon, though," he said. "You're already at twenty-eight weeks and twenty-nine is our cutoff. And you need to understand that although fetal surgery's been around for a while, it's considered experimental for this condition," he cautioned. "Frankly, it's been unsuccessful elsewhere, for the most part, but we're getting encouraging results here at Lincoln. The technique I'm using is particularly new and we're hopeful. We've performed the surgery in only nine cases so far and none of those babies has been born yet, although a couple should be very soon and we're extremely optimistic. But you need to know that three of the babies we operated on have died in utero."

"Three!" I said, horrified.

"Yes," he responded soberly. "I want you to know the risks. One died during the surgery, the other two a couple of weeks after. The reality is, though, that those babies wouldn't have survived more than a day or two after they were born." He then showed me diagrams as he explained what he would do—what he would *attempt* to do—to my baby's tiny, fragile heart. I heard some of what he said. "A wire as thin as a human hair" and "inflate a tiny balloon to force the valve open." The images blurred in front of me. Three babies had died. Had I come all this way to lose Joanna to the surgery I thought would save her?

When he was done telling me about the surgery, he sent me back to Liz who congratulated me on making it into the study.

"I'm happy for you," she said, taking a seat in the office with the leather straight-backed chairs. "Dr. Perelle is excellent and he'll give your baby her best chance."

I had trouble smiling back at her, I was so overwhelmed

by the last few hours. All the tests. All the information. The disheartening statistics. "I'm scared," I admitted, lowering myself to one of the chairs.

"We'll take good care of you," she said. She was looking down at her clipboard and I noticed that my file had grown over the last few hours. "Now, you may know your insurance won't cover this procedure or any of the follow-up care because it's experimental," she said, "but it's a study, so you don't need to worry about that. You said you don't have family or friends in New York, right?"

"Right."

"But you need to stay nearby—that's a requirement of the study that you'll have to agree to. We can get you a reduced weekly rate at nearby corporate housing, which will come in at around four-fifty a week. And you have eleven or twelve weeks left in your pregnancy. I know that adds up. Can you manage it?"

That was the reduced rate? I nodded uncertainly. "I think so," I said. I thought I'd been wealthy when Hunter gave me that thousand dollars. It would only cover a couple of weeks in New York. But Myra had said Temporal Solutions could help me. I hated to ask her for that much.

"It'll be a studio apartment with a little kitchenette," Liz said. "Once you have the surgery, you'll need to be on modified bed rest and—"

"Bed rest!" I said. How was I going to manage that with no one to help me?

"Modified," she assured me. "That means you can get up, move from room to room ... although the studio apartment is only one room ..." She chuckled. "You can go to the bathroom, take a shower, make yourself a meal, take a cab back and forth to the hospital. You just can't go sightseeing or shopping. Your building will have concierge service to bring in groceries, though of course that will cost you extra. Can you manage it?" she asked again.

"Yes," I said. I would make this work, though I was frankly terrified. This was going to be more complicated than I'd anticipated.

"We're scheduling you for Tuesday, May eighth," she said. "That's a little over a week from now and you'll need to check into the hospital the day before. All right?"

"Yes," I said again.

She gave me more details about the surgery and all it would entail, and although I nodded and reassured her that I understood, I felt as if I were inside a dream. All I hoped was that it wouldn't turn into a nightmare.

16

By the time I arrived back at Myra's house in Princeton, it was nearly six o'clock. Myra ordered pizza and she and Hunter and I sat around the small table in the kitchen as we ate it.

"So what did they tell you about where you'll live?" Myra asked, balancing a slice of pizza on her fingertips.

"It'll be a studio apartment not far from the hospital," I said, "but I'm afraid even with the reduced rate, it'll be expensive and I'll understand if you can't help me financially. It's four hundred and fifty a week, and I don't—"

"For a studio apartment in the Upper East Side?" she interrupted me. "That's nothing. Don't worry about it. Use your money for food and incidentals. Temporal Solutions will pick up the tab on your housing."

My eyes burned with gratitude. "Thank you," I whispered.

"How do they do it?" Hunter asked. "How do they get to the baby to operate on it?"

I could see the wheels turning inside his head as he considered the mechanics of the surgery, and I smiled. "Through my abdomen," I said, and I tried to repeat back to them what I'd learned that day. "But three of the nine babies the doctor's performed this surgery on have died before they were born," I said. "So I'm pretty nervous."

"Wow," Hunter said. "Thirty percent? That sucks."

"Hunter," Myra chided, "that doesn't help. Nearly sixty-seven percent have survived. Let's focus on that."

"None of the babies have been born yet, though," I said. I felt particularly disheartened tonight, exhausted from negotiating Manhattan and the corridors of the hospital, and all the tests, which now blurred together in my mind. When I thought of having to go back to New York and live alone for months in that huge, crowded, cluttered, noisy city, I felt overwhelmed with longing for the peace of the Outer Banks, and especially for my sister. But it seemed as though every time fear seized me, Joanna gave me a little kick to remind me why I was here.

The week sped by. I continued what I was coming to think of as my "2001 lessons" by watching plenty of TV and reading the *Times* online. I read everything I could find on HLHS and fetal surgery. It encouraged me to find Dr. Perelle's name in much of the literature. His experience went back twenty years and he was clearly well respected.

In the evenings, I spent as much time as I could with Hunter. If he wondered why this woman, twelve years his senior, took such an interest in him, he didn't let on. I wanted to feel the comfort of being close to him, and I thought he enjoyed the attention. His favorite topic was music, and he told me about all the bands featured in the posters on his walls. Myra was badgering him to take those posters down to get his room ready for their upcoming move, but he was in no hurry.

"I finally got them just right," he griped to me. "Now I'm going to have to start all over again."

"Are you sad about moving to Virginia?" I asked him. "Leaving all your friends?"

He shrugged. "No big deal," he said. "I'm pretty good at making new friends."

I asked him if he had a girlfriend and he said he was interested in several girls and hadn't decided which one he'd focus on yet. He seemed to think it was a fait accompli that whichever girl he chose, she would like him back. In many ways, adolescent Hunter seemed like an entirely different person from the grown-up Hunter, but the one characteristic both of them shared was that self-confidence. He could have his pick of girlfriends. He would ace his exams. He would make friends wherever he went. Just as the grown-up Hunter was confident he could bring me— and Joanna—home from 2001.

So my daytime and evening hours were full. I was learning what I needed to learn and getting to know my future brother-in-law better. But at night, I lay alone in bed trying not to panic. I felt trapped, and I hadn't even left Princeton yet. Once I had the surgery, I wouldn't be leaving New York until Joanna was born . . . if she made it that long. I tried to stop myself from ruminating on the worst that could happen, but only daybreak seemed to put an end to my nighttime fears.

On Sunday morning, Myra gave me one of her old suitcases for my new clothes. The suitcase was on wheels—a brilliant invention. I packed it, then sat in the living room as I waited for the taxi that would take me to the train station. Myra and Hunter waited with me. They shared the sofa, both of them reading the print version of the *New York Times* while I stood at the window watching for the cab. It was going to be particularly hard to leave Hunter. Would I ever see him again in 2001? I wanted to ask him to come to New York to visit me, but I thought that would strike him as odd. Could I at least hug him good-bye? That would probably embarrass him. So when the taxi arrived, I simply said good-bye to them both and walked out the front door to change my life once again.

17

MAY 2001
NEW YORK CITY

I arrived at the Fielding Residential Hotel wearing my mustard-yellow backpack and rolling Myra's suitcase by my side. The building was eight stories high and old, the brick front dark with age. A doorman—the first I'd ever seen in the flesh—opened one of the double doors for me and offered to help me with my suitcase, but I told him I was fine. Inside, the small, spotless lobby was nothing like the aging exterior of the building. It gleamed with white marble on the floor and walls, and an elaborately carved wooden registration desk nearly ran the length of the room. The young woman behind the desk told me it was too early for me to check in.

"Check-in is at three," she told me. Her name tag read *Becky Danson*. I asked if she could make an exception, explaining that I had to check in at the hospital at three. Becky didn't exactly roll her eyes, but she did sigh in annoyance as she poked a few keys on her computer with her very long fingernails. Those nails were painted in a red and white striped design, vivid against her dark skin. "Give us an hour," she said. "You can leave your suitcase here."

Outside, I was still amazed to find so many people on the sidewalk. This was going to take some getting used to. On a busy day in downtown Raleigh, I might pass five or six people in the space of a block. Where were these people all going? Some were dressed to the nines, others in shorts and T-shirts—the day was quite warm—and no one looked at anyone else. There would be eye contact in Raleigh. Smiles and nods. None of that here. A few people wore headphones similar to Hunter's. Two of the men I passed looked like they were talking to themselves and I wondered if they were mentally ill, but when I saw a third person—a woman—also talking to herself, I realized they were actually speaking into microphones attached to their phones. There was still so much—too much—about this future world that I didn't know or understand. I'd learned a lot about 2001 by watching the news and reading the paper, but I wasn't sure I'd learned how to actually live in it.

I found a bank close to the hotel and opened a checking account with eight hundred dollars of the money Hunter had given me. Between that account and the credit card from Myra, I felt financially secure. It was the only sense of security I had.

There was a restaurant on the corner near the hotel, and though I was too anxious to be hungry, I thought I'd better eat. I had no idea if they'd give me a meal at the hospital the night before a surgery. The restaurant seemed to have no name. The sign on the awning out front simply read DELICATESSEN. I'd never seen a delicatessen in North

Carolina; I didn't think they existed. I stepped inside and found it packed with people, the mouthwatering scent of pickles strong in the air. I sat at a small table near the window and studied the menu. Knishes and kugel and latkes. I had no idea what they were. Was this a Jewish restaurant? I'd never even met a Jewish person, as far as I knew, and I felt even more out of place and conspicuous than I had out on the sidewalk. Glancing around, though, I could see there were all types of people dining here. Men and women. White and black and brown. Some of the women looked like they'd stepped out of a high-powered business meeting with their impeccable suits and high heels, while the woman at the table closest to me wore a sleeveless white T-shirt, and a tattoo on one of her bare arms read SAUCY BITCH. *I could fit in here*, I thought, relaxing. *Anyone* could fit in here.

Feeling momentarily adventurous, I ordered matzo ball soup. I wasn't sure what it was, but I'd heard of it and it sounded comforting. The waitress didn't bat an eye as she wrote down my order. She had no idea I was any different from anyone else in this place.

The soup was delicious and I ate nearly all of it, suddenly glad my apartment would be so close to this deli. Maybe walking the short distance to it from the hotel might count as part of my modified bed rest. Paying my bill, I felt the tiniest sense of having a home. The tiniest sense of being safe.

The studio apartment was small and clean with a huge bed, a sofa, a dresser, a flat television even larger than the one at Myra's house, a small refrigerator, and a microwave oven. No stove. I would have to master cooking in that microwave. I opened the curtains to reveal a view of the fire escapes attached to the building behind me. Becky at the front desk had informed me the apartment came with daily maid service, a doorman, and that concierge service Liz had told me about. She gave me a cable I would need to use to connect my iBook to the internet, since the hotel didn't have Wi-Fi. The apartment was really quite nice, I thought, though it was hard for me to imagine living here for the next ten weeks. That was what I needed to hope for, though. The only way I'd be leaving any sooner was if my baby didn't survive the surgery. *Thirty percent.* I wished I could get that number out of my head. Right now, Joanna was alive inside me. Would she still be alive after tomorrow? I hoped I wasn't making a terrible mistake. A small and ever-shrinking part of me was still in denial that there was anything wrong with her. She was so lively and she'd looked perfect to me on the ultrasound. I was blind to whatever Dr. Perelle had seen that was so ominous. But I had to face facts. The surgery was the only chance my baby had.

It was a few minutes before two as I hung my clothes in the tiny closet and folded my underwear into the dresser. There was a safe on a shelf beneath the TV and after a few false starts, I figured out how to open it. I put my iBook inside and wondered if I should leave my phone there as well. "Don't bring valuables to the hospital with you," Liz had told me as I was leaving her office last week. "Just your ID and insurance card in case it's needed." So I put my phone and wallet in the safe as well, tucking my ID and insurance card in the pocket of my new straight-legged jeans. Then I took one last look around the apartment and headed for the door. My hand was on the knob when I heard my phone ring. I raced back to the safe, struggled with the combination, and answered the phone on the fifth ring.

"Calling to wish you luck tomorrow," Myra said, and I began to cry. Whether it was from fear or loneliness or simply the sense of being estranged from all the people and places I knew and loved, I couldn't have said, but it was a moment before I could pull myself together.

"Thank you," I said finally.

"You'll be fine," she said with such firmness that I wondered if she somehow knew my future.

"Do you know that for a fact?" I asked. "I mean, have you seen me in the future sometime with my baby?"

She laughed—or at least she made a sound that approximated laughter. Myra was not a lighthearted woman. "No," she said. "I'm in the dark as much as you are. But it sounds like you're in good hands and I think it's going to go well for you."

I sniffled like a child, trying to keep the sound from reaching the phone. "I hope you're right," I said.

"Call me when it's over," she said.

"All right. Thank you so much for calling. I needed it . . . I needed to hear a familiar voice."

"You'll be fine," she said again, and then she was gone without saying "good-bye."

*

I decided to walk to the hospital. It was less than a mile and I knew this would be the last decent walk I'd be able to take for a while—as long as things went as they should.

I checked into the hospital without a problem and was disappointed when I was taken to a private room. I would have liked to have a roommate. Someone to talk to. Someone I could get to know. I changed into the silly hospital gown—one thing that was no better in 2001 than it had been in 1970—and noticed my hands were already shaking. A nurse took my temperature and blood pressure, which was much higher than it should have been. Liz came in to tell me everything was ready for my surgery in the morning. She had one of those faces that always wore a smile, even when she was talking about something mundane.

"You'll be given general anesthesia before the surgery and will stay overnight tomorrow night," she said. "We'll want to be able to monitor you and your baby for at least twenty-four hours. In a little while, they'll bring you a light dinner, but you can't have anything to eat after that." She patted my foot through the blanket. "Hope you have a good night's sleep," she said.

Dinner was chicken and potatoes and Jell-O. I tried to watch a movie on TV after I'd eaten, but I couldn't concentrate, and I was happy when the nurse brought me a sleeping pill. I took it gratefully. I wanted time to speed up now. I wanted tomorrow to be over.

18

The following morning sped by as I was readied for surgery. Nurses bustled around me, hooking me up to an IV, shaving my belly, taking my blood pressure, and asking me for the hundredth time to tell them my name and my new birth date—which I had to struggle to recall. Someone wheeled me into the operating room, where it seemed like a dozen people stood in masks and blue gowns, waiting for me. I turned my head from side to side to take them all in. My teeth chattered and my body trembled uncontrollably, I was so anxious and cold.

Dr. Perelle leaned over me, recognizable only by those blue-green eyes that smiled above his mask.

"You ready to do this?" he asked.

I nodded, and the next thing I knew, I was waking up, groggy, nauseous, and disoriented. I blinked against the bright lights in the ceiling above me. The whole world seemed to be pale yellow. I heard voices. Beeping sounds. Low chatter.

"Cough," someone instructed me, and I did. My belly felt bloated and my skin stung beneath the hospital gown.

"You're in the recovery room," a nurse told me. "Your surgery's over."

"My baby?"

"Dr. Perelle will be in shortly to talk with you," she said.

"But . . . is she okay?" I tried to grab her hand but missed.

"Your surgery went well," she said. She was doing something—pushing buttons or turning knobs on a piece of equipment behind my head. "Dr. Perelle can give you more specifics. Cough for me again, now."

She left me alone to worry, and I slowly became aware of the IV still attached to my arm and monitors hooked up to my belly. Some sort of compression device tightened and loosened on my legs. Something else—an oxygen tube, I guessed—pressed into the skin below my nostrils.

I must have dozed off and when I woke up again, Dr. Perelle was standing next to my bed in his white coat.

"It went fantastically well," he reported. "I'm very pleased. Your baby cooperated in every way. I can honestly say it was the smoothest I've done of this procedure."

"Do you say that to all your fetal surgery patients?" I tried to smile.

"I wish I could," he said, "but no. Just to you."

"Is she . . . do you think she'll survive?"

"I think we've given her the best chance she could possibly have at survival and a healthy heart, Caroline," he said. "We'll keep an eye on her as well as on you for the next ten weeks. Right now I have you on antibiotics and medication to prevent preterm labor. You feel a little nauseous at the moment?"

I nodded.

"That's more from the medication than from the anesthesia, so I'll get you something to deal with it. You'll be on that medication till tomorrow morning. Then home . . . or in your case, the Fielding Hotel, right?"

I nodded again.

"I'll be frank with you," he said, two sharp lines between his eyebrows. "I don't like that you have no help here in the city. If there's anyone you can call to come lend a hand, please do so. Bed rest is no picnic when you have to do everything yourself."

"I'll be okay," I said. At that moment, I felt sure I would be. If Joanna was okay, so was I.

I barely remembered the rest of the day. Whatever Dr. Perelle prescribed to be added to my IV for nausea helped, and by that evening, I ate half the meal brought to me in my room. In the morning, a technician performed yet another echocardiogram, this one through the transparent bandage that now covered my belly. Then Liz stopped in to give me discharge instructions and my next appointment, just three days away. She told me how to do leg exercises while on bed rest and said I should eat six small meals a day, drink six to eight glasses of water, avoid very hot bath water, and lift nothing over ten pounds.

"And I know you lost your husband, Caroline," she said, a serious expression on her face, "but I still need to tell you: no sexual activity of any sort."

I looked away from her. I was not prudish—that wasn't it—but my heart broke a little at the mention of Joe. The mention of intimacy. It was a reminder that I was alone in all of this.

"And you can't take a taxi home alone," Liz said. "If you give me the number of your New Jersey friend, I'll contact her to come take you to the hotel."

"No," I said. "It's too far for her to come. Too much of an imposition. I'll be fine." There was no way I was going to lean on Myra any harder than I already had.

"I understand, but you'll have to sign a form saying you've been advised against taking a cab alone."

"That's fine," I said. "And since this is only modified bed rest . . . there's a delicatessen on the corner by my hotel," I said. "It's only half a block. Could I—"

She was already shaking her head. "Have them deliver," she said. "When you go out, it's only to come here for your checkups, okay?"

"Okay," I agreed. Except for taking the cab alone to the hotel from the hospital, I was going to be the most compliant patient they'd ever had.

19

I fell into a routine over the next few weeks. I got up, showered, had breakfast, and went back to bed to watch TV. I was hooked on the *Today* show with Katie Couric and Matt Lauer. The soaps were my afternoon entertainment. It was so easy to get sucked into their ridiculously engrossing stories and I wished I had a camera so I could take pictures of Bob and Lisa and Nancy on *As the World Turns* to show Patti when I got home.

If the Fielding Hotel's purported concierge service truly existed, I could have asked someone to buy me a cheap camera, but there was no individual actually assigned to handle that sort of request. Instead, all needs were met either by one of the two people working at the reception desk—businesslike Becky or a sleepy-looking young guy named Dennis—or the doorman, Raoul. Raoul, who was about forty years old and handsome in his gold-trimmed blue uniform and cap, was quickly becoming my lifesaver. He accepted my deliveries from the deli or the little market down the street, and if no one was around to bring them up to the eleventh floor for me, he did it himself.

"They did *what*?" he asked, wide-eyed, when I told him

about the surgery and why I couldn't leave the apartment. He seemed to take on my welfare as his personal responsibility then. Besides bringing me the sandwiches and soups and salads I ordered, he was quick to flag down a cab for me when I needed to go back to the hospital for an appointment. He wouldn't take my tips. I didn't know if I was offering too much or too little, but either way, he didn't want my money. He told me about his wife, Corinna, and his five children. He showed me a picture of the whole family, and it was strange to see him out of his uniform. He told me Corinna had to be on bed rest with her last pregnancy and how hard that had been for the whole family. Every few days, he'd bring me something Corinna had sent with him to give to me. Stew or cold fried chicken or a big slab of cake. Sometimes Corinna would include a note: *You're in our prayers* or *Let us know what you need*. I was touched. I'd never even met the woman.

Most days, Raoul was my only contact with the outside world. He couldn't believe I'd never been anywhere in New York. "You've never been to Times Square or the Empire State or the World Trade Center or any of the museums?" he asked in disbelief. "And now you're sitting here in the greatest city in the world for months and months and you might as well be back in your podunk little town in North Carolina, for all the good it's doing you."

It was so strange to hear black people like Raoul and Becky speak with New York accents. I was surprised every time they opened their mouths. And while I felt defensive when Raoul made fun of North Carolina, I began to think that my life in my home state had been very small and insulated indeed. I wondered at Hunter's willingness to trade in the excitement and energy—not to mention the technological advances—of the twenty-first century for the slower, quieter life of the sixties and seventies. It told me how much he adored my sister, in case I didn't already know.

Raoul asked me if I'd like to try a meal from a different restaurant for a change, but I had a paper menu from the deli and hadn't come anywhere near to exhausting their options. After I'd been ordering from them nearly every day for a few weeks, Ira, the deli's short, gray-haired owner, showed up at my door.

"I wanted to meet the Southern girl with the miracle baby," he said, and I knew Raoul must have told the delivery boy from the deli about me. "I threw in a couple extra bagels and a nice slice of New York cheesecake for you, honey," Ira said. "You let us know if you need anything."

Then there was Angela, the housekeeper. I looked forward to the half hour she spent in my apartment each day. She cleaned the bathroom and kitchenette, vacuumed the area rug on my hardwood floor, and made my bed with fresh sheets every Tuesday and Friday, but she spoke no English and I spoke no Spanish, so we just smiled when we caught each other's eye. Every once in a while she would touch my shoulder to get my attention, and when I looked at her, she'd make a rock-a-by-baby motion with her arms. I'd laugh, unsure if she was trying to tell me something profound or if she was simply sharing her anticipation that soon I would have a baby with me in the apartment. *Only for a very short time,* I thought, my mind on the date of the first portal Hunter had given me.

One day when I was feeling particularly low and lonely, Angela arrived carrying a wicker bassinette. It looked old, the wicker a little worn in places, the mattress clean but a bit ragged, and I wondered if the bassinette had been in Angela's family for generations. I was so touched I couldn't speak. I took the bassinette from her, set it on the dresser, then hugged her. She didn't seem to want to let go.

My appointments at the hospital were long and filled with tests—blood work and urine, ultrasounds and fetal echocardiograms. I only saw Dr. Perelle once, when he stopped by to check one of the echocardiogram results. I could tell he was very pleased.

"How are you doing all alone in the hotel?" he asked, as I sat in the lab, waiting for yet another blood draw.

"Fine," I assured him. "And thanks to you, I'm not really alone." I patted my belly and he smiled. I wished he could be the one to deliver my baby, but his job was done. I'd been turned over to a perinatologist and an entire team of doctors who would be there at Joanna's birth, ready to jump into action if she—or I—had any problems. The perinatologist was a woman, which surprised me. She reminded me a little of Myra: not very warm but clearly intelligent. If I had to choose between those two qualities in the person responsible for bringing my baby into the world, there was no contest.

A month into my stay at the hotel, I discovered a support group on the internet for pregnant women on bed rest. "Stir Crazy Mamas," it was called. At first I was timid about participating, but I devoured every comment left by the participants and pored over the baby pictures posted by the women who'd successfully delivered their healthy babies. I avoided reading about those women who were having problems and completely skipped the distressing thread started by a woman who'd had a stillborn infant. There was even a woman in California whose baby had had fetal surgery, but for something far less ominous than a heart problem. After a week of reading and rereading every post, I tiptoed into the group, introducing myself, telling them about my baby and the fact that I was on bed rest alone in New York. Within another week, I felt as though I had a dozen or so friends as we compared our experiences. There were black women in the group and a woman who called herself a "Latina" and a French woman who typed in broken English, and at least one lesbian. Everyone treated everyone else with the same caring and respect and acceptance. I was so touched by that. I wasn't sure that would have been the case in 1970.

I was the only person in the group living entirely alone, my caretakers a doorman, a housekeeper, and a sweet old deli owner who tossed a bagel or a fat kosher pickle into my dinner order from time to time. They admired me, my new online friends said. They were praying for me. I checked in with them nearly every hour. Was it possible to love people you had never met, I wondered, or had my loneliness gotten the better of me?

One of the Stir Crazy Mamas made and sold baby slings and she posted pictures of them online. The slings consisted of a slightly complicated-looking length of fabric you slipped over your head and wore across your chest. The baby would rest snugly inside the sling, close to your body.

You could even nurse while carrying your baby, the woman said. I ordered one with the credit card Myra had given me, and when it arrived, I practiced putting it on until I had it mastered. I couldn't wait to be able to carry Joanna that way, next to my heart.

Most of the Stir Crazy Mamas were hungry for sex, it seemed, and I quickly realized that I was, too. I must have blocked thoughts of intimacy after losing Joe, but now it seemed to be all I could think about. *No sexual activity of any kind,* Liz had told me. I was attracted to half the men on the soaps, and I was practically living for Wednesday nights when I could see Rob Lowe on *The West Wing.* Yes, the Stir Crazy Mamas and I were horny and we couldn't do a thing about it. Some of them wrote about ways they were "taking care of" their husbands, and they complained about how frustrating it was for them to give and not be able to receive. I stayed quiet during those conversations. I only wished Joe were alive for me to "take care of."

Although I was grateful to have found the Stir Crazy Mamas, I discovered that the internet could be a double-edged sword. One evening when I was feeling particularly low and missing Joe, I made the mistake of Googling "Vietnam" and "Pleiku" and "bridge" and "explosion" and "1969." I found a 1999 article written by a soldier who had been there. In a stroke of luck, he'd been a short distance away from the bridge during the explosion; if he'd been any closer, he wouldn't have survived to write about it. As a survivor, he was one of the soldiers who had to "clean up" afterward and he said he'd never recovered from the experience. He wrote about men who'd been burned alive.

About the severed arms and legs. About a head he accidentally stepped on. His descriptions made me wonder what exactly the army had sent back to us in Joe's coffin. How did you piece together the puzzle of a man's body when it had been blown apart? The author said he often wished he was dead and that he was now being treated for PTSD, an acronym I'd never heard before and had to look up. He'd thought of killing himself more than once, he said. He was grateful to his wife for sticking by him through the worst of it.

I should have stopped reading the article as soon as I realized the story would do me no good, but I kept going. That night, I couldn't get the images the author described out of my mind. That severed head. Whose was it? I could only hope Joe's death had come quickly. That he never knew what hit him. I finally turned on the TV and watched an old Alfred Hitchcock movie, trying to get the horrible images out of my mind. I knew, though, that the vivid pictures the soldier had painted were never going to leave me.

On the nineteenth of June, six weeks into my bed rest, Myra showed up at my apartment door. She'd called me about once a week since I left Princeton, but this was her first visit and I was happy and relieved to see her.

"You're really getting big," she said when I let her into the apartment.

"Hard to believe I still have five weeks left to go," I said, my hand on my stomach. My enormous belly overjoyed me. I was uncomfortable and bored, yes, but Joanna was growing, her development right on target. All her tests were encouraging, and according to the cardiologist who did her echocardiograms, her heart was "as close to normal as we can hope for at this point."

"Can I get you something?" I asked as I motioned for her to sit down on the sofa. "I have water and orange juice and—"

"Nothing," she said, sitting down. "I had a meeting in the city this morning so thought I'd stop in to check on you. I'm trying to wrap things up before our big move to Virginia."

I sat down on the sofa myself. "When do you go?" I asked.

"Hunter's done with school, but he has a job as a counselor at a day camp in Princeton, so I don't think we'll be able to leave until the end of July."

"I wish you weren't going," I said. Right now, Myra and Hunter were only an hour train ride from me—not that I was free to go to them if I wanted to. But once they were in Virginia, they would be five hours away. I'd probably never see them again—at least not in 2001.

She shrugged off my concern. "I'll be an email or phone call away," she said.

"You're not planning to go . . . *far* away anytime soon?" I said. "As in 2050 or something." I smiled, but I was genuinely worried she would simply vanish on me.

"I've traveled four times," she said. "No fifth trips, remember?"

"Good," I said, but I remembered that she did indeed take a fifth trip, one she would never return from. Of course I said nothing about it. "I'd like you to stay in 2001, please," I said instead.

"I have something for you," she said, digging in the large tote bag that served as her purse. She pulled out a small yellow cardboard box. "It's a disposable camera," she said, handing it to me. "I thought you'd want to take pictures of your baby when she arrives."

"Thank you!" I said, staring at the small camera in wonder. I turned it over in my hands. "How do I get the film in and out?"

"You don't. The film's already in it. You mail the camera to the address on the back and they'll send you the developed photographs. Then you just buy another camera at any drugstore. They're cheap."

"Wow," I said. Sometimes I really loved 2001.

"By the way," Myra said. "I checked out the Gapstow Bridge on my way here. The bridge Hunter wants you to step off from?"

I nodded. I'd pulled up pictures of the Gapstow Bridge from the internet. The images were not terribly helpful. They'd been taken from a distance, and while they showed the handsome arched stone bridge and the pond below it, I couldn't gauge how high the bridge's walls were.

"You're going to need a small stepladder to get to the top of the wall," Myra said, addressing my unspoken concern.

"Hunter told me that," I said. "I'm worried about how I'll do it with a baby, though I bought a sling to carry her in."

With some effort, I stood up from the sofa and walked over to the dresser, where I pulled the handmade fabric sling from the top drawer to show her.

"That's perfect," Myra said, taking it from me and looking it over. "Your hands will be free. Excellent."

"I landed facedown on my chest in Princeton, though," I said, lowering myself to the sofa again. "I'm afraid of crushing my baby when I land."

"No worries," she said. "You didn't land hard, right? There's actually no impact at all." She stood up, checking her watch. "I need to catch a train, so I'll be on my way. You'll let me know when the baby comes?"

"Of course," I said, starting to get to my feet to let her out.

"Stay," she said. "No need to get up."

"Thank you for the camera," I said.

"No problem," she answered, and I watched her leave, the door clicking into place behind her. I sat there a few minutes feeling terribly alone. I knew Myra wasn't my friend, exactly. She was more than thirty years older than me, to begin with, and her personality was always cool and professional. But she was the only person in 2001 who truly knew who I was. I wondered where Hunter had gotten his warmth from. That sperm-donor father, I guessed. Bless that guy, whoever he was.

The last few weeks of my bed rest were filled with TV shows and takeout meals, and my Stir Crazy friends. Some of them gave birth to their perfect babies and their good news encouraged me. Bed rest was worth it.

By the beginning of July, there was talk of inducing my labor. Joanna's due date was two weeks away, but the doctors—I had too many of them to count at this point—were nervous and they were making me nervous as well, especially the pediatric cardiologist.

"There's a chance she may require a small intervention once she's born," he told me. "We need to wait and see."

"Intervention?" I asked him. "What does that mean?"

He shrugged. He was not a very communicative man. "A procedure," he said. "Possibly surgery or just a dilation. That wouldn't be unexpected. We need to wait and see," he said again.

Oh, no. Dr. Perelle had told me it was possible Joanna would need more treatment after she was born, but I'd hoped he was simply informing me of every possible complication. I planned to hang on to that hope.

The perinatologist scheduled the induction for the following Friday, which was only a few days before my actual due date. When I told the Stir Crazy Mamas about the upcoming induction, several of them wrote back over the next few hours, sending encouragement. One woman, who had already had her baby but still visited the group, told me she'd been induced as well and she described the whole process, which I nervously skimmed to get to the very end: a healthy baby boy.

The morning before I was to have the induction, though, I was brushing my teeth when my water broke. It startled me as it puddled around my feet and it explained the backache that had kept me awake for most of the night. I stared at my reflection in the mirror, heart pounding.

This is it, I thought. I was finally going to meet my little girl.

20

"You're doing beautifully," the nurse said in my ear. "Push! That's it. That's it. Good, Caroline. Very good."

I held the nurse's hand in a death grip. I would never let her leave my side. I couldn't remember her name. Donna? Diana? It didn't matter. What mattered was that she was there. At that moment, her voice in my ear, her hand in mine, was all that was keeping me sane and grounded against the pain. I was having a quick labor, she'd told me. A short labor. Progressing very well. It didn't seem short to me. It seemed to last a lifetime and the pain was the least of it. I knew Joanna was fine inside me, but I was terrified about sending her out into the world where I could no longer control what happened to her. I felt unbearably alone. The desperate longing I felt for Joe to be there with me seemed never-ending. I wanted *him* to be the person whispering in my ear that I was doing well. I wanted *him* to tell me he was right there with me. *Right there.* There were moments—crazy moments—when I actually thought he *was* there. Behind all the medicinal smells of the labor room, I was certain I detected his aftershave.

I reached for Joanna when she was born. Reached for her beautiful, glistening, pale—too pale?—little body. Someone held her close enough to me that I could touch her foot, but that was all I could do before she was whisked away into the hands of the gaggle of pediatric specialists waiting to examine her.

I must have fallen asleep after she was born—had they given me something? I didn't know. All I knew was that I woke up in a room by myself, attached to an IV, the sound of babies crying in the distance. I gasped, remembering. *Joanna.* Where was she? Was she all right?

I gazed at my fingers. I could still feel the silkiness of her foot against my fingertips. I looked from my hand to my arm, where the IV tethered me to a pole that rose above my bed. I needed to be set free. I needed to find my baby.

I fumbled around on the bed until I found a call button for the nurse. I was already sitting up, woozy-headed, my legs dangling over the side of the bed when she arrived. She nearly bounced into the room.

"Ready to use the bathroom?" she asked. She was younger than me. Petite. Blond. Too perky, though I saw that as a good sign. Would she be perky if Joanna was not okay?

"I just want to see my baby," I said.

"One step at a time," she said, checking a machine attached to my IV pole. "Let's get you cleaned up and then you can visit her."

"Is she all right?" I asked.

"They'll be able to update you on her condition when you go over there," she said.

An unsatisfactory answer, I thought, and I was ready to head out the door and find my own way to the nursery, but I felt so shaky when I stood up that I knew she was right. She unhooked me from the IV and I let her lead me into the bathroom, where I rushed through brushing my teeth and washing up as quickly as I could. My hair was a straggly mess and I didn't bother to comb it. My whole body ached.

The nurse had a wheelchair ready for me when I came out of the bathroom, along with a robe made of the same thin fabric as the hospital gown. I slipped awkwardly into the robe, my hands and arms so tremulous that I had trouble finding the sleeves. Then I sat down in the chair, wincing from the pain, and the nurse pushed me into the hallway.

After a short distance, we entered a small foyer, the walls lined with lockers and a couple of sinks. Through the large glass windows, I could see into the nursery, which was filled with wall-to-wall isolettes and recliners and people dressed in yellow gowns. I knew immediately which isolette held my baby because it was surrounded by the yellow-gowned people, masks over their noses and mouths, yellow hats covering their hair. Doctors and nurses.

"Is that her?" I asked my nurse. "What are they doing to her?"

"Perfectly normal," she reassured me. "There are always lots of tests when a new baby comes to the CICU."

"Sick-U?" I asked.

"PCICU, technically," she said. "This is the Pediatric Cardiac Intensive Care Unit."

A dark-haired nurse who looked to be in her mid-thirties opened the door between the foyer and the CICU. She smiled at me. "Who's this?" she asked the nurse pushing my chair.

"I'm Joanna's mother," I said, those wonderful words leaving my mouth for the first time. "Joanna Sears's mother."

"Welcome," the nurse said. "I'm Celeste Purvis. I'll be Joanna's primary nurse for the next few days."

I loved that she used Joanna's name so easily. My baby had been real to me from the moment I knew I was pregnant. Now she was real to someone else.

"She's being evaluated," Celeste continued. "She had a little trouble breathing when she first arrived but we've stabilized her and she's being hooked up to monitors right now. You won't be able to get very close but you can come in and watch if you like."

"Yes, absolutely," I said.

"I'll be back in a little while," the nurse pushing my chair told me. She squeezed my shoulder and left.

"You need to wash your hands really well," Celeste said. She instructed me to use some special antiseptic soap up to my elbows for two full minutes. She told me I had to remove my wedding rings and Hunter's chronometer before I washed, although she said I could put them back on when I finished. I stayed in the wheelchair while I scrubbed. I couldn't seem to stop trembling or move my gaze from where the crowd in yellow stood around my baby.

Once I'd dried my hands and put the rings and watch back on, Celeste helped me slip into one of the yellow gowns.

"Are you okay to walk or would you rather use a wheelchair?" she asked.

"I'm fine," I said. I just wanted to get to Joanna.

Celeste must have seen that I was not as fine as I said. She held my elbow as she opened the door to the nursery and we walked inside. I was immediately assaulted by the sound of alarms going off and the wail of babies crying. We walked toward Joanna's cubicle, passing some unbelievably tiny infants, no bigger than my hand, in their isolettes.

Curtains were pulled around some of the cubicles, but not Joanna's. Celeste guided me closer, but there was no way I could see my baby through the sea of people surrounding her.

"This is Joanna's mom," Celeste interrupted them. "Can she say hello to her daughter for a second?"

The people turned to look at me, only their eyes visible between their masks and hats, and I realized there were only four of them. Two men and two women. I looked past them to my daughter as Celeste nudged me closer to the isolette.

I knew she would be connected to some monitors and perhaps to oxygen, and yet the sight of my baby wearing only a diaper and a pink hat, hooked up in a dozen different ways, was more shocking than I'd expected. There was a sort of masklike device on her face holding things in place.

A tube in her nose. Another in her mouth. A network of wires crossed her little chest and tummy, and another tube ran into her navel. I couldn't even see her face behind the mask. She lay still and quiet, eyes closed. Sedated, I was sure. My throat tightened and I heard myself whimper. The muscles in my legs shook as I reached over the side of the isolette to touch her cheek with the back of my fingers. She was perfect beneath all the paraphernalia, I was certain. I felt tears roll silently down my own cheeks.

They were speaking to me, those people in yellow, but their voices were a white noise in my head.

". . . and we're keeping an eye on it," one of them said.

"I'm your daughter's cardiologist," a woman said. She was not the pediatric cardiologist I'd been seeing during my pregnancy. "Give me a few more minutes with her and then we can talk."

"Talk about . . . ?" I asked.

"The condition of her heart," she said. I couldn't read her expression from her eyes alone. "She looks quite good," she reassured me, "but we need more information."

"All right," I whispered.

From somewhere, Celeste produced a wheelchair and I sank into it. She pushed me to a lounge at the side of the CICU. The room held six green recliners, small tables between them. Celeste sat on the edge of one of the chairs, while I remained in the wheelchair.

"She weighs six pounds, two ounces," Celeste said, as if to make conversation. I thought they'd told me that in the delivery room, but I couldn't remember. "And her APGAR scores were pretty good, given what she's been through."

"Is she going to be all right?" I asked, cutting to the chase.

"She's off to a good start," Celeste hedged. "Let's see what Dr. Wynn has to say."

"Can I go back to her?" I looked toward the door. We'd only been in the lounge a few minutes, but I already wanted to go back. Why was I in here when my heart was out there?

"Yes, as soon as they're finished evaluating her, you can spend as much time with her as you like and I'll explain what all those things she's connected to are doing for her. It'll be less intimidating once you know. Before we do that, though, you'll need to return to your room to have your breakfast and get ready to be discharged."

"I don't care about breakfast." I waved a hand through the air dismissively. I didn't want to go back to my room. I wanted to stay as close to Joanna as they'd let me.

"I understand your husband passed away," Celeste said, bringing my attention back to the lounge.

I nodded. *They've been talking about me,* I thought. *About how I'm alone.*

"But you have a sister . . . ?" She didn't finish the sentence.

"We're estranged," I said. "And she's in North Carolina."

"Maybe this would be a good time to mend fences," she said.

"It would be harder on me to try to do that right now than to be alone," I said. If only I had a sister nearby with whom I could mend a fence! I didn't like lying, digging myself in deeper with every embellishment of who I was.

"Hey." One of the doctors came into the room. Without her mask on, I could see she was Asian. Petite, fair-skinned. Almond-shaped eyes. She pulled off her yellow cap to reveal shimmery black hair swept back in a ponytail. With her hand outstretched, she walked straight across the room to me, smiling.

"Amy Wynn," she said, shaking my hand. "Let's talk about Joanna's heart." She looked like she might only be a year or two older than me. How could she possibly know what she was doing?

"Dr. Wynn is terrific," Celeste said as if she read the worry on my face.

Amy Wynn brushed aside the compliment with a wave of her hand. Like Celeste, she took a seat on the edge of one of the recliners and leaned toward me. I expected her to have a Chinese or Japanese accent when she spoke, but her voice was pure New York.

"You made a very good decision to have fetal surgery on your baby," she said. "Frankly, I think you saved her life. The repair looks excellent."

I choked up again as I had when I stood next to Joanna's isolette. *Thank you, Hunter,* I thought. Suddenly I knew that everything I'd been through during these past few months had been worth it.

"Is she . . . is she going to be all right, then?" I asked.

"Her problem now is relatively minor," Dr. Wynn said, "and it's fixable. The aortic valve is still narrower than we'd like to see. We'll make sure she's stable over the next few days and then we'll do a dilation."

"Is that surgery?" I asked, thinking, *No, please, no.* I

didn't want Joanna to endure anything more than she already had.

"She'll be asleep," Dr. Wynn said, not really answering my question. "But we can do it through a catheter placed in the umbilical artery. I expect it to be successful and it'll make a big difference as far as her leading a normal life with a normal heart goes." She stood up. "There's always a chance of valve insufficiency—leakage—after a dilation," she said, "and we'll watch for that, but I believe the chance of that is small in Joanna's case."

I thought I should ask more questions, but I felt too overwhelmed to know what those questions might be. Dr. Wynn left us, and the nurse who'd brought me to the CICU from the maternity unit returned.

"Ready for discharge?" she asked brightly.

I shook my head. "Can I just stay here in the nursery?"

My nurse smiled. "You can come right back," she assured me.

Reluctantly I got to my feet, aware for the first time of how sore I felt. How tender. How tired. My nurse had left the first wheelchair outside the nursery, and as we walked through the CICU, I looked over at Joanna's isolette. For the first time in nine months, I was separated from her. I could barely stand the feeling.

My phone rang when I was packing my few belongings in the hospital room. I thought it would be Myra—who else would call me?—but it was Becky from the hotel registration desk.

"Raoul told me to call and check on you," she said. "He

thinks you must have had your baby. He said he called you a cab to go to the hospital and you didn't come back."

"I did have her," I said, sitting down on the edge of the bed. "She's in the Cardiac Intensive Care Unit and has to have a . . . a procedure, but hopefully then she'll be all right."

"Good news," Becky said in her unemotional voice. "I'll pass it along."

"Thank Raoul for me," I said.

"Will do." She hung up without saying good-bye. Becky always acted as if she were very busy, even when she was not.

When I hung up with Becky, I dialed Myra's number. She answered right away and I told her I'd had Joanna and how she was doing.

"Well, congratulations," she said. "That's excellent news. So what do you think? Will you be able to make that first portal?"

I had the impression she was anxious to get me back to 1970 where I would no longer be her responsibility.

"I don't know," I said. "She won't have that dilation for a few days and then she'll need to recover from it." Today was July 12. The first portal was nearly two weeks away, but it sounded like Joanna had a long way to go before then. I tried to imagine tucking my fragile-looking little baby into the sling and stepping off the wall of the Gapstow Bridge. Impossible.

"Well," Myra said. "Keep me posted."

For the rest of the day, no longer a patient in the hospital myself, I sat next to Joanna's isolette. Celeste explained the function of every lead, every wire, every tube. She told me to expect Joanna to be an irritable little thing for a while, tethered to so much equipment and struggling to breathe. "After the dilation, her heart rate and breathing will settle down and you'll see a calmer baby," she said. "You should be able to hold her then. For now, just talk to her. Let her get to know your voice."

Joanna couldn't have been calmer than she was at that moment. Her eyes were closed, and she appeared to be sleeping like an angel behind the mask and tape and tubes. I reached into the isolette and moved the edge of her little knit hat aside enough to see the fair hair on her head. Pale peach fuzz. That was exactly how my mother had described my own hair when I was a newborn. She had perfect ears. Her little hands and feet, fingers and toes—all perfect. Behind all the paraphernalia that was layered and taped over her body, she was beautiful. I touched her hand. Held her small fingers. She didn't try to pull away from my touch.

When Celeste left us alone, I began talking to her. I chattered in a nearly constant stream of words. I told her about her father. How I taught him to use sand fleas as bait the first time I met him. How we fell in love. How much he would have adored her and spoiled her. What a brave soldier he had been. I whispered that part to her. To the outside world, Joe hadn't been a soldier at all. I told her about her cousin John Paul and described the bond I was sure would soon exist between the two of them. I talked about her aunt and uncle, Patti and Hunter. I told her she'd soon be living next to the sea and I described the animal life of the beach and the maritime forest. I couldn't stop talking to her. I had so much to say. When Celeste pulled the curtains closed around Joanna's cubicle, I thought it was to give me privacy, but then I wondered if the nurses and other parents in the CICU were simply tired of listening to my chatter. I didn't care. I was with my baby. My very nearly healthy baby. *Frankly, I think you saved her life.*

I had the disposable camera with me, taken from my purse before I secured it in one of the small lockers provided for parents in the foyer, but I couldn't bring myself to take a picture of Joanna tied up the way she was. Most of the time, she didn't appear to be struggling in any way, but every once in a while she screwed up her tiny face as though she wanted to wriggle out of her wiry prison. As I was trying to comfort her with my voice, Celeste pulled open the curtain and came to my side, a chart in her hand.

"Sometimes she needs quiet time," she said. "Time to help her heal."

I smiled. "Have I been talking too much?" I asked.

"Let's give her some rest." She returned my smile without really answering the question.

"It's just that I've been saving up so much I want to tell her," I whispered.

Celeste touched my shoulder. "You'll have the rest of your life to talk to her," she said. She hung the chart on the side of the isolette and I saw the name "Amy Nguyen, MD" below my daughter's name. I frowned. "Is that the cardiologist?" I asked. "I thought her name was Amy Wynn?"

"N-G-U-Y-E-N," Celeste said. "It just sounds like Wynn to our ears. It's a very common Vietnamese name. I think about half the Vietnamese population has that name." She checked the tape holding one of Joanna's wires in place. "No Nguyens in North Carolina?" she asked me.

I couldn't find my voice. Dr. Nguyen was Vietnamese? North or South or . . . ? Was it ironic that she might be the person to save the life of Joe's child? It didn't matter, of course. I just wanted someone to make my little girl well.

"No," I said. "No Nguyens in North Carolina."

Not in 1970, anyway.

Celeste set me up with a breast pump, although she said it would be a while before Joanna could have my milk— and probably a while before my milk actually came in. "She needs more calories than breast milk can provide, initially," she said. "But we'll freeze your milk for when she's ready." She helped me figure out how to use the pump, but my breasts were dry as bone.

"Stress," Celeste said. "Not at all uncommon. You need to go home . . . go to your hotel . . . and get a good night's sleep."

I protested. I couldn't imagine leaving Joanna.

"You really have to," Celeste said. "She'll be fine and you'll come back refreshed in the morning."

I knew she was right. My obstetrician had called in a prescription for a breast pump to the hospital pharmacy, so I picked it up, then headed outside where I blinked against the hot, gold sunlight. It felt strange to be outside among the throngs of strangers again when my whole world was in the hospital behind me. I found a cab and rode back to the hotel. I was disappointed to find that

Raoul was not on duty. When I got into my apartment, though, there were flowers—a huge bouquet of them—on the table in the dining area. *Congratulations from your admirers, Raoul, Angela, and Ira,* the card read. I stared at the enormous bouquet, smiling tiredly to myself. I had friends. I had a beautiful daughter. In that moment at least, I no longer felt alone.

21

The next four days passed by in a blur. I spent them sitting in the recliner next to the isolette, talking to Joanna, holding her hand or simply watching her sleep. The longer I stayed with her, the more aware I became of the discomfort Celeste told me Joanna would experience. Sometimes, she'd screw up her little face behind the mask and tubes as though trying to expel them. My heart broke for her. I couldn't imagine how it felt to be so trapped. So helpless. When she grew irritable like that, her monitors pinged and beeped as her heart and lungs protested. I hated that breathing was such a struggle for her. I wished I could give her my own breath.

Every once in a while, she'd open her eyes. Not wide, and not with any purpose. She'd open them just enough for me to see her blue-gray newborn eye color, her tiny pale lashes fluttering. I learned how to take her temperature and change her diaper, gingerly at first, afraid of disturbing everything she was hooked up to and setting off an alarm. Now that I could see—from an emotional perspective— past the wires and tubes to her little face, I took pictures of her. I used up all the film in the camera, mailed it off, and bought another disposable camera in the hospital gift shop. *Yes,* I thought to myself with some delight, *I'm one of those parents who can't stop snapping pictures of her baby.* I pumped my breasts at the hotel as well as at the hospital, and my milk finally came in three days after Joanna's birth. It was being saved for her in the CICU freezer. Meanwhile, Joanna was fed through a tube, her heart not yet strong enough to try the bottle or breast.

I was growing increasingly anxious about the dilation, having made the mistake of Googling the procedure. It was more serious than Dr. Nguyen made it sound. It would take a few hours and there were risks involved. Serious risks. At the same time, it was hardly elective surgery. This needed to happen. On one hand, I wanted Dr. Nguyen to get the dilation over with so Joanna could start down the road to recovery . . . and the road home to 1970. On the other hand, right now she was alive in front of me. I could see her and touch her. I was so afraid of losing that.

Dr. Perelle stopped by the CICU to congratulate me. He reassured me about the dilation. "Dr. Nguyen is excellent," he said. "You couldn't ask for better care for Joanna."

I asked him how the study was going and he told me that five of the HLHS babies he'd operated on had been born so far. "Three of them, including your Joanna, required the dilation," he said. "One had to have a different type of surgery. And unfortunately, we lost the fifth baby, who died at three days old."

"Oh," I whispered. I appreciated that he didn't mince words with me, yet I ached for those parents. Joanna was four days old today. I felt safe, as though she and I had dodged that three-day bullet.

On the fifth day, Joanna had a different nurse. Deirdre. She was older, about fifty, with gray streaks in her brown hair, and she was extremely efficient. I felt confident in her care, but she lacked Celeste's warmth. She reminded me of an older version of Becky from the hotel. Efficiency without warmth. I told myself efficiency was what Joanna and I needed, but I missed Celeste for the few days she was off duty.

The day before Joanna was to have the dilation, I decided to check out the Gapstow Bridge where I would be stepping off. The first portal was only a week away and it seemed impossible we'd be ready to go. But Deirdre said Joanna would most likely be feeding from the bottle or even the breast once she had her strength back after the dilation. It seemed unimaginable that Joanna would be free of her wires and tubes in a week, but I needed to plan our escape from 2001 just in case. The thought of going home filled me with hope and wonder.

I'd walked to the hospital the last couple of days, now that I felt much stronger. After being cooped up for so many months, I liked the freedom of the walk, although my experience of the city remained limited to those few blocks between the Fielding Residential Hotel and Amelia Wade Lincoln Hospital. If anyone had asked me what New York was like, it was those clean, not-too-congested, tree-lined blocks I would describe to them. I had no interest in the rest of the city right now. I wasn't there to sightsee.

So on that morning, I surprised Raoul when I turned right instead of left as I left the hotel.

"Hey!" he called after me. "Aren't you going the wrong way?"

I turned to smile at him.

"I'm just going for a little walk before I go to the hospital," I said.

"Hey, that's wonderful," he replied. "Missy must be doing better for you not to rush over there like you do." He'd taken to calling Joanna "Missy" for some reason.

I nodded. "She has to have a procedure tomorrow, so I'm a little nervous," I said. "But right now, yes, she's doing better."

"Good news, good news," he said. "You go have a New York adventure now, Little Mama. You deserve it."

I'd memorized my route from the online map. I walked up East Sixty-seventh Street in the direction of Central Park. The scenery was very much like the walk to the hospital, with the small trees, now lush and green, lining the broad sidewalk. I made a left when I reached Fifth Avenue, then entered the park. In front of me, to my left, stretched a long line of benches. People sat on them reading or talking. Aside from those benches, though, I was surrounded only by trees and shrubs and grass. I had the strangest feeling then, nature all around me. I might have been back in Raleigh. I drew in a long homesick-yet-happy breath and kept walking. The deeper I got into the park, the more that sense of being home filled me with both comfort and longing. I couldn't believe that this wonderland had been only a few blocks away from me for the past few months and I'd never known it.

I passed people pushing strollers or walking dogs or jogging. Others carried shopping bags or briefcases. I made a turn on the path, relying on my memory of the online map. Then another turn. One more turn, and I knew I was good and lost. I asked a woman who was walking her boxer to point me in the direction of the Gapstow Bridge, and she told me of a few more turns I needed to make. I continued on the path, walking past enormous boulders, dense thickets, and a statue of a dog. Every few yards, I passed a tall cast-iron streetlight. Reassuring, those lights. I didn't feel the least bit uneasy walking through the park in daylight, but I couldn't imagine what these confusing paths would be like at night. I'd have to be more certain of my way than I was today.

The entrance to the small Gapstow Bridge finally appeared ahead of me. I slowed my pace as I walked onto the stone bridge, trying to look nonchalant to the few people who passed by me. At the apex of the bridge—the location where Hunter planned for me to step off—I turned and looked into the distance. It was a pretty view. Buildings rose high above the treetops, and below the bridge, a pond was carved into the trees and overgrowth. I rested my arms on the top of the stone wall. It was about chest high. As Myra had said, I would need a stool or ladder to be able to climb onto the wall, but at least the area where I would stand was broad. It was hard, though, to imagine Joanna as she was now, so vulnerable, still tethered to oxygen and feeding tubes and hooked up to too many monitors to count, being able to make this trip in less than a week. Not just hard, I thought sadly. Impossible. There was no way I could take her home using this first portal. But we had others. Plenty of others. We were safe.

Celeste returned to work the following day, the day Joanna was to have the dilation. I was a wreck that morning, literally sick to my stomach. Celeste asked me what I'd eaten the night before, but I knew my chicken salad sandwich from Ira's deli wasn't the cause of my problem. It was nerves, pure and simple. Joanna and I had come so far in so many ways. This final step—the dilation—simply had to be successful.

Celeste wheeled Joanna's isolette to the Cardiac Catheterization Lab, with me walking beside her. I sat in the waiting room, too nervous to read or do much of anything other than worry. Celeste had returned to the CICU, but after about an hour, she brought me a cup of tea, which was so sweet of her. Two more hours passed, maybe longer, before Dr. Nguyen finally emerged from the double doors, dressed in her surgical gown and cap. I stood up and she smiled at me.

"Everything went very well," she said. "We'll be moving her back to the CICU in about thirty minutes, so you can wait there for her. She'll need to rest quietly for the next twenty-four hours, but we can already see improved heart and lung functioning."

I couldn't speak at first, my throat was so tight. I smiled and nodded and finally found my voice. "You can already see it?" I asked. "The improvement?"

"Definitely," she said. "Breathing should be much easier for her now."

I started to cry. "It's been so hard for her," I said, as though I was telling her something she didn't know. I blotted my eyes with the tissue I'd been clutching for the last two hours. "How much longer do you think she'll need to be in the CICU?" I asked.

"We should keep her there at least another week," she said. "Then she can go to the step-down unit."

My own heart sank. I hadn't even thought of the step-down unit. I'd heard other parents talk about how great it was that their baby was ready for less intensive care, but somehow I hadn't thought about *my* baby making that transition. How long would Joanna need to be in *that* unit? I opened my mouth to ask Dr. Nguyen that question, but she was already turning back toward the catheterization lab. I stood there watching her walk away, wondering if Joanna and I would even be able to make our *second* portal.

22

Hunter

"I've got the water." Patti stood next to the sink in the kitchen, tightening the lid on the thermos. "What else will she need?"

"Nothing right away." I'd walked into the room carrying my sleepy son. "And please don't get your hopes up, babe," I said for at least the fifth time. "Her arrival today would be the best-case scenario."

For Carly and the baby to be able to show up this morning, everything would have to have gone perfectly in 2001. The fetal surgery would have been a complete success. The baby would have been born early—or at least no later than Carly's due date—and she'd have to be healthy enough for Carly to step off with her on the first portal. It had been optimistic of me even to include this portal in the list I gave her. Nevertheless, as Patti and I drove the very short distance through the early dawn light toward Jockey's Ridge, I felt hopeful. I imagined a joyful reunion with my sister-in-law on the dunes and the relief I would feel now that this grand experiment was over. In my mind's eye, I saw Patti embracing her sister. Cuddling her new niece in her arms.

For the past few months, Patti had vacillated between anger at me for—as she put it—risking Carly's life, and excitement over the possibility of Carly having a healthy baby. I never knew which Patti was going to greet me when I walked in the door—the furious, frightened woman or my grateful, loving wife. Patti's anger was new to me. In the nearly five years we'd been married, I'd never experienced it. But I supposed I seemed like someone new to her as well. I had to remind myself that her anger was born of fear. I didn't let on that I shared some of that fear. I knew I had to get Carly to 2001. I knew it because that was where I'd met her for the first time, and how could she have gotten there without my intervention? But I wished I knew what happened next. My mother had never mentioned her again after she left our house, and even though I'd liked Carly and all the attention she'd lavished on me, being the self-absorbed kid I was at the time, I'd never thought to ask my mother about her once she was gone.

"Let's park as close to the dunes as we can get," I said, maneuvering the car to the side of the road, careful not to get the tires stuck in the sand. "She won't be feeling terrific when she lands and she's going to get worn out when she has to walk over the dune."

"Could she be there already?" Patti asked as we slipped off our sandals and got out of the car. I took John Paul from her arms for the hike up the dune. He was fussy from being awakened so early and he wriggled in my grasp.

"I doubt it," I said. "I predicted she'd land sometime between six o'clock and seven."

"I can't wait to see her!" Patti said, and she quickened her pace as we began to climb. The temperature had to be eighty degrees already, but the sand was cool on our bare feet. The dawn light turned the dune a vivid pink as we climbed. By the time we reached the peak, the rising sun behind us glowed on the sand.

"She's not here," Patti said, bending over to catch her breath, the thermos upright in the sand at her feet.

I stood next to her, scanning the broad sandy valley between the dunes. That was where I'd planned for her to land, though I'd known it would be iffy. Working out calculations on living dunes—sand that shifted daily depending on the weather—was dicey at best. My biggest concern was that she might land high on one of the dunes and end up rolling down the sandy slope before she was fully conscious. I hoped she had that baby secured tightly to herself.

I set John Paul down beside me. Giddy at finding himself on five hundred acres of sand, he began crawling and tumbling and giggling. Patti kept a watchful eye on him, trying to prevent him from rolling all the way down the dune. Finally she sat down on the sand and lifted John Paul into her arms.

"Where is she?" she asked, more to the air than to me. A rhetorical question.

"I don't think she could make this portal," I said. "It was just too soon." I sat down next to her, my arm around her shoulders. The sun bored into the back of my neck.

"Sorry, babe," I said. "I know you were hoping this would be the one."

Patti stiffened. "What if something terrible happened?" she asked. "What if she had an accident up there"—she constantly referred to 2001 as "up there"—"or she didn't do the stepping off right and ended up someplace else entirely?"

"I told you, everything would have had to be perfect for her to make this first portal," I said. "She has three left. I don't think there's anything to worry about." Though I was thinking: what if I screwed up and Carly was right this minute lying on the far side of the second dune where we couldn't see her? What if she'd landed beyond the dunes in the sound? I kept my voice calm when I spoke. "Just to be absolutely sure," I said, getting to my feet, "I'm going to walk to the top of the other dune and take a look around."

"Should I come?" she asked.

I shook my head. "I'm ninety-nine-point-nine percent sure she's not there, but just in case. Be right back." I ran down the first dune, enjoying the rush of it even though I knew I was risking a twisted ankle or worse. Then I started the arduous climb up the second dune. By the time I reached the top, the sun was well above the horizon and my T-shirt was soaked with sweat. She wasn't there, of course. The sound side of the dune was a blank slate of gold sand. I turned around and headed back to my wife and son.

When I finally reached them, Patti was on her feet, the sun pinking her cheeks and John Paul's arms, and I had the ludicrous thought that I should have asked Carly to bring some 2001 sunscreen back with her. I nearly said as much to Patti, but one look at her face told me she was not in the mood to hear what I was thinking, ludicrous or not.

"When is the next goddamn portal?" she asked. My wife, who never, ever swore.

"Two weeks," I said.

I waited for her to respond, but she said nothing at all, and that was even worse.

I had the feeling the next two weeks were going to be the longest of my life.

23

Carly

JULY 2001
NEW YORK

Kangaroo care.

I'd never heard of it—I guessed it didn't officially exist in 1970. But a couple of days after Joanna's dilation, Celeste told me to wear a shirt that opened in the front when I came to the CICU the following day. Then, finally, I was able to hold my baby. It took Celeste and another nurse to juggle all the tubes and wires, taping them and clipping them to my yellow gown as they set my sweet little girl against the skin between my breasts.

"Skin to skin," Celeste said. "This is the best thing for her and for you." She went on to tell me all the benefits to both Joanna and me of kangaroo care, but quite honestly, I wasn't paying attention. I was so lost in the bliss of finally holding my little girl. It was magical, the way she settled down against my skin, and I settled down as well. It was as though this was the moment we'd both been waiting for. I could feel her heartbeat against my skin and I imagined she could feel mine. We both felt safe now, I thought.

"Hold her like that at least an hour to get the full benefits," Celeste said.

No problem, I thought. I never planned to let her go.

The little pink cap was off her head and I could lean over to touch my lips to her soft, almost invisible, hair. I fantasized about what it would be like when I had her home with me. My real home. My 1970 home with no iBook, no microwave, no cell phone. Just my family and an abundance of love. Imagining that life brought me such a sense of calm and joy. In all the months I'd been in 2001, I'd never felt the sort of peace I experienced at that moment. I only hoped Hunter and Patti were not too upset that I hadn't made that first portal. Hunter knew it had been unlikely, yet I couldn't help but imagine their disappointment.

The social worker, Ellen Cathcart, met me in the CICU that afternoon when Joanna was back in her isolette, sleeping soundly. I'd met Ellen shortly after Joanna was born when she wanted to make sure I had transportation to get back and forth to the hospital.

"Do you have a minute to chat?" she asked me now, then added before I could answer, "Let's go into the lounge."

I followed her to the lounge at the side of the CICU and was glad to see that we had it to ourselves.

"How are you doing?" she asked as we sat down on the recliners. She was an attractive woman who reminded me a little of my mother, with short-cropped light brown hair and the dark brown eyes I'd inherited. "I hear Joanna's procedure went very well."

I nodded. "They expect to move her to the step-down unit by the end of the week," I said.

"That's great news." Ellen smiled. She glanced down at the notepad on her knees. "I need to talk to you about a couple of things," she said. "You were part of the fetal surgery program, which is what allowed you to have that reduced rate at the Fielding Hotel, but that rate was only good for two weeks after your baby's birth, so now you'll have to start paying the hotel's going rate. I'm not sure what that is, but I *am* sure it's going to be pricey. Would you like me to look into space at the Ronald McDonald house for you?"

"Um," I said, thinking. This wasn't a surprise. I'd known from the start that I only had two weeks of the reduced rate after giving birth, but I'd frankly forgotten about it. I hadn't expected to need the hotel very long after Joanna's birth and I wasn't sure how to answer Ellen's question. I knew about the Ronald McDonald House from other parents, but I needed to check with Myra to see what she'd like me to do. I hoped I could stay where I was. I felt safe there and it would be a hassle to move and start over someplace new when I wanted my time and energy to go into being with Joanna. "I need to make a phone call and then I'll let you know," I said.

"All right." She tapped her notepad. "Just know that the higher rate will start immediately."

"I understand."

"I know you have no family in the area, Caroline." Her eyebrows knitted together in sympathy. "And I'm concerned about what this is like for you. It must be very difficult."

I gave a small nod to acknowledge the truth in her statement, but added with a smile, "I'm doing fine."

"Joanna's nurse, Celeste, tells me you're a devoted mother—she's actually very impressed with you"—she smiled—"but this has to be so challenging and tiring."

My throat suddenly tightened and my eyes stung. I didn't want to cry, but her words tapped into the exhaustion I kept hidden even from myself. Every stressor from the last few months suddenly washed over me at once. "Yes, it's been a challenge," I managed to squeak out, "but she's worth it."

Ellen smiled again. "We have volunteers here who love nothing better than to hold babies," she said. "Why don't you take a few hours off each afternoon? Go back to the hotel—or the Ronald McDonald House or wherever you end up—and rest, knowing that Joanna is getting plenty of care and attention?"

"I'd rather be here with her," I said. "I hate even leaving her at night." I didn't give voice to my irrational fear—that I would come in one morning and she wouldn't be here. That after all this, I would lose her. I'd seen other babies die. I'd witnessed other mothers endure that horrible shock.

"Well, I want you to know it's an option," Ellen said. "She's well cared for here, and you'd be just a phone call away."

"I know."

She shifted position on the recliner, smoothing her skirt

over her knees, and I sensed she was about to change the topic. "It's got to be hard for you, losing your husband so recently," she said.

I nodded. "I wish he could see her," I said.

"It was a car accident?" she probed. I knew she was trying to help, but she didn't know the depth of what I was going through and there was no way I could tell her.

"Yes," I said.

"You have a sister, right?"

"In North Carolina."

"Would you like me to contact her? Explain what you're going through?"

Good luck with that, I thought. "No, thank you. It would only make things worse."

"Would you like to talk about whatever it is that's driven a wedge between you?"

I shook my head. "It's old history," I said. "And I'm afraid nothing will change it, but I'm fine, really." I held up my hands to acknowledge the truth and put an end to her questions. "Yes, I'm tired, and yes, I'm scared about my baby," I said, standing up, "but I'm holding it together. And I'll check into the hotel situation and let you know."

"All right," she said, reluctantly getting to her own feet. She handed me her card and I slipped it under my yellow gown and into the pocket of my jeans. "I admire you for your independence and gumption," she said. "Just know that there's help available if you need it."

"I know." I smiled, more to myself than to her. I *did* have gumption, didn't I? How many people would leap from an ocean pier in the middle of the night? "Thank you," I said. "I'll be in touch."

Once she left the lounge, I took my phone from my pocket, sat down again on the recliner, and dialed Myra's number. I'd spoken to her once since Joanna's dilation to tell her we wouldn't make the first portal. She'd sounded disappointed, but not terribly concerned. "Let's get that baby healthy," she'd said. "That's the main thing." I'd been relieved by her attitude. I hoped she'd be as unfazed when I told her I would need more money to be able to stay in the hotel.

"I have an idea," she said when I explained the situation. "I don't know why I didn't think of this earlier. Remember I told you about the New York traveler I have in the 1800s?"

"Yes," I said, although my memory of that conversation was vague.

"Well, he's not due back until next year and I'm one hundred percent certain he'd let you use his condo in Sutton Place," she said. "He told me to use it anytime I'm in the city. It wouldn't cost you a thing."

"Are you sure?" I asked. "Wouldn't it be weird moving into someone's home without his permission?"

"I'm absolutely sure he'd be fine with it," she said. "He stayed with Hunter and me for months when Hunter was little. I know he'd like to return the favor, even if he won't know about it for quite a while." She chuckled. "I'll take care of having his electric turned back on, et cetera, and the housekeeping set up."

"I won't need housekeeping," I said. "I spend all my time at the hospital."

"You won't be there that long," she said, as if I hadn't spoken. "Hopefully you'll make the next portal. It's next week, right?"

"August eighth," I said. "Almost two weeks away." I pictured Joanna, still wired up, still tube fed, still in the CICU. Celeste said they'd be removing the feeding tube soon and they were already adding a bit of my breast milk to her formula, but I had to face reality. Would she really be able to leave the hospital in two weeks? "She still may not be able to be released by then," I said.

Myra said nothing for a couple of seconds. "No problem," she said finally, though her tone of voice told me it *was* a problem. "Now back to the condo situation. I have my friend's keys and codes. I can come up to the city tomorrow and get you set up. Then Hunter and I take off for Virginia next Thursday."

"Already?" I said. I was going to feel even more alone once they were gone.

"I'll email you the condo address and we can meet there tomorrow. Ten A.M. It's about a mile, mile and half from where you are."

I wanted to be in the CICU at 10 A.M. tomorrow. But then there was *no* time I didn't want to be in the CICU and I had to make this move while I could. "All right," I said. "Thank you."

I spent the rest of the day with Joanna, breaking away from her only to grab a quick lunch and call Becky at the hotel. "I'll be moving out tomorrow morning," I told her.

"Your hospital rate's ended, you know, so today's charges will be on your credit card."

"That's fine," I said. "Thank you." I wouldn't miss Becky, but I would miss Raoul and Angela and Ira at the deli. I wasn't sure how I would have made it through the last few months without them.

In the morning, I packed my few belongings into my suitcase and Hunter's backpack, left a ten-dollar bill for Angela, and took the elevator to the lobby. I balanced Angela's bassinet on top of the rolling suitcase, and as Raoul opened the hotel door for me, he looked despondent.

"We're going to miss you, Little Mama," he said.

"I'll miss you, too," I said. "Thanks for everything, Raoul." I let go of the suitcase handle long enough to give him a hug I could tell he wasn't expecting.

"You Southern women," he said, shaking his head. His dark skin made it hard to tell, but I thought he was blushing. "You're somethin' else."

I planned to walk to the condo where I'd meet Myra, but Raoul insisted I take a taxi.

"Too far to drag a suitcase and that baby-bed thing," he said. So he bundled me into a cab and in a few minutes I was in front of a towering brick-and-glass building. I paid the cab driver, then carted my belongings into the three-story lobby where I was overjoyed to find Myra standing inside the door. I wanted to hug her, but knew better. She wasn't even smiling, and I knew in that moment that I had become more of a burden to her than she wanted. Her mind must have been full of her move to Virginia, her work, and taking care of Hunter.

"Thanks for doing this," I said instead of hello.

"No problem," she said. She took the bassinet from me and we walked across the lobby to the bank of elevators. "Let's go up."

Inside the elevator, Myra used a key to access the button for the top floor. The penthouse? Seriously? My ears popped as the elevator rose silently through the building, and when the doors opened, I realized we were inside the condominium itself. I could see nearly all of it from where we stood when we stepped out of the elevator. In front of us was a living room with a beige leather three-sided sofa and a couple of chairs upholstered in beige and black fabric. The floor was covered with plush white carpeting. To our left was an open kitchen area with dark cabinets, and to the right, a long, slender dining room table. But I barely took all of that in. My eyes were drawn to the wall of glass in front of us. The view of the city made me gasp.

"This is it?" I asked, incredulous. "Your friend's condo?"

"Howard is our biggest benefactor," Myra said as she walked into the living room with a familiarity that told me she'd been to the condo many times before. She set the bassinet down near the long glass-topped coffee table. "Mostly because he wanted to travel himself," she said. "This is his second, and therefore final, round trip, of course, so I'm sure he's milking it for all it's worth. His return portal isn't until next year, so no worries about him walking in and surprising you."

"Well, it's amazing," I said. I left my suitcase on the

marble floor by the elevator and stepped onto the plush carpet, walking across it to the glass wall. I could see buildings in all shapes and sizes spread out in front of me. In the distance, the windows of the Empire State Building glittered in the sunlight. "I can hardly believe this," I said.

"So, that baby of yours." Myra sat down on the three-sided sofa, her voice businesslike. "You don't know if you'll make the next portal?"

I shook my head, reaching into my purse for the packet of pictures I'd taken of Joanna. I sat next to Myra and opened the envelope.

"I hope so, but no, I don't know for sure," I said. I handed her the stack of photos. "These are from a week ago, before her dilation. She looks a little bigger and healthier now." I smiled down at my daughter over Myra's shoulder.

"Wow," she said, sifting through the photos, too quickly for my taste. Did she even notice how beautiful Joanna was? "This level of care certainly wouldn't have been possible in 1970," she said.

"She's alive because of Hunter. And you," I said.

"She's still very . . . hooked up, isn't she," Myra said, studying one of the pictures. It wasn't a question. "This doesn't look like she'll be leaving there anytime soon." She let out a heavy sigh. "That concerns me."

"Well, these pictures are a week old." I tried to sound reassuring. "They're giving her time off oxygen each day now and she's improving practically by the hour. If we don't make this next portal, there are still two more," I said. "The last one isn't until September ninth, six weeks away. I think we'll be fine." I felt antsy sitting there with her now. Looking at the pictures of Joanna made me want to be with her. "I'm still worried about landing with her," I admitted. "The portals are for Jockey's Ridge—these giant sand dunes. But sand is hard, and—"

"I told you," she said. "It's not like you land with a thump, squishing her beneath you." She handed the stack of photos back to me. "It's more as though you . . . materialize. You can stop worrying about it. As long as she's securely attached to you with that sling, both of you will be fine." She reached into her purse and handed me a key and a slip of notepaper with numbers written on it. "This is the code to let you into the building," she said. "And this is the elevator key." She stood up. "If, God forbid, you run out of portals, you call me," she said. "I'll set you up with a new one."

"Thanks, but she's doing so well, and with three more portals, I think—"

"Well, you know how to reach me," she said. "I have no plans to change my phone number when we move."

"How is Hunter?" I asked. "Is he excited about moving to Virginia?"

"He's not thrilled, but he'll be fine." She lifted her tote bag and slung it over her shoulder, clearly ready to leave. "Hunter is all about loud music and girls. He just coasted by in school this year. It's a good thing he's bright because he hates to study. He's just lucky things come so easily to him." She looked toward the glass wall for a moment, and when she spoke again, her voice sounded far away. "I don't like knowing about the future from my travelers," she said, "but I have to admit that you've reassured me about him."

"He's the best," I said, standing up myself. "And I can't wait . . . absolutely can't wait . . . to see him and my sister and nephew again and to show off Joanna. Thank you for making all this possible."

She looked at me without speaking for a moment, then nodded. "No problem," she said, although I had the feeling she saw Joanna and me as a very big problem indeed.

24

For the first and probably last time in my life, I was living in unbelievable luxury. I had no time to relish it, though, since I spent nearly all my waking hours in the tight quarters of Joanna's cubicle in the CICU, taking my quick meals in the brightly lit hospital cafeteria. There was no place I would rather have been than holding Joanna in my arms. At night, though, back at the borrowed condo, I moved one of the comfortable beige and black chairs close to the windowed wall, turned off all the lights, and stared out at the spectacular light show that was New York City.

I felt like an old pro in the CICU now. I could ask Dr. Nguyen and the pediatrician intelligent questions. I knew what caused each beep and alarm on the monitors. I helped other parents learn the routines and keep their fears in check. It was the fathers that got to me the most. The dads. When I'd see a man holding his baby against his chest, providing kangaroo care for his son or daughter, I had to look away. *Oh, Joe,* I'd think. *You should have had that chance.* I'd read that Robert McNamara, the man who'd been secretary of defense during the Vietnam War and who'd pushed us to get more and more involved over there, recently admitted he'd been wrong. The fury I felt reading his statement nearly paralyzed me for a full day. I wanted my husband back. Fifty-eight thousand wives and mothers and children wanted their loved ones back. *You bastard*, I thought, reading the article. *You son of a bitch.*

I was such a fixture in Joanna's cubicle that Celeste and Deirdre and the other nurses started telling me I should take a day off. "There are no prizes here for the most devoted mom," Celeste said. "Get out of the hospital. See the city, for heaven's sake. You can't go back to North Carolina and tell them you spent months in New York and never saw the Empire State Building. You need a break, Caroline." But I didn't want a break. I was right where I wanted to be—holding my baby in my arms.

A couple of days after I moved into the condominium, the pediatrician in the CICU removed Joanna's central line. They did it before I arrived that morning. She now had a line taped to her hand, and I had the feeling they'd gotten all that taken care of before my arrival so I didn't have to witness what must have been torture for my little girl. Her cheeks were still splotchy from crying by the time I arrived. I knew it was a milestone, though. A very good one, and I told Joanna how well she was doing as I held her. The very next day, Joanna's three-week birthday, they removed the feeding tube. She'd been making little rhythmic sucking motions with her mouth and Celeste said it was time to try nursing her. For the first time, I was able to see my daughter's face without the tubes and the mask that held all the apparatus in place. Oh my God, she was even more beautiful than I'd thought! Her face was round, filling out in a healthy, pudgy-cheeked sort of way. Her eyes with their pale lashes stared into mine when I held her, and even when she was not in my arms, her gaze followed me. She sought me out. She knew her mama. I thought she smiled at me, but couldn't have sworn to it. Was she mimicking my expressions, raising her eyebrows when I raised mine? Sticking out her tongue when I stuck out mine? Maybe I was only seeing what I wanted to see.

"Breastfeeding can be a challenge at first," Celeste warned me, setting Joanna in my arms. The curtains were closed to the cubicle and the front of my yellow gown was open. I'd been reading up on nursing practically from the moment I learned I was pregnant and I expected the challenge Celeste talked about, but as soon as I touched my nipple to Joanna's lips, she latched on. I was delighted. My breast felt a little pinched and tingly as she sucked, but soon the discomfort passed and I felt only warmth. "Is she getting any milk?" I asked Celeste. "How can I tell?"

"She's doing beautifully," Celeste said. "And so are you. I'll leave the two of you alone. Just give a shout if you need me." She slipped out of the cubicle and I looked down at Joanna. Her blue-gray eyes locked onto mine and they didn't leave my face until she'd finally had enough to eat and fell asleep in my arms.

Late that afternoon, Dr. Nguyen stopped in the cubicle while I was holding my sleeping daughter skin-to-skin.

"Joanna's doing so well that she'll probably be released

directly from the CICU," she said. "There's no reason to put her and you through the hassle of a move to the step-down unit for only a couple of days."

"A couple of days?" *Oh my God,* I thought. That would mean I could take her to the condominium on Sunday or Monday. The second portal was Wednesday. I felt my heartbeat quicken at the thought of actually doing it. Actually stepping off the bridge with Joanna in the sling.

"Uh-huh," Dr. Nguyen said. "She should be ready to go by then. Celeste said you're already a breastfeeding champ. She says you two are a great team."

Her words made me feel like crying and I forced a smile to keep the tears at bay. Joanna and I were a great team! I loved taking care of her. Bathing her. Changing her. Cuddling her. Nursing her. I loved the intimacy. The undeniable bond between us when she looked into my eyes.

"Thank you for making her well," I said.

"My pleasure," she said. "I'll keep you posted on when she'll be able to go home."

That evening, I left the hospital early enough to walk to a children's store where I bought everything I'd need to have Joanna in the condo with me for the few days before we stepped off. I knew the hospital wouldn't let me take her without one of those car seats for the cab, so I bought the least expensive one they had, knowing I would use it once or twice at the most. Buying the car seat made me laugh to myself. The hospital was worried about me transporting my baby a few blocks in a cab. Imagine what they would think if they knew I planned to jump off the Gapstow Bridge with her.

I bought disposable diapers—I wished I could take a crate of them back to 1970 with me. Patti used disposable diapers with John Paul but they were much bulkier than the 2001 variety and they needed to be secured with pins rather than tape. I bought diaper cream, a thermometer, two bottles, a few burp cloths, and a couple of onesies. Everything else could wait until I got to North Carolina. The salesgirl tried to sell me a baby-care book, but I already had two of them that I'd read cover to cover.

I was both excited and nervous about the thought of having Joanna alone with me in the condo. Although I was doing most of her day-to-day care now that she was free of her tethers, I was used to having the nurses nearby to answer any questions that arose. The thought of being entirely alone with her, feeding her every two hours, getting little rest for myself, was exhausting. I reminded myself that wouldn't be the situation for long. I would soon be home in the Outer Banks where I'd have all the support I needed. How I missed my family and the simplicity of my old life! I missed my beloved Outer Banks and the never-ending sound of the surf. The only things I could imagine missing from 2001 were my iBook and the microwave, which I'd come to love despite my early misgivings. But I would trade in both of them, plus my phone and more, to be in our beach cottage with my daughter.

The day Joanna was to be released, two days before the second portal, I arrived in the CICU carrying the car seat, my nerves tied in a knot. I walked through the unit to Joanna's cubicle only to find her isolette gone. I stopped short, my heart in my throat. I remembered two times I'd seen a parent walk into the CICU only to find their babies missing. Neither of those situations had a good outcome. Maybe the nurses were getting Joanna cleaned up and ready to go?

Then I heard Joanna's cry. I knew that cry. To another person, it might have sounded like every other cry in the nursery, but to me it was distinct. I looked in the direction of the sound—the front right corner of the CICU—and saw Celeste and a couple of other yellow-gowned nurses or doctors huddled over an isolette. I raced toward them.

"What's going on?" I asked. I actually pushed a nurse aside so I could see my baby and my heart sank. She had those blotchy red cheeks that told me she'd had a good crying session and there was a new IV in her arm, the little oxygen cannula at her nose. "Oh, no," I said. "What's wrong?"

Celeste stepped away from the isolette, tugging me with her, hand on my arm.

"Joanna had some blood in her diaper this morning," she said.

"What?"

"They have to take her for an X-ray to rule out enterocolitis. Just as a precaution. She—"

"What's that? Enterocolitis?"

"A type of colon disease. I think it's unlikely in Joanna's case, though, so let's not borrow trouble. It usually happens to preemies, not term infants, and not as old as Joanna." She glanced over her shoulder toward the isolette. "Although I've seen it happen with an older infant who had a heart defect," she said. She was thinking out loud now, talking more to herself than to me, unaware of how she was escalating my panic.

I watched as a nurse wheeled Joanna's isolette out of the CICU. It reminded me of the only other time I saw her leave the unit: the day she had the dilation. I wanted to follow her, but I had too many questions for Celeste. "Where are they taking her?" I asked. "And if the entero . . . whatever it is, isn't the problem, then what would cause the blood?"

"Milk allergy," Celeste said. "Think about it. We started adding some of your milk to the formula in her feeding tube at the end of last week. Then you just started nursing her full-time. She also had a mild rash . . . a hivelike rash . . . on her neck early this morning. So an allergy is my best guess, but we'll know very soon."

"Would that mean I can't nurse her?"

She nodded. "Possibly, though Dr. Davidson might want you to try changing your diet first. But I think this was an extreme enough reaction that he'll say it's not worth the risk. Why don't you go to the cafeteria and have a cup of coffee and then come back down? We should know something very soon."

I nodded, but instead of going to the cafeteria, I walked back to Joanna's cubicle and sat down in the recliner. I didn't shut the curtain. Instead, I riveted my gaze on the door to the CICU, waiting for my baby to come back to me.

"The X-ray was clear," Dr. Davidson, the pediatrician, told me nearly an hour later, "so it looks like your little one is allergic to your breast milk. This may clear up over time, but for now, you shouldn't try to nurse."

"Can I eat differently?" I asked, remembering what Celeste had said, but he was shaking his head before I even got the question out.

He pulled a prescription pad from inside his yellow gown. "I'm afraid this is a pricey formula, but it's the best," he said, handing me the piece of paper with the name of a formula written on it.

"Is there a substitute for this?" I asked. "A ... less expensive substitute?" I wasn't worried about the cost. I wanted to know what on earth I would be able to feed Joanna in 1970. I doubted this formula existed then.

"They have rebates," he said, "so let's get her started on that and see how she does over the next week or so while she's still here in a controlled environment."

"The next week or so?" I nearly shouted. "She was supposed to be discharged today."

"You can understand why that needs to be postponed, can't you?" He looked at me curiously.

Of course I could understand it. I was just miserably disappointed. The next portal was August 22, two weeks away. Two more weeks in 2001 when I'd had my heart and mind ready to see my family. My home. I was ready to start my real life with my daughter.

"Yes," I said. "I understand." My breasts felt suddenly heavy and full, and Dr. Davidson almost seemed to sense my discomfort.

"Get yourself the tightest sports bra you can find," he said. "It shouldn't take too long for your milk to dry up."

I spent the rest of the day holding Joanna. I could see the remnants of the rash on her neck, the fading pink spots. I fed her from a bottle, which she didn't like any more than I did. Plus I was depressed that it would be two more weeks before I was able to take her home. I thought of Hunter and Patti waiting for me once again, hoping this time that I'd show up. They'd worry something had gone wrong when I didn't. Something more ominous than Joanna needing more time in the CICU. I felt a tear roll down my cheek and watched it land on Joanna's nose. She didn't seem to notice. Her gaze was riveted to my face, her little lips not moving on the nipple. She was truly looking at me, truly seeing me, and I suddenly felt the attachment between us in a new, intense way.

"Hush, little baby, don't say a word," I sang softly to her. "Mama's gonna buy you a mockingbird." She seemed to study me with fascination as I continued the song, and I smiled down at her. "If that mockingbird don't sing, Mama's gonna buy you a diamond ring." Her lips spread across the nipple, let it slip from her mouth. Crinkly-eyed, she let out a little gurgly sound. "And if that diamond ring turns brass, Mama's gonna buy you a looking glass." I touched my finger to her nose. She gurgled again, following the sound with the most beautiful gummy smile I could imagine.

Oh, my baby. Tears burned my eyes and I hugged her to me tightly until she wriggled in protest. Then I patted her back, burying my face against her sweet-smelling neck.

"I will never, ever let you go," I whispered.

25

Myra was not pleased when I told her I'd missed the second portal.

"That's ridiculous," she said angrily. "You said she's fine now. Why do they need to keep her another week?"

"They want to be sure she's handling the new formula well," I said. "I'm upset, too, Myra. I was all set to go, but we have two more portals. Hunter thought of everything."

She didn't speak for a moment. "All right," she said, surrender in her voice. "The next one is . . . what? The twenty-second?"

"Yes."

"All right," she said again.

"There's no problem with me staying longer in your friend's condominium, is there?" I wondered if she was uncomfortable having me stay there for so long a time.

"No, no problem."

"How was your move?" I asked. "How's Virginia?"

"Hot as blue blazes," she said, clearly in a sour mood. "I've got to run. Do what you can to make that portal."

"I will," I said. "Don't worry."

As usual, she left the line without saying good-bye. I felt

a flash of sympathy for Hunter, growing up with so little warmth from his mother. I hoped she treated him with more kindness than she did me. He was her son, after all, while I was nothing but a nuisance to her by now.

On the fourteenth, one week after Joanna's allergic reaction, she was discharged. I was a wreck, far more nervous than I'd anticipated being. I'd worn the sling to the hospital, and for the first time, I slipped her into it. "Slipped" was probably the wrong word. For months, I'd imagined sliding her easily into the sling, but when it came right down to it, "wedged" was the more accurate word to describe the experience. Joanna whimpered as I tried to balance her and pull the sling open at the same time, but once I finally had her in place she settled down quickly—magically, it seemed—and I drew in a long breath of relief.

Celeste and a couple of the other nurses hugged us good-bye. They let me take a donated mobile of cute little sea creatures with me.

"To hang over her crib," Celeste said. I had no crib, of course, but I would find a way to rig it up over the bassinet for our final week in 2001.

Outside, one of the hospital volunteers found a taxi for me, but the driver was impatient as I struggled with the car seat with a seven-and-a-half-pound baby hanging from my chest. I'd studied the instructions for attaching the car seat to the seatbelt, but the belt on the taxi was twisted and old and I finally gave up, cursing under my breath. "Just go," I told the driver, who was by that time muttering to himself in a language I didn't understand. I braced myself with an arm against the back of the front seat as he dodged in and out of traffic, and I breathed a sigh of relief when he finally pulled up in front of the condominium.

I had the elevator to myself and peeked inside the sling to be sure Joanna was breathing, she was so still. *Whoever invented the whole sling idea was a genius*, I thought, watching my daughter breathe in and out, in and out. She was as still and calm as she was during kangaroo care. I leaned over to kiss the top of her head.

Inside the condo, I hated to disturb her by transferring her to the unfamiliar bassinette so I left her in the sling as I curled up in one of the corners of the three-sided sofa. Using the remote, I turned on the TV, leaving the volume soft as I switched the channel to a soap opera I hadn't seen since the day Joanna was born. Then I promptly fell asleep.

For two days, everything went perfectly. Joanna and I fell into a routine. Feeding, changing, napping, bathing— which she hated. Other than bathtime, she was good-natured, her smile increasingly easy to elicit now. *I have a good baby*, I thought. For all she'd gone through in her first five weeks of life, it seemed a miracle that she was so easygoing. On the third day, though, that changed. She woke up crying and nothing I did soothed her. She fought the confines of the sling. She turned her head away from the bottle. When I held her as I walked back and forth across the living room floor that evening, the lights blinking on in the sea of buildings outside the windows, I felt the heat of her temple against my lips.

Fever.

I found the thermometer, laid her down on the blanket I used for her "tummy time," and took her temperature: 102. Horrified, I called Dr. Davidson, berating myself the whole time for not checking for fever earlier.

"Get her back to the CICU right now," Dr. Davidson said. "I'm already at the hospital. I'll meet you there."

I wedged Joanna into the sling, noticing with some horror that she was no longer crying or even whimpering. Instead, she'd grown terrifyingly limp and listless and I rested my hand against her back through the sling as I rode the elevator down to the lobby. I wanted to be able to feel her breathing.

I told the cab driver it was an emergency and he whipped through traffic like a professional hot rod driver and refused to let me pay him when he dropped me off at the hospital. While I was touched by his kindness, I was too frantic by that point to do much more than thank him as I raced out of the car.

Dr. Davidson was waiting for me in the CICU, and once again, Joanna was placed in an isolette. She was wheeled into one of the isolation rooms and I wasn't allowed to follow her. In all the time Joanna had spent in the CICU, she'd never had to go into one of those rooms. I knew what would happen there. A spinal tap, among other things. I knew of two babies who'd been diagnosed with sepsis after visiting that room, and I knew that one of those babies never recovered. I stood near the CICU doorway, my fist pressed to my lips.

"Did you scrub in?" a nurse my own age asked me. I'd seen her once or twice before but didn't know her name.

"Oh," I said, shaking my head. "Sorry."

"Go do that." She pointed behind me to the foyer and the sink. "Then you can wait in the lounge."

It was nearly midnight by the time Dr. Davidson joined me in the lounge. Although a couple of other parents had come and gone as I sat there feeling alone and scared, he and I now had the room to ourselves.

"It's not meningitis." They were the first words out of his mouth. "But she has a bacterial infection. It'll be a day or two before we get the lab results, but we're starting her on IV antibiotics and I'll readmit her."

"How serious?" I asked.

"In another baby, I wouldn't be too concerned," he said. "But given Joanna's heart history, we need to treat this aggressively."

"Will her heart be all right?" I asked. "Will *she* be all right?"

"We're going to do everything in our power to make sure she is," he said.

"How long do you think she'll have to be here?" I asked. "I mean, if everything goes okay."

"She'll be on the antibiotics a couple of weeks," he said.

I shut my eyes as panic bloomed in my chest. We wouldn't make the third portal.

"You're exhausted," Dr. Davidson said. "Go home. Get some rest. You can come back in the morning."

"I want to stay with her," I said, opening my eyes.

"Go home," he said again, this time with a small smile. "Doctor's orders. She's in good hands here. If anyone should know that after the past five weeks, you should."

26

Hunter

The hardest thing about time travel was being completely out of touch with the traveler. I should have worked harder on that when I was with Temporal Solutions in 2018. My mother should have worked harder on it. Maybe they were working on it now. I hoped so, but that wouldn't do me any good at this moment. Not when I wished like hell that I could get in touch with Carly.

Three portals down and only one to go. I was sitting in my RTP office, staring numbly into space—something I seemed to be doing a lot of in the week and a half since the third portal. Carly'd been in 2001 for four months now and Patti was barely speaking to me. "If you've lost my sister, you've lost me," she told me as we once again waited in vain for Carly to appear on Jockey's Ridge. "I'm serious, Hunter," she'd said, her gaze on the dunes rather than on me. "I'll never be able to forgive you." Her voice sounded cold. It was a voice I'd never heard her use before. We hadn't made love since the day Carly left. We'd barely even touched, and our only conversations centered around John Paul. "It would be like you killed her," she added, finally turning to look at me. "Maybe you have."

Maybe you have.

I looked down at the client file on my desk. I needed to open it and start working on that company's project. Instead, I folded my hands in my lap, shut my eyes, and tried to think.

Had something gone terribly wrong with one of the portals? It could happen. Or maybe the problem had nothing to do with the portals at all. My sleep these days was filled with nightmares. I'd had a horrendous dream that Carly lost the baby—literally. She lost it and couldn't find it. Neither Patti nor I could eat, and we'd each dropped over ten pounds. John Paul picked up on our fears and had become a finicky eater as well, even turning away from the brownies Patti baked the other night. The pediatrician told us he was simply having a growth spurt. Not to worry. The pediatrician had no idea how much there was to worry about.

I tried to picture Carly there, in 2001. She was in touch with my mother, wasn't she? That reassured me. Surely my mother could help her out of any jam she found herself in. Unless ... Carly'd died. During childbirth? A car crash? So much might have gone wrong. And if she'd died, we would never know.

Instead of focusing on the work I should be doing for my clients, I ran the portal calculations over and over again. They were correct, every one of them. Yet I knew from experience that many variables outside my control could interfere with a well-calculated stepping-off or a meticulously plotted landing and I began to seriously doubt myself. Doubt the whole plan. My thinking became circular and I couldn't escape it. So what if I'd met Carly in Princeton when I was fifteen? I should have just forgotten about it. Put it out of my mind. What was the big deal if I'd changed that little bit of the future? She would have lost the baby if she'd stayed in 1970, true. But I worried that the baby might not be all she'd lost now.

All I'd caused her to lose.

27

Carly

The fourth and final portal was tomorrow, Sunday, at 11:14 P.M. and everything was finally falling into place.

Joanna had spent the last three and a half terrifying weeks in a battle against some mutant bacteria that seemed resistant to every antibiotic the doctors had in their arsenal. Even the infectious-disease specialist that Dr. Davidson called in struggled to find the magic bullet that would make my baby well. It was the most frightening few weeks of my life as we all worried the infection would travel to her heart. After all I'd been through with her, was I going to lose her? She'd turned from an easygoing, sweet-natured baby to a wan and listless little thing, sick from whatever infection she was fighting as well as from the medications that ravaged her body as they worked to make her well. I spent nearly every second in the isolation room with her, even sleeping there at night, and I had dark circles beneath my eyes that I was certain made me look thirty-seven instead of twenty-seven. Like every mother of a sick infant, I was terrified. Unlike every other mother of a sick infant, I had the added fear of not being able to take her home with me to the place and time where she belonged.

A week ago, though, she finally turned the corner. I'd kissed a listless baby good night and a smiling baby good morning. When I saw the light in her eyes and the energy in her reaching arms and kicking legs, I ran from the isolation room into the CICU to find Celeste.

"She's better!" I nearly shouted. "Come see!"

She *was* better. Her fever had broken, and while her blood work wasn't perfect, it was moving in the right direction. For the first time in too long, she wanted to interact with me and I spent the day cuddling her, feeding her, singing to her, all the while counting and recounting the days until tomorrow, the final portal. She was moved out of isolation, and with every passing day, she grew stronger. She was on oral antibiotics now, the IV gone, and her discharge from the hospital was planned for tomorrow morning. Sunday, September 9. I'd been a wreck all week, worrying they wouldn't discharge her until Monday, a day too late. This seemed like a miracle. It had been a rough few weeks, yes. A rough few *months*. But in a little over twenty-four hours, we'd be going home.

Yesterday, Celeste and several of the other nurses presented me with an envelope. Inside was a ticket for a bus tour of the city.

"You've been in New York all this time and haven't taken a moment for yourself to see the sights," Celeste said. "We want you to have a little chill time before you have to head back to North Carolina. You know we'll take good care of Joanna while you're enjoying the city."

I was touched, but playing tourist was the last thing on my mind. I had a very full day planned that allowed no time for a city tour or anything else that would divert my attention from the work at hand. First, I needed to pick up a box of the special formula Joanna was on. Then I needed to carefully pack Hunter's mustard-yellow backpack with the formula and a few other necessities to be sure I could manage it as well as the sling. Joanna was a little over eight pounds now and I worried that all the weight could throw off Hunter's calculations.

Perhaps the most important thing I needed to do today was buy a small stepladder, which I planned to take to Central Park to hide in the brush near the Gapstow Bridge.

Myra called that afternoon while I was walking to the hardware store. "Are you set?" she asked, cryptically. I knew what she meant was, *Are you ready to step off tomorrow night?*

It was noisy on the sidewalk, the sound of cars zipping by making it hard to hear. I stepped into the entryway of a pharmacy, holding my hand over my free ear. "Yes, everything's fine," I said. "Joanna will be released tomorrow morning. I'll keep her at the condo for the day and then, tomorrow night, we'll *finally* head back to—"

"Shh!" she hissed. She sounded angry and I frowned. What had I said to set her off? "I just wanted to be sure everything's on schedule for you," she said, and I heard the tightness in her voice.

"Myra, is something—"

"Enough," she said. "Is there anything else you need from me?"

"No, but I—"

"I need to go now," she said.

"All right," I said. "And thank you so much for everything." Her end of the line clicked off before I'd even finished the sentence.

At the little neighborhood hardware store, I bought a flashlight and a three-foot-high lightweight stepladder. Leaving the store with the ladder, I was torn between joy and terror. It seemed to have taken forever, but Hunter's scheme was going to be a success: I had a healthy, beautiful baby, and I was about to take her home. The terror came from the mechanics of the task I was facing: with perfect timing, I needed to climb onto that stone wall and leap into darkness, my precious baby in a sling on my chest. *Dear God.* It sounded so impossible! What if it was too much for Joanna? Myra didn't seem to think it would be a problem, but she didn't realize how sick Joanna had been. I was terrified at the thought of harming her after her long struggle to get well.

From the hardware store, I walked the mile and a half to Central Park. One thing I was coming to appreciate about New York: no one gave a woman carrying a stepladder a second glance. I entered the park from a different direction than I had nearly two months earlier when I first checked out the bridge. I wound my way along the trails, transferring the ladder from hand to hand, as I followed the map in my head. Once again, I got lost and had to ask a woman pushing a stroller to point me in the right direction. I would need to carefully memorize the directions for tomorrow night. I couldn't afford to get lost in the middle of the night with the minutes ticking down to 11:14 P.M.

I finally reached the bridge, but I was not alone. It was a beautiful Saturday and it seemed that everyone had decided to cross the small Gapstow Bridge at that moment. Women pushed strollers. A boy sailed by on one of those crazy skateboards. Two women walked arm in arm, one of them talking on her cell phone. I leaned against the southern wall of the bridge, looking toward the buildings in the distance, feigning nonchalance. The stepladder hanging over my forearm was beginning to cut off circulation. How was I going to do this? My plan had been to hide the stepladder in the brush along the path, and while I'd noticed the perfect spot for it as I'd approached the bridge, I could hardly tuck it away there with all these people around.

I leaned the ladder against the wall and pulled out my phone, pretending to make a call so I didn't look peculiar—I hoped—as I dawdled on the bridge. After ten minutes or so, the path was suddenly clear of people. I carried the stepladder to the area of overgrowth I'd spotted, then darted into the brush and tucked the ladder behind some shrubbery. I slipped back onto the path as a man jogged by. He didn't give me a second look, but I was trembling. I wasn't much good at subterfuge, and it suddenly occurred to me that there might be a security camera nearby. Was that possible? Those invasive cameras seemed to be everywhere in 2001. What if I arrived tomorrow night with

Joanna in tow only to find the stepladder gone? How would I get onto the stone wall without it?

Stop worrying, I chided myself. *Everything's going to be fine.*

When I left the park, I felt too tired to make the walk to the hospital, so I took a cab. I rode in the backseat thinking, *This is my last taxi ride in New York City. Hallelujah!* When I picked up Joanna in the morning, I'd walk back to the condo carrying her in the sling. We'd spend the day there together until it was time to head to the bridge. I no longer felt anxious about taking care of her on my own. Other than the medical care, I'd been doing everything for her myself these last couple of weeks in the hospital. I imagined sitting in one of the cushy beige and black chairs in the condo, feeding her and burping her and cuddling her to sleep. I'd be worried, I knew. Worried about our trip in the dark to Central Park. Worried about stepping off at the precise moment. And worried about not injuring Joanna when we landed on the dunes. But I no longer had any worries about caring for her myself. I only wanted the chance.

I spent a few hours with Joanna in the hospital, then headed back to the condominium, where I drank a special tea Celeste had told me would help me sleep. I wanted to be well rested for tomorrow.

In the morning, I dressed in jeans and a T-shirt and light jacket—the air had taken on a sudden early fall chill. I bundled up the sling in my purse. I probably should have purchased a diaper bag like other mothers I saw on the street, but it would have been a waste of money. I'd only be using it today to look like a typical mom. If anyone asked, I'd say I'd left it home. That was the sort of mundane thing I thought about as I walked to the hospital. A couple of people I passed on the street smiled at me and I thought that was a bit unusual until I realized that *I* was smiling myself. Smiling at the world. Finally, our ordeal was over.

I stopped in the hospital gift shop and picked out a small stuffed teddy bear for John Paul that read I LOVE NEW YORK across its chest. Then I bought a huge box of candy for the nurses. They deserved much more than that, but it was the best I could do. I crammed the teddy bear into my over-stuffed purse, then took the elevator to the tenth floor.

I put my purse in the foyer locker I had begun to think of as mine, then scrubbed my hands up to my elbows for the very last time. I knew Celeste was off today, so I sought out Deirdre once I walked into the nursery. She was sitting in one of the recliners, gavage-feeding a preemie.

"I'm ready to take Joanna home," I announced with a smile.

Deirdre looked up at me in surprise. "Didn't anyone call you?" she asked.

I froze. "About what?"

"Joanna spiked a fever during the night," she said. "It seems to be coming down now, but she's back in isolation. Dr. Davidson wants to keep an eye on her for another forty-eight hours."

28

I stared dumbly at Deirdre. *This cannot be happening,* I thought.

"I have to take her today," I said.

She shook her head. "I'm sorry. I know you had your heart set on her coming home today, but it's not possible."

"I'll call Dr. Davidson." My hand shook as I pulled my phone from my jeans pocket.

"You can do that," Deirdre said as she checked the level of formula in the syringe she was holding. "But I know what he'll say."

As I dialed the phone, I walked into the isolation room where Joanna lay on her back, sound asleep. I rested my palm against her temple while I was on hold. She was warm, but not hot. Her cheeks had the ghost of the blotchy redness she'd get when she was feverish. They were right to keep her. Right to observe her. But I couldn't let her stay.

I sat in the recliner, waiting a very long five minutes for Dr. Davidson to come on the line.

"She needs just a few more days," he said. "It'll be worth it to know she's fine before you take her to North Carolina.

You don't want her to end up back in the hospital down there, do you?"

I don't have a few days, I thought. Sitting there, clutching the phone, I felt dizzy with panic.

"I know you've been through so much with her," Dr. Davidson continued when I didn't respond. "One scare after another. But she's doing well and hopefully the fever is just a fluke. But we can't know that for cer—"

"What if I insist on taking her home today?" I asked.

He didn't respond right away. "That would be a mistake," he said finally. "Come on, Caroline. Don't risk all the progress she's made by taking her home too soon. I'd have to fight you on that decision," he added.

I felt like crying. Then I thought of Myra. I could call her. I could get another portal from her. It would worry Hunter when I didn't show up on this final portal, but at least I'd still have a way to get home.

"Okay," I said to Dr. Davidson. "I understand." I was anxious to get off the phone now that I had a plan. Anxious to call Myra.

I shut the door to the isolation room as I dialed Myra's number. I didn't want this call overheard. Her number rang only once before I was greeted by a mechanical voice.

The number you have reached is not in service and there is no new number.

Had I misdialed? I tried the number two more times with the same result. How could this be? Myra had called me from this number only yesterday. I remembered how odd she'd sounded, though. How short she'd been with me. She hadn't wanted me to say too much over the phone.

Heart thumping, I sent her an email from the phone. *Please respond,* I typed. *It's urgent.*

Almost immediately, I received a message back saying that my email had bounced. I pressed my hand to my mouth, staring at my phone. I vaguely remembered something Myra had said a few months ago about having to change everything when someone—the military or the government or someone—got too close to Temporal Solutions' secrets. Was that what had happened?

Is there anything else you need from me? she'd asked me yesterday. Did she actually mean, *Is there anything else you need from me before I'm unreachable?* I'd told her everything was set for this portal. She thought Joanna and I were ready to go. She thought she could disappear without worrying about us any longer.

I went through the motions of taking care of Joanna that morning. She slept more than usual, and although her temperature was barely elevated, she wasn't her usual smiley self. She turned away from the bottle after only a few minutes and she showed little interest in my songs or my chatter. Dr. Davidson was right: she needed to stay in the hospital. I thought briefly of stealing her. I'd steal her, then I could—quite literally—disappear with her into thin air tonight and no one would ever be able to find us. But at what risk? I would never forgive myself if I did something to harm her already fragile health.

I had two choices, I thought, as I sat next to her isolette. I could stay in 2001 with Joanna. I'd have no job, no usable degree, no way to make a living, no friends or family, and after Myra's time-traveler friend returned, no place to live. Most likely, my credit card would soon be cut off since Myra expected me to be gone.

My only other choice was to take the portal tonight by myself. I could get a new portal to return to 2001 from Hunter. I'd ask for the soonest he could come up with. It didn't matter where he had me land. I would find my way back to the hospital and Joanna. I could return with a few new portals to take her back to 1970. How I was going to leave 2001 and my daughter, though, I didn't know.

At six o'clock, I kissed my sleeping baby good-bye, tears running down my cheeks and spilling onto hers. "I'll come back as soon as I can, sweetheart," I whispered to her. "I love you more than you'll ever know."

I left a note for Celeste telling her I had to help a friend who was having a medical emergency and that I'd be back in a couple of days. Then I slipped out of the CICU, not wanting anyone to see my tears, and I cried as I began walking to the condominium. People on the street turned away from me, uncomfortable at witnessing my grief.

Think about what you need to do, I told myself as I walked. *Focus. Focus.* I wiped the tears from my eyes with my fingertips, stiffening my spine, and by the time I reached the condo, my eyes were dry and my plan in place.

29

It was a long, long wait until nine o'clock, when I planned to leave the condominium. I hadn't eaten anything since breakfast and I looked in the refrigerator to see if something would pique my interest, but I couldn't muster up an appetite. There were only a few things in the refrigerator anyway: milk, half a block of cheddar cheese, a carton of eggs, a plastic container of strawberries. I would leave it all behind in a show of optimism that I'd be back long before the food went bad. I'd also leave my clothes and Angela's bassinet here, I thought, along with the iBook and my phone. The gadgets would do me no good in 1970. The one thing I would make sure to take, though, was the packets of photographs I had of my daughter.

I sat on the three-sided sofa, watching darkness fall and the lights blink on in the sea of buildings in front of me, but it wasn't the buildings I was seeing. Instead, I pictured Joanna alone in the isolation room. The nurses would take good care of her in my absence, but not the way I would.

At eight forty-five, I put on my jacket. I looked down at the coffee table where I'd left my phone and iBook and the sling and had a sudden idea. Slipping the sling on over my jacket, I headed for the kitchen, where I reached into the refrigerator for the carton of eggs. I slid the carton into the sling with a sense of satisfaction. The eggs would tell me for certain if Joanna would be safe when I landed on the dunes.

I walked the mile and a half to Central Park with resolute steps, going over and over the path I would take through the park to the bridge in my mind. There were not many people on the street at this hour and I was glad. I didn't want to be observed as I concentrated on what I needed to do.

It took some courage to walk onto the dark path that led into the park. There were streetlights, yes, but they were not close to one another and the pools of light they cast were a good distance apart. My flashlight was heavy and sturdy, and if anyone came near me I would whack the hell out of them with it. It wasn't so much my safety I cared about as Joanna's. I needed my plan to work. I didn't have time for a trip to the emergency room. I wasn't going to let any Central Park hoodlum get in my way.

I came to a fork in the path and felt a moment of self-doubt. I didn't recall this fork in my memory. I turned right and felt a flutter of anxiety in my belly as two young men appeared in the darkness in front of me. *Touch me and I'll kill you,* I thought to myself. They were holding hands and they dodged me on the path, and I imagined they were no happier to see me than I was to see them. I looked over my shoulder to be sure they were still walking away from me. They were. I was safe.

At nine fifty, I spotted the bridge ahead of me, illuminated in moonlight. I let out my breath in relief, knowing that I'd taken the correct path. I'd imagined waiting on the bridge until I could step off at eleven-fourteen, but now that I saw how exposed it was, I needed a new plan. Looking around to be sure I was alone, I slipped carefully into the brush near the entrance to the bridge, my flashlight darting though the confusion of shrubs and vines in front of me. I found the stepladder, opened it, and sat down on it, turning off my light and reaching behind me to slip it into Hunter's yellow backpack. I would wait there until a few minutes before I was to step off.

Only now did my heart start to race at the thought of leaping from the bridge. It had been frightening to step off from the end of the Nags Head pier, but I'd had Hunter's hand to hold. Now that experience felt like a dream, an impossibility, and I was suddenly glad I didn't have Joanna with me. I didn't want to risk her life as well as my own.

By the time eleven o'clock rolled around, I'd convinced myself I would fall into the pond when I stepped off. How deep was it? Would I drown in the darkness or was it so shallow that I'd break a leg and have to somehow drag myself to the weedy shore? I swallowed against the rising panic, my imagination out of control.

When the illuminated face of my chronometer read 11:05 and I could feel my heart pounding in my temples, I heard chatter on the path leading toward the bridge. I looked down at my body and the ladder, making sure I was covered by darkness. The street lamp caught the intruders: a young couple—teenagers?—both dark-haired and slender. They held hands, pressing their shoulders up against each other. The girl laughed, the sound echoing in the darkness. Not a soul had passed by in the hour and a half I'd been sitting there and now this?

In a moment, they fell out of my view, but I could hear them talking. I strained to listen. The chatter grew quieter, but it never ceased, and I knew they had stopped on the bridge.

Quietly, I stood up. The ladder made a barely perceptible squeak as I folded the legs together. I put it over my arm and walked as slowly and softly as possible to the edge of the brush so I could see the couple between the branches of a tree. They leaned against the north side of the bridge, chatting softly between kisses. The half-moon outlined their bodies in silver.

Go, I thought. *Leave.*

My knees shook as I balanced myself in the overgrowth, trying not to make a sound. The couple had stopped talking now. They were deeply entwined in each other's arms and showed no sign of leaving.

At ten minutes past eleven, I could wait no longer. I lifted the stepladder over my arm again and walked resolutely out of the trees and onto the path. In a moment I was on the bridge. The couple was so absorbed in each other that they didn't notice me at first, but as I neared the center of the bridge, they turned to face me, the moonlight reflecting off their startled faces.

I smiled at them as though I was doing nothing out of the ordinary as I set the stepladder in what I hoped was the exact center of the south-facing stone wall of the bridge. I opened it slowly, glancing at my chronometer. Two minutes.

"Don't mind me," I said to the couple with a smile that belied the nausea I was fighting.

"What are you doing?" the girl asked.

"Just getting ready to take a picture," I said. "Sorry to disturb you." I wondered if they could tell I was wearing a baby sling over my jacket? I hoped the carton of eggs wasn't visible or they'd really think I was crazy.

"Be careful," the guy said as I stepped onto the first rung of the ladder, then the second. I would need to step on the top of the ladder to be able to get onto the broad surface of the wall.

"I do this all the time," I said.

"She doesn't have a camera." The woman spoke in a near whisper to her partner.

Thirteen after eleven.

I stood on the top of the ladder, leaning over, my hands on the smooth stone. One more step. Just one. I lifted my leg.

"Hey, stop!" the guy said. I heard him start toward me, his feet scraping on the pavement as I raised myself onto the top of the wall. Thirty seconds left. He grabbed for my leg. I kicked his arm away.

"Leave me alone!" I said. "I'm fine."

"Call 911!" he shouted to his girlfriend, then to me, "This bridge isn't even high enough to do the job, lady!" he said. "You'll just hurt yourself!" He reached for me again, but I jerked my leg away from him and stepped forward into the air. Somewhere behind me, I heard the girl scream and the world went white, as though I'd stepped into the moon.

30

Hunter

This was Carly's last chance.

Mine, too, I supposed, at least in Patti's eyes. She'd still been in bed when I left the house before dawn and drove to Jockey's Ridge. We'd stayed up most of the night, talking in bed or staring at the ceiling, both of us with the same fear: Carly wouldn't show up.

"I can't bear it," Patti had said. "I can't sit on the dunes for a fourth time and watch her not come."

I couldn't blame her. I felt the same way.

I parked the Impala near the dunes. For the fourth time, I kicked off my sandals, grabbed my flashlight and thermos and began walking up the first dune, the circle of light from my flashlight bouncing against the sand. The morning was chilly. Cold for September, actually, and it was a reminder of how long Carly had been gone. The first time I'd waited for her to arrive I'd been sweating.

I didn't feel optimistic. If everything had gone according to plan—a successful surgery, a healthy baby—wouldn't

Carly have taken an earlier portal? If she didn't show up this morning, could I make myself go to 2001 to try to find her? I could send her back, although I wouldn't be able to return myself. Which of us would Patti want? I knew my wife still loved me, despite her recent anger, but there was no contest when it came to which of us she would want to save.

I climbed higher, my thoughts and fears a jumbled mess. I was glad Patti hadn't come with me. I needed to feel the fear all on my own.

I reached the top of the first dune as dawn was breaking and I could finally get my bearings in the gray light. Below me, in the valley between the two dunes, there was a patch of color in a sea of pale sand. A pile of clothing maybe? It was not moving, but as the sky lightened over the ocean behind me, I made out Carly's long blond hair spread out like a fan against the sand. *Thank God!* Was she moving? *Yes, just a little.* I dropped my flashlight and half ran, half slid down the dune, calling her name.

31

Carly

I dreamed I was sitting in the CICU, Joanna in my arms. She reached a hand toward my mouth the way she did sometimes, her blue-gray eyes locked on mine. I gently nibbled her fingers with my lips. Then I lifted my head, puzzled by a sound. Someone was calling my name.

Carly!

The voice came from far away. Another part of the hospital? Or through the trees in Central Park? Or . . . *Oh!* My eyes fluttered open. I remembered!

My head felt so heavy. My hands clutched sand as I tried to sit up.

"Carly!"

Hunter. It was Hunter calling me.

"Here," I tried to shout, but the word came out as a whisper. I managed to push myself up, my hands pressing hard into the sand, until I was sitting. I was surrounded by the dunes and a sky the color of peaches. Hunter ran toward me. He was a hazy image, sand spraying behind him, and I must have briefly lost consciousness because one moment he was flying down the dune, the next he had his arms around me. I grabbed his shoulders, pressed my face into the fabric of his shirt, and sobbed.

"Where's the baby?" he asked.

He would have to wait for the answer. Right now, I just needed to touch him. Touch 1970. The weight of knowing I was an impossible distance from Joanna squeezed my heart. She was hundreds of miles and thirty-one years away from me. I choked on my tears with grief and fear.

Hunter drew back from me. Looked into my eyes. "The baby?" he asked again.

"I had to leave her." My voice came out in a husky dry whisper. I cleared my throat. "She wasn't ready to leave the hospital yet."

"Oh, no," he said. "Oh, damn. I should have given you more portals. I—"

"You have to get me back there, Hunter." I clutched his arm. "Now. Right away. Please."

He stared at me as though he didn't understand what I was asking. Then he nodded. "All right," he said. "First, let's get you home. Then I'll go . . ." He frowned, touching the lump jutting from the sling at my chest. "What's this?" he asked.

I'd nearly forgotten. My fingers moved jerkily as I reached into the sling and withdrew the carton of eggs.

"What the . . ." Hunter said.

I rested the carton on my lap and worked the lid open. The eggs were perfect, every one. "I wanted to know if Joanna would be safe when I traveled with her."

Hunter laughed and hugged me again. "I told you she would be," he said.

I looked into his blue eyes. "Get me back to her."

He nodded. "I will. I promise." He unscrewed the top of the thermos he was carrying, poured water into the cap and handed it to me. I drained the cup, then leaned heavily against him as I struggled to my feet.

"Hmm," he said, looking up at the dune we would need to climb. "Maybe the dunes weren't the best idea."

"I can do it," I said.

He helped me take off my sneakers. He carried them along with the thermos and the carton of eggs, and with one arm around me, led me up the dunes. I lost track of how many times we had to stop so I could catch my breath. I felt as though I was on another planet with nothing but sand on all sides of me, no landmarks to let me know exactly where I was. Finally we crested the dune and I saw the ocean. *Home.*

"Hold on for a minute," Hunter said. "I see my flashlight."

I stood still, not completely sure of my balance yet as Hunter left my side to pick up the flashlight.

"I can carry the eggs," I said as he neared me again, laden down with my sneakers, the thermos and flashlight, and the carton of eggs. I smiled as he handed them to me. They seemed so ludicrous now, eggs from 2001. "Can we have these for breakfast?" I joked.

Hunter stopped walking, and when I looked at him, his eyes glistened in the early morning light. "You don't know how scared I've been," he said. "How scared *we've* been. I knew you got there. Of course I knew that, since we met there, as you now know. But after that, I didn't know what happened to you."

I wrapped my arms around him. At that moment, I felt like the strong one. The one who knew exactly what needed to happen next. "I'm all right," I assured him. "And Joanna is all right. You saved her life, Hunter. You saved both of us. Now please, just get me back to her."

The sun was a yellow streak in the pink horizon as we pulled into our driveway. Patti ran from the cottage and swept me into her arms, crushing me to her. I quickly told her why Joanna wasn't with me and she pulled away, holding me at arm's length to study my face.

"I don't care about the baby!" she said. "I just wanted *you* back."

Her words stung me. "*I* care," I said, but she didn't seem to hear me. She grabbed my free hand and walked with me into the house.

"What are you wearing?" she asked, pointing to the sling when we'd reached the porch. "And why are you carrying *eggs*?"

"The sling's for carrying a baby," I explained. "A lot of women—and some men—use them in 2001." I told her about the eggs. She didn't smile. There was something new in Patti, I thought. She was prickly. Angry. At me? At Hunter? I didn't know.

John Paul was in his playpen and Hunter lifted him out and plunked him in the high chair.

"Hi, sweet baby boy," I said, leaning over to cover his face with kisses. Or at least to *attempt* to cover his face with kisses. He pulled away from me as if I were a stranger, and I felt a twinge of sadness. I'd been gone a good chunk of his little life. I took off my backpack and pulled out the small stuffed I LOVE NEW YORK teddy bear. He reached for it and I finally got a smile from him.

Patti made bacon, eggs, and grits for breakfast, using eggs she had in the refrigerator. "No way I'm using *those* eggs." She took the 2001 carton from where I'd left it on the table and threw it in the trash. She kept stopping to touch me as she cooked. She'd squeeze my shoulder. Lean over to kiss the top of my head. It was as though she wanted to be sure I was truly there.

I struggled to eat, my fork trembling in my hand. I was shaky with anxiety, hyper focused on my need to get back to Joanna. I ate one egg. Half a strip of bacon. A forkful of grits. Patti sat across from me at the table, filling me in on John Paul's milestones: he was walking all over the place now and he knew eight words as well as the phrase "I love you." He adored strawberries and she couldn't keep enough of them in the house over the summer. I'd never heard her prattle before but she was prattling now, acting as though I'd been on a trip to the next state rather than thirty-one years in the future. Hunter was quiet, as if letting her get it all out.

"Patti," I said finally. "I . . . we . . . need to figure out how to get me back to 2001 and my daughter."

She looked down at her plate, cheeks crimson. "I don't want you to go back," she said. "It's too dangerous."

Hunter finally spoke up. "You could have contacted my

mother to get a later portal so you could stay with Joanna," he said. "Did you think of that?"

I nodded. "She was a huge help, but I lost touch with her," I said. "By the time I realized I needed a new portal, it was too late. I'd already told her I was all set and then she moved and must have changed her phone number. She thought I had everything ready to go."

"Ah, so that's what happened," he said, setting his fork on his clean plate. "We moved to Alexandria, Virginia, outside Washington in September that year. I think she had some government connection there, though I never knew much about it. Sometimes things got too close for her and she'd shut everything down. Change her number. Leave town. She liked to make herself hard to find. Where did you go when you left our house in Princeton?"

"First to a hotel that the fetal-surgery study helped pay for," I said. "Then your mother moved me into a condo owned by a friend who was time-traveling." I glanced at Patti. She was feeding John Paul applesauce now, her lips tightly pressed together. "The guy must be a multimillionaire because his condo is beautiful. I left my things there. My iBook and phone and some clothes."

Hunter grinned. "I remember our iBook lessons," he said. "You were a quick study."

"And you were a patient teacher," I said.

"What the hell are you two talking about?" Patti asked.

"Hunter was there, Patti," I said. "He was only fifteen, but—"

Patti set down John Paul's spoon and put her hands over her ears. "Stop it," she said. "Stop talking about this like it was a lark. Do you have any idea what this has been like for us?" she asked, lowering her hands to the table. "What it's been like for me to discover the two of you had been plotting behind my back? Then my sister disappears into the ether? I can tell no one what's going on. I have to make up where you are. Why you're gone. It was like you were dead. I was afraid you *were* dead."

"I'm not though, honey," I said. "And I have to go back. Just for a little—"

"No!" She shouted so loudly that John Paul jumped, his small face scrunching up as he began to cry. Patti lifted him into her arms from the high chair. "You're not going back," she said.

"She has to," Hunter said firmly. "Her baby's there. I'm driving to RTP as soon as we're done with breakfast so I can work out some new portals for her."

"No," Patti said again, quieter this time. I saw tears in her eyes. "I can't go through this one more time." She looked at me. "Don't go, Carly," she pleaded. "Please. Don't do this again. It's way too risky."

"I can't leave my daughter there," I said calmly. "I need to bring her home."

"You almost got stuck there!" she said.

"I didn't almost get stuck there," I said. "I could have safely taken any of the portals if only Joanna had been well enough to come with me." I got up from the table and reached into the backpack where I'd left it on the counter. "Let me show you pictures of your niece," I said.

"Frankly"—Patti set John Paul on the floor, then folded her arms across her chest—"I don't care if she's the most

beautiful child on earth, you shouldn't go back. Let someone in 2001 adopt her. She'll be all right."

"*Patti,*" Hunter chided.

Her words cut through me. I couldn't simply pretend
she hadn't spoken them.

"I get that this has been hard on you," I said, sitting
down again, the packets of pictures on the table in front of
me. "But I can tell you right now, it's been harder on me.
First, I lost my husband. Then I'm told my baby will die.
Then I stepped off the railing of the damn pier in the
middle of the night!" My hands were knotted in fists on my
lap. "Then I had experimental surgery with no idea if it
would work or not. I lived all by myself in a strange city
and a strange *time* with no family or friends around me, all
the while watching my baby fight for her life. I've risked
everything for her and if you think I'm leaving her in 2001
when I have the ability to go back and get her, you're
crazy!"

Patti stood up without a word. She lifted John Paul into
her arms again and walked across the kitchen and out the
back door to the beach.

I looked across the table at my brother-in-law.

"Give her some time," he said. "She's been a mess ever
since you left." He nodded toward the envelopes on the
table. "Show me the pictures."

I showed him the photographs, half of my mind out on
the beach with Patti. "Joanna had a couple of serious set-
backs," I said. I skipped over the one picture I'd kept of
Joanna wired and tubed and tethered. I hated looking at it.
Instead I showed him what she looked like now . . . or at

least, what she looked like in September 2001. Healthy. Strong. Smiling.

"She looks a little like John Paul, don't you think?" Hunter asked.

I hadn't seen the resemblance until he mentioned it, but now I did. Something about the shape of her nose. The roundness of her cheeks.

Hunter tugged at the end of my hair. "We'll get her home," he promised.

"Is there a chance I could go back tonight?" I asked. "I know it takes time to do the calculations and everything, but—"

He shook his head. "Very doubtful," he said. "The problem is not just finding a portal that will work from the end of the pier and put you somewhere safe in New York, but I need to figure out some new return portals as well." He looked at his watch. "It's nearly seven. If I leave right now, I'll get to RTP before eleven and can start working on it." He looked down at the top picture of Joanna again. I was holding her in it, her downy hair against my lips. Celeste had snapped it for me. "I'll make a final portal for you as long as a year out," he said, "just in case."

I groaned. "I hope I'll be back much sooner than that, but it's probably a good idea. I just wish I could leave tonight and arrive tomorrow morning. I don't want them to think I deserted her. I left a note, but still. I don't know what would happen if she's ready to be discharged and I'm not there."

He nodded. "I'll get you a portal as soon as possible," he said, getting to his feet. He squeezed my shoulder. "Be kind to Patti," he said. "This has been harder on her than either of us anticipated."

"I will," I said. "I didn't expect her to be so angry."

"We shouldn't have left her out of everything."

I nodded, then watched him head toward the doorway to the living room, my future quite literally in his hands.

"Hunter?" I said, and he turned to look at me. "I don't care where I land," I said. "I can get a train or a bus or something to New York City from nearly anyplace, so please just get me there as soon as you can."

He grinned at me. "You've gotten gutsy, woman," he said.

I thought of how I kicked away that guy on the Gapstow Bridge. How I leaped into the dark air from the top of the stone wall.

"Yeah." I smiled. "I guess I have."

32

Hunter

My nearly four-hour drive to RTP sailed by, my mind wrapped up in Carly's return. Thank God she was back, safe and sound. I wished she would stay put now, but I understood her need to get back to her daughter and I admired her for her courage in being ready to go as soon as I could make it possible. I only hoped her return would save my marriage as well as her daughter.

Before I left Nags Head, I'd found Patti sitting on the chilly dune behind our house, watching John Paul as he played in the sand.

"You okay?" I asked, squatting down beside her.

She nodded without looking at me. Her cheeks were dry, but I could tell she'd been crying. I leaned over to kiss her cheek. "I'm going to RTP," I said. "If at all possible, I'll be back tonight."

She turned to look at me, grabbing a handful of my shirt in her fist. "Be careful," she said. "Be careful driving and plotting those . . . portals . . . and everything. Please?"

"I love you," I said. We kissed for the first time in a long time. "I'll be careful," I promised.

Yes, I thought now as I drove, *I'd be more careful this time than I was the last time.* I could have kicked myself for not giving Carly a later portal. I should have thought it through better. She'd had a very sick baby. I should have guessed that baby might have needed to stay in the hospital longer. If only Carly'd been able to reach my mother, she could have gotten a later portal for herself ... but then she wouldn't have returned this morning and Patti would have walked out the door. Or rather, since the cottage was technically hers and Carly's, she would have kicked *me* out the door. And I would have thought I deserved it.

My mother. I felt envious that Carly had gotten to spend time with her. I wished I could. I wished I could slip back to 2001 and tell my mother how much I appreciated and admired her. All those things you don't think of telling a parent until it's too late. She was sixty-eight years old when she took that fifth trip, and I sometimes wondered if she chose to stay wherever she landed. If it was actually her choice. Although it hurt to think that she would have deserted me that way—even though I was well into adulthood by then—I hoped that was the case. I hoped she landed someplace that made her happy.

I reached RTP and my office a few minutes before eleven. Gloria wasn't there, of course, since this wasn't one of my usual work days, and I was glad to have the office to myself. I called Duke to reserve some time on the mainframe and was pleased to hear they had a cancellation for one thirty that afternoon. I would have to work fast to be ready for that time slot. I locked the office door behind me, turned on my radio, and set to work with my maps and the giant coffee-table book filled with photographs of New York City. I opened the book at random and there was a picture of the Sheep Meadow in Central Park. I knew about the Sheep Meadow only because it had been in the news the last few years. Demonstrations against the war were held there, along with love-ins and other massive gatherings. I would have to assume it was still there in 2001. The vastness of it would give me a lot of wiggle room in planning Carly's landing.

I worked out as much as I could on paper, then drove to my appointment with the mainframe at Duke. I plugged in times and longitudes and latitudes and nearly whooped out loud when I realized that Carly *could* step off tonight, a few minutes before midnight. We'd have to time her stepping off nearly to the second, but as long as we did, she'd land early in the morning in the Sheep Meadow.

I was exhausted, though. I hadn't slept much last night, worrying about whether or not Carly would show up this morning, and my adrenaline was pumping now in a way I knew could cause mistakes. So I went over and over my calculations until I was absolutely sure I was right about tonight's portal. Then I spent another hour figuring out Carly's returns, again from the Gapstow Bridge. I gave her five this time, making the final one for September 2002. If her baby wasn't ready to leave the hospital by then, I thought, Carly would have bigger problems than I could solve.

33

Carly

I made two mugs of tea and carried them, along with Joanna's photographs, out to the beach where Patti sat on our dunes and John Paul played nearby with a plastic pail and shovel. I handed Patti one of the mugs like a peace offering, then sat down next to her, the envelope of photographs on my thigh.

"I'm sorry I was short with you," I said.

"I'm sorry I was a bitch," she responded.

I put my free arm around her. "There's so much I want to tell you," I said. "Share with you. I'm a mother now, too. I want to share that experience with you. Please let me."

She leaned her head against my shoulder. Let out a sigh. "Of course," she said. "I just . . ." She raised her head and turned to look at me and I dropped my arm. "You vanished, and then I learned that my husband isn't who I thought he was. That he'd been lying to me ever since I met him and that the two of you plotted your . . . your *disappearance* behind my back. It was all too much." She looked down at the mug she held between two hands. "I've been so depressed and angry and . . . Then you finally show up this morning, and you're alive and I'm so happy, but all you talk about is wanting to leave again. Leave *me* again. I'm just afraid something will go wrong and I'll lose you forever." Her voice broke. "I couldn't take it, Carly."

"You don't need to worry," I said. "I'm going to get Joanna and come back the instant I can." I put my arm around her again. "You know this is where I want to be, right?"

She nodded, an attempt at a smile on her lips.

I looked out toward the water. This *was* where I wanted to be. I'd missed our beach. The ocean. The salty air. The seabirds and the peace, absolute peace, of September on the Outer Banks. I imagined the day when John Paul and Joanna would play together out here. They'd grow up together, as close as siblings.

"Let me see the pictures," Patti said, setting her mug down on the sand.

I reached into the envelope and handed the stack of photographs to her, watching as she studied each one. A tear slipped down her cheek. "She's so beautiful," she said finally.

I looked down at the picture of my little girl. "Imagine how you'd feel if John Paul was there," I said. "Could you stay here if you had the chance to bring him home?"

"No," she admitted quickly with a shake of her head. She handed the pictures back to me. "But Hunter should go with you," she said. "Keep you safe."

"He can't," I said. "Did he tell you about the 'fifth-trip rule'?"

"Oh." She nodded. "I forgot. If I didn't have John Paul to take care of, *I'd* go with you. Though it would terrify me." She glanced at me. "You're braver than I am."

"It's amazing what you'll do for your child, isn't it?" I said.

She nodded, then looked out to sea. "So . . ." she said. "What was Hunter like as a teenager?"

I laughed. "I wish you could have seen him at fifteen, Patti," I said. "He wanted to be a music producer. He was just like you at that age, with his walls covered with music posters, although I didn't know who any of the groups were. All those 2001 musicians. Except for the Beatles. He did have at least one Beatles poster. He said he'd just discovered their music."

"It's so . . . crazy," she said. "So hard for me to imagine you were actually in 2001."

"And guess what?" I said. "*As the World Turns* is still on in 2001!" I told her about the actors who still played their same old roles.

"You're kidding!" She laughed her boisterous Patti laugh and I was so happy to hear that sound.

I told her about my iBook and the internet and email and my little cell phone, wishing I'd thought to bring it with me to show her. She shook her head in amazement, then suddenly sobered.

"When does the war end?" she asked.

I didn't want to talk about the war. I shut my eyes, thinking of Joe. Thinking of his sacrifice. "Not for another few years." I looked at my sister. "So many more are going to die before it's over," I said, suddenly choking up. "I can't talk about it. It's too . . . I just don't like to think that Joe died for nothing."

"He died defending his country," she said firmly, even

though I knew she'd never believed in the war. She was just trying to comfort me.

I nodded. I would leave it at that.

"Anyway"—I cleared my throat—"people are more accepting of other people in 2001," I said. "I mean, I know I was in the North, but blacks and whites get along a lot better, though there's still problems. And now I know why Hunter always calls black people African Americans. That's the correct term in 2001. And homosexuals are more open. There's this show on TV called *Will and Grace*, and Will is gay and it's no big deal. A lot of people, especially young people, have tattoos and it's not considered strange at all."

"You're kidding," she said again.

"And a lot of doctors are women. And some men are nurses."

"A male nurse?"

"Yes, there's one in the CICU. The nursery." My mind slipped back to the CICU. At how alone I'd felt there at times. "I missed you so much," I said. "It was hard, being by myself there. Having a baby alone. No family with me. I wanted to share it all with you and had no way to do that. I love you so much, sis."

"Joanna should sleep in the little fourth bedroom," she said suddenly. "Hunter will have to move all his junk out of there, but that would be perfect, wouldn't it? She'd be right next to your room."

I grinned, knowing Patti was finally seeing my daughter as a real person—a real person who would be living with us very soon. "That sounds great," I said.

"Should we buy a crib and paint the room before you go?" she asked.

"I'm hoping I won't have time to do any of that before I go back," I said gently.

"All right," she said, smacking her hands lightly on her thighs, "then that's what I'll hope for, too. How about I paint the room while you're gone? Or wallpaper it. Some cute girly wallpaper! Will you let me fix up the room for her? Or do you want to do it yourself when you get back?"

"I'd love you to do it for me," I said, touched by her change of heart. "Fix it up however you'd like."

We sat side by side, our arms touching, as we watched the waves begin to pool around John Paul's chubby legs, and I had the strongest feeling that everything was going to work out just fine for all of us.

Patti and I spent the day talking about the past and the future as we started to straighten the room that would be Joanna's. We took long breaks, walking on the beach with John Paul in our arms or toddling along in front of us. We talked about Joe and how Joanna would always be a beautiful, living, breathing reminder of him. When we got back to the house, there was a message on the answering machine from Hunter. Patti pressed the replay button.

"Hey, Patti," he said. "Good news for Carly. Tell her I've got a portal from the pier to Central Park tonight around midnight that'll put her in New York early tomorrow morning. I worked out several return portals for her plus one a year from now. I have a little more to do here and then I'll head home. I should be there by ten. Love you."

My stomach contracted at the thought of stepping off the pier in a few hours. It was what I wanted, yet I couldn't help that visceral reaction.

"Thank God," I said, as Patti switched off the machine. I would be back with my baby in the morning. I would have her in my arms again, and with any luck, she'd be healthy and ready to come home.

Patti, John Paul, and I took naps late that afternoon. I fell instantly into a dreamless sleep and awakened to the sound of voices downstairs. It took me a moment to get my bearings in the dark. *September 1970. My bedroom.* I looked at my chronometer. It was already ten o'clock.

I jumped out of bed and ran barefoot down the stairs.

Patti and Hunter were sitting in the living room where Hunter had a plateful of lasagna balanced on his knees. He grinned at me. "Just call me your personal travel agent," he said around a mouthful of lasagna. "You're all set."

"Thank you, thank you!" I said, sitting down on the sofa next to Patti.

He nodded. "Your first return date is Friday, if she's ready."

I leaned against the back of the cushion, shutting my eyes and letting out my breath. I felt as though I'd been holding it in since I walked out of the CICU the day before. "I'm pretty sure she'll be ready," I said.

He swallowed a bite of lasagna. "And if she's not," he said, "I've got plenty of other options for you. Plus, I'll write down my mother's Alexandria address just in case you end up needing it. I don't remember her phone number from back then, though."

I lifted my head to look at him, wondering if he knew something he wasn't telling me. "Do I ever see you again in 2001?" I asked.

He shook his head. "Not that I remember."

"Do I see your mother?"

"I don't know. I don't think she ever mentioned you to me again. Hopefully you won't need to see her." He reached for a plump envelope on the end table next to him. "Seven hundred dollars for you," he said. He tried to give it to me, but I held up my hand to stop him.

"Oh, Hunter, thank you, but I won't need it, especially if I'm coming back Friday. I still have more than five hundred in my New York bank account from the money you gave me last time. And I have that credit card your mother gave me, as long as she hasn't canceled it."

"Humor me," he said. "When you didn't come back and didn't come back, I started worrying about your finances. How are you paying for the hospital?"

"Your mother took care of the insurance for me."

"Okay," he said. "But it's still hard to predict what you're going to need. Just take this. I'll feel better if you have it."

"All right." I took the thick envelope from him. I would bring every penny of it back to him.

34

Hunter

I felt a little cocky as I drove the mile and a half to the pier late that night. Carly sat beside me, her backpack clutched in her arms. Every few seconds, she checked the chronometer on her wrist. Our target was 11:57 and she needed to be pretty exact with it tonight.

Patti was in the backseat, John Paul asleep in her arms. She'd wanted to be with us this time.

"I have to see Carly do this with my own eyes before I'll believe it," she'd said.

I thought it was a good idea to have her with us. She'd been so upset that we'd left her in the dark the last time.

Everything felt right with my world at that moment. I was proud of myself for whipping out five portals in record time that afternoon and I was one hundred percent certain of their accuracy. My wife was back in love with me. My sister-in-law thought I'd hung the moon. My son was walking and talking. Best of all, the night was clear. Nothing to get in the way of a perfect launch for Carly. It didn't get any better than this.

Carly was antsy, tapping her foot against the floorboard and smoothing her hands back and forth over my old yellow backpack. We had half an hour to spare and I knew she was worried something—or someone—would get in our way. After her experience with the guy who grabbed her leg on the Gapstow Bridge, I couldn't blame her. But unless there were fishermen at the end of the pier—always a possibility—we would be fine. Her courage was stunning to me. If I'd learned anything in the last day, though, it was that the love of a mother could make a hero out of an everyday woman.

I parked the car and got the stroller from the trunk. John Paul didn't wake up as Patti tucked him into the stroller and we began walking toward the pier. The night was dark, the lights on the pier giant white puffballs in the air.

"Fishermen," Patti said quietly as we started walking onto the pier.

I squinted down the length of the pier. There were indeed a few fishermen scattered here and there at the sides of the pier, but I couldn't make out any at the end, and that was where it mattered.

"What if one of them sees the three of us walking to the end of the pier and only two of us walking back?" Patti asked in a near whisper.

"We'll tell them they were seeing things," I said. "They were here last time, too, and gave us no problem. All they care about is their fish."

Carly was quiet. She had turned in on herself, I could tell. In her mind, she was probably already in New York. Probably already holding her baby in her arms again.

We reached the end of the pier. We'd walked far past the last fisherman and although there were a couple of the tall puffballs of light above us, the spot where Carly would step off was in the safety of darkness. Nothing to worry about at all. Still, my heart pounded as it always did leading up to a launch, whether it was my own or that of a fellow traveler.

"My God, my God," Patti said quietly as she looked over the railing. She turned to Carly. "It's so high," she said. "How can you make yourself do this?"

"In a few hours, I'll be with Joanna," Carly said with a shrug. "That's how." For the hundredth time, she looked at her chronometer. "Four minutes," she said, slipping the backpack onto her shoulders. She looked like a seasoned time-traveling pro.

"When she steps off, don't yell or scream or anything," I said to Patti. "I know it'll be tempting but we don't need any attention."

"I won't," she promised. She reached for Carly, pulling her into a hug. "I love you," she said. "Hurry home."

"Love you, too," Carly said. Then she turned to me. "Help me up?"

I held her hand as she climbed onto one slat of the railing, then another. I could see the illuminated second hand on the chronometer as she took the final step onto the top of the railing. I was vaguely aware of Patti next to me, covering her mouth with her hand, ready to catch her scream. The second hand ticked to 11:57.

"It's time," I said, and Carly let go of my hand as she rose to her full height. She took one step forward and then she was gone. I let out my breath.

Patti nearly collapsed against me, a moan escaping her lips.

"Oh, Hunter," she whispered. "Bring her back."

I wrapped my arms around her, wondering if she could tell that I, too, was trembling. "Shh," I said. "She's fine. It'll all be fine." I let go of her and turned the stroller around. "Let's go home," I said. "It's all in Carly's hands now."

Patti cried quietly as we walked the length of the pier, and as far as I could tell, none of the fishermen paid us any attention. She put her hand on my back, her fingers tucked inside my belt, and I thought, *Tonight, we'll make love.* It had been so long. Finally we could get back to being happy. Being together.

It wasn't until I'd pulled into our driveway that I had a horrific thought. I had to be wrong. I pressed the brake. *God, please let me be wrong.*

"What was today's date?" I asked. I thought my voice sounded remarkably calm as I turned off the ignition.

"September tenth," she said. "Why?"

"No reason," I said, but I couldn't seem to move from behind the wheel, my body cold with fear.

I'd just sent Carly to New York City on the morning of September 11, 2001.

PART TWO

35

Carly

NEW YORK CITY

When I came to, I lay on my side in cool grass that tickled my nose. I sat up quickly with a gasp, then groaned, my stomach out of sync with the world as it spun around me. I was in a sea of green. Was this the Sheep Meadow where Hunter had told me I would land? Yes, it had to be. The grass stretched away from me in all directions and in the distance I saw trees and the tall buildings of New York. I wanted to leap to my feet and run from the park to find the hospital, but I knew better. Instead, I sat still, trying to get my bearings. I wasn't alone in the meadow. People walked across the vast lawn. A young couple sat on a blanket nearby, sipping coffee, most likely, from cardboard cups. Two women walked past me, a gaggle of children in tow. The women glanced in my direction. They were both blond, both wearing baseball caps, long ponytails bouncing from the openings in the back. One of the women pointed to me and said something to her friend, who nodded, then jogged toward me.

I smoothed my hair, wondering how disheveled I appeared to her.

"You all right?" she asked as she neared me.

I smoothed my jacket and checked that my backpack was still attached to my shoulders as I smiled up at her. "Yes, I'm fine," I said. "I was just resting."

She looked at me doubtfully. "All right," she said, then turned to go.

"Wait!" I said, realizing I had no idea how to get to the hospital from the Sheep Meadow.

The woman looked down at me again, waiting.

"Can you point me toward the exit, please?"

"Which one?"

"Just the nearest."

She pointed toward my right. "See that road there? If you follow it, you'll come to Central Park West."

From where I sat, I couldn't see the road she was indicating, but I would find it . . . as soon as I was certain my legs would hold me up when I tried to stand.

I waited until the woman and her friend had moved a good distance away before I dared try to get to my feet. I took a few steps across the grass. I was fine. Still a little woozy, a little nauseous, but I ignored the feeling as I headed in the direction she'd sent me. Central Park West. I knew that was the wrong way if I wanted to go to the hospital, but I would be able to find a cab there. That was all that mattered.

By the time I reached Central Park West, the muscles of my legs were shaking from my ankles to my thighs. I had to hold on to a lamp post as I tried ineffectually to wave down a cab. I definitely felt worse than I had the first two times I traveled. I needed rest, but it was the last thing I wanted. All I wanted at that moment was to get to Lincoln Hospital and my daughter.

I felt the eyes of a suit-clad businessman on me and knew I didn't look well. The man was gray-haired and carrying a briefcase and he, too, was trying to catch a cab, though with far more energy than I possessed. He was out in the street, arm up, practically stopping traffic with his body. When a cab finally pulled over for him, he walked to my side, wordlessly took me by the elbow and guided me to the door.

"This one's yours," he said. "I can catch another one."

"Thank you," I whispered, surprised and hugely grateful. I felt like crying over his kindness as I sank down in the backseat.

"Where to?" the driver asked.

"Amelia Wade Lincoln Hospital," I said.

"Well, hallelujah," he said. "If one more person asked to go to Lower Manhattan today, I was gonna find a new job." He put the taxi in gear and pressed the gas. "Practically every fare so far this morning took me down there and you can't get within five blocks of the memorial."

"What memorial?" I asked, to be polite.

I saw him frown at me in the mirror. "Where're you from?" he asked. "Alabama? You sound like Alabama."

"North Carolina," I said.

"Well, it's that 9/11 remembrance day they're having down there," he said. "You know, September eleventh? Ring a bell?"

Okay, I thought, this was something I was supposed to know. "Oh, right," I said. "Sure." I tried to smile at him in the mirror. "Well, I don't need to go to Lower Manhattan," I said, "so you're safe with me."

In the mirror, I saw him frown again, his eyebrows knitted together. "You're a strange one," he said, and I thought it was best to keep my mouth shut for the rest of the drive.

Something seemed different to me as the cab pulled in front of the hospital. Was the driver dropping me off at a different entrance? There was a new Mexican food cart on the corner that looked like it had been there forever, and next to the sidewalk stood a life-sized bronze statue of a woman and child I could swear I'd never seen before. But the actual entrance with its huge double glass doors looked the same. I paid the driver with fumbling fingers, then got out of the cab and headed for that familiar entrance.

The lobby comforted me with its piano music, reception desk, and familiar congestion. I walked to the bank of elevators, joined several other people in one of the cars, and pressed the button for the tenth floor. I felt woozy again as we began to rise and I leaned against the side wall. *In one minute you'll be with Joanna,* I told myself, and I felt a tired smile spread across my face.

I got off the elevator on the tenth floor and felt immediately disoriented. The sign on the wall, the sign that was supposed to read MATERNAL AND FETAL CARE CENTER instead read ONCOLOGY. Had I gotten off at the wrong floor? But no. The placard next to the elevator clearly read "10."

One of the elevators opened and a young man, an orderly, I guessed, walked out pushing an empty wheelchair.

"Excuse me," I said. "Isn't the nursery that way?" I pointed down the hall.

"Sixth floor," he said, brushing past me.

"No . . ." I started to argue with him, but he was already dashing down the hallway.

Had something jogged loose in my memory when I traveled from 1970? Two days earlier, the nursery had definitely been on the tenth floor.

Nevertheless, I rode the next elevator to the sixth floor. There was the sign . . . no, it was a different sign: MATERNAL AND FETAL HEALTH, with an arrow pointing left. NURSERIES with an arrow to the right. Completely disoriented, I turned right and headed down the hall, stopping at the double doors marked "PCICU." I felt as though I was in a completely different hospital than Amelia Wade Lincoln. Everything was wrong. The counter where the receptionist sat? Gone. The glass window that allowed you to see the babies? Gone.

I pushed open the double doors to find myself in a small, windowed foyer where a nurse sat at a long counter operating a computer. I could see into the nursery. Into the sea of isolettes, no longer separated by curtains but rather by screens that formed walls between the cubicles.

The nurse smiled up at me. "Can I help you?" she asked. I knew nearly every nurse in the CICU but I'd never seen this woman before.

"I'm a mom," I said, trying to smile. I felt unsteady and held on to the edge of the counter. "A mother. My baby's here. Joanna Sears. And I'm a little confused. Did the nursery suddenly move to the sixth floor?"

She frowned at me. "It's been on the sixth floor as long as I've been working here," she said. "And that's five years." She tapped the keys on the computer in front of her. "Joanna Sears," she said, typing. "Joanna right? Not Johanna? And Sears is S-E-A-R-S?"

"Yes." I gripped the counter harder. I wished there was a second chair in the foyer because I desperately needed to sit down.

"No, I'm not finding her." The nurse frowned at her computer screen.

"She's here," I argued. "I had to go away for a couple of days, but she's still here. She was in isolation."

"I'm sorry but I think you're mis—"

I swept past her chair and pushed open the door to the nursery.

"Hey!" she said, and I heard her shout into the phone or an intercom or something. "Security!"

Another unfamiliar nurse pushed an isolette past the door to the nursery and she looked up at me in surprise.

"Where's the isolation room!" I shouted. It was as if another woman inhabited my body. One who shouted. One filled with panic.

"You can't be in here," the nurse said. "You need to get a gown and—"

"My *baby* is here," I said. "Where's Celeste? She can tell you."

I walked into the sea of isolettes, many of them closed off by those new screens. My eyes searched the perimeter of the nursery for the isolation rooms. I spotted one, but the door was open and from where I stood, I could see it was empty.

"Where's my *daughter*?" I asked the nurse. Other nurses—and some parents—were looking at me now. One nurse took my arm and tried leading me back to the door, but I pulled away from her, suddenly furious. "Where *is* she?" I shouted. "What's going on?"

"Celeste's the NICU supervisor," the nurse at my elbow said calmly. "Let me take you to see her."

And then I saw the clock. It was on the far wall, huge blue numbers stating the time, and below them in smaller numbers, the date: 9–11–2013.

They were the last thing I saw before my world went black.

36

I was in a wheelchair. Someone held a cool cloth to my forehead. My backpack was on one side of my lap, an empty emesis basin next to it. A man in uniform stood nearby. He had a gun on his belt. Around me, people talked over one another.

"I remember her," a woman said.

I knew that voice.

"Celeste?" The name came out of my mouth in a whisper. "Celeste?" I said, looking around in desperation, my mind beginning to clear.

"Yes." She was in front of me. Leaning toward me. "Carol, right? That's your name?"

"Caroline, yes," I said. "And my baby Joanna is supposed to be here." My body trembled with the need to hold my daughter in my arms.

Celeste stood up straight. She looked both different and the same. Her brown hair was shorter. Redder. There were wrinkles at the corners of her eyes. Of course she was older. It was 2013. *Oh my God.* I tried to get out of the chair. "I have to go," I said. "I have to get back to—"

"No, no," someone said from behind me, holding my shoulders down.

"Take her to the ER," the man with the gun said.

"No," Celeste said. "Take her to my office. I remember her well now. Let me talk to her." She leaned toward me again. "You're agitated, Caroline," she said. "Let's get you settled down and we can talk."

I nodded woodenly, hoping there was something she could say or do that would erase this nightmare. How had this happened? How had I ended up in 2013? I couldn't believe Hunter could have been that off in his calculations.

Someone I couldn't see wheeled me down a corridor and into a small office. Behind me I heard Celeste's voice.

"She has to be close to forty," she said quietly to the person pushing the chair. "But she still looks exactly like she did back then. I remember that long blond hair. That flawless skin."

I was wheeled to the side of a desk. Celeste dismissed whoever had been pushing me, shut the door and sat down at the desk, turning her chair to face me. We were nearly knee to knee. "Here." She opened a bottle of water and handed it to me. I drank nearly half of it in a couple of gulps, the dehydration suddenly overwhelming.

"Not so fast," Celeste said. "You don't want to be sick."

I drank more. I couldn't help it, the thirst was so great.

"My God," Celeste said, shaking her head. "You haven't aged a day. And I'm mystified." She leaned toward me. Took the emesis basin from my lap and set it on her desk. "Whatever happened to you, Caroline?" she asked gently. "I remember you very well now. You were so devoted to your little girl. You were in the nursery nearly every hour of every day, weren't you? Then suddenly, you stopped coming. I remember it was right before 9/11, and we all figured you must have been one of the victims. We'd given you a gift certificate for the city tour and we worried you'd picked that day to take the tour and something happened to you. That was the only possible reason we could think of for you to disappear like that. What actually happened?"

That "9/11" again. A victim? I stared at her blankly, unsure how to respond. Clearly, this "9/11" was something I should know about. Maybe, though, she was giving me my story. The reason I disappeared.

I nodded. The water sloshed around in my stomach. "Yes," I said. "I was . . . a victim."

"Oh, no, how terrible." She shook her head, an expression of great sympathy on her face. "Thank God you survived, though."

"Where is Joanna?" I asked. That was all I really cared about.

Celeste hesitated a moment as though she wasn't certain she wanted to answer me. "When she was well enough to be discharged," she said slowly, "the hospital social worker contacted Child Protective Services and they took her."

I pictured the scene. My baby, waiting for me to come cuddle her and sing to her, instead being trundled off into the arms of a tired, overworked, indifferent social worker and taken . . . where? A whimper escaped my throat. My eyes burned.

"And then what?" The words came out in a small voice

I barely recognized as my own. "What did they do with her?"

"Once a baby leaves us, we have no way of knowing," Celeste said. "I think what you need to do is imagine that Joanna landed with a loving family. She'd be what? Twelve now? I bet she's having a wonderful life with parents who are thrilled to have her."

Joanna was twelve? With a loving family? *No, no, no.*

"She already *had* a loving family," I said, my voice breaking. I needed my baby back! The sense of loss I felt was unbearable. I had to get back to 2001 and my little girl! I thought of the list of portals in my backpack and with sudden horror, I realized all those dates were to return me to 1970 from 2001. Not from 2013. I was stuck here.

The nausea came back with a vengeance. Celeste seemed to sense it and handed me the basin. I clutched it, shutting my eyes, my breathing so rapid I was nearly choking on it.

"Deep breaths," Celeste said calmly. "Fill your lungs nice and slowly."

I barely heard her, my mind racing with the horror of my predicament.

"Where were you when the planes hit?" Celeste asked gently. "Did you sustain a head injury?"

What planes? What the hell was she talking about? I shook my head slowly, staring down at my lap, thinking, *Twelve years.* I was twelve years too late for my baby. Another small, agonized sound escaped my lips.

"Thank God you weren't killed," Celeste continued. "I wanted to go to the remembrance service this morning so much, but I can't leave here. I was able to go last year, though." She paused. "I lost five friends when the towers came down," she said.

I felt the blood rush from my head. The towers? The only towers I could think of were at the World Trade Center. They came *down?* Planes hit them? How? *Why?*

"We don't need to talk about it," Celeste said kindly. "It must be very hard to think about. It was just so shocking to us when you didn't come back. But then, everything was shocking during that time, wasn't it?" She leaned forward to touch the back of my hand. "Where did you go?" she asked. "Were you hospitalized? As I recall, you were from out of the area. North Carolina, right? Is that where you're living now?"

She'd asked too many questions at one time for my frightened brain to process. I needed to get out of here. Needed to figure out how to get back to my baby. I started to get out of the wheelchair but she stood up quickly, holding me down by the shoulders.

"No, no," she said. "I can't let you go like this. Obviously you had some sort of traumatic brain injury, since you didn't realize the date," Celeste said. "Do you remember what happened?"

I was going to have to make something up. Something to explain my behavior. "I don't really remember," I said, settling into the chair again. "But when I . . . I came to, they told me I'd been hit in the head by . . . I don't know what. They took me to my sister's house in North Carolina." The fake story spilled from me. "I've been there all these years. I guess I had . . . amnesia. I forgot I had a baby." I could never, ever, in a million years forget I had a baby.

"Didn't your sister tell you?" Celeste asked.

I looked away from her. Licked my lips, scrambling for an answer to her question. "She didn't know," I said. "We'd been estranged for years. Though now we're close, and I began to remember Joanna and felt confused about what year it was. What year it *is*, I mean." I felt a sob rising in my chest and fought to keep it down.

"Have you been treated for PTSD?" Celeste asked.

I remembered reading about PTSD in an article written by a Vietnam veteran. Could you have it if you hadn't gone through a war?

I nodded. It was easiest to go along with her.

"I imagine today's date brought it all back for you, huh?" she asked. "Left you pretty confused?"

I nodded again. *Let me out of here,* I thought.

"Here's what we should do," Celeste said, shifting both her position in her chair and her tone. "I'll take you down to the ER. I'll ask them to have a psychologist stop in to talk to you, and—"

"No," I said quickly. I had no time for this. I had to get out of here. I had to figure out what to do. "I'm not crazy, Celeste," I said, hoping I sounded saner than I had a few minutes earlier. I remembered when I was a physical therapy student and we learned about working with the elderly or people who seemed confused. We'd have to give them a mental status exam. *What month is it? Who is the president?* I had no idea who the president was. They'd drag me off to some psychiatric hospital.

"I'm not saying you're crazy," Celeste assured me. "PTSD has nothing to do with—"

"I'm all right. Really." I set the basin on the edge of her desk again, preparing to stand, but she rested a hand on my knee.

"It's 2013 and you thought it was still 2001, Caroline," she said gently. "You thought your—"

"It was being back here," I said. "Just for a moment, I remembered coming to the hospital every day. Being with Joanna." *Joanna.* I could see her so clearly. Feel the weight of her in my arms. *Kangaroo care.* Her soft skin against mine. Her gummy little smile. "I know it's 2013," I said, my voice husky. "I know where I am. Who I am. I'm fine."

"I'm worried about just letting you walk out of here." Celeste frowned. "Where will you go? Where are you staying? How about I get the social worker up here and she can call your sister for you?"

"I'm fine," I said again.

"You need to think about Joanna in a positive light," she said. "Imagine she has a good life."

"What if she doesn't?" I asked. "What if she didn't get adopted by some wonderful family? What if they didn't take good care of her? Didn't get her medical care? Made sure her heart was okay?" I choked up with panic. "I didn't abandon her! I would never abandon her."

"Oh, Caroline." Celeste folded her hands awkwardly on her lap. "You *do* need some help to work all this through," she said. "Have you seen a therapist at all?"

"Yes, I've seen one." I'd go along with her. It seemed the best course of action right then. I flipped up the footrests on the wheelchair with my feet and shifted forward, hoping I could stand without getting too dizzy. "And you're right. That's a good idea. I'll call my therapist and tell her what happened here today." I spoke quickly as I stood up and Celeste looked at me uncertainly, unsure how to respond to the fact that I was getting ready to leave. "She's a wonderful therapist and it'll be good to talk to her." I smiled, trying to look perfectly sane. It was killing me. I wished I *did* have someone I could tell everything to.

"You're sure you're okay to leave?" Celeste asked, standing up herself.

"Yes, and I'm sorry I was so messed up when I got here," I said, heading for the door. I had to get out of here. I had to think. "I feel like a fool now."

"No, no. No worries," Celeste said. "That day messed all of us up." She lifted the phone on her desk. "Let me ask someone from security to make sure you get downstairs and outside all right."

"No," I said quickly. "Really, Celeste. I'm fine. Thank you."

I turned and walked out of her office. In the hallway, I heard the cries of babies. My breasts ached. My belly contracted. Only two months ago, I gave birth to my baby girl. I needed her back in my arms. Eyes burning, I turned in the direction of the elevators. I felt stiff and scared as I rode down to the lobby. If anyone was playing the piano, I didn't hear it. I walked through the front door, then leaned against the cool outside wall of the hospital and shut my eyes.

Joanna.

I started to cry. I covered my face with my hands and sobbed my grief into them, not caring who saw me. I must have stood there for five miserable minutes. Slowly, my weeping stopped. I wiped my cheeks with my fingertips. People glanced at me as they passed me by. I looked straight through them, my mind not here on this street. Instead, I was thinking of the one person with the power to get me back to my baby: Myra.

I needed to clear my head. Think things through. I needed a plan. The bank where I had my account was only a couple of blocks away. First, I would go there and withdraw the money I'd left in the account. Then I'd go to the condo and get my iBook and phone.

I pressed my hand to my mouth. What was I thinking? Twelve years had passed. My iBook and phone were long gone. I doubted the key I had would even let me into the condo and surely by now it was no longer vacant. Oh my God, what a horrible mess I was in!

I slipped off my backpack and pulled the list of dates Hunter had given me from the outside pocket. Turning the paper over, I saw his mother's address. Alexandria, Virginia. Was she still there? I'd get my money from the bank. Then I'd catch the next train to Alexandria, and—as long as Myra was still living at this address—I would beg for her help to somehow, some way, get my baby girl back again.

37

"When an account is abandoned for three years, we close it and turn the money over to the state," the bank manager explained. He'd been called over by the teller when I began to cry with frustration over not being able to get my money.

There was that word again. *Abandoned.* "I didn't abandon it," I argued. "I was injured in the . . . in the 9/11 thing, and I had to go away to get better. And I need that money."

The manager frowned at me. "I can give you a form you can use to contact the state," he said, "but I'm afraid they'll say it's far too late. I'm sorry."

I left the bank without taking the form. So I was five hundred dollars poorer. What did it matter right now? What the hell did anything matter?

I took a cab to Penn Station and was relieved to see that at least the train station looked familiar. I needed *something* to look as I remembered it. I studied the timetables. One hundred and fifty-six dollars to get to Alexandria. I shut my eyes, upset all over again at my lost five hundred dollars. The train would leave in twenty-five minutes and arrive in Alexandria a little after five. The credit card Myra had given me such a short time ago had long since expired, so

I paid for the ticket with some of the precious bills Hunter had given me, grateful now that he'd forced that money on me.

I reached the correct platform and joined the line of people as they boarded the train. I found a window seat and was glad when no one sat next to me. It would be a four-and-a-half-hour trip. I had nothing to read. Nothing to distract me from thoughts of my baby. My missing daughter. My chest tightened in agony every time I pictured her in her isolette, waiting for her mama. Waiting and waiting. I turned my face to the window and let the tears stream down my cheeks.

The train began chugging its way out of the station through a dark tunnel, and I squeezed my eyes shut. *Hunter.* I didn't want to be angry with him, but he'd screwed this up. I'd pressed him to work fast, though. Pressed him too hard. I should have been more patient. Given him more time. I'd trusted him to do it right. He always did everything right. He was the smartest person I'd ever known. How could he have gotten this so very wrong?

The train stopped at every town we passed through, or so it seemed. People got on and people got off, but the seat next to me remained free and I could only guess that, with one look at me, passengers decided it was best to give me a wide berth. I didn't look like a good traveling companion.

As we neared Virginia, I had a sudden thought. It was 2013. Twelve years since I'd last seen Myra. Maybe by now she'd figured out a way for a traveler to take a fifth trip. Maybe she could get me back to 2001 to find my baby and then home safely to 1970. I filled with hope then, until I remembered that Hunter had arrived from 2018 and not only had the fifth-trip rule still been in place then, but Myra had somehow gotten herself trapped by it that year and disappeared.

"Shit!" I said, out loud. And the woman in the seat across the aisle turned to glare at me. What did she see? A disheveled twenty-seven-year-old woman with tear-streaked cheeks, well-worn blue jeans, and a grass-stained backpack who now cussed out loud to the air. I turned my face back to the smeared window.

I found a cab at the Alexandria station and gave the woman driver Myra's address. She glanced at me in the rearview mirror.

"Long trip?" she asked pleasantly. I knew then that I looked even worse than I thought.

"You could say that," I said.

"Going home or visiting?"

I didn't understand the question at first. My brain was not in this cab at all. "Visiting," I said. I hoped this wouldn't be a long trip and a long conversation. She seemed to pick up on my mood and fell quiet. We were driving on a busy street, hitting every red light. Rush hour. After ten very slow minutes, I had to know how close we were.

"How much farther is it?" I asked.

"We're almost there," she said. "This is Old Town Alexandria and the address is just a few blocks away."

Thank God. She turned onto a cobblestone street, driving downhill, and we bounced with such force my teeth knocked together. I could see the glint of water—a river?—ahead of us. Then she turned onto a paved street and stopped in front of a row of narrow, ancient-looking town houses.

"This is it," she said, pointing to a beige brick town home squished between two others.

"Thanks," I said. I handed her more of my precious cash, then climbed out of the cab lugging my backpack over my shoulder as I walked to the red door. I pressed the doorbell as the cab drove away. No answer. I pressed it again. Held it down. I could hear it buzzing inside the house.

A man in a suit eyed me as he walked up to the sidewalk to the town house next door.

"Excuse me!" I called to him. "Can you tell me if Myra Poole lives here?"

He nodded as he reached into the mailbox next to his door. "When she's in town, yes," he said.

Oh, no.

"Is she . . . do you know if she's in town?"

"No idea." He pulled a few pieces of mail from the box. Glanced at them, then back at me. "She keeps to herself." He frowned. "You all right?"

"It's just been a long day and I need to see her." I forced myself to smile to fend off more questions.

"Well, maybe she'll be home soon." He slipped a key into his lock and gave me a quick wave as he opened the door. I nearly asked him for some water, but thought better of it. I was afraid of too many questions. Afraid of seeming out of it.

I looked down the street once he'd closed the door to his house. I could see some shops in the distance. I walked in that direction and found a bakery, where I bought a bottle of water and a slightly stale blueberry muffin. I devoured the muffin and gulped down the water as I walked back to Myra's. As I neared the house, I saw a woman approaching the front door. Her hair was white but she was unmistakably Myra. I began to run.

"Myra!" I called.

She'd opened her door but turned to look at me. Daylight was beginning to fade and she squinted. Cocked her head. "I remember you," she said, and I could tell she was hunting for my name.

"Caroline Sears," I said. "Carly. Hunter's my brother-in-law."

"Shh!" She glanced behind her as though someone might have heard me. "Come inside," she said, then whispered, "Don't say things like that outside the house."

"Sorry," I said, walking past her into a long, skinny living room. The sides of the room were windowless, as they would have to be, since the house was tucked between two others. But the far wall was nearly all glass and looked out over the darkening river. "I need your help." I was suddenly filled with hope at seeing her. "Desperately!" I said. "I was supposed to—"

"Slow down." She set her briefcase on a table inside the door, then motioned toward the living room. "Have a seat and I'll be right in. Do you want something to drink?"

"Just water."

I sat impatiently on the edge of the long off-white sofa, my hands knotted together in my lap. She finally came into the room and handed me a glass of water before sitting down in a chair by the window. "The year 2001, wasn't it?" she asked. "You had fetal surgery, followed by a healthy baby, and you returned with the baby to 1970, correct?"

I shut my eyes, gathering all the words I needed to explain what had happened. I told her about returning to 1970 without Joanna. "So Hunter sent me back to 2001 to get my baby, but when I arrived in New York this morning and went to the hospital to see her, I discovered it was 2013."

She stared at me, mouth open, clearly stunned. "Hunter wouldn't make that gross an error," she said. "Off by twelve years? It wouldn't happen. He's working with me in the program now and he's very good. Better than me. He's also married to a woman who is not your sister, so don't go telling the neighbors he's your brother-in-law, for Christ's sake."

"But I'm here in 2013, so yes, he made a mistake," I insisted. She didn't seem to understand my desperation. I sat forward on the sofa, my hands in fists on my knees. "And now I'm stuck and I need to get back to my daughter. I have to—"

"Wait a minute," she said, getting to her feet, tapping her finger against her chin. She was clearly deep in thought and she paced the room. "Holy shit. It was this morning you landed in New York?"

"Yes."

"You were aiming for 2001?"

"Yes, but—"

She held up a hand to cut me off. "Do you know what happened in New York on September 11, 2001?" she asked.

"I . . . people kept saying something about '9/11' and those towers. The World Trade Center towers, I guess? A plane flew into them or something like that?"

"*Yes*," she said excitedly. "Oh, this is beyond fascinating!" She nearly ran back to the table by the front door for her briefcase. Returning to her chair, she pulled a laptop computer from the briefcase, flipped it open, and began tapping the keys. "It was an attack by this Islamic terrorist group called Al Qaeda," she said. "Both towers completely collapsed to the ground. Thousands of people were killed."

I was stunned into silence. It sounded impossible.

"The day the planes hit, the smoke and debris in the air was unbelievable." She glanced up at me over the laptop. "Imagine those huge towers being suddenly vaporized, turned into a toxic plume of concrete dust." She stood up and carried the laptop to the sofa. Sitting down next to me, she set the computer on my lap. On the screen, I saw a picture of people running from thick black smoke that seemed to be chasing them, the crumbling towers in the background. It looked like something from an end-of-the-world movie. I pressed my hands over my mouth.

"My God," I whispered. "Did they . . . we . . . ever catch the people who did this?"

Myra brushed aside the question with a sweep of her hand. "Very long story," she said, moving the computer from my lap to hers. "Back to your time travel. We've learned that it doesn't take much to throw off our calculations when it comes to atmospheric disturbance," she said. "Even a good rainstorm can do it. So I think we have our answer. I'm sure Hunter had the correct calculations, but he couldn't—or didn't—account for what was happening in the air around New York that morning. And it threw your travel off and you landed here." She shut the lid of her computer, looking pleased with herself.

"But what do I do now?" I asked. "I have to get back to 2001 and my baby!"

"You can't do that," she said. "First of all, the last place on earth you want to be is Manhattan in September of 2001, trust me, and—"

"Yes, I *do* want to be there," I insisted. "No matter what's happening, my daughter is there. I need to be with her."

"Also, if you go you'll be stuck in 2001," she said as though I hadn't spoken. "That would be your fourth trip, right?"

"Yes, but . . ." I imagined what it would be like to be stuck in 2001 with no hope of ever seeing Patti or Hunter or John Paul or my friends, ever again. Unbearable. But so was the thought of losing my daughter. "I can't just leave my baby there." My voice broke. "They thought I abandoned her and they turned her over to Child Protective Services."

"Think," Myra said, a bit impatiently. "Your baby is no longer a baby. Your baby is now twelve years old. Most likely she was adopted by someone who adores her. You have to think about it that way and let it go. We don't tamper with—"

"Let it *go*?" I argued, annoyed she was making the same worthless argument as Celeste. "If you gave birth to Hunter and a couple of months later you couldn't find him, would you just let it go?"

She stared at me and I thought I'd gotten through to her. "I would accept the fact that I could do nothing about it," she said in that matter-of-fact tone I'd come to associate with her. "The ship had sailed and I would hope he was being well cared for and happy."

"But what if—"

"No arguments," Myra interrupted me, opening her computer again. "I'll find a portal to take you back to 1970 where you belong, and that's that," she said. "You can stay here until I come up with something. If you see any of my neighbors, tell them you're a friend. No more information than that. All right?"

No, it wasn't all right. I looked down at my hands, fighting tears. I needed my baby. My body ached with the need for her.

"Right now, you're very emotional and not thinking clearly," Myra said, as she tapped her keyboard. "I need you to look at this satellite image." She moved the screen so I could see it once again. "The Outer Banks, right, if I'm remembering correctly? Where do you want to land?"

I stared at the astonishing map. I was looking at Nags Head from outer space and the sight was breathtaking. I thought of trying to make out our cottage, but decided against it. I didn't want to know if a storm had taken it in the last forty years. That was not only possible, but likely.

"Come on, now," Myra prompted. "Show me where."

I saw the white blanket of sand that had to be Jockey's Ridge. For a long moment, I stared numbly at it before I touched the screen with my hand.

"What is that?" she asked. "Sand?"

"Dunes."

"Excellent." She shifted the computer back to her own lap. "I'll get something worked out for you, hopefully very soon. We use the roof of a hotel here in Old Town for the stepping-off, so—"

"It needs to be over water."

"What?"

"I have to step off over water. I can't do it over . . . a street or concrete or—"

"What does it matter?" she asked. "It's not like you're going to land on the street."

"It's psychological," I said. "I need it to be over water."

She sighed. Closed the computer. "Fine," she said. "I'll see what I can do." She stood up. "Help yourself to anything in the refrigerator or pantry and let me show you the guest room. I keep it made up because I frequently have visiting physicists passing through, so it's all set. It has its own small bathroom and there are toiletries in the shower."

I stood up. My body felt as though it weighed two thousand pounds as I followed her up the narrow staircase.

"Maybe no one wanted to adopt a baby that had heart problems," I said from behind her. "Maybe she's spent her entire life moving from one crappy foster home to another." I pictured my little girl poor and struggling— struggling in every way possible. No parents. No friends. No money. No love. "What if I could find her?" I said. "Then she could go back with me."

"Oh, no." Myra gave her head a vigorous shake as we reached the top of the stairs. "You need to move past this. We don't tamper with people's lives. Accept that she's most likely fine and healthy and happy. Think positively. And let it go."

"Please, Myra," I begged as we reached the second story.

"Wherever that girl is, you can't mess with her life," she said, guiding me down a hallway. "It's best if you pretend none of this ever happened. Pretend she never existed. She was a glimmer of your imagination. I won't help you do anything other than get back to 1970."

The guest room was sterile. Nothing on the white walls. A few plastic hangers hung in the otherwise empty closet. The double bed was covered by a thin, plain gold spread, the corners crisp. There was one night table. A small TV, the only frivolous trapping in the room, sat on the dresser. A frameless mirror above the dresser revealed how long and hard this day had been. My eyes were rimmed with red, the skin around them swollen and damp, and I was pale, my summer tan completely gone. My limbs felt as though they were moving through mud as I set the backpack on the dresser and pulled out my nightgown and brush. *A glimmer of my imagination.* How dare she refer to Joanna that way?

I brushed my teeth and splashed water on my face, then I drank two glasses of water and climbed into the bed. There was a remote for the TV on the night table, and I turned it on. It was set to CNN and I realized I was in the middle of a program that recounted the events of 9/11, twelve years ago. In horror, I watched a film of the towers coming down, so much more real than that still image on

Myra's computer. The loss of life was impossible to comprehend.

But the World Trade Center had been far from Lincoln Hospital, I thought. I would have been safe there with Joanna. Shaken by what was happening, yes, but we would have been safe. I would have been holding her as I had every day since her birth. I'd touch the silky skin of her cheek. Hold her tiny hand and sing to her. I'd watch for her smile, waiting for it to light up my heart. I wanted my baby back. I *needed* her back.

I turned off the TV, crawled under the covers, and cried myself to sleep.

38

I slept far more deeply than I would have thought possible. When I got up in the morning, Myra was gone but she'd left a note on the kitchen counter next to the stove, promising to bring me a portal that would take me home to 1970.

I ate an orange from the fruit bowl on the kitchen table only because I knew I needed to have something in my stomach besides tea. I had to find a phone. I had to call Child Protective Services in New York to find out what they'd done with Joanna. I wasn't going anywhere until I knew what had happened to my daughter. Carrying my cup of tea from room to room, I hunted for a phone without success. Even Myra's small home office had no phone. It was a remarkably pristine room, the shelves filled with books on astrophysics. The only sign that a human being ever used the room was a framed photograph on Myra's desk: Hunter and a dark-haired woman I guessed to be Rosie, both of them smiling. Looking happy. The picture made me uncomfortable and I couldn't give it more than a glance.

Bright sunlight filled the living room and I looked out

the rear windows to the small brick patio and the river beyond. I spent the rest of the morning sitting on the sofa, staring at that water. Kayakers passed by and birds flitted through the trees at the water's edge, but my mind wasn't truly on the river. It was in grimy foster homes. I imagined tasteless food and terrible nutrition. I imagined the lonely heart of a child who thought her mother had abandoned her way back in 2001. I had to find that child. If I was going home, I thought, she was going with me.

Shortly before noon, Myra returned to the house with two sandwiches and bottles of Coke. We sat at the kitchen table, unwrapping the thick white paper from the sandwiches.

"Turkey and cheese," Myra said.

"Fine," I said, though I knew I could only pick at the sandwich.

"So," she said, reaching into the briefcase next to her chair. She pulled out a small phone and a driver's license bearing the picture she'd taken of me a few months ago. "If you're willing to step off the hotel, I can get you a portal on Saturday."

"No," I said stubbornly. "I can't do that."

"That's what I figured. So, I was able to get you a portal off the Arlington Memorial Bridge. It's going to be tricky because there are always people on that bridge, even at night, but it should be workable. Unfortunately, the soonest date I could make it work is over a week away, on the twentieth. And if you're going to be here that long, I thought you'd better have an ID and a prepaid cell phone, unless you want to stay cooped up in the house."

I stared hungrily at the phone. As soon as I had a moment alone, I would call Protective Services.

"Do you have to go back to work this afternoon?" I asked. I took a bite of the sandwich. The thought of making that phone call, getting some answers, piqued my appetite.

"I can work here," she said, disappointing me. I needed privacy.

Neither of us spoke for a couple of minutes. "Where is Hunter?" I asked, making conversation. "Does he live nearby?"

"You don't need to know about Hunter. I don't want you to look for him."

"He told me I don't see him again in the future."

"Good. So let's not talk about him."

"Can I go for a walk?"

"Of course," she said, deep frown lines between her eyebrows. "You're not my prisoner. Old Town has a lot of charm, so enjoy it. Just be careful what you say to people. Do you need money?"

I shook my head. "Hunter gave me some before I left."

Myra picked up the phone. "My number's already programmed in here," she said. "And your number's here, too." She flipped open the phone to show me her number as well as my own. Then she stood up abruptly, wrapping the uneaten half of her sandwich. "These are huge," she said. "We'll finish them for dinner."

"Good idea." I began wrapping my sandwich as well, glad this lunchtime chat was over. I couldn't wait to get outside with the phone.

*

I supposed Myra was right about Old Town having charm, but it was lost on me as I walked past the small shops, hunting for a quiet place to make my call. I found an area on the riverfront where people sat on benches, eating or talking, and I walked past them until I spotted an empty bench. Sitting down, I pulled the phone from my jeans pocket. I dialed information, and in a few minutes, I was connected to Child Protective Services in Manhattan. The woman who answered the phone sounded both bored and annoyed with her job.

"I hope you can help me," I said, my heart thumping. "Back in 2001, I had a baby at Amelia Wade Lincoln Hospital and the baby had to stay in the nursery for a few months. I was with her every day. When September eleventh happened . . . 9/11 . . . I was injured and unable to get back to my baby. It took a long time for me to recover, and I only recently learned that my baby was turned over to Child Protective Services. So I'm trying to find out what happened to her."

There wasn't so much as a peep from the other end of the line. I stared anxiously toward the river where a small boat, its motor sputtering, sailed by.

"Hello?" I asked. Had I lost her?

"I'm not following you one bit," the woman said. "You left your baby in the hospital on 9/11 and only now remembered?"

"I was injured. I didn't intentionally leave her there. And it was a head injury, so I had amnesia for a long time and I thought it was still 2001. That my baby was still a baby and I—"

"Hold on," the woman said.

I closed my eyes, waiting. I knew I sounded like an idiot. Worse. I sounded insane.

Another woman came on the line and I went through the whole explanation again, trying to the best of my ability to sound like a normal, healthy woman who had simply lost twelve years of her life to a now-resolved injury. Finally, the woman broke in.

"So what is it you want?" she asked.

"I want to know what Protective Services did with my baby," I said.

"We can't tell you that."

"But I'm her mother. I didn't abandon her." How I hated that word! "I couldn't help what happened. I just want to know if she . . . if she's in a foster home, or . . ." I couldn't bring myself to ask if she was still alive. "If I tell you her name, can you at least tell me what happened to her? Just generally?"

"No, ma'am, we don't do that. You want any information on her, you'll have to get a lawyer, but we don't just give out information to someone who calls in, twelve years after the fact, or even twelve *days* after. Sorry."

She hung up. I stared at the phone in my hand, tempted to heave it into the river. Instead, my mind filled once again with images of Joanna in her isolette, waiting, waiting, waiting for her mother to come and take her home.

When I returned to Myra's, I found her in her small office on the second story. She looked up from her desktop computer and I knew she could tell that something had shifted in me.

"What's wrong?" she asked. "What's happened?"

I clutched the new phone in my hand. "I called Protective Services in New York to find out what they did with my baby," I admitted, "and they wouldn't tell me anything. I didn't abandon her! They made me feel like I was lying." I looked at the ceiling, letting out a sigh. "Well, I *was* lying," I said, "but not the way they think."

Myra stared at me, her thin lips in a tight line, her fingers tapping on the arms of her chair. I waited for her to chew me out.

"I'm worried about you being here a whole week, stewing over this," she said finally. "It would be best if you took the Saturday portal from the roof of the hotel. I need to get you out of here."

"No," I said.

"You're just torturing yourself by staying in 2013."

I looked away from her. My eyes lit on that photograph of Hunter and Rosie again.

"You need to find a way to spend your time," Myra said. "Go into D.C. Go to the museums."

"I'm not the least bit interested in the museums!" I said. "Don't you understand, Myra? I've lost my baby!"

She let out a weary sigh. "I get it," she said. "And I also get that there's nothing you can do about it. So go find a book to read. Or here—" She reached into her briefcase and pulled out the laptop computer, handing it to me. "Read the news. Surf the internet." She jotted a long password on a small yellow square of paper. "You just click on Safari."

I took the computer from her and turned on my heel to leave the room. I had no idea what Safari was but I was too upset with her to ask. I'd figure it out myself.

I carried the laptop into the guest room and propped myself up against the headboard. The internet was a different animal than it had been in 2001 and I stumbled around in confusion, clicking on icons, finally finding something familiar: *Google*. I clicked on it. Biting my lip as I stared at the empty search box, I typed in "Joanna Sears."

It was clearly not an uncommon name. Many websites popped up and I scrolled through them all, but every Joanna Sears was an adult. If my Joanna were still in foster care, I doubted she'd have access to a computer at age twelve, and if she'd been adopted, she'd have a different name. And if she'd died?

I shuddered.

Then I typed in "Joanna Elizabeth Sears" and "obituary." All that came up were websites that wanted me to pay for information, which I would have done if I could have figured out how to pay without a credit card.

I stared at the Google screen for a long time. I could type in my name. I could type in Patti's. The thought of what I might find, of seeing our future laid out in front of me, was so mind-altering that a wave of nausea washed over me. I closed the computer, lay down on the bed, and shut my eyes. I had to figure out what to do, but for now, all I could imagine doing was sleep.

When I opened my eyes, Myra stood in the open doorway of the room, arms folded across her chest, and I realized she'd been calling my name. I raised myself to my elbows.

"I've done some thinking," she said, her voice softer than it had been earlier. "I tried to imagine my life without Hunter in it when he was a child. I could have survived without him as long as I knew he was okay. That's the real issue, isn't it?" she asked. "You need to know your daughter is safe?"

I nodded, although that was only half of the issue. I needed her safe with *me*.

"I'm going to pull some strings to find out what happened to her," she said, and I sat up fully now, my eyes wide.

"How will you do that?" I asked.

"I know people," she said cryptically. "People in high places who owe me favors." She shrugged. "I can't promise anything, but I'll try. Then hopefully you can return to 1970 with an easy mind. All right?"

"*Yes.*" My voice was husky. "Thank you."

39

Two days passed. Two days during which I pestered Myra relentlessly to see if she'd learned anything about Joanna.

"I'll tell you if and when I do," she said. "Someone's looking into it for me, but it's taking some time, plus it's the weekend. Be patient."

In five days, I was supposed to use the portal from the bridge to go back to 1970. I couldn't imagine returning to my old life with empty arms. In the meantime, I had new energy knowing Myra was working on tracking down my daughter. I spent my time walking through Old Town Alexandria until I knew every street by heart. In the little shops, I saw crocheted baby clothes that made my heart ache. And I saw trinkets I wished I could buy for a twelve-year-old Joanna. A bracelet. A little statue of a dog. Did she like dogs? Cats? Was she horse-crazy the way I had been at her age? I saw tasteful little earrings and wondered if her ears were pierced. It seemed as though every girl about Joanna's age had pierced ears in 2013.

And every girl I saw who was about Joanna's age became my daughter in my eyes.

When I opened the door to the guest room on Monday

morning, I heard Myra talking on the phone downstairs. I stood very still in the hallway, leaning closer to the head of the stairs, trying to listen.

"That's right," Myra said. "I don't know what her middle name was, but I'm sure that's it. Thanks, Terri. I owe you."

I raced to the stairs and nearly slid down them to the kitchen. Myra looked up at me from her seat at the table. She tore a sheet of paper from the small notepad on the table and crumpled it in her hands as she smiled one of her rare smiles at me.

"I have some news for you," she said.

I sat down across from her. "Joanna?" I asked.

She nodded. "She *did* go into foster care for a time, but then she was adopted by a family in New Jersey when she was ten months old."

My tears were instantaneous. I pressed my fists to my mouth. I hadn't anticipated the extraordinary sense of loss that came over me. Joanna wasn't mine. She'd only been mine for two months. Those precious two months were all I would ever have of her.

Myra watched me with concern.

"Is there any more?" I asked, blotting my eyes with my fingertips. "Do you know if she has siblings? Or what her parents are like? Or if she's . . . healthy?"

Myra got to her feet. "That's all we get," she said. I watched as she tossed the crumpled paper into the trash can beneath the sink. "And it's a miracle we were able to get that much information, so you'll have to be satisfied with knowing she was wanted by someone and is, in all likelihood, being raised in a good family. That's all you really needed to know, right?"

I nodded, although she was wrong. That wasn't all I needed to know. And when Myra left for her office an hour later, I slid the trash can from beneath the sink and pulled out the crumpled piece of paper. I spread it flat on the counter and saw what Myra had scribbled: *adptd 10 mths. Van Dyke. Summit, NJ.*

Van Dyke. Was that the name of the people who adopted her? Were they good people? Was she well? Was she happy? Did she know her biological mother would miss her every moment of every day for the rest of her life?

I studied the piece of paper again. There was only one way to learn the answers to those questions. How far was it to Summit, New Jersey?

40

Myra had taken her laptop to the office with her, so I spent the afternoon on the huge computer on her desktop, happy to discover I didn't need a password. Would she know I'd been on it? At first, that worried me and I tried to think of ways to mask what I was doing, but after a few minutes I gave up. I didn't care. What I was doing was too important.

Summit, New Jersey. It sounded like it should be a small town on a mountaintop, but I didn't get that feeling from the photographs that popped up when I Googled it. It had a pretty downtown and lots of trees. Were the website pictures carefully selected to make the town look classy and clean when in reality it had rough schools and a dangerous underbelly? What conditions had Joanna been living in all these years?

I typed "Joanna Van Dyke" into Google's search box and was greeted by a few adult Joannas, as I had been when I typed "Joanna Sears" a couple of days earlier. Clearly none of these Joannas was my daughter. What was the likelihood her name was still "Joanna"?

Then I hunted for addresses. There was only one Van Dyke in Summit. *Brandon and Michelle Van Dyke*. Were they Joanna's adoptive parents? I stared at their names, my chest tightening with envy and anger. *She's* mine, *damn it!* Tearing a sheet of paper from Myra's small yellow notepad, I jotted down the address: 477 Rosewood Court, Summit, New Jersey.

I checked the train schedule, clicking through screen after screen until I found the information I needed. I'd have to take the 9:05 train tomorrow morning from Alexandria back to Penn Station in New York, but from there it was less than an hour to Summit. I'd arrive a few minutes to three tomorrow afternoon. Staring at the screen, I twisted my hands together with nerves and excitement. Could I really do this? And why *would* I do it? What did I hope to gain?

"I need to know she's okay," I said softly to myself, my gaze still on the computer screen, the train schedule blurring in my vision. "That's all." But even as the words left my mouth, I wasn't sure I believed them. All I knew was that I couldn't stay here in Alexandria when my daughter was only a few hundred miles away.

I searched for hotels in Summit and found only one anywhere near the train station. It looked beautiful but was shockingly pricey to my 1970 mind. Between the hundred-and-twenty-two-dollar train ticket and the hotel room, I'd be wiped out in days. I couldn't ask Myra for money now when she expected me to return to 1970 at the end of the week. Money didn't matter, anyway. I would sleep on the street if I had to.

I looked up the Van Dyke address on the computer map and hit that "satellite" button. The neighborhood was a blanket of trees, the houses barely visible among them. But a red dot appeared above one house and I could see a roof, quite large and multileveled, and what was probably a grassy green yard behind it, surrounded by those thick trees. Was this Joanna's house? Joanna's yard? I needed to know.

I studied the route from the Summit train station to the Van Dykes' Rosewood Court address and saw that it was less than a mile. Less than a mile! I felt Joanna growing closer. I struggled unsuccessfully to figure out how to print the map from the computer, so I found a sheet of paper and drew a map from the train station to the address. I folded it up. Slipped it in my jeans pocket.

How I would get through the evening with Myra, I had no idea. In the morning, I would leave her a note. I'd thank her for all she'd done for me but tell her I wasn't ready to return to 1970. I hoped she wouldn't try to find me. I replaced the crumpled piece of paper in the kitchen trash can. She'd have no reason to think I'd learned where Joanna lived. She'd be angry, but at that moment, I didn't care. I was going to find my daughter.

41

I left the house at seven the next morning, grateful that Myra was not yet up. The train station was a little over a mile away and I had plenty of time to catch that 9:05 train. I stopped at the bakery for two muffins and tea, devouring all of it as I walked, my backpack slung over my shoulder. My appetite was suddenly insatiable. I was nervous, yes, but energized as well.

The train station was crowded with men and women dressed for work. I bought my ticket, then found a free seat on a bench where I took stock of my plan. I had my phone. I still had nearly four hundred dollars. I had my hand-drawn map. First thing I'd do when I arrived in Summit, I told myself, would be to go to that expensive hotel and see if I could talk the price down for tonight. Who was I trying to kid? First thing I'd do would be to walk directly to 477 Rosewood Court.

The hours on the train to New York slipped by, the Van Dyke address a mantra in my brain. I was coming up with "my story" as we passed through town after town—the story I would tell anyone I met who asked me what someone like me was doing in New Jersey. My husband died, I would say, and I wanted to get away from the reminders and start over. I'd heard about a wonderful rehab center in New Jersey and wanted to work there. That was partially the truth. I had heard about the Kessler Institute and knew it was one of the best in the nation—at least it had been back in 1970. Did it still exist? It had been someplace in New Jersey, though I had no idea if that someplace was anywhere near Summit. I should have thought of my story earlier and Googled Kessler. Of course I could never get a job there. I had no current credentials to show. No current license. But I hoped the story would be good enough to get me by for now.

I had a sense of déjà vu in Penn Station, as if I were back in 2001 and could grab a taxi to Lincoln Hospital where I would find my sweet baby waiting for me in the nursery. My eyes stung by the time I climbed aboard the commuter train to Summit. I felt dispirited, as though I was leaving my baby behind in New York again. *That's over,* I told myself. *She's not there. She's not a baby any longer.* I was going to have to accept it.

While waiting for the train, I ate a pastrami sandwich that reminded me of Ira and his deli, and I wondered how he was doing. Was he even alive? The thought jarred me. He'd been pretty old in 2001. When I got back to 1970, I would never again take time for granted. I would never again try to rush it.

I bought a couple of apples, bottled water, a candy bar, and some packages of cheese crackers, shoving them all in my backpack. I didn't know when I'd next have a chance to buy food. Then I joined the line of people, most of them clearly commuters, waiting for the train.

As the train pulled into Summit, I knew at once the online pictures of the town were accurate. It bustled with shops and restaurants and well-dressed people. I was going to look sloppy and out of place here, carting my grimy mustard-colored backpack around like a homeless person, which, I guessed, I was.

Once off the train, I stood on the platform to study my hand-drawn map, trying to get my bearings. I figured out the direction I needed to go, aiming for Rosewood Court, and began walking. Summit was not neatly laid out and I turned one corner after another after another, following the pencil lines of my map. All around me were beautiful, impeccably maintained older houses, surrounded by manicured lawns and voluminous trees, and the closer I got to Rosewood Court, the bigger the houses, the more sprawling the yards. It comforted me, thinking of Joanna growing up in the safety of a neighborhood like this, growing up with this beauty around her.

Finally, I reached Rosewood Court. I studied the house numbers. Number 477 would be across the street, probably a block away, and I continued walking. I was drawn to the gray colonial with the red front door even before I saw the house number. The house was huge. Stately-looking, it was set back from the street by a long expanse of vivid green lawn. A driveway ran down the right side of the building and I guessed the garage must be in the back of the house. I could see more of the emerald lawn back there, surrounded by a virtual forest of trees. Except for the

Unpainted Aristocracy, I knew little about architecture, but I knew beauty when I saw it, and this house and its setting quite literally took my breath away. I stood there both gawking and gasping. I bit my lip, wishing a twelve-year-old girl would run out that front door and into my arms.

And now what? This wasn't the sort of neighborhood where a young woman could stand idly in front of a house unnoticed. Nor could I walk back and forth, back and forth, waiting for ... waiting for what? I wished I had a car. I could park on the side street with a view to the house and watch and wait. I looked at my chronometer. Nearly four thirty. I needed to find that hotel that would cost me an arm and a leg, get a room for the night, and then figure out my next step.

I checked my map again and saw I had another mile or so to walk to the hotel. I set out in that direction, suddenly very tired. I'd found her—at least I hoped I had—and yet I hadn't found her at all. And I needed to.

I was only a few blocks from the hotel when I spotted an old Victorian house across the street from where I was walking. A sign on the front lawn read SLEEPING DOG INN. Was this one of those bed-and-breakfast places? I crossed the street and walked up the sidewalk. Close up, I could see that the house needed work, but its old bones were stunning. Climbing the slightly lopsided steps to a narrow porch, I saw a handwritten COME IN sign next to the doorbell. I pulled open one of the double doors, which stuck slightly and needed a bit of forcing. I stepped into a dimly lit foyer. A long, highly polished wooden counter stood a few steps in front of me, its surface littered with papers. To my right was a living room or parlor, where a young man sat on a sofa working on a laptop computer, a German shepherd asleep at his feet. Neither the man nor the dog looked up when I walked in.

I tapped the bell on the counter and was greeted by yapping from behind a curtained glass door at the rear of the foyer. In a moment, a woman walked through the door, a young golden retriever on a leash at her side. The golden retriever did what young golden retrievers do, tugging excitedly at the leash, yapping and yipping, paws up on the counter in an attempt to greet me. The woman, with her gray-streaked dark hair and amused-looking eyes, held up a finger to keep me from speaking.

"Sit, Poppy," she told the dog. "Hush."

It took a few seconds for Poppy to give in, but she finally sat down and I lost eye contact with her behind the counter.

"She's a good girl," I said with a smile.

The woman rolled her eyes. "I hope someday I'll be able to say that about her," she said. "She's only six months old and it takes goldens forever and a day to grow up. I don't know what my niece was thinking."

"She's your niece's?" I asked politely.

The woman laughed. "I wish! No, my niece gave her to me. My husband died a year ago, not long after our last dog died, and my niece thought I needed a companion." She looked down at the dog I could no longer see, then she smiled. "Maybe I do," she said. "But the work! I'd forgotten the work."

I returned her smile. "I had a golden when I was a child," I said. "I remember." *And I'm a widow, too,* I thought, but I said nothing about that.

"So how can I help you?" the woman asked, but before I could answer, she held up a hand. "If you're looking for a room, I'm sorry but all five rooms are full," she said. "I need to get my NO VACANCY sign out there."

"Oh," I said, my hopes dashed. "I *was* hoping to find a room. I checked online and only saw that one hotel, the Grand Summit, so I guess I'll head over there. I didn't see your inn on the computer."

"Well, if you look up 'pet-friendly inns,' you'll find us," she said. "We don't advertise much. We're not that big and most of our guests are repeats, since they know they can bring their pets here." She gave me a curious look. "What brings you to Summit?" she asked. "You're from one of the Carolinas, right? I know that accent."

"You have a good ear," I said, but I was unprepared for the question and tried to remember the story I'd come up with on the train. "I needed a change of scenery," I said. "I have a physical therapy degree and thought I'd get licensed up here and hopefully get a job."

Her curious look only intensified, and I couldn't blame her. I needed a change of scenery? It sounded suspicious even to my own ears. "Do you have friends up here?" she asked.

"No." I smiled as though acknowledging the craziness of my plan. "But there's a really good rehabilitation center— the Kessler Institute—and I'd love to land a job there eventually." I watched her face for a reaction, hoping she wouldn't tell me Kessler had shut down twenty years ago.

"Oh, yes, that's a great place," she said, and I let out my breath in relief. "I know a couple of people who had rehab at the West Orange campus after their hip replacements."

West Orange. Wherever that was. I'd have to remember that name.

"Is it just you?" She peered behind me as though I might be hiding someone.

"Yes, just me."

The woman smoothed a strand of her salt-and-pepper hair back from her cheek and gave Poppy a preemptive "hush."

"I tell you what," she said. "The only room I have left I don't usually rent out because it only works for a single traveler and doesn't have much room for a dog crate. It's a twin bed up three flights in an attic room, not much more than a closet, and the bathroom is a bit compact"—she winked at that—"and just has a shower. No AC up there, either, so the room is pretty unusable in the summer, but it should be fine now. I can let you have it for sixty."

"I'll take it," I said, trying not to sound as desperately excited as I felt. "Can I have it for two nights?" That would give me all day tomorrow to ... to what? Try to get a glimpse of my daughter, I guessed. I wished I had some idea of what I was really doing here. What I really wanted. Well, I knew what I wanted. My baby girl back. And that I could never have.

"Oh, sure," the woman said. "I'm Winnie, by the way."

"Carly," I said.

"Do you want to see the room first?"

I shook my head with a smile. "I'm sure it'll be fine." I slipped off my backpack and reached inside it for my wallet.

"You can park in the lot behind the—"

"I don't have a car," I said.

"Oh, that's fine. I need your driver's license, though. For the registration."

I handed over my driver's license as she moved some of the papers from the countertop to uncover a registration book. She wrote down my name and my fake North Carolina address from my license. "What type of credit card?" she asked.

"Cash," I said, taking one hundred and twenty dollars from my wallet. "Is there tax?"

She told me the amount, which I paid from my shrinking funds. My phone rang as I handed her the money. *Myra*. I turned it off.

"On the other side of the living room is a dining room," Winnie said, pointing to my right. "I serve breakfast there from six thirty to eight thirty." She gave a tired shake of her head. "So I'm up at the crack of dawn to take care of this one"—she nodded toward the dog, who was still behind the counter and who I thought was behaving remarkably well for a six-month-old puppy—"then I make a full breakfast, then clean the place." She sighed, but she still wore a good-humored smile. "My husband and I used to split the work and now I do it all. And my niece doesn't understand why I didn't want another dog." She chuckled. "'You're lonely, Aunt Winnie,' she said. 'You need a companion.'"

"When Poppy gets a little older, you'll be happy to have her," I said, thinking that all I wanted at that moment was to find my little closet of a room, sink onto a bed, and imagine what it would be like to find Joanna.

"I know you're right," Winnie said as she handed me a key on a key chain shaped like a Shetland sheepdog. "Hope you don't mind a few stairs." She pointed to the narrow staircase at the side of the foyer. "There should be towels and toiletries and whatnot up there. And here's my number if anything's missing." She handed me a business card. "You can call me instead of climbing down fifty flights of stairs."

I was out of breath by the time I reached the stuffy little attic room. The scent was musty but I didn't really care. The room was at the front of the house where the ceiling was sharply pitched and the one window, which was in need of cleaning, overlooked the street. The window was screened and, with some effort, I managed to open it. A small fan sat on the dresser next to the window. I turned it on and felt the air quickly cool, the musty smell dissipating. I pulled down the quilt and top sheet on the narrow bed and gave the linens a cursory check for bugs. All clear. Except for the window, the room appeared quite clean, actually. There was not even any dust on the dresser. I pictured Winnie keeping this room clean on top of everything else she had to do. Everything else she used to share with her husband.

I sat down on the bed and looked at the business card she'd handed me. *Winnie and Bill Corman,* it read, followed by the address of the Sleeping Dog Inn and a phone number. My heart twisted, seeing her husband's name alongside her own. I wondered if she'd had no time to get new cards made or if she couldn't bear to let go of "Winnie and Bill." I knew how that felt. We'd been Carly and Joe for so long. It had been unbelievably painful to suddenly change from "we" to "I."

I set the card on the dresser, exhausted from the long day. I ate a package of my cheese crackers and drank my bottle of water. Then, although it was still very early, I climbed into bed. Despite my tiredness, though, I couldn't sleep as I tried to figure out my next move. How many nights could I afford this little room, plus food? Along with saving enough money for an eventual train ticket back to Myra so I could return to 1970? Maybe enough for *two* train tickets back to Myra.

What the hell are you thinking, Carly? What are you dreaming about? Are you losing your mind?

I had the feeling I'd lost it long ago. Maybe the day they came to tell me Joe was dead. Or the day they told me my baby was doomed. Or a few days ago—had it only been a few days?—when I discovered I'd landed in 2013 instead of 2001. I'd had plenty of opportunities to lose my mind, but to be honest, I didn't care if I was crazy or not. All I wanted right now was to see my daughter.

The next morning, Winnie served fruit salad and a frittata in the dining room, which was a pet-free zone. I sat at the table with three other guests: an older couple, Betsy and Tom, who were in town visiting their grandchildren, and a businessman who sat at one end of the table reading the *Wall Street Journal* instead of conversing. My fictional life story crystallized in my mind as I described the loss of my husband in a car accident and my plan to get my New Jersey physical therapist license and a good job.

Winnie floated around us, pouring juice and coffee, taking away dirty plates and chatting easily with her guests.

"You didn't tell me you were widowed," she said as she refreshed my juice, and I knew she felt an instant connection to me.

"Sometimes it's hard to talk about," I said.

She nodded with understanding. "Don't I know it," she said, giving my shoulder a gentle squeeze.

I kept glancing at my chronometer as I ate. I wanted to get to Joanna's neighborhood before she left for school. I pictured her leaving her house to . . . to what? Catch the school bus? Walk a few blocks to a neighborhood school?

Meet friends for a ride in a car pool? I didn't know. All I knew was that I needed to lay my eyes on my daughter.

"How long are you staying in Summit?" Betsy asked me.

I thought of the portal Myra had given me to return to 1970. It was only two days away and I doubted I'd be ready to leave by then. Not nearly ready. There would be other portals. Myra would be angry when I returned, asking for them, but I was certain she would give them to me. She would want me gone. I was safe . . . as long as Myra didn't pick up and move again. If that happened, I didn't know what I would do.

"I'm not sure." I tried to think of how to answer in light of my fabricated story. "I need to research the licensing exam and figure out the best place to live while I'm doing that, and find a job to tide me over," I said.

"Oh, I'm sure you'll be able to find something," Betsy said. "There are all those stores and restaurants in town."

"You're already licensed in North Carolina?" Tom asked.

"Yes," I said. *In 1970.*

"Isn't there reciprocity between the states?" he asked.

I had no idea, but I shook my head. My story needed to make sense. "Afraid not," I said, not having a clue if there was reciprocity. "New Jersey has its own exam."

"I had physical therapy after I hurt my knee," Winnie said as she poured the *Wall Street Journal* guy another cup of coffee. "That's a hard job." The man didn't even raise his eyes from the paper to acknowledge her.

"I enjoyed it," I said. God, it felt like a lifetime since I'd last worked! The day I found out that Joe had died had been my last day. I thought I'd take a couple of weeks off to try to pull myself together. Then I learned I was pregnant and my emotions went into a tailspin. I didn't like to remember those weeks and months of emotional numbness when I wanted my husband home with me, whole and healthy. The last thing I'd been thinking about then had been my job.

"I bet that's your husband's watch you wear." Winnie nodded toward my wrist and the chronometer.

I nodded, wishing it *had* been Joe's watch. I had nothing of his with me here. "Yes," I said. "It is."

She set the pitcher of orange juice down on the table and lifted a chain from around her neck until a gold wedding band appeared from beneath her blouse. "This was my husband Bill's," she said. "Nice to keep that connection to our men, isn't it?" She smiled at me and I returned the smile. I felt a surprising, deep kinship with her.

"When we lost our last dog," Tom said, "Betsy carried his dog tag around in her pocket for months."

"I sure did," Betsy agreed.

If either of them saw the disparity between their lost dog and our lost husbands, they didn't acknowledge it. I caught Winnie's eye and she winked at me.

It was seven thirty before I could easily extricate myself from the dining room and leave the house, and ten to eight by the time I reached Joanna's street. I walked casually up her block, my gaze on her front door. Was anyone watching me? Who walked this slowly so early in the morning? Anyone taking a walk at eight in the morning would be doing so for exercise, not sauntering along the way I was. The house looked still, and there was an emptiness about it. It might even be vacant. They might have moved away. I walked a block past the house, glancing over my shoulder every few seconds. Then I turned around and walked past the house again. I was too late, I thought. She'd already left. Or maybe she was staying home, sick today. Or maybe she didn't live here at all. For all I knew, I thought with a shudder, Joanna could be dead.

I found the library and spent an hour huddled over a computer. After one of the librarians helped me figure out how to get online, I once again Googled "Joanna Van Dyke," this time adding "Summit, NJ." A single entry popped up on my screen: the July 2013 church bulletin from a Catholic church in Summit. My anxiety mounting, I scrolled through the bulletin, reading about the Fourth of July picnic and the chorus rehearsal and the mass schedule as I hunted for her name. And there it was, in the list of birthdays: Joanna Van Dyke. July 12.

For a moment, I simply stared as though I couldn't believe what I was seeing. Then my throat tightened and I felt tears on my cheeks before I even realized I was crying. Pressing my hands together hard beneath the table, I looked at her name as it blurred before my eyes.

Joanna. My baby. She was alive.

Swallowing against the ache in my throat, I quickly got to my feet and raced through the shelves of books until I reached the restroom, glad to find I had it to myself. Inside one of the stalls, I sat down fully clothed on the toilet, head buried in my hands as I sobbed. My whole *body* ached with longing as I felt the loss of my baby girl all over again.

But she's *alive,* I told myself. She's *here.*

And she almost certainly lived in that big beautiful house on Rosewood Court, no more than a few miles from where I sat.

The librarian told me that schools let out at three o'clock. Joanna was Catholic, though. She might attend a Catholic school and get out at a different time, but I would plan my afternoon around that three o'clock dismissal time. I left the library with a sense of excitement and purpose. I bought a yogurt for lunch, but I had no appetite and ended up throwing half of it away. Then I spent the afternoon walking methodically from store to store asking if they were hiring. If I worked during school hours, I'd be free in the afternoon and evening to . . . to what? I didn't know. I didn't have a plan. All I knew was that I wanted to be near her, and if I was going to stay in Summit for now, I would need money.

No one was hiring, though, or at least, they weren't hiring me. I fended off question after question about my accent. My past experience, or lack thereof. "I was a PT in 1970" was not an answer I could give to that question. One of the restaurants asked if I could work evenings, but I turned that down. Another needed help in the morning, but my lack of waitressing experience put them off, understandably so.

I was tired but excited as I walked back to Joanna's neighborhood, reaching Rosewood Court a few minutes past three. This time there was an empty blue van in the driveway. I walked past the house, trying to act nonchalant as I looked toward the front door from the corner of my eye. I peered down the driveway and as deep into the lush green backyard as I could see. I kept walking. After a block, I turned around and started walking toward the house again.

I was a few houses away when I saw a girl in the driveway. She walked past the blue van toward the sidewalk, an energetic brown dog tugging on a leash in front of her. *Oh my God, is that her?* My heart sped up until I could feel it beating in my throat. Biting my lip, I forced myself to hang back. I pretended to study the leaves of a shrub, but my eyes were on the girl as she reached the sidewalk. She had the same pale blond hair I'd had at that age. Long, well past her shoulders. She walked with a bounce. A happy bounce. She had the look of a healthy child, and I felt overwhelmed with both gratitude and longing.

"Come this way," I whispered to myself. "Turn this way."

But she didn't. Instead, she turned in the opposite direction, away from me. I didn't know what to do. Follow her? Try to bump into her?

I had a better idea, though. It would mean waiting until tomorrow afternoon. It would require patience. But the wistful joy I felt at seeing her, even from this distance, was enough for now.

43

When I returned to the inn, I was happy to find Winnie behind the counter in the foyer. I had a proposal to make her. Winnie smiled at me, but it looked as though it took some effort. She seemed exhausted, actually, dusky circles around her eyes. I could hear Poppy barking from behind the glass door at the rear of the foyer.

"Winnie," I said, "could I take Poppy for a walk sometime tomorrow? I'd love the exercise."

Winnie's eyes widened in surprise. "Heck, yes!" she said. "This poor dog." She took a few steps to the rear of the foyer and opened the door. Poppy came bounding across the room toward me and I braced myself. "No jump!" Winnie commanded. The dog stopped short of leaping on top of me, but her entire body wriggled back and forth with the effort.

Laughing, I squatted down on the floor to cuddle her, letting her lick my face. She was a wired bundle of energy, knocking me over and stepping on top of my legs in her effort to get as close to me as possible.

"I love her to pieces," Winnie said, "but I'm seriously

thinking of sending her back to my niece. I just don't have the time."

I looked up at her, my hands deep in Poppy's golden fur. "I was also wondering if you'd consider a kind of bartering arrangement with me," I said. "I can help you clean and cook . . . and give Poppy walks . . . in exchange for the attic room. Would that be possible? I tried to find a job today with no success."

Winnie leaned her elbows on the counter and laughed. "You and I are definitely on the same wavelength today," she said. "I've been thinking about exactly that ever since breakfast this morning, when you talked about looking for work. I've thought about hiring help. Bill always handled the reception counter and record keeping and maintenance and I handled making breakfast, grocery shopping, and cleaning. I just can't do it all myself. But I would pay you," she added quickly. "That's only fair. I've talked to some friends who run B and Bs and I think for this size place, four hundred a week plus your room and breakfast is fair."

Four hundred a week! It sounded like a dream. "What would I be doing?" I asked as I got to my feet, dusting off the back of my jeans. Poppy looked up at me, waiting for another pat.

"Housekeeping in the morning," Winnie said. "Cleaning the rooms and bathrooms, changing the sheets of the guests who are moving out. I'll take care of the kitchen and making breakfast. I still enjoy making my semifamous Sleeping Dog Inn breakfasts." She smiled. "In the afternoon, you'd shop for the groceries and paper goods for the following day. Maybe walk Poppy, if you're willing. Any time after that would be your own. I can't offer you health insurance, but soon you'll be able to apply for Obamacare."

I had no idea what "Obamacare" was, but knew better than to ask. I didn't care, anyway. This was an amazing break. I didn't want to take advantage of Winnie, though.

"I'd really like to do this," I said, "but I don't know how long I'll be in the area. I can't guarantee that—"

"That's all right," Winnie said. "That's why I suggested a weekly salary rather than monthly. I know you're most likely here temporarily, but you could start right away and I like you, so that's what's important. We have some struggles in common, don't we." She gave me an understanding look and I knew she was thinking of her Bill and my Joe.

I nodded, although she really had no idea the extent of my struggles. "Yes," I said.

"What do you say, then?"

"Is there a grocery store in walking distance?" I asked. "I don't have a car, remember."

"Oh, you can use mine. No problem."

My heart was thumping. With a car, I could more easily watch Joanna's house. *My God,* I thought. *I've turned into a stalker.*

I smiled at her. "I accept," I said, and Poppy began leaping around me at the change of tone in my voice. "Thank you."

Winnie gave me some papers to fill out to make my employment official, and as I signed my name to the documents, I knew for certain that I wouldn't be taking that portal back to 1970. My stomach flipped at the realization that I now had no certain way to go home. I couldn't have said if I felt more terror or joy.

44

Winnie guided me through my work the next morning. I changed two sets of linens, preparing the rooms for new guests who would arrive that afternoon. On each pillow, I left little dog treats wrapped in white plastic imprinted with the Sleeping Dog Inn logo on them. I made the other beds—the slept-in beds for the guests who were not yet checking out. In one of the rooms, an elderly boxer watched me from his crate. I scrubbed toilets and sinks and tubs and I vacuumed the threadbare carpeting in the bedrooms and the beautiful oriental rugs in the living room, dining room, and foyer. I'd never been much of a housekeeper and it was hardly rocket science, but the work—the perfection it required—didn't come naturally. It was a little nasty, too, cleaning up after people. I didn't mind, though. I couldn't believe my good fortune that I now had a job and a place to live so close to my daughter.

At three o'clock, I buckled Poppy into her collar and we set out for our walk. I didn't think Poppy had ever heard the word "heel," and I kept tripping over her, repeatedly saying "Don't pull!," the command falling on deaf ears. I would have to do some work with this dog to be able to walk her every day. She'd been cooped up too much for such a young pup. Her boundless energy had no place to go. But she was also beautiful and sweet and I could tell she wanted to please me. She'd try to heel, succeeding for ten or so yards, before reverting to her wild furry self.

When we reached Joanna's neighborhood, the car was once again in the driveway, but there was no sign of life. I circled the block twice before I saw her walking down the driveway, the brown dog on a leash. Quickly, I crossed the street so that we'd be walking toward each other. My heart pounded as she drew closer and the dogs began straining to get to each other. I could see now that her dog was a chocolate Lab, not much older than Poppy and no better behaved. Joanna had to use two hands to stem him in.

"Heel, Jobs!" she shouted ineffectually. "Heel!"

By the time our dogs were nose to nose, then nose to butt, tails frantically wagging, Joanna and I were laughing, although my laughter was a bit more like crying. I trembled all over and a wave of nausea passed through me. I was breathing hard, as if I'd run a mile, and my heart pounded against my ribs. I'd longed for this moment and now that it was here, I worried I would faint on the sidewalk and frighten her, my precious child. How I wanted to reach out to touch her, to pull her to me! Instead I stood frozen in place trying to tamp down the nausea.

Joanna knelt down to untangle the leashes. I couldn't seem to move or speak. Helplessly, I watched her. She wore tan shorts, a blue T-shirt, and sandals, seemingly oblivious to the September chill in the air. Her ears were indeed pierced, tiny blue stones in each lobe. A week and a half ago, I'd held baby Joanna in my arms. She'd smiled at me, her blue-gray eyes fixed on my face. She'd been so helpless then. Now look at her. She was a stunning whippet of a girl.

She finally untangled the dogs. "You're good at that," I managed to say.

"I can't believe he wants to play with your dog," she said. "He's usually afraid of other dogs and hides behind my legs. He's scared of everything. He even failed his good citizenship test at puppy class because he was so afraid of the other dogs. Yours is the first dog he likes, for some reason. Weird."

"He's beautiful," I said, reaching down with a tremulous hand to pet the dog's head. *You're the beautiful one*, I was thinking. *Oh, Joanna, I love you so much!*

"Thanks," she said. "Yours is, too. What's his name?"

"It's a girl." My voice sounded strained to my ears. Did she notice? "Her name is Poppy."

"That's cute," Joanna said.

"And yours is named Jobs?" I managed to ask.

"Right," Joanna said. "After Steve Jobs." She looked at me expectantly as if waiting for my reaction to the name.

I had no idea who Steve Jobs was and I didn't dare ask since it was clear that I should know. Some singer or actor? A heartthrob of twelve-year-old girls? I felt suddenly sad. She was my child and I didn't know her. I had no idea who or what she liked. What activities did she love? What did she like to read or watch on TV? Did she have a lot of friends? What did she long for? I had no way of knowing. All of that had been stolen from me.

"You're the first person who hasn't looked at me like I'm crazy for naming him after Steve Jobs," Joanna said, oblivious to the turmoil going on inside me.

"Well, I figure you must really admire him," I said.

"Oh, yeah, I do," she said. "I love everything Apple. I have a MacBook Air and an iPad and an iPhone and an iPod."

I still felt lost, but I couldn't help grinning. I loved her utter lack of guile. Her lack of shyness. And I thought I was catching on. I remembered the apple on the lid of the iBook Myra had given me in 2001.

"I used to have an Apple computer," I said.

"*Used* to have?" Joanna asked, eyes wide in feigned shock.

"I'm between computers right now." I couldn't take my eyes off her. She looked so much like I had at twelve. Skinny. Long legs. Small, almost nonexistent breasts. That long fair hair. Dark eyes, darker than the sleek brown fur on her Lab.

"Well, you've totally got to get another Apple," she said as though I'd be a fool to consider anything else.

My daughter is a precocious little thing, I thought, pleased. Someone had given her self-confidence. I would have done the same.

"I'll see what I can do," I said. "My name is Caroline, by the way." I thought of reaching out to shake her hand, but she might find that strange . . . and I might not be able to let go. I studied her face carefully. Did she know that her birth mother had been named Caroline? "My friends call me Carly," I added.

"I'm Joanna," she said, not reacting to my name. Maybe she didn't even know she was adopted. The thought made me feel cut off. Cut out.

"Joanna is a pretty name," I said, and she shrugged noncommittally. "Are you in . . . what? Sixth or seventh grade?"

"Seventh." She looked a little insulted that I might have guessed she was a sixth-grader. "I go to a Science and Technology Middle School."

"Wow," I said. "Is that a special . . . a private school?"

"Yeah." She ruffled the fur on Jobs's head. "I love techie stuff."

"I see that." I smiled, but I was thinking about that private school, wondering if the people who adopted her were giving her more than I ever would have been able to.

Joanna gave me a puzzled look. "Do you live in this neighborhood?" she asked.

I shook my head. "About a mile away. I work at the Sleeping Dog Inn." I pointed in the direction of the inn and saw that my hand was still shaking. I lowered it quickly to my side.

Joanna's face lit up. "I know where that is!" she said. "I love that name."

"They allow dogs," I said. "Isn't that cool?"

"Totally! Do you take care of the dogs there?"

"No, I'm the housekeeper. And Poppy belongs to the owner, but I get to walk her."

"Awesome," Joanna said. She looked down at her own dog again, and I had the feeling we'd reached the end of our conversation. "I better walk him," she said. "I can tell he has to pee."

"You're right," I said, but I didn't move. How I wanted to touch her! Her slender shoulder felt like a magnet to me. I tightened my hand around the leash instead. "It was nice meeting you, Joanna," I said.

"Yeah," she said over her shoulder as she and her dog headed away from me.

I turned in the direction of the inn, away from Joanna and her beautiful neighborhood. I fell apart quickly as I walked, as though I'd been holding myself together with rusty nails that were popping out of my body one by one, until by the time I was a block from Rosewood Court, my shoulders were heaving with my tears.

I dropped Poppy off at the inn, then walked into town to buy a new phone so Myra would no longer be able to call me. I was careful, though, to transfer her number to the replacement phone before I did anything else. While I didn't want Myra to be able to reach me, the last thing I wanted was to lose her again.

With the new phone in my pocket, I walked to the library where I looked up "Steve Jobs" on the computer. He'd cofounded Apple and had died a couple of years ago. And he'd been adopted. Was that one of the reasons Joanna liked him? I winced when I read his description of his birth parents as a "sperm and egg bank." I pushed my chair back from the computer and stared into space. Would Joanna ever think of Joe and me that way?

In my narrow bed that night, I lay awake for hours, playing my short meeting with Joanna over and over again in my mind. A sense of disorientation teased me. She was still my little baby in my imagination one minute, cooing at me as I changed her diaper, studying my face carefully as I sang to her. Five minutes later, she was this young girl, fully formed, with a world of knowledge and passions inside her head. I loved them both with an intensity that was almost too much to bear. They were both my daughter. Both my little girl.

I could get to know her, I thought, as I stared up at the dark, sloped attic ceiling. *I could take her back with me*. I doubted there were any science and technology middle schools in 1970, no, but I would find her the best school possible, even if it meant private school. Even if it meant leaving the Outer Banks and moving back to Raleigh where she could have any opportunity she wanted.

I imagined Joanna with us at the beach, being doted on by Hunter and Patti and besotted with her little cousin John Paul. I could see her romping in the ocean. Sunning on the beach with new friends. It was impossible, wasn't it? But I let my imagination fly. *Just for tonight*, I thought, curling myself into a ball, hugging my pillow. Just for tonight, I'd allow myself to imagine my daughter and my real life coming together in harmony.

But how did you steal a child away from the world she knew to take her to the world where she belonged?

45

As I scrubbed toilets and dusted dresser tops the following day, I imagined Myra was cursing my name. Tonight I was supposed to step off from the Arlington Memorial Bridge and surely by now she realized that was not going to happen. Did she have a clue where I was? I knew she felt responsible for me and wanted me—an interloper in her time-travel program—out of her hair.

I could still make it to the portal. All I had to do was get on a train and I could be in Washington in time to step off, but even if I could only see Joanna one more time, for one more minute, it would be worth missing that portal. Insane, I knew, but seeing her again was all I could think about as I cleaned the rooms and shopped for the groceries for tomorrow's breakfast.

I finished my duties at the inn a few minutes before three and clicked the leash onto Poppy's collar. She danced around me in the foyer, then tugged me toward the front door. It was only our third time walking together but she already knew the drill. She made a right turn when we reached the sidewalk and fell into heel position next to me.

"Good girl," I said, slipping her one of Winnie's home-made dog treats from my pocket. "Good heel."

We walked the short distance to Rosewood Court, my anticipation building. I was trying to think of questions I could ask Joanna without seeming too nosy when I spotted a woman walking a brown Lab. It was Jobs, I was sure of it. *Damn it.* I was both disappointed and anxious. Was this Joanna's adoptive mother? I felt suddenly guilty about what I was doing. Manipulating a meeting with Joanna. Trying to insinuate myself into her life. It felt very wrong, and yet, damn it! She was my daughter. I never abandoned her. I never would have abandoned her.

I thought of crossing the street to avoid a meeting with the woman, but Poppy and Jobs had other ideas. They barked and strained to get to each other, and though I held my ground, trying ineffectually to get Poppy to settle down, the woman began laughing as she headed in my direction, her silky dark bob picking up a breeze. I stiffened, my nerves on edge.

"Hi!" she said as she neared me. She was quite a bit older than me. Late forties, I thought. Maybe even early fifties, although except for a few fine lines around her eyes and at the corners of her mouth, her skin was satin smooth. She was slender in her jeans and form-fitting long-sleeved pink jersey. An undeniably pretty woman who took care of herself. I suddenly felt young and sloppy.

She nodded toward Poppy. "I bet this is Poppy," she said.

I tried to smile. "It is," I said. "How did you know?"

"Joanna told me about meeting her yesterday," she said.

Not about meeting me, I thought, *but the dog.* That was okay. Of course a twelve-year-old would find Poppy more interesting than me.

"Your turn to walk Jobs?" I put on my friendliest voice. It sounded false to my ears.

"Joanna's talking to a friend about an assignment, so yup," she said. She had the whitest teeth I'd ever seen on an adult. "I get to walk the little scaredy-cat this afternoon." She smiled down at Jobs who was bowing to Poppy, enticing her to play. "I can't believe this, though." She motioned toward the dogs. "Joanna said Jobs finally met a dog he likes and I see she was right." She looked up at me. "She said you work at Winnie Corman's Sleeping Dog Inn?"

It sounded like she knew Winnie. "Yes, I'm the house-keeper," I said. "And resident dog walker."

"I'm Michelle," she said. "I don't think Joanna told me your name?"

For a moment I wondered if she suspected me of being Joanna's mother trying to worm her way into her life. But I was only twenty-seven. I had to seem very young in this woman's eyes. I would have been fifteen when I gave birth to Joanna. Not impossible, certainly, but . . . how much did Michelle know about Joanna's mother?

"I'm Caroline Sears." I felt shaky as the words left my mouth. There it was. My full name, out there in the open like a dare. I waited for a reaction, but there was none. Either she'd never known the name of her daughter's bio-logical mother or she'd long ago forgotten it. Forgotten me.

"Pretty name," she said.

I recovered my composure. "You have a very bright daughter," I said. "I enjoyed meeting her." *Understatement,* I thought.

"She's scary bright," Michelle said. "We can't keep up with her sometimes."

"Do you have other kids?" I hoped that didn't seem like too personal a question.

Michelle shook her head. "Just Joanna," she said and I waited, hoping for more information. I wanted her to talk about the adoption, but why would she mention that to a perfect stranger?

At that moment, the red front door opened and Joanna came flying across the lawn toward us.

"Poppy!" she called, and in a moment she was down on the sidewalk being gently mauled by both dogs. Poppy's tail whacked against my legs. Again, I felt that shaky, near-nausea anxiety, being this close to her. The sensation felt like fear, as though I didn't trust myself to stay in control. To resist touching her. Resist shouting to both her and her mother, *She's mine!*

"Did you get that homework assignment squared away?" Michelle asked her.

"Yeah." Joanna giggled as the dogs licked her face. "See, I told you, Mom? Jobs actually *likes* her!"

"I can see that," Michelle said, then added, "Can you say hello to Caroline?"

Joanna looked up at me.

"Hi," she said.

"Hi." Those dark eyes connecting with mine made my heart speed up. Such an unusual combination, pale hair and dark brown eyes. I'd seen a bit of Joe in her face when she was an infant. Now I saw only myself. Did she see it, too? Did she recognize herself in my face? Did Michelle?

"I have a great idea," Michelle said suddenly. She looked at me. "Tomorrow's Saturday. I don't know what your schedule is like, but maybe you could bring Poppy over after lunch and she and Jobs could play together in our yard? It's fenced."

Joanna sucked in her breath. She looked up at us, eyes wide. "Cool!" she said.

Oh my God, I thought.

"We're supposed to be socializing him, but it's hard when he's afraid of his own shadow," Michelle said. "He obviously likes Poppy, though." She pointed to her dog, whose tail was whipping back and forth as he and Poppy tried to get to each other. "Plus he needs to work off some energy. He nearly ate the entire throw rug in the master bathroom last night." She looked from the dog to me. "Do you think you could manage it?" she asked. "Is it too much of an imposition?"

"Not at all." I kept my expression as neutral as I could, while inside I was shouting with an anxious sort of joy. I'd have to rush through my work at the inn, but that would be no problem. "It'd be great for Poppy, too," I said. "I could make it at two. Is that too late?"

"Mom, it won't work," Joanna said suddenly, looking up at her mother from where she was detangling the dogs. "Programming," she added.

"Oh, that's right," Michelle said. "Joanna has a computer-programming workshop tomorrow afternoon." She looked at Joanna. "Well, you wouldn't need to be here," she said, and my heart sank.

"Mom, I do *too*," Joanna said in a pathetic-sounding little wail. My heart did a jealous twitch every time the word "mom" came from her mouth.

Michelle looked thoughtful. "We could do it around four thirty," she said, then wrinkled her nose in an expression of worry. "Is that too late for you?" she asked me.

There was no time Michelle could mention that would be too late or too early or too anything. I would be there, no matter what. "It's perfect," I said.

"Awesome!" Joanna said, and she cuddled the two dogs as they crawled all over her.

When I returned to the inn, I brought Poppy into Winnie's private living room. Winnie had her own space in the inn—a small apartment behind the curtained glass door at the back of the foyer. I let Poppy off the leash and she ran to Winnie who was sitting on the sofa, laptop computer on her knees. She set the computer aside and told Poppy to sit before she petted the dog's head.

"Did you have a good walk?" she asked. I wasn't sure if she was talking to me or Poppy.

"Very good," I said. "And I wanted to ask if you'd have any objection to Poppy playing with another dog in a fenced yard tomorrow afternoon. I met a woman— Michelle Van Dyke—and her daughter while we were on our walk. They have a chocolate Lab and Michelle suggested the dogs get together."

"Oh, Michelle," Winnie said. "On Rosewood Court,

right? I knew her when I used to volunteer on the Historic Preservation Committee, which I haven't had time for in years. She was a volunteer at the same time. Tell her I said hello."

"I will."

"And as long as there's a fence for the dogs, it sounds like a great plan. The more exercise this girl can get, the better." She bent over to give Poppy a kiss on the nose. "I hate for you to ruin your whole Saturday, though. You should be able to have time just for yourself after you clean."

"I enjoy the time with Poppy," I said. "Truly."

"Well, you're definitely a keeper," she said. "I hope you stick around for a good long time."

"I expect I will," I said.

Winnie's expression was somewhere between curious and sympathetic. "What was his name, honey?" she asked. "Your husband?"

The question took me by surprise. "Joe," I said. As soon as I said his name, an image of him slipped into my mind. He was wearing his khaki pants and shirt, ready to get on the plane for the first leg of his journey to Vietnam. I was trying unsuccessfully not to cry, and he gave me that sexy grin of his, this one belying some of the anxiety he had to be feeling. He pulled me to him with a one-armed hug and a quick last kiss. Our very last kiss.

"How long has it been?" Winnie brought me back to the here and now. I was gritting my teeth together hard, trying not to cry, and I must have looked at her blankly, because she added, "Since you lost him?"

"Not quite a year," I said.

She nodded. "A year and two months for my Bill," she said. Then she sighed. "The anniversary will be hard," she warned me. "You let me know when it is and take that day off. Spend it by yourself. Grieve your heart out."

"Is that what you did?" I asked. Poppy walked back to me to lean against my leg. I bent over to scratch her behind the ears.

"No, actually." She laughed. "I spent it painting a couple of the bedrooms." She grinned sheepishly. "Do as I say, not as I do," she said.

"Do you have children?" I asked, curious.

"I wish we'd taken the time to have kids," she said with a sigh, "but we were workaholics. We owned a rug company and when we weren't working in the store, we were traveling abroad to find new rugs, which was great fun but it was a lifestyle that didn't fit with having a family. When we retired, we bought this place"—she waved a hand through the air to take in the inn—"and ran it together. It was a wonderful life, but now that he's gone, it's a bit lonely. At least we had forty-five years together. You must have only had a handful. And to lose him in an accident, so young. It breaks my heart for you."

"Thank you," I said, giving Poppy a final ear rub as I straightened up. Winnie wanted us to confide in each other, I knew. To commiserate. I would have liked that. I wished I *could* commiserate with her, but my tangle of lies made it impossible. I was becoming such a deceitful person.

"It's hard to talk about, I understand," Winnie said. "Just remember, my door is always open."

I thanked her again, then left her apartment and climbed the three flights of stairs to my little attic room, where I flopped onto my bed. My life was full of impossible magic these days, I thought. I'd traveled through time not once but three times. I'd met my twelve-year-old daughter only a few days after I'd held her in my arms as an infant. But there was still one little bit of magic I wished I could experience: I wished Joe could see her. I wished I could take a picture of Joanna and send it to him. Let him see what we created together. I lay awake much of the night, fantasizing that there was a way to do that. I could imagine his reaction. He'd fill with the same love that was overflowing inside of me at that moment. The love that, in reality, had no place to go.

46

Michelle opened the front door when Poppy and I arrived the following day. Again, I was struck by her beauty and the way her simple beige T-shirt and blue capris accentuated her athletic-looking body. The day was warm and I'd worn my best sleeveless red blouse and cleanest jeans, not wanting to look like a slob next to her.

"Joanna's so excited," she said, stepping back to let us in. She tucked a lock of her silky dark hair behind her ear. "She's out back with Jobs. This way."

She led me through a large foyer rich with hardwood floors, a red oriental carpet, and a wide staircase with a thick white bannister. We walked into a huge kitchen that sparkled with cleanliness, not an errant spoon or glass or plate on any of the black granite countertops. The air was filled with a savory aroma. Despite the almost clinical look of the kitchen, something was cooking in here.

Michelle pointed to a large metal pot on the island. "I've become a lazy cook since going back to work," she said with a chuckle. "If I can't make dinner in the Crock-Pot, we get takeout."

"It smells delicious," I said absently. My gaze was on the

windows that overlooked the expansive backyard as I searched for my daughter.

Michelle grabbed two bottles of water from the enormous refrigerator and handed one of them to me. Then she opened the sliding glass door and we stepped onto the deck. From the middle of the yard, Jobs spotted us. He hesitated for a moment and I caught a glimpse of the shyness Joanna had told me about, but then he seemed to recognize us. He bounded across the grass, leaping up the four steps to the deck to greet Poppy. Joanna followed him at a run, laughing, her fair hair waving like a flag behind her.

"Poppy!" she called.

"You can let Poppy off," Michelle said.

I didn't hear her at first, or at least, her words didn't register. I was mesmerized by the sight of my daughter running toward us, all long legs and arms and joy.

"Her leash." Michelle lightly touched my arm. "You can let her off."

"Oh, right." I reached down and unsnapped the leash from Poppy's collar. She looked up at me as if to say, *You're kidding, I'm free?* and I realized that she'd probably never had the chance to run and play outside before. She'd never had the chance to simply be a dog.

"Go on," I said to her. "You're free."

"Come on, Poppy!" Joanna said, and she ran back into the yard, both dogs bounding after her.

The yard was quite extraordinary. It was large, the grass thick and emerald green in the late afternoon light, the perimeter lush with trees and shrubs. From where we stood, no other houses were visible and it appeared that the rear of the yard abutted some massive forested natural area. In the far right corner of the yard, an enormous tree house was nestled among the branches of a couple of oaks, the top of the house so high I couldn't see it from the deck.

"What an amazing tree house," I said.

"Brandon and his cousins built it," Michelle said. She motioned to the chairs at the glass-topped table and we sat down.

"Brandon's your husband?" I asked, setting my water bottle on the table.

"Yes. He's a software engineer and a frustrated carpenter." She glanced at her watch. "He's playing golf right now," she said.

"I guess that's where Joanna gets her interest in computers," I said, thinking Joanna would have developed an interest in bridges and architecture and tennis from Joe. My eyes threatened to fill and I quickly blinked. How had everything gone so terribly wrong?

"Most definitely." Michelle took a drink from her bottle. "She sure didn't get it from me. I'm an aesthetician at a dermatologist's office three days a week and I teach yoga on Saturday mornings."

"Wow," I said. No wonder she was in such great shape. I felt a stab of envy. Her life seemed so easy. She and her husband clearly had tons of money and a gorgeous house. And my daughter. They had my daughter. "You have a full schedule," I said, trying to keep up with the conversation.

She shrugged. "Brandon and I tag team in taking care of Joanna, so it all works out."

That's good, I told myself. It was good that they both loved her. They both took care of her. Then why did hearing about it make my heart hurt?

Michelle told me about some of the women in her yoga class, but I wasn't really listening. Chatting with her wasn't what I'd expected to find myself doing on this visit. I'd hoped to spend the time with Joanna, but I could see now that would have seemed strange—a twenty-seven-year-old woman showing too much interest in a twelve-year-old girl. I would have to be careful. Anyway, Joanna was in her own world, happily throwing a ball for the dogs. I wouldn't have much of a role to play out in the yard. I needed to settle for being this close to her.

"Poppy's loving this," I said, when Michelle seemed finished with her story about her yoga class.

"It's definitely good for Jobs, too," Michelle agreed, "but it's even better for Joanna." Her voice had sobered.

"What do you mean?" I asked.

Michelle looked thoughtful, her head cocked, her gaze on Joanna rather than me. "We bought her the dog to try to get her nose out of her electronics," she said. "And to give her a friend, really." She glanced at me with a quick smile. "Oh, she actually has tons of friends, but we moved her into a private school the middle of last year on the recommendation of a counselor we saw. Joanna was bored to tears in public school and her grades were tanking, but all her friends are there, at that old school. In her new school, she's thriving academically—she adores the work and the teachers—but she's having a hard time making friends. All she does is homework, and when she's not doing homework, she's texting her old friends or reading on her iPad or researching something on her computer. Thus, we decided to give her a dog so she'd have something she can't program."

I ached at the thought of Joanna struggling to make friends, but I loved that she was a brainiac. I wanted to know more about her. I wanted to know *everything*. And I wanted Michelle to talk about the adoption, so I fished.

"She's very cute," I said. "She has your dark eyes, doesn't she."

Michelle laughed. "People tell me that all the time, but the truth is, Joanna's adopted."

"Oh?" I held my breath.

"We adopted her when she was less than a year old. The most wonderful day of my life." Michelle smiled, while my heart contracted in my chest.

"I bet it was," I said, and I found myself once again fighting tears.

"She was in a foster home," Michelle continued. "She was an orphan, actually. Her father was dead—I don't know how. I only hope it wasn't drugs." She gave me a worried look. "And her mother died in 9/11. I think she was working in one of the towers or something."

"How terrible," I said. Beneath the table, I dug my nails into my palm.

"I *know*," Michelle said. "She was in foster care for nearly a year and I hate to even think about what that was like for her. She had some health problems that got in the way of her being adopted right away, plus I think they were trying to track down relatives who might take her in, but they couldn't find any."

Oh, my poor baby. I never should have gone back to 1970. Why didn't I just stay with her? Why did I risk losing her?

"What sort of health problems?" I asked, not caring if I sounded nosy. I had to know what Joanna went through.

"It was her heart," Michelle said. "She had some problems when she was born that were taken care of back then. When she was ten, she had some related issues and had to have her aortic valve dilated, but she's perfectly fine now."

Now my own heart sped up. If I'd managed to take Joanna back to 1970 with me, would I have been able to get her the medical help she'd needed?

"Ugh," Michelle said suddenly. She nodded toward the yard. "See what I mean?" she asked. Joanna had stopped playing with the dogs to check her phone. "She can't stay off that thing."

You could always take it away from her for a few hours each day, I thought of saying. *You're the grown-up.* But I kept my mouth shut. I didn't get to make the rules here.

"I feel like she's not getting a real childhood, you know?" Michelle said.

"Maybe this is a real childhood in 2013," I said. "It's just not the childhood we had."

She smiled at me. "Well, it's definitely not the childhood *I* had. I grew up in the sixties and seventies. It was a totally different world. Joanna thinks I'm ancient, and compared to her friends' mothers who are all in their late thirties and early forties, I am. But you . . . how old are you? Twenty-five?"

"Twenty-seven." I realized this was the first question she'd asked me about myself since we'd sat down. She was the sort of woman who liked to talk about her own life. That was probably for the best. All I had to share was lies.

"So you came of age in the nineties."

Not really, I thought, but I nodded. "Yes," I said.

"That dog!" Michelle suddenly frowned toward the yard where Jobs was merrily digging in one of the flower beds, dirt flying out behind him. "Joanna!" she shouted, and Joanna looked over at us. "Don't let him dig!"

Joanna grabbed Jobs's collar and shouted something at him we couldn't hear. Jobs stopped digging for a couple of seconds, then went right back to it.

"We need to get him back into obedience class," Michelle said, "but now that school's started, there's no time."

I stood up, reaching into my jeans pocket for a handful of dried-liver treats. There were bowls of it all over the inn.

"Let me see if I can help," I said to Michelle, relieved to have a reason to join Joanna in the yard.

"Hey, Joanna," I called, walking down the steps from the deck. She looked toward me, the late afternoon sun turning her hair gold. *The most beautiful child in the world.* "Let's do some recall training with them." My voice had a shiver to it. Looking at her, moving toward her, was literally stealing my breath away.

"How do we do that?" Joanna asked.

Both dogs rushed toward me, Jobs leaving the hole he'd

been working on in the flower bed to see what I had in store for them.

I walked close enough to Joanna to give her a fistful of liver treats. Our hands touched, and I longed for more. I wanted to fit her slender hand into mine. Raise her fingers to my lips. I took a step away from her. "You stand on that side of the yard and I'll stand over here by the tree house, and we'll call them back and forth and reward them with liver," I said. "Break the treats into little pieces so they last."

"Okay!" She seemed to like the idea and ran toward the shrubs at the far side of the yard. The dogs leaped around her, and she giggled as she held the treats high above her head to protect them.

I bent over, holding out my hand with the liver. "Poppy! Jobs! Come!" I called.

Jobs understood first, his training, however minimal, kicking in, and he ran toward me, Poppy on his heels. I made them sit—no easy feat—before rewarding them with the treats, then nodded to Joanna. "Your turn," I called.

"Jobs! Poppy! Come!" she said, and the dogs ran back to her.

"Make them sit first," I said, and she did.

There followed one of the most blissful fifteen-minute periods of my life as we sent the dogs back and forth between my giggling daughter and me. Joanna's laughter reminded me of Patti. I felt homesick then. I wanted Joanna to meet my family. I wanted them to be able to meet her.

Michelle walked toward me across the lawn as our game of recall wound down. "Can you stay for dinner?" she asked.

"Oh, no," I said, glancing at my chronometer. It was nearly five thirty. I'd overstayed my welcome. "No, we should get back."

"Oh, stay!" Joanna pleaded and my heart soared. She wanted me here. My smile was so broad, I probably looked ridiculous.

"Yes, you'll stay," Michelle said, clearly accustomed to getting her way. "Brandon can drive you and Poppy home after dinner."

"Are you sure?" I asked her. "I don't want to impose."

"There's plenty of cacciatore in the Crock-Pot," she said.

"Okay," I said, torn between joy and anxiety. "I'll call Winnie and let her know where we are. She says 'hello,' by the way." I pulled my phone from my rear pocket.

"Tell her 'hi' back," Michelle said. She turned to Joanna. "Why don't you show Caroline your tree house?" she suggested. "We'll have dinner at six. Dad'll be home any minute."

"Her name's Carly," Joanna said. She looked at me. "Right?"

"Right." I smiled. "And I'd love to see your tree house."

The two-level tree house was astonishing. Although it was still daylight, the structure was nestled so deep in the trees that sunlight strained to reach it. Joanna flicked a switch as we reached the first level and the room filled with light. A tree house with electricity! The room was nearly twice the size of my little attic room at the inn, big enough for two twin beds and a small table and chairs. The ceiling was low, six and a half feet at best. We were about to climb the circular wrought-iron staircase to the second story when Joanna's phone chirped and she pulled it from the pocket of her shorts to check the screen. She slipped it back into her pocket without responding.

"Is that your ring?" I asked. "That chirpy sound?"

"It's a text," she said.

"Oh," I said. "I've never texted."

She looked at me like she couldn't believe I was for real. "You've never sent a text?"

I shook my head. "I don't even know how."

"Give me your phone," she said.

I handed her my phone and watched as she deftly tapped a few keys. She handed it back to me, then pulled out her own phone and tapped another few keys. My phone chirped.

"Now look at your phone and hit that icon that says 'Messages.'"

I obeyed her directions and saw a message from her. U need an iPhone, she'd written, and I laughed.

"Send me a message back," she commanded.

I looked at my little keyboard. *I love you* would be inappropriate, of course, so I settled for Today was fun.

Her phone chirped and she looked at the screen. "Awesome," she said, then added matter-of-factly, "Now you know how to text." Turning, she climbed the circular staircase with me close on her heels.

The second level of the tree house was simply an open space filled with windows and a pitched ceiling. No furniture. We sat down cross-legged on the floor to look out the window toward the house, where lights shone from the kitchen.

"What do you use this space for?" I asked.

"Sleepovers, mostly."

We watched a silver car pull into the driveway, making a U-turn to face the garage, where it stopped.

"Daddy's home," she said.

I watched a man get out of the car and head toward the rear of the house. He was too far away and too blocked by the branches of the tree for me to make out his features. Brandon, the software-engineering, golf-playing man. I felt hurt all over again that this strange man got to be called "Daddy."

"Two people can sleep in the beds downstairs"—Joanna continued her conversation about sleepovers—"but we all usually stay up here in our sleeping bags so we can be together." She touched the window with her fingertip, idly tracing a line I couldn't see on the glass. "I'm having a sleepover tomorrow night, actually, since Monday's a school holiday." She folded her hands in her lap.

"With friends from your new school?" I asked hopefully. I wanted her to be happy.

She wrinkled her nose. "I don't have any friends at my new school," she said. "They're all totally weird."

"How are they weird?"

She shrugged. "They just are."

"Sometimes people seem weird until we really get to know them," I counseled.

"And sometimes they're even *weirder* when we really get to know them," she shot back, but she was smiling. She wasn't going to buy into my insipid platitudes. I liked her feistiness.

"True," I agreed. I looked down at the smooth expanse of wooden floor between us. "This is the perfect spot for playing jacks or Scrabble or cards," I said.

"What's jacks?" she asked.

"You've never played jacks?"

Her phone chirped again and she pulled it from her pocket. "Mom says it's dinnertime," she said, hopping quickly to her feet. She was so agile. So *healthy*.

We descended the circular staircase and then I followed her down the steep steps to the ground, where Poppy and Jobs waited for us. Joanna and the dogs ran ahead of me. Watching them—watching *Joanna*—I felt overwhelmed by loss. She was a beautiful girl. An amazing girl. But I had missed twelve years of her life. Twelve years! All those firsts I'd looked forward to. First steps. First words. First tooth. First day of school. I'd missed everything.

I followed her across the lush grass of the darkening backyard, once again blinking back tears.

I didn't want to miss anything else.

47

Brandon Van Dyke didn't seem pleased to find a stranger at his dinner table. I met him in the dining room as the four of us sat down to eat. He was a tall, angular man who had to be twice my age, and I felt very young in his presence. He had handsome, serious features and the sort of pale hair that may have been either gray or blond. His eyes were a steely blue, but in spite of his eye color, I thought he could easily pass as Joanna's father. Or more likely, as her grandfather.

"Caroline, this is Brandon," Michelle said rather formally as she began dishing out the aromatic cacciatore from the serving bowl on the table. "Brandon, this is Caroline."

"Carly," Joanna piped in. She smiled at me and my heart melted.

"Hi." I smiled at Brandon, and he nodded to me as he sipped red wine from his glass. I sensed suspicion and distrust in his reserved greeting . . . or maybe it was only my guilty conscience at work. Joanna and I sat across the table from each other. Did he see the resemblance between us? I wasn't sure how anyone could miss it.

"Jobs actually likes her dog Poppy," Joanna said. "And she's helping me train him," Joanna said. "We did recalls in the yard."

"Good luck with that," Brandon said dryly, setting down his glass.

"He's a good dog," I said. "Just still has a lot of puppy in him." At that moment, both Jobs and Poppy were—I hoped—sprawled out on the deck, exhausted from their time in the yard.

As uncurious about me as Michelle had seemed, Brandon was the opposite.

"Michelle said you work at the Sleeping Dog Inn," he prompted as he cut his chicken.

"Yes," I said. "Do you know Winnie Corman, too?"

"I've referred a few people to her inn over the years." He lifted a piece of chicken from his plate with his fork. "Clearly you're not from around here," he said, referring to my accent, I supposed. "How did you end up at the inn?"

"I'm from North Carolina," I said. "I needed a change, and a friend once lived up here and she told me how nice Summit was, so I thought I'd come see what it was like for myself."

"You say 'ah' instead of 'I,' " Joanna said. "It sounds so funny."

"Joanna, that's rude," Michelle scolded.

"Sorry," Joanna said, but she was smiling to herself.

"No problem." I winked at her, thinking that if things had gone the way they were supposed to, she, too, would be saying "ah" instead of "I."

"Your friend's not still living here?" Brandon asked.

"No," I said.

"Do you know anyone in the area?"

"Actually, not a soul." I smiled, but his questions were putting me on edge. "Sometimes you need a complete change of scenery." There I went with that stupid "change of scenery" again.

"What are you running away from?" he asked, throwing me completely off guard.

"Brandon!" Michelle said. "What kind of question is that?"

"I hope I'm not running away from anything," I said, trying not to bristle. "I like to think I'm running *to* something. I have a degree in physical therapy and hope to eventually get a job at the Kessler Institute up here."

He stared at me, fork halfway to his mouth, and I knew I'd surprised him.

"Good place," he admitted. "You're not married?"

"Widowed," I said.

"Oh, no." Michelle set down her own wineglass. "I'm so sorry."

"Does that mean your husband died?" Joanna asked.

I looked across the table at her. *Oh, sweetie,* I thought. *It's your daddy I'm talking about. You would have loved him so much.* "Yes," I said. "It's been a while now." As in forty-four years or ten months, depending on how you counted. It felt like only yesterday to me, though, and once again I bit back tears. I was acutely aware that a little bit of Joe sat across the table from me.

"Accident?" Brandon asked.

"Drunk driver." I nodded.

"How tragic," Michelle said.

"So," I said, looking directly into Brandon's piercing blue eyes, "if I ran away from anything, it was from a lot of sadness. I needed to get away from the reminders for a while, and I knew about Summit and—"

"No children?" he asked.

Damn. This man was not going to let me off the hook. I shook my head. "I wish," I said.

"How about some more chicken?" Michelle asked me, although I still had plenty on my plate. I was grateful for her awkward attempt to take the heat off me.

"I'm fine," I said. "Thanks."

"Carly said we should play cards and checkers and things on the second story of the tree house," Joanna said, and Brandon laughed.

"Honey," he said to Joanna. "The day you actually play cards with a real deck instead of on a computer screen is the day I'll eat my hat." He leaned over to brush a lock of hair from her cheek and I saw his affection for her. Real affection. His voice was completely different from the voice he'd used to interrogate me.

"And what was the other thing?" Joanna ignored his teasing as she looked across the table at me. "Janks?"

"Jacks," I said. "You have the perfect floor space for a good game of jacks up there."

"Jacks!" Michelle laughed. "That brings back some memories."

"How do you play?" Joanna asked.

Michelle and I tried to explain the game to her. "It's easy," I said, "but it takes coordination."

"You know," Michelle said, "I'm pretty sure I have some jacks in the attic. My mother gave me a box of my old things when I got married and I stuck them up there."

"We should look," Joanna said.

"All right." Michelle sounded pleased. "We'll look after dinner."

Michelle and I did the dishes, while Brandon and Joanna took the dogs for a walk.

"You have the magic touch with Joanna," Michelle said as she slid a plate into the dishwasher. "If I'd been the one to tell her about jacks, she would have rolled her eyes at me, thinking, 'boring old mom.'" She laughed.

"Well, when she sees the actual game, she'll probably roll her eyes at *me*," I said, but I loved what she said about my magic touch. I wanted that. I wanted that so much.

When Joanna returned to the house, and the kitchen was back in order, she and Michelle and I climbed the stairs to the neatest, most orderly attic I'd ever seen. Still, we had to move aside at least a dozen plastic tubs of Christmas decorations to get to a cardboard box marked simply *Michelle*.

Michelle dug through high school yearbooks, an old teddy bear, a faded pom-pom—I should have guessed she'd been a cheerleader—and ancient photograph albums, and there in the bottom of the box was a small brown paper bag containing a set of jacks. Joanna peered inside the bag, clearly unimpressed.

"That's it?" she asked, disappointment in her voice.

"That's it," Michelle said. "Come on," she added, getting

to her feet. "Hours of fun await." Suddenly her gaze lit on a large white plastic bag near the top of the stairs. "Joanna, when are we going to take that bag to the shelter?" she asked.

Joanna gnawed her lip as she eyed the bag. She glanced up at me. "That's my dolls and stuffed animals and things," she said. "I'm going to donate them." She walked over to the bag, opened the top, and pulled out a small stuffed cat and I watched as she smoothed the faux fur on the cat's head.

"Why are you giving them away?" I asked.

"Because I'm practically thirteen and nobody thirteen still plays with stuffed animals," she said simply, but I could see the ambivalence in her eyes as she tenderly returned the cat to the white bag. It made me smile.

I love you so much, I thought. *I love you so damn much.*

Joanna's room was very girly and very purple. The walls were lavender, the spread on her big bed a deep plum. On the wall above the bed was a giant wooden purple *J*. In spite of the donation bag of toys in the attic upstairs, there were still a few stuffed animals in front of the mountain of pillows on the neatly made bed. This was a child's room, I thought. Joanna was still more little girl than teen.

Michelle pushed aside one of the furry white throw rugs to make room on the hardwood floor for our game of jacks, and the three of us sat down to play. Michelle and I were more into the game than Joanna, but I saw a competitive side to her that I liked. She was terrible at first while Michelle and I seemed to have muscle memory for the game, but she studied our techniques and slowly improved. She seemed determined not to let us show her up.

"I'll practice," she said to me, "and next time I see you, I'll beat you."

"You think so, huh?" I teased.

Brandon poked his head in the room and leveled his blue eyes at me. "I need to run to the store, so why don't I take you home now?" he asked.

"No!" Joanna said. "Not yet, Daddy. I'm finally almost winning."

"Let us finish this game, hon," Michelle said as she scooped up seven jacks. "Just a few minutes."

He looked at his watch and I thought he was going to protest, but he nodded. "Okay," he said. "I'm in my study."

We wrapped up the final game, which Joanna came close to winning, and the three of us got to our feet. Michelle returned the throw rug to its rightful place on the floor. "This might be a weird question to ask a grown woman, but while you're waiting to find a PT job, would you ever consider babysitting?" she asked as she straightened a corner of the rug.

"Yes!" Joanna said. "Say yes."

I laughed, touched that she wanted more time with me. "I'd love to," I said.

"Tuesday night when you go to New York?" Joanna asked her mother.

"Well," Michelle hedged, "we have Deanna lined up for Tuesday night." She looked at me. "Brandon and I have tickets for *Kinky Boots*," she said.

I guessed I should have known what *Kinky Boots* was.

"That should be fun," I said, hoping that was the appropriate response.

"Could we cancel Deanna and make it Carly?" Joanna asked.

Michelle seemed to think it over. "Does Tuesday night work for you?" she asked me.

I was a little appalled at Joanna's power. At the same time, I was thrilled at the thought of spending an evening with her, just the two of us.

"That should be fine," I said.

"Awesome!" Joanna said.

We left Joanna in her room and Michelle and I walked downstairs, Michelle telling me about the woes of finding decent babysitters in the neighborhood. "Once they're old enough to be responsible, they're old enough to want to spend Saturday night with their friends," she lamented. "I'll tell Brandon you're ready," she said when we reached the kitchen. "You can get Poppy and meet him in the driveway."

I thanked her for dinner, then walked out the back door. Although the deck was well lit, the yard had grown dark and I couldn't see the dogs. Poppy came running when I called her, though. By the dirt on her muzzle, I guessed Jobs had taught her the joys of digging. I was brushing the dirt from her face when I heard voices coming from the garage. I held on to Poppy's collar as I straightened up to listen.

"We don't even know her," Brandon was saying.

"You're being ridiculous," Michelle said. "She works for Winnie Corman, for heaven's sake. She's very nice, and I think she'll be a healthier, more mature influence on Joanna than Deanna Gladstone. When Deanna babysits, she spends the whole night on her phone while Joanna's on hers. Carly didn't even glance at her phone while she's been here. Not once. Did you notice that?"

"On our walk, Joanna told me she uses a prepaid cell phone," Brandon said. "Who uses prepaid phones these days? Only transients or people without the means to sign a contract."

I bit my lip, listening, afraid Michelle would give into him and I might never be able to see my daughter again.

"I'll call Winnie and see what she has to say, all right?" Michelle said. "Just to put your mind at ease? Winnie would never hire someone who wasn't trustworthy."

"There's something strange about the whole . . ." Brandon lowered his voice and the rest of their conversation was lost on me. Poppy, most likely tired of me standing there frozen with my fingers around her collar, let out an impatient bark.

"Ready!" I called out as I clipped Poppy's leash to her collar. I crossed the deck, heading for the driveway. A light mounted on the outside corner of the garage illuminated Brandon and his car. Michelle must have slipped inside the house through the garage and Brandon was laying a blanket across the backseat of the car by the time Poppy and I reached him. He opened the back door wide.

"For your dog," he said.

Poppy hopped into the car and I shut the door behind her before getting into the front seat. The car smelled new.

"Thanks for doing this," I said, as Brandon pulled out of

the driveway onto the road. I wished I could find a way to win him over.

"No problem." He adjusted the rearview mirror while I tried to think of something I could say that would put his mind at ease about me. But he spoke up first.

"What's your last name again?" he asked.

"Sears," I said. I watched his handsome profile, waiting for a reaction. Did he know the name of Joanna's mother? Could he have known it and kept it from Michelle? Or maybe Michelle had simply forgotten it.

"What nationality is Sears?" he asked. I let out my breath. He didn't know who I was.

"Irish," I said, "but that was actually my husband's name. My surname was Grant. It's Scottish." Was he going to try to Google me? He'd never find me. Not the twenty-seven-year-old me, at any rate. "I guess Van Dyke is Dutch?"

"Right. It was the name given to people who lived near dikes in the Netherlands, which I suppose was just about everyone." He glanced at me. "How long before you can get a PT job?" he asked.

"Well, first I need to get licensed in New Jersey," I said. "I'm licensed in North Carolina, but there's no reciprocity. Then, of course, I'll need to find an opening."

"Seems like you're making life hard on yourself," he said, turning a corner. "Leaving the state where you're already licensed."

"Well, I figure I'm young enough to start over," I said, thinking that he had no idea exactly how hard my life was right now.

"Where did you go to school?"

"University of North Carolina," I said. "Chapel Hill."

"Really." He sounded surprised. "Good school." Did he have a way of looking up alumni at UNC? He'd think I was a liar. I *was* a liar.

"I loved it," I said, for something to say. We were already at the inn, and he pulled into the driveway.

"I'll pick you up at five thirty Tuesday night," he said. "You can bring the dog if you like."

"Oh, Poppy and I can walk over," I said.

"No, I'll pick you up."

I knew better than to argue. "All right," I said. "Thanks."

"And Caroline," he said, as I opened the door. I looked over at him, struck by his serious tone. "Joanna means everything to us," he said. I felt a chill run up my spine.

"Of course she does," I said. "She's a wonderful girl."

I got out of the car, surprised to discover I was trembling as I let Poppy out of the backseat.

"Good night," I said to Brandon before shutting the rear door, and I felt his eyes on me as I walked toward the front steps of the inn, thinking, *She means everything to me, too.*

48

Hunter

Carly was a no-show. Again.

I'd been staring at the sand between the two giant dunes for the past hour and a half. Now I lay back, not caring that I was getting sand in my hair. I stared up at the early morning sky. The clouds hanging thick, gray, and low above me matched my mood.

Two portals down; three to go.

Was it the baby? Was Joanna so sick that she needed more time in the hospital than Carly had anticipated? Much as I wanted that baby to be healthy, I hoped that was the problem. Carly's delay would be much more ominous if it had nothing to do with Joanna's health. It would mean I'd screwed up by sending her back on 9/11. That was my big fear—one I hadn't dared to share yet with Patti.

I remembered being in my social studies class when the planes hit the towers, but I couldn't remember the exact time, so I didn't know how the event might have influenced Carly's landing in New York. Our teacher had turned on the TV in the classroom and we all watched in horror. The fallout from the towers' collapse—all that smoke and ash and debris—had blown in the opposite direction of Central Park, I was quite certain, and yet there may well have been enough of an atmospheric disturbance to throw off my calculations. I kept telling myself there wasn't a thing I could do about it now. I could obsess about it every minute of every hour of every day and that would do nothing to help Carly and only serve to paralyze me. Already, my work was suffering and I was behind on a couple of contracts with important clients. I wasn't used to this miserable feeling of helplessness.

Patti'd cleared the rest of my crap out of the spare room and covered the walls with pink and white striped wallpaper. We'd put together a crib that stood ominously empty on one side of the room, and Patti was now crocheting a sweater for the baby, keeping her hands and mind occupied while we waited. I dreaded coming home from the dunes alone again this morning, manufacturing more benign reasons why Carly wasn't with me.

The next portal wasn't for a month. I wasn't a praying man, but I found myself uttering pleas to God as I drove home from the dunes. If Carly didn't make that next portal, I wasn't sure what I would do.

49

Carly

Poppy followed me around the inn Sunday morning as I vacuumed the living room, made beds, and wiped strangers' hair out of the showers. It made me uncomfortable, seeing personal glimpses into the lives of the guests as I cleaned their rooms. I felt intrusive and tried to turn away from things I had no business noticing. Yet there they were: the birth control pills on the dresser. The false teeth container on the nightstand. The hemorrhoid cream on the toilet tank.

An older couple had checked into the inn on Saturday night. I hadn't yet met them and they'd already eaten breakfast by the time I got downstairs, but Winnie told me they'd driven up from Virginia.

"Nice couple," she said. "They'll be here for nearly three weeks visiting family and going to some sort of reunion with friends."

As I cleaned their room, I noticed a black baseball cap on the dresser, VIETNAM VETERAN embroidered above the brim. My heart stopped for a moment, seeing that hat. I touched it with tentative fingers. Our guest had served in Vietnam? When? Could he possibly have known Joe? *Don't be silly,* I thought to myself. Of course he hadn't known Joe. Joe hadn't even been in Vietnam two weeks when he was struck down. My throat instantly tightened and my eyes burned, and I was angry at myself as I continued cleaning, this time with a vengeance. Was I going to fall apart every time I heard the word "Vietnam"?

I bumped into Winnie in the upstairs hallway as I finished cleaning the bedrooms. She laughed when she saw Poppy glued to my side.

"I think she's more your dog than mine, now," she said. She didn't sound the least bit bothered by the thought.

"She's a good girl." I tried to match Winnie's light tone, hoping there was no trace of my small breakdown in my face. I reached over with my free hand—the hand not carrying my caddy of cleaning supplies—to rub Poppy's head. She'd slept with me last night after we got home from Joanna's house and I'd welcomed her on my tiny bed. She was cuddly and I'd needed something to cuddle.

"I hear you're going to babysit for the Van Dyke girl," Winnie said.

"Did Michelle call you?" I asked.

Winnie nodded. "I told her what a big help you are to me and that she has nothing to worry about."

"Thanks." I smiled. I hadn't even known Winnie for a week and it was kind of her to give me such a sterling recommendation. I would do my best to live up to it.

*

When I finished my work for the day, I was finally free to take Poppy for a walk. I tried not to get my hopes up that I might see Joanna when I reached Rosewood Court. It was Sunday, after all, and her schedule would be different, yet I wanted to try. Just a quick wave as I passed by her house would be enough. Maybe a glimpse of her in the yard with Jobs. Anything. I would take anything.

I walked the mile to Rosewood Court and started slowly past the Van Dykes' house. When I was even with the side of the house, I saw all three of them—Joanna, Michelle, and Brandon—in the far corner of the yard by the tree house, probably getting it ready for Joanna's sleepover tonight. Joanna was climbing the steps up to the first level, and she reached down to take something from Michelle's hand. Brandon was hunched over at the base of the steps, hammering. I was ready to wave should one of them turn in my direction, but none of them did and I kept walking, the vignette of the three of them stuck firmly in my mind. The little family. The 2013 family I was no part of.

You have to let her go, I thought to myself. *She's not yours.*

"Shut up!" I said out loud, and Poppy looked up at me as if wondering what I could possibly mean by this new command.

That night, Poppy lay next to me on my bed in the attic room. I wondered if I should contact Myra this week. I really should let her know that I'd need a portal back to 1970 . . . eventually. I'd tell her I wasn't ready to go yet, though. I was nowhere near ready to leave, but I worried about her disappearing again. Changing her phone number. Her address. I needed to get in touch with her before she made another of her great escapes.

Yet I was afraid to contact her. She was going to be furious about my disappearance and would want to know what I was up to. She'd insist I take the first portal she could find for me and I would have to refuse. How could I leave Joanna forever? All I knew was that I was not yet ready to go and I couldn't take her with me. How had I ever imagined that I could? It would be cruel. A ridiculous idea.

I sank my fingers into Poppy's coat, pulling her big body close to me, resting my chin against the soft slope of her forehead, searching for comfort. I missed Patti. I missed Hunter.

I was losing my mind and I had no one to talk to about it.

50

"She needs to go to bed at nine," Michelle told me in the kitchen Tuesday night. She wore a sleeveless, shape-hugging black dress, an artsy-looking silver necklace, and unbelievably high high heels. I was stunned to see a small tattoo on her left shoulder. From where I stood, it looked like an upside-down V. It seemed to me that nearly everyone had tattoos in 2013. "She's still making up for getting zero sleep during that sleepover Sunday night," Michelle added.

"Mom!" Joanna protested as she walked in the room. "I did so get sleep!"

"I heard you out there in the tree house," Michelle said, her scolding voice betrayed by her smile. "You and your friends kept me awake all night long, so unless you were asleep and everyone else was awake, you had little to no sleep, and I know you didn't get enough last night to make up for it, since you were still dragging today. So no later than nine tonight." She looked at me, and I nodded.

"Nine o'clock," I assured her. She noticed me staring at her tattoo and she turned so I could get a better look at it.

"It's a downward dog," she said. "You know . . . the yoga pose?"

"Ah," I said, though I'd never heard of a downward dog. I could see now that it was a tiny figure of a woman bending over, her bottom high in the air.

"I should have gotten it bigger." Michelle laughed. "No one can ever tell what it is." She turned to Joanna again. "And stay off the phone," she said. "If you haven't noticed, Carly isn't a phone addict, and it would be nice if you'd actually interact instead of burying your nose in the—"

"*Mom,*" Joanna wailed. "All right. I get it."

It was a prickly side to her I hadn't yet seen and Brandon walked in the room to put an end to it with a hug.

"Good night, sweetheart," he said. "Love you."

Brandon had driven Poppy and me to the house and he'd been cordial, if not exactly friendly, in the car. I'd asked him about his work but immediately zoned out as he tried to explain it to me. I didn't truly understand what "software" was and his explanation went way over my head. Clearly, though, his work had influenced Joanna.

"'Night," Joanna said to him now as their hug ended.

"You two have fun," Michelle said as her husband gallantly wrapped a black cape around her shoulders. He took her hand and they headed for the door to the garage.

"You ready to lose at jacks?" Joanna asked as soon as her parents had left. Her hair was damp and she gave off the scent of shampoo and soap. I realized the loose cotton shorts and matching tank top she was wearing were most likely her pajamas. The tank top hugged her small breasts, but her legs were still the long gangly legs of a child. She was adorable and I once again felt the urge to scoop her into my arms and cover her with kisses.

"No," I said instead, "but I'm ready to continue my winning streak."

"Don't get your hopes up!" she said as she headed for the stairs at a trot.

I followed her upstairs to her room, Poppy and Jobs at our heels. The throw rug was already folded out of the way and the set of jacks was on the floor. She'd been practicing.

We played five games. I'd been tempted to let her win a couple of them until I realized that she was now better than me. She won three.

"In October, we're going down the shore," she said as we wound up our final game. "I can't wait."

"Does that mean the beach?"

She nodded. "Yeah, Long Beach Island. Have you ever been?"

I shook my head, distressed by the thought of her going away.

"It's so awesome in the fall," she said. "Sometimes it's even warm enough to go swimming, but not usually. We have, like, a mini family reunion with my cousins and everybody, and Mom and Dad and my aunt and uncle run in a race and it's so cool. Want to see where it is?" She jumped to her feet and clambered onto her bed where she had her laptop. Poppy leaped onto the bed with her and I made her get off. I'd created a monster, letting Poppy sleep with me.

Reclining cozily against the mound of pillows in front of her headboard, Joanna began tapping the keys on the computer. "Come look," she said, patting the bed next to her.

Hesitantly, I sat down next to her on the double bed, our bare arms touching. I felt intrusive, as though I was invading her personal space. This was where I belonged, I reminded myself. I deserved this intimacy. Joanna didn't seem the least bit concerned as she zipped around the computer screen, her arm gently knocking into mine. I watched her hands, a smaller version of my own. Her nails were short and unpainted, like mine. Around her slim wrist she wore a decorative bracelet that looked as though it was made from pink and purple rubber bands.

"I can't wait," she said again, as houses began appearing on the screen. She scrolled rapidly through the images. "We go to LBI every summer, too. All my cousins and everybody are there then, and my best friend Gayla goes with us. We get the same humongo house every year. It has a million bedrooms and is right on the ocean with a pool and everything."

I felt her damp hair against my shoulder. The sweet smell of her filled my head and I breathed it in, nearly intoxicated by the scent. "How long will you be gone in October?" I asked, my heart tightening in my chest at the thought of her being more than a mile away from me.

"A week," she said, "though my cousins can't stay as long. I have a school holiday."

A week. I missed her already.

"Here it is!" she said, enlarging the photograph on the screen. The house was unlike any summer home I'd seen in the Outer Banks. It was almost comically huge, with numerous decks and balconies jutting from every angle. The exterior was a soft peach color with white trim, and a broad staircase led up to the double front doors. The house looked very new to me, but then every house built after 1970 struck me as new.

"That's a beautiful house," I said.

"You can't tell, but it's right on the ocean. I'll show you." She tapped a few more keys and suddenly we were looking down at the beach from above. Satellite view. "See how close the house is to the water? It's so cool. I can't wait."

"My house is that close, too," I said, forgetting to censor myself.

"Your house? Don't you live in the Sleeping Dog Inn?"

"Right now I do, yes, but where I lived in North Carolina is right on the beach."

"Cool!" she said. "Show me. What's the address?"

"What do you mean . . . Oh! You mean we'll look at it from the satellite?"

"Yes," she said, her fingers waiting above the keyboard.

I hesitated and my heart gave a thud in my chest. Did I want to see what Nags Head looked like in 2013? How many storms had passed through the Outer Banks since 1970? I was so afraid my house would be gone.

Finally, I gave her the address, and she laughed.

"Nags Head! That's a weird name. Like a horse?"

"Like a horse," I said. "The legend is that pirates hung a lantern around a horse's neck and walked him back and forth at night to trick ships into thinking the light was from another ship. Then the duped ships would run aground and the pirates would pillage them."

"Is that true?" Joanna looked up at me with those big dark eyes, and I shrugged.

"Who knows?" I said. "But that crazy name had to come from somewhere."

Joanna hit a few more keys and in a moment we were looking down on the roofs of the Unpainted Aristocracy. Taking the computer onto my own lap, I anxiously moved the screen until I spotted the roof of my house. I let out my breath in relief. It was still there. I recognized the square shape of it. The dormer windows. The ocean appeared to be no closer to it than it had been in 1970. "This is it," I said, excitement in my voice as I pointed to the roof.

"Wow, it's like right in the water practically," Joanna said. "Let's look at the street view." She took the computer back from me.

"Street view?" I asked.

"Haven't you ever used the street view?" She clicked a key and suddenly we were on the beach road, looking at cottages I recognized as my neighbors'. I felt both afraid and curious to see my own house now, forty-three years after I'd last seen it. Joanna clicked on an arrow, moving the screen along the road. There was a split-rail fence I didn't recognize and some of the houses had changed the color of their hurricane shutters, but everything else appeared to be remarkably familiar.

"Oh my God, there it is!" I said as my house came into view. I pointed to the screen. The image of the house was big enough that I could make out my bedroom window on the northernmost side. An unfamiliar red car was in the driveway. "That's my nephew's room," I said, pointing to one of the street-side windows before clamping my mouth shut. John Paul would be in his forties by now. Who knew what room was his, if any of them? For that matter, was the house still in my family? Were we all still alive? I trembled, almost sick with nostalgia.

"Those houses look really ancient," Joanna said. "How come none of them are painted?"

I imagined the modest cottages looked very plain to her compared to the whale of a house her family rented.

I swallowed against the sick feeling that still teased me. "The houses are called the 'Unpainted Aristocracy,'" I said. "They're very old. They were some of the earliest cottages in the Outer Banks and people wanted to keep them just as they were. You know, preserve the history? My family has owned our cottage since the thirties."

"The nineteen thirties?" Joanna asked, and I knew that had to seem like ancient times to her. "Wow."

"Uh-huh."

I felt her gaze on me. "Are you homesick?" she asked. "You sound kind of sad."

"I *am* a little homesick," I admitted. I touched the screen lightly with a fingertip. "To me, this is the most beautiful place in the world." I smiled at her, but my eyes burned. If everything had gone as planned, she and I would be in that house right now, my baby and me. "But I'm happy to be here now," I said. "Sometimes you wish you could be in two places at once."

"Why didn't you stay there?" she asked. "Does it remind you too much of your husband who died?"

Because you're here, I thought. "Yes," I said. "Someday I'll be ready to go back, but not yet." How could I ever go back?

How could I ever leave her? Suddenly desperate for a change of topic, I touched the bracelet on her wrist. "This is so cute," I said. "Is it made of rubber bands?"

She lifted her hand to study the bracelet herself. "Gayla made it for me on her Rainbow Loom," she said. "It's my friendship bracelet."

"What's a Rainbow Loom?"

"I'll show you." She hopped off the bed, the dogs instantly on their feet, circling her legs, as if waiting to see what fun thing we had in store for them next. I watched as Joanna rummaged around in the lower drawers of her dresser as if she couldn't quite remember where she'd put the loom. Finally, she found what she was looking for and brought a narrow pegboard and a plastic case to the bed. She climbed back to her roost against the pillows, and the dogs settled down again on the floor.

"I haven't made one of these in forever." She opened the case to reveal about two dozen compartments filled with tiny colored rubber bands. "I'll show you how to make a simple bracelet," she said. "This one"—she held up her arm to show me the bracelet Gayla had made her—"is an inverted fishtail and it's way complicated, but I'll just show you how I make a plain old one."

She spent the next half hour demonstrating how to make a bracelet, this one in blue and pink. I watched her as she worked. My daughter. *Our* daughter. So extraordinarily beautiful. Her profile was perfection. Her nose had the tiniest bump at the bridge. Her lashes were pale but long, downcast right now as she threaded the bands over the pegs on her loom. Her lips were cherry colored, slightly parted, her white teeth visible. *We created her, Joey,* I thought to myself. *I wish you could see her.* I was tempted to lift my hand to her cheek. Run my fingers over the smooth, fair skin. But I kept my hands folded tightly together in my lap.

When she'd finished her bracelet, she slipped it on her unadorned right wrist. Then she put away the loom and rubber bands and asked me to paint her nails, assuring me that her mother would approve "as long as it's not black or something." We sat on her bed again and I held each of her hands steady while painting her short nails a pale lavender, treasuring every minute her fingers were in mine. Then she put music on her CD player and showed me a dance routine she and Gayla had performed at a talent show in their old school. She was a ball of energy, this daughter of mine, cramming as much activity as she possibly could into our few hours together before that nine o'clock bedtime.

"I'm not tired," she said, when nine finally rolled around. "Mom doesn't realize that I really got a lot of sleep last night." She was sitting on the chair at her vanity dresser by then while I stood near the door of the room, feeling like the mean mommy.

"Come on." I smiled at her lame attempt to weasel out of going to bed. "Don't get me in trouble with your parents."

"All right," she said, dragging herself from the chair as if her body was made of lead. "Maybe we can get a mani-pedi sometime," she said. "Mom's always too busy to take me."

"What's a mani-pedi?" I asked, and by the way she stopped walking and the look of disbelief on her face, I knew I'd asked an idiotic question.

"You know," she said. "It's when they do the manicure on both your hands and feet."

"Oh." I smiled, loving that she would want to do that with me. Loving that she wanted to do *anything* with me. "Why don't you ask your mother if that would be okay."

"All right," she said, trying to mask a yawn. She slithered under the covers and I resisted the urge to walk over, tuck her in, and give her a kiss on the forehead—all those things I would have been doing if she'd grown up being mine. "Turn on the night-light for me?" She pointed to the small red-haired princess-shaped night-light plugged into the outlet next to her dresser. "Please," she added. "I can't sleep in the total dark."

My chest tightened in sympathy as I turned on the little light. I thought of the first few months of her life when she'd slept under the bright lights of the CICU. Was that why she still needed light now? How else had those early months of pain and helplessness affected her?

I stepped back to the doorway and turned off the overhead light. "Good night," I said, the word barely making it past the knot in my throat. "I had fun."

"Me too," she responded, her voice muffled by the covers as she snuggled beneath them.

The dogs followed me downstairs and I let them outside for a few minutes, giving them treats I found in the pantry when they came back in, my actions mechanical. My mind was still upstairs in Joanna's bedroom. Then I went into the room the Van Dykes called the "family room" and tried to read the book I'd brought with me, but I couldn't concentrate. I set the book aside and went upstairs again, opening Joanna's bedroom door quietly to peek inside. She was sound asleep. The faint light from the princess nightlight dusted her blond hair where it spilled over her blanket. Her left hand with its stubby lavender nails was balled into a fist near her cheek.

Stepping back into the hallway, I shut the door quietly behind me. I intended to go downstairs again, but my knees suddenly gave out on me and I sank to the floor. Burying my face in my hands, I wept, overwhelmed by my daughter's preciousness. Overwhelmed by her very existence. Overwhelmed by everything I'd lost.

Back in the family room a while later, I didn't bother picking up my book again. Instead, I studied the floor-to-ceiling bookshelves that lined one wall. Were there photograph albums? I wanted to see pictures of Joanna's childhood— her growing-up years—even though I knew it was going to hurt to see those pictures that should have been mine. I could find no albums, though. I supposed they kept all their pictures on their computers these days. But I spotted a book that didn't seem to fit among all the others, and when I pulled it from the shelf, I realized it was a baby book. The design on the cover consisted of white polka dots on a pale blue background, and at an angle, in large navy blue and white striped letters, was the name *Joanna*. I carried the book to the couch and the dogs rested at my feet as I opened it. On the first page, Michelle's and Brandon's names were handwritten in the blanks for "parents." The names of strangers were in the blanks for "grandparents."

Did I really want to torture myself with this book? I thought, but my hand was already turning the page.

There was a "first photograph" of Joanna. Ten months old. She sat on what looked like a big white chair cushion wearing a sleeveless pink jumper. A hairband adorned with a pink bow was wrapped around her head, her pale hair almost invisible beneath it. She looked like she might be giggling, her cheeks pudgy, her chocolate eyes squinty with joy. I could see the tops of two tiny white teeth in her mouth.

Below the picture, there was an inscription in what I imagined to be Michelle's meticulous handwriting:

This is how you looked when we first brought you home.
You were so adorable!

Another photograph: Joanna standing in a blue dress, barefoot, holding on to the white picket of a fence, a stuffed zebra in her free arm. That same captivating little smile.

This is how you look a month after we brought you home.
You have five teeth and have started walking, already getting
into everything! Your favorite word is "Dada." Your favorite
food is blueberries and you make a mess with them!

The subject of the next page was "How We Found You."

We tried for years and years to have a baby. Then Mom got
very sick and had to have a hysterectomy and that was the
end of our dream of having a family, or so we thought.

I stopped reading for a moment. "Very sick." Cancer? Michelle seemed so vibrantly healthy to me and I hoped she was. No matter how much I wished Joanna were mine, I'd never want her to lose the only mother she'd ever known.

But we still longed to share our lives with a child, so we talked to agencies and social workers and one of them told us about you. When we heard about you, how you were a miracle baby who had surgery while still inside your birth mom, how you had to be in the hospital for a long time, and how you lost your mom and dad before you could even get to know them, our hearts filled with longing to take care of you and love you forever. That was even before we met you. When we met you, you reached for me (Mom) and cuddled up in my arms like you knew that was where you belonged. Daddy cried, he was so happy. We were instantly a family.

I shut my eyes, my chest and throat too constricted to continue reading. I was filled with both envy and gratitude, each emotion so strong it couldn't be crowded out by the other. Joanna had belonged in *my* arms, and yet I felt grateful to Michelle and Brandon for taking her. Accepting her and her damaged heart. Loving her.

I rested my head against the back of the sofa. I knew I could never take Joanna away from Michelle and Brandon. I couldn't take her away from her computer and her science and technology school and everything 2013 could offer her.

But I could stay here, couldn't I? I could stay in 2013. My

breathing quickened at the thought. Maybe I could get fake documents from Myra that would let me go back to college. I could earn a current degree in physical therapy. Get a legitimate license. Try to get the job I lied about wanting at Kessler or some other place nearby. I could build a life here that included my daughter, if only as a family friend. A *close* family friend.

The unbearable pain of never seeing Patti, Hunter, and John Paul ever again washed over me, but I swept it from my mind. I wouldn't let it in. It would derail me if I did.

Joanna would be in my life. If I stayed here, I would have my daughter. That was all that mattered.

51

I met the Vietnam vet and his wife over breakfast at the inn on Wednesday morning. We were the only three people eating that early and I sat across the table from them. The woman, Linda, who had to be at least sixty, was petite, chatty, and very cute, her hair dyed a vibrant reddish-purple that matched her personality as well as her V-neck T-shirt. By contrast Gary, her husband, was quiet, seemingly content to let her do the talking for them both. He was clean-shaven, his complexion very tan, almost ruddy, and set off by his thinning white hair. The skin around his eyes was lighter, as though he always wore sunglasses when he was outside. He had on a green and yellow short-sleeved Hawaiian shirt, and his left forearm was covered by a tattoo, too blurred by time and the furry gray hair on his arm for me to decipher.

They were in town to see Linda's family and spend some time in New York, Linda told me. "But the real impetus for our trip is Gary's reunion this coming weekend with other vets," she added. "Those boys have a tighter bond with one another than they do with their wives," she said with a smile. I was surprised to see her taciturn husband wink at her. They might have very different personalities, I thought, but clearly they got along.

I tried not to stare across the table at Gary as I ate Winnie's blueberry pancakes, but I caught my gaze drifting in his direction over and over again, wondering if Joe would look or act anything like him by now if he'd lived. Of course that didn't make sense. They were different men with different life experiences. Yet they had Vietnam in common, and if there was one thing I'd learned since coming to the future, it was that veterans from that war bore shared scars, whether physical or psychological. Gary caught me staring at him and he offered me a small nod I couldn't read. I wished I knew what his experience had been like, but it wasn't the sort of thing you could ask about out of context.

I took Poppy for her walk after finishing my work that afternoon. I still felt warm and happy at the memory of my time with Joanna the night before, yet I was anxious about my nascent decision to stay in 2013. The decision both terrified and thrilled me . . . and made me miserable every time I thought of Hunter and Patti and their confusion and grief when I never returned. They'd wait until I didn't show up on that last portal, many months from now, and then what? Would they have to report me missing? Go through the charade of an investigation? How would they explain not reporting my disappearance for so long? Would suspicion fall on them? I wanted to think through every possible ramification of my decision before I made it, but I always came back to the one certain fact: I would be living in the same world as my—and Joe's—daughter and that trumped any obstacles I could think of.

Poppy and I reached Rosewood Court at three thirty, as I'd planned, but I saw no sign of Joanna or her parents. There were no cars in the driveway, either, although I wasn't able to see the garage at the rear of the house. Then I remembered Brandon mentioning something about a family get-together as he drove me home last night. His brother-in-law's birthday party? Something like that. I imagined Joanna with Michelle and Brandon at that party now. I pictured her surrounded by aunts and uncles and cousins.

By bedtime, I was mired in depression. I wanted my daughter, damn it! I wanted her to be with me in Nags Head, with Patti and Hunter. It was where she belonged. Where *I* belonged. I didn't belong in Summit or in 2013. I pulled the covers up to my chin. Squeezed my eyes shut as I sank even deeper into depression. Only Poppy, pressed against me in bed, saved me from a brutal loneliness.

I threw myself into my work on Thursday, doing extra tasks around the inn to try to keep my mind off Joanna. I washed windows and laundered quilts in the inn's huge washer and dryer in the basement. I found a hundred things to do to keep me busy until three o'clock, when I could take Poppy for her walk.

My timing was perfect. Joanna and Michelle were getting out of the blue van in the driveway just as I began passing their house. Joanna dropped her backpack on the ground and ran over to me. Poppy jumped on her and I made the dog sit.

"Can Poppy play?" she asked.

"Is it okay with your mom?" I glanced at Michelle, who walked toward us, a bag of groceries in her arms, a welcoming smile on her face.

"We don't want to take advantage of you," she said, "but if you have time, Jobs could really use the exercise."

She thought *she* was taking advantage of *me*? "That would be great," I said happily. I looked down at my daughter. "Why don't we let them play for a little while and then do some training?" I suggested.

"Cool," she said.

So, I had my hour of bliss with my daughter until Michelle called her in to do her homework. Michelle walked with Poppy and me down the driveway and out to the sidewalk.

"I worry you'll start avoiding our street, thinking we'll drag you into the yard every time you pass by." She laughed.

"Poppy loves it," I said, amazed at how backward Michelle had it. "And Joanna's such a doll."

"She had fun with you Tuesday night," she said. "Thanks again for sitting. I think you're good for her." She looked over her shoulder toward the house, as if she could see Joanna through the exterior walls. "Yesterday she used her Rainbow Loom for the first time in ages," she said. "She pretty much gave it up when she got her phone and started texting every two minutes."

"Call on me anytime," I said. "I don't have friends here

yet and no obligations other than my job, plus Joanna's a pleasure to be with."

"Well"—she smiled—"if you're serious about that, we'll be going out again Tuesday night. Tuesdays are our date night and—"

"I'd be happy to," I interrupted. *How about every Tuesday night for the rest of my life?*

"She won't need a sitter much longer," Michelle said, as if reading my mind. "I have no problem leaving her alone during the day, but nighttime"—she shook her head—"not yet. Maybe when she's thirteen."

"That's just around the corner," I said, for something to say.

"Ugh, don't I know it." She wore a worried grimace, unconvincing given the smile in her eyes. "She already gets moody and grumpy and obstinate sometimes. I'm reading all the books on parenting teenagers that I can find."

"I bet you'll be good at it," I said, and I meant it. I only hoped I could play a part in those teenage years. I was determined to find a way to make that happen.

52

I woke up the following morning feeling strong about my decision to stay in 2013. I wondered if Myra might know of some way to get word to Hunter and Patti that I was okay? It seemed impossible, but so did traveling through time. I teared up, thinking about them. I wanted to let them know how much I loved them and would miss them, but that I needed to be with Joanna. I had to be close to her forever. That was all there was to it. Maybe someday, far in the future, I would even be able to tell her the truth.

Lying there, I thought of the things I needed to do. First and foremost, I had to get my courage up and contact Myra to ask for her help in getting me the false documents I needed. College transcripts, maybe? Could she possibly get me a fake degree in physical therapy? No, I thought. That would be akin to malpractice, since I had no idea what advances had been made in PT in the last forty years. But maybe I could already have an associate's degree. Shave a couple of years off the education I'd need. Hopefully I could still live and work at the inn while going to school. And what was I going to do about health insurance? I now understood what Obamacare was and I'd checked the application process on the library computers. I could never get it. They required a wealth of documentation, none of which I had. Employment records, tax returns. I couldn't ask Myra to provide all of that for me . . . though she *had* managed to get insurance for me when Joanna was born. Maybe she could get it for me again? Maybe I could just skip it? I was healthy and always had been, but my work as a physical therapist had taught me that you could be perfectly healthy one day and hit by a bus the next. I added insurance to my ever-growing list of things I needed to talk to Myra about. I also needed a credit card so I could buy my own computer. I was certain Myra could get the card for me, but this time I would tell her I'd pay my expenses myself. I wouldn't use Temporal Solutions money again, not that I had any illusion she'd offer it.

I got out of bed, grabbed the small notebook I'd started carrying around with me, and began writing down the things I needed her help with. I wouldn't call her until I was certain my list was complete, although I knew I was kidding myself. That was just a way to put off the phone call. The thought of it turned my stomach upside down. I would be asking her for a great deal to help me stay in 2013, when I was afraid she'd refuse to help me stay here at all.

That morning, I received my first paycheck from Winnie. What taxes could do to a four-hundred-dollar check was a shock, but it still left me with more money than I'd made for a week's work as a physical therapist in 1970 and I was grateful to have it. I opened a savings account, planning to sock away every penny of it except for what I needed for food and some thrift shop clothes.

Over the next few days, I walked Poppy every afternoon, but there was never a sign of life at Joanna's house. I thought of texting her, but Michelle had mentioned that they'd somehow arranged for Joanna's texts to go to Brandon's email account. "That was our agreement when we began letting her text," she'd told me. I didn't want Brandon seeing my texts to her. The idea of texting her felt a little creepy, anyway. A little stalkerish. If texting her felt inappropriate to me, I was certain Brandon would find it doubly so.

I babysat again for Joanna that Tuesday night while Michelle and Brandon went to the movies for their date night. Michelle was racing to get ready to meet Brandon at a restaurant when I arrived.

"Date night keeps a marriage healthy," she said as she applied lipstick in the foyer mirror. I saw her face quickly pale in the reflection. "I'm so sorry," she said, turning to me, touching my wrist. "I keep forgetting about your husband."

"It's all right," I reassured her.

"You seem so strong and independent and happy that I forget about . . . I forget what you've gone through."

"It's all right," I said again, thinking she couldn't begin to imagine what I'd been through. "And date night sounds like a great idea."

Especially if they called on me to babysit every time they went out, I thought.

Joanna came running into the foyer. "I have a surprise for you!" she said.

"You do?" I asked, delighted.

"She does." Michelle gave me a surreptitious wink. "You two have fun." She gave Joanna a kiss on the temple, then headed for the door.

"Come on," Joanna said, tugging my arm toward the stairs. "I'll show you the surprise."

The dogs had been rambunctious when I first arrived so we'd put them in the yard. Now I peeked out there to be sure they were all right before following Joanna up the stairs. She again wore what I guessed were pajamas, only this set had long pink pants and a short-sleeved pink and white polka-dotted top.

"Sit down," she commanded when we reached her room. She motioned toward her neatly made bed and I sat on the edge of it. With her back to me, she moved things around on her dresser top, then handed me one of those rubber-band bracelets. "I made this for you," she said.

This one was different from the others she'd shown me the week before, the bands almost disguised in a tight blue and green pattern.

"It's called the snake-belly pattern," she said. "It took me forever because the stupid bands kept breaking. Do you like it?"

"It's beautiful," I said, a little overwhelmed. My daughter had made me a friendship bracelet. "I love it." I slipped it over my wrist.

"It goes with your shirt," she said.

She was right. The blue was a perfect match to my T-shirt.

"Can you do a French braid on my hair?" she asked.

"I don't know what that is."

She proceeded to show me an elaborate hairstyle on some "beauty and hair" site on the internet. "Could you do this to my hair?" she asked. "It has directions."

I laughed. I was never any good with my own hair. In my teens in the late fifties and early sixties, I struggled to get my fine hair into a beehive and then a few years later, into a flip that always flopped within hours. I was so happy when the style changed to long straight hair. That I could manage.

"I can't promise anything," I said, studying the picture, "but let's give it a try."

I sat on her vanity bench and she dragged a beanbag chair across the room, sitting down on it in front of me. I spent the next half hour with my fingers in her hair, loving the intimacy of it, smiling every time I glimpsed my new friendship bracelet.

"You have lovely hair," I said. "It's perfect for this."

I laughed with her when I screwed up and cheered with her when I finally got it right. We both agreed the braid looked beautiful.

"Take my picture," she said, handing me her phone. I snapped a couple of shots of the back of her head and she texted one of them to her parents.

"Can you text it to me, too?" I asked. She did, and I heard the chirping sound on my phone where it rested in my jeans pocket.

"Let's do a selfie with both of us," she said, squeezing next to me on the vanity bench. We tipped our heads together as she held her arm out in front of us and snapped the picture.

"Awesome," she said, checking it out. She handed the camera to me to see.

Beyond awesome, I thought, looking at the screen. How could anyone look at this picture and not realize Joanna and I were related? The blond hair. The dark eyes. The pointed chins. It was so obvious to me.

"Want me to text it to you?" she asked.

"Yes," I said. "That's a great picture."

She hit a few keys on her phone. "Done," she said. "Let's see how it looks on your phone."

I pulled my prepaid cell phone from my pocket and she wrinkled her nose at the picture. "You need to get an iPhone." She spoke like a child who didn't know the meaning of the term "money problems."

"Someday," I said. "Do you know how or where I can get a print of this?" I asked. I missed the disposable camera I'd used in the nursery and wondered if they still made them.

"A print?" She looked at me as though it was a bizarre question. "You can just put it on your computer and . . . oh, I forgot." She rolled her eyes at the fact that I had no computer. "Never mind. I'll just make you a print." She sat down at her desk and I watched her pull up the picture of both of us on the computer screen, put some special paper in her printer, hit a few buttons. In a few seconds, she handed me a five-by-seven shot of the two of us.

"Thank you!" I said, impressed and, to be honest, thrilled that I now had a picture of us together.

"Oh, here, do you want to see pictures from my sleep-over?" Joanna asked, scrolling through other pictures on her computer screen.

"Of course," I said. I stood behind her as she showed me pictures of the innocent-looking preteen party in the tree house. I asked her to tell me about each of her friends and she seemed to enjoy filling me in on the seventh-grade gossip. Then she showed me pictures of Jobs as a puppy, and finally, a picture of a smiling dark-haired girl from her new school.

"She's a potential friend," she said.

"Really!" I said, pleased. "That's wonderful."

She turned around from her computer, though it looked as if it took some effort to tear herself away from her photographs.

"What should we do now?" she asked.

"Hmm," I said, sitting down on the end of her bed. I thought we may have worn out jacks. She hadn't mentioned them all evening, and the throw rug was back in place on her floor. "Have you ever played Spit?" I asked.

"What's Spit?"

"You're going to love it," I said. "But we need two decks of cards. Where can we find them?"

"Real cards?" She wrinkled her nose in disappointment.

"Real cards." I suddenly wondered if anyone played cards anymore in 2013. "I promise you. You'll like it."

"I think there's some in the family room," she said, and I followed her downstairs and into the room I'd come to think of as her Baby Book Room. My gaze instantly went to the bookshelf, where I could see the polka-dotted cover of the book that was filled with so much love for my little girl. Joanna dug around inside the cupboard beneath the bookshelf, finally producing two decks of cards, the packages still covered in plastic wrapping. Clearly, this wasn't a card-playing family.

"Should we play here?" She pointed to the carpeted family room floor, a distinct lack of enthusiasm in her voice.

"Uh-uh," I said. "We need a slick surface. How about the dining room table?"

In the dining room, we sat on the very edge of our chairs while I taught her how to play the fastest, liveliest, and most addictive card game I knew. Once Joanna got the hang of it, our cards flew all over the place as we battled each other, and I couldn't stop laughing at her unexpected enjoyment and killer instinct.

We played until Joanna's bedtime, which was nine thirty tonight. When we'd finished the last game, I started to gather the deck but she quickly stopped me, her hands on mine.

"No!" she said, a devilish grin on her face. "Wait here. Don't put them away."

She disappeared for a moment, then returned with a gold baseball cap, setting it on the table next to the cards. Across the front of the cap, embroidered in brown script, were the words MASSEY'S GOLF PARK.

I looked at the hat, then at her. "I don't get it," I said.

"Do you remember when Daddy said he'd eat his hat if I ever played cards with a real deck?"

I laughed. "Maybe you'd better let him off the hook on that one," I said.

"No way," she said, checking the arrangement of the cards and hat on the table. Once she was pleased with it, she told me good night and headed up the stairs to her room.

When Brandon and Michelle returned home a short time later, they laughed when I showed them the cards and the hat.

"That's my clever little girl," Brandon said with a smile, his arm around Michelle's shoulders.

I turned away quickly so they didn't see the tears in my eyes.

53

Wednesday morning, I found only Gary, the Vietnam vet, at the breakfast table when I came downstairs. He was reading the paper and he grunted a hello to me. If Linda had been there, she would have filled the room with her usual chatter—what they'd done the day before, the people they'd seen, the food they'd eaten. I hadn't heard more than a few words from Gary since their arrival. Yet he fascinated me. He was so connected to Joe in my mind.

I helped myself to a scone from the plate in the middle of the table and poured a glass of juice.

"Is Linda sleeping in this morning?" I asked him.

He glanced up from the paper. "Yeah," he said. "This is vacation for her and that woman loves some extra shut-eye."

"She still works?" I asked, then wondered if that was insulting. Maybe they weren't as old as I thought.

"She's a nurse," he said. "Works the night shift in the ER. She needs the time off."

"Oh, I bet," I said. He returned his attention to the paper. I wished I could really engage him but it was clear he wasn't interested, so I focused on eating my scone. I was nearly finished with it when Gary suddenly let out a guttural sound of annoyance.

"Disgusting," he said.

"What is?" I asked.

"Some asshole threw white paint on the wall."

"What wall?" I asked.

He frowned at me above the paper. "*The* wall," he said. "The Vietnam Veterans Memorial?"

"Oh," I said. "Where is that?"

He set the paper on the table next to his empty plate and stared at me. "Tell me you're kidding," he said, and I knew this was definitely something I should know.

"I just . . . I forget exactly where it is."

He shook his head slowly, his eyes narrowed to slits. "That's *exactly* the problem with this country," he said. "People your age don't give a shit about the past. About *history*. About the sacrifices my generation made so you could sit here in this pretty inn and be ignorant." His nostrils flared. "Do you know anything about the war in Vietnam?" he asked. "Anything at all?"

I was trembling, shaken by his outburst, and trying to hold in what I wanted to say. *Yes, I know about the war!* I wanted to shout. *I know even better than you do what it cost.* I was tired of keeping so much of myself hidden. If I stayed in 2013, this would be my life. I'd always be tiptoeing around the truth, unable to be open about who I really was.

"My uncle died in Vietnam," I said, turning Joe into an uncle I'd never had the chance to know.

The vet's eyes widened. "Where was he?" he asked. "What year?"

"Pleiku," I said, wondering if it seemed weird that I didn't know about "the wall" but I knew exactly where my "uncle" had been struck down. "Nineteen sixty-nine."

"Damn." He sat back from the table and studied me. "Then you should know about the wall, little girl," he said. "Your uncle's name is on it."

"His name is . . . ?" I pictured a white wall in a museum covered with small engraved placards bearing the names of fallen soldiers.

"Yes," he said, and he picked up the paper, folded it in half, and handed it to me. "That picture there at the top," he said. "The wall. In Washington, D.C."

It was hard to tell what I was looking at in the black-and-white photograph. I guessed it was a section of the wall he was talking about. It was gray or maybe black, and appeared to be outdoors. It looked as though a bucket of milk had been tossed over it.

"My uncle's name is on this wall?" I asked.

"If he was killed in Vietnam, yes, ma'am."

My heart pounded as I got to my feet and handed the paper back to him.

"You're right," I said, already halfway out of the room. "I need to learn about the wall."

I raced through my work that morning and when I took Winnie's car to buy groceries, I stopped first at the library. I sat down at one of the computers and typed "The Vietnam Wall" into Google. Hundreds of websites popped up. I read about the wall's creation. The controversy over the design, which seemed to go on for years. There were photographs of it, and it took me a minute to realize that what I first thought was a design in the glossy stone was actually engraved names. *Your uncle's name is on it,* Gary had said.

Oh my God. Joe's name was on a monument in Washington, D.C.

I folded my hands together. Pressed them to my lips. I needed to see his name. *Touch* his name.

I read on. People came from all over to make rubbings of their loved one's name on the wall, the article said. Could I make a rubbing of Joe's name? Something I could keep with me always?

I pushed away from the computer. Sitting back in my chair, I shut my eyes, not caring if anyone noticed that I had moved far, far away from the library and Summit, New Jersey.

I wanted to see Joe's name.

I had Monday and Tuesday off. I would go then.

I only wished I could take Joanna with me. I wished I could point to Joe's name on that glossy black wall and say to her, "This is your father."

I wished I could tell Joanna everything.

54

Mom says to ask can you come to dinner tonight.

I was walking down the stairs for breakfast the following morning when the text came from Joanna, and I stopped and leaned against the bannister. I read the few words over and over again, loving that she'd written to me, even if it had been at Michelle's request. And that in and of itself— Michelle asking me to join her family for dinner, as a guest, not as a babysitter or a provider of exercise for their dog—warmed my heart and gave me hope.

Love to, I texted back.

There's something funny.

What was she talking about? Something funny about me? Were they on to me? But seriously, how could anybody possibly be on to me?

Funny? I texted. It took me so long to text just that one word along with the question mark. I envied Joanna for how her fingers flew over the keys on her phone.

You'll see.

What time?

Hold on . . . She says 6:30.

See you then, I wrote, a big smile on my face.

After work, I walked into town, thinking I'd pick up some candy or something to take to the Van Dykes' tonight. With Joanna there, a bottle of wine wouldn't be appropriate. I was stewing over what to get when I noticed a tiny store tucked between a tailor shop and a shoe store. FRESH BARKED BISTRO. I'd seen the shop before and always read the small sign as FRESH BAKED BISTRO. Now I clearly saw that it read BARKED and there was a poster of a dog in the window. On a whim, I went inside, where I discovered a bakery devoted to pets. I couldn't begin to imagine such a thing in 1970. I spent half an hour admiring all the treats displayed in glass-fronted cases, as if this was a regular bakery. In the end, I bought a pretty display box with four adorable peanut-butter treats shaped and iced like a penguin, a cat, an owl, and a turtle. I hoped it made sense that my hostess gift was for Jobs and that I wasn't committing some major social faux pas.

With that errand taken care of, I stopped in a drugstore and bought a simple gold frame for the photograph of Joanna and me. I smiled as I imagined slipping the picture into the frame and placing it on the dresser in my little attic room. I'd see it when I woke up every morning.

Then I headed to the library to research the train schedule to Washington. I'd have to go back into New York to change trains, and then it would be three and a half hours to D.C. Three and a half hours and a lot of money. I googled hotels and the cheapest I could find that sounded safe and was within walking distance of the wall was a bit over one hundred and fifty dollars a night. This little trip was going to clean out the bank account I'd just opened and then some, but it was an absolute necessity. I wasn't even sure how I was going to wait until Monday to go. If I could, I would go right now. I was glad to have the invitation to the Van Dykes' for tonight to give me something else to think about.

The three Van Dykes were impressed by the dog treats. We were all in the large, always clean kitchen, the scent of beef stew rising from the Crock-Pot, when Joanna opened the box. The dogs clamored around her legs.

"They're really too cute to give to the dogs," Michelle said, peering into the box as she chopped cherry tomatoes in half.

Brandon poured himself a glass of red wine. "I bet Jobs'd like that turtle," he said.

Joanna looked up at me. "Can I take it?" she asked.

"Absolutely." I held the box steady so she could reach in and pull out the treat.

"You need to offer one to Poppy, too," Michelle said as Joanna lifted the turtle from the box. Joanna studied the treats for what seemed like a full minute before deciding that Poppy could have the penguin. We gave the cookies to the dogs and sent them out into the yard.

I wondered why I'd been invited to dinner here tonight. It seemed almost too good to be true. Being here with them, with Joanna, felt like a dream. This was what I wanted, to be part of Joanna's family. I couldn't believe it was becoming a reality so quickly.

Brandon set down the glass of wine and put his arm around Michelle's shoulders. "How can I help?" he asked.

I didn't hear Michelle's answer because I was too busy filling up with envy. Not that I wanted Brandon. I wanted *Joe's* arm around my shoulders. I wanted Joe to ask me how he could help. I just wanted Joe.

Together, the four of us finished making the salad, setting the table, filling glasses with water, dishing the savory stew into gigantic soup bowls, and carrying the bowls to the dining room table.

"So what's the 'something funny' you told me about?" I asked Joanna as we began to eat.

"You'll find out," she said mysteriously, and she and Michelle exchanged a smile.

"What are you guys talking about?" Brandon asked.

"Nothing," Joanna said, digging into her stew, and I realized I may have let the cat out of the bag.

"I'm going to Washington, D.C., Monday morning," I said to change the topic, "but I'll be home in time Tuesday to babysit."

"Yay!" Joanna said.

"Oh, that's crazy," Michelle said. "You can't go to Washington just for one day! Don't worry about sitting. We can get someone else."

"No," Joanna whimpered.

"I have to work Wednesday anyway, so it's fine," I said. "I'm just going to Washington to visit the Vietnam Memorial."

"Very moving," Brandon said with a solemn nod.

"Why there?" Michelle asked. "I mean, why make that long trip just for that one stop?"

"There's a Vietnam veteran staying at the inn," I said. "When I talked to him, I remembered a promise I'd made to my father that I'd go to the wall one day and make a rubbing of my uncle's name. My father's older brother. So that's what I'm going to do." Lies seemed to flow out of my mouth these days. It was almost as if I believed them.

"That's a really nice gesture," Michelle said, her voice sincere.

"That's the wall with all the soldiers' names on it?" Joanna asked.

"Right," Brandon said. "All the men—and women—who were killed in a war that never should have happened."

My jaw clenched. I'd come to agree with that sentiment, yet it hurt every time I heard it or read it.

"Is a rubbing like what you did on Poppop's grave?" Joanna asked Michelle.

"Exactly," she said.

"Do you remember when we went to the Air and Space Museum in Washington?" Brandon asked Joanna.

Her eyes lit up. "Totally!" she said, and she began telling me everything she saw and experienced in the museum. All the simulators she was able to use. All the exhibits she seemed to have memorized. She loved seeing the Wright Brothers' plane, and she told me nearly every detail about the exhibit of the Apollo 11 astronauts who walked on the moon. Hearing about that felt spooky to me, knowing I was the only person in the room who had seen that event live on television barely a year ago. Joe and I had watched it together. To Joanna, it was ancient history.

"We couldn't tear her away," Michelle said. "I swear, her birth parents must have been astronauts or something."

I smiled. *No,* I thought. *Just a physical therapist and a structural engineer.* God, how Joe would have loved this girl!

"Did you know that Kitty Hawk, where the Wright Brothers made their first flight, is only a few miles from where I lived in the Outer Banks?" I asked Joanna, intentionally using the past tense, curious to see how it felt. It didn't feel good or right and I nearly winced as the words left my mouth.

Joanna's eyes widened. "You're kidding!" she said. "That is so cool."

"The place they took off from is no longer a part of Kitty Hawk, though. It's now called Kill Devil Hills, and there's a monument there to mark the spot."

"That's another crazy name," Joanna said. "Tell them the name of your city. The horse name."

"Nags Head," I said. And then I went through the whole "how Nags Head got its name" story again. When I finished, Michelle stood up.

"I think it's time for dessert," she said.

I pushed back my chair to help clear the table, but Joanna stopped me. "You stay here with Daddy," she said. "Mom and I've got this."

Brandon gave me a shrug and we watched Michelle and Joanna whisk away the bowls and salad plates.

"They have something up their sleeves," Brandon said to me with a smile. "Been whispering ever since I got home."

In another minute, Michelle brought out a plate covered by a box. Joanna giggled at her side, a stack of dessert plates and forks in her hands. Michelle set the plate on the table in front of Brandon. With a flourish, she lifted the box from the plate to reveal a cake in the shape of a yellow baseball cap, "Massey's Golf Park" written in a shaky brown script on the crown.

I started laughing immediately, though it took Brandon another second to catch on. "Oh, good God," he said finally, grabbing Joanna around the waist and hugging her to him. "You two are crazy! Which one of you made this?"

"We did it together," Joanna said. "I frosted it but Mom did the writing."

Michelle handed Brandon a knife. "Hope you'll share," she said.

I was still chuckling as Brandon began cutting oddly shaped pieces of the cake, but before I knew what was happening, my laughter turned into tears.

"Why are you crying?" Joanna stared at me from her father's side at the head of the table, and Michelle and Brandon looked over at me.

I couldn't answer her. I wasn't even sure why my tears were falling. I felt overwhelmed with joy at being with my Joanna, seeing this family, witnessing their love, knowing my daughter was safe. At the same time, I remembered holding her, my tiny newborn infant, such a short time ago. She'd been trapped in a network of tubes and wires. I remembered her light weight in my arms. The scent of her. The feeling of her smooth temple against my lips. I thought of all I went through to give her life.

So worth it, all of it, I thought. *Even if she's no longer mine.*

Brandon had stopped cutting, the knife halfway through the cake, and all three of them stared at me.

"I'm all right," I reassured them, trying to smile. I scrambled for a way to explain my tears. "I'm just touched by this family," I said. "You're all so perfect."

"Oh, honey." Michelle laughed. "We are so not perfect! Nobody is."

"I don't mean 'perfect,' as in you don't ever make mistakes or . . . not that kind of perfect." I stumbled over myself. I couldn't possibly explain what I meant. What I meant was that if I had had to give Joanna up and could have handpicked a family for her to grow up in, I would have picked this family, where she was so perfectly loved.

"We are *totally* not perfect," Joanna agreed with her mother.

There ensued a good-natured listing of everyone's imperfections: Michelle was scatterbrained and spent too much money on yoga clothes, Brandon talked too much about work projects, which put other people to sleep, plus he burped too loud, and Joanna read in bed when she was supposed to be sleeping and she was lazy when it came to cleaning her room. They were the tamest of imperfections, presented with good humor and laughter. I was certain that, beneath the surface, there were shortcomings and failings, weaknesses and inadequacies, flaws that gnawed at each of them, heavier imperfections not fit for the ears of a guest. That was to be expected. But sitting there with the three of them, the cute cake hat ready to be devoured,

I found that all I wanted from them and for them was to be a happy, healthy family.

"Round up your dog and I'll drive you home," Brandon said, after the four of us had cleaned the kitchen and straightened the dining room.

"All right," I said, walking onto the deck. I called Poppy and she came running to me across the dark yard. Snapping on her leash, I headed toward the driveway where Brandon was once again covering the backseat of the car with a blanket. Poppy hopped in and I closed the door behind her, then sat down in the front seat.

Brandon was quiet as he turned the car around in the driveway and I spotted the dark tree house in the far corner of the yard, its windows picking up a glint of light from the deck.

"That tree house is amazing," I said, thinking the tree house was neutral conversational territory.

"I always wanted to build one." He turned onto the road. "My father built one for my siblings and me when I was a kid. Not as . . . high-end as this one." He chuckled, and I knew I'd picked the right topic. "But I wanted to build one for a child of mine. It was one reason I wanted us to buy this house. Michelle and I were only in our twenties back then, and when I saw this beautiful yard and all the trees. All the oaks . . . I knew this was it. The only problem was getting the kid to go with it." He glanced at me. "You think that'll be easy. 'Oh, we'll get married and have three kids.' And then it doesn't work out the way you planned." He drew in a breath and let it out as a sigh. "It was a tough time. Then we finally got Joanna and I started building."

"How long did it take you?"

"To get it to the state it is now? A couple of years of pretty intense weekends and evenings." I could see his smile as we passed beneath a streetlight. "She loves it," he continued. "Someday she'll outgrow it. Or more likely, she'll turn it into a make-out den or something." He laughed, lost in memory, I thought. "That's what I did with mine, anyhow."

"I think you're a good dad," I said sincerely.

"Thanks," he said. We were at a stop sign and he looked directly at me. "I didn't trust you at first, you know," he said.

Of course I knew, but I played dumb. "What do you mean?" I asked.

He pressed the gas and we started moving again. "When you adopt a child, you're always afraid," he said. "Afraid that child is never truly, one hundred percent yours and that someday, someone will come and take her away. The way you just showed up . . . And you look like her." He shook his head. "Rationally, I know her parents are dead, plus you're not old enough, but I thought you might be a long-lost, much older sister or an aunt or . . . I don't know. Related in some way. It scared me and I didn't trust you." He glanced at me. "Sorry if I was a jerk to you."

"You don't have anything to apologize for." I felt so guilty. I'd won him over under false pretenses.

"I didn't want you around her," he continued, "but Michelle told me I was crazy, and she was right. You're good for her. I can imagine you becoming an older mentor type of friend to her. Jo has a lot of pressure in her life, from her school and from us. Everything at her school is tough. All the science and math." We'd reached the inn and he pulled into the driveway. "What other kid names her dog after Steve Jobs, for Pete's sake?" He laughed, and I heard his love for Joanna in the sound. "Thanks for giving her a little balance."

"She's giving me some balance, too," I said, my throat tightening again as I opened the car door. "And thanks for the ride. I'll see you Tuesday night."

My tears started again as soon as I began walking up the sidewalk to the inn with Poppy. I was thinking about Joe. He would have been this same kind of father as Brandon, I thought. Protective. Loving. Kind.

If he'd only had the chance.

55

I was up early Monday morning for the long train trip to Washington. I should have been tired, but I was too geared up for the day ahead. I only had my backpack with me— Hunter's old backpack, which I washed in Winnie's washing machine but which still looked pretty grimy. I didn't need much. Just my nightgown and toiletries, two bottles of water, two apples, two of Winnie's scones, and a plastic bag of almonds. As the miles zipped by, though, I began to think I should have brought a suitcase with me. How was I going to carry the rubbing of Joe's name in a backpack without destroying it?

I imagined making that rubbing. I'd read that if the name was up too high, a park ranger would make the rubbing for you, but I hoped Joe's name was low enough for me to do it myself. I needed to touch his name. It was crazy how much I needed to do that. For other visitors to the wall who'd lost loved ones, the loss would be old. For me, it was fresh and new and terribly, terribly raw.

I arrived in Washington a little after eleven and found a taxi outside the train station. I asked the driver to take me to the memorial, so I was surprised when he tried to drop me off in an area that looked like a park. He must have misunderstood me.

"I want the Vietnam Memorial," I said. "The wall."

"This is it," the man said, pointing. "Can't see it from the street. Just follow that path."

I paid him, got out of the taxi, and fell into step with several other people who were walking along the path, the sound of traffic fading behind us.

I'd seen pictures of the wall online, but nothing prepared me for seeing it in person. It was a deep scar in the earth and looked like a long black mirror reflecting the puffy white clouds, the blue sky, the trees and grass. It reflected the things people left at its base—small flags and stuffed animals and photographs. And it reflected the faces of the people who stood in front of it, looking, pointing, weeping.

It reflected me.

The wall grew taller as I walked. It grew and grew until it overwhelmed me with all the thousands and thousands and thousands of names engraved on its surface. I couldn't wait to see Joe's name. He'd believed in his country. He'd believed he was doing the right thing when he left for Vietnam. He deserved to be honored on this wall.

I scanned the surface of the wall as I walked, even though I knew that spotting Joe's name among fifty-eight thousand others was impossible without some guidance. I knew there was a register at the end of the walkway that would tell me where to look, but I tried to slow down. I didn't want to rush hungrily to the wall to look for his name. I felt a duty to pay respect to all the men whose names rose above me as I walked.

There were two registers at the end of the walkway, both in use at that moment. A park ranger—a woman in a broad-brimmed straw hat—stood between them. She offered me a somber-looking smile as she motioned me toward one of the registers, and I queued up behind a man and woman who were jotting something down from the book. I clutched my hands together in front of my chest, feeling both anxious and excited. *It's only his name,* I reminded myself. *Not him.*

It was my turn. I knew the book was in alphabetical order and I quickly paged through it looking for the *S*s. I found a Benjamin Sears and a Devon Sears, but no matter how hard I stared at the page, there was no Joseph Sears.

"I don't understand," I said, looking over at the ranger.

She walked toward me. "Need some help?" she asked.

"I must be doing this wrong," I said. "It's alphabetical, right? I'm trying to find my uncle, Joseph Michael Sears, but he's not here."

I stepped aside to let her look herself. "Here's a Joseph Spears," she said. "Could that be him?" I looked where she was pointing.

"They got his name wrong," I said, my heart aching, my hands again clutched at my chest. Then I saw Joseph Spears's birthdate. "This isn't my hus . . . my uncle's birth-date. My uncle was twenty-six. This guy was . . . twenty."

"Come with me to the kiosk," the ranger said. "I have some other ways of checking."

Please, please, please, I thought as I walked silently next to her down the path. *Please don't take this honor away from him.*

At the kiosk, the ranger told me to wait in front of the glass window while she stepped inside. "Now let me check a different way," she said from her side of the window. She began tapping keys on a computer. "Joseph Sears, right?"

"Right."

"Birthdate?"

"January 8, 1943."

"Army or . . . ?"

"Army."

"Hm."

I could tell she wasn't having any luck. I dug the nails of my right hand into the palm of my left.

She glanced up at me. "Do you by any chance know when he was killed?" she asked.

"November 28, 1969."

The ranger pressed a few keys. Frowned at her screen. "Maybe you need to check on his name," she said. "Talk with your relatives. Maybe Joseph was his nickname and—"

"It was *not* his nickname!" I snapped, angry now. "He deserves to be on that wall!"

"I'm sorry, miss," the ranger said calmly. "This happens sometimes. You think you have the correct information, but—"

"Who do I contact about this?" I asked. "How do I make this right?"

She stared at me for a moment. Then she gave me a brochure about the wall, circling an email address at the bottom of the last page. "Try contacting them," she said. "I'm sorry we didn't have any better luck."

I left the kiosk, heartsick, and headed back toward the wall. This was so wrong. I would do whatever it took to get Joe's name up there where it belonged.

I walked the length of the memorial again, thinking I would keep walking until I reached my hotel. I needed to work off my anger and disappointment. This time, I didn't even glance at the wall or the thousands of names or the reflection of myself as I walked. I was too upset.

"Miss!"

I turned to see the ranger coming toward me at a trot. I stopped walking and she caught up to me, a slip of paper in her hand.

"I think I found him," she said. "He's not on the wall because he wasn't killed."

"But he was," I said.

She shook her head, handing me the paper. "He was a POW," she said. "Prisoner of war. He came home in February of '73."

I stared at the paper where she'd written *Joseph M. Sears, POW, 2/12/1973* and my knees threatened to buckle. I grabbed her arm.

"Miss?" she asked. "Are you all right?"

"This is impossible," I said, letting go of her arm, testing my balance to be sure I wasn't going to keel over. "They told us—my family, I mean—that he was killed."

She nodded in sympathy. "Every once in a while, there's a mistake," the ranger said matter-of-factly. "It's rare, but it happens. I checked another source to verify this information, though. He definitely came back in '73." Her expression turned quizzical. "I wonder how come you didn't know that?" she asked.

"I . . . I don't know," I said. My mind was racing too quickly to come up with a lie. Joe came home? He *came home?*

"I guess it's possible no one knew, if he kept to himself," the woman mused. "Some of those guys were in pretty rough shape after spending years as POWs and each of them had to find a way to deal with what happened to them. Maybe that's your uncle's story. Maybe he . . . moved away, or . . ."

I wasn't listening. Muttering my thanks, I turned and continued walking past the wall, then along the sidewalk, and then all the way to Union Station. It took me an hour, but I was so lost in thought that I didn't notice the time. All I knew was that I needed to get back to Summit. Back to my little room with the picture of Joanna and me on the dresser. Back where I would burrow into my now familiar narrow bed and figure out what I needed to do next.

Waiting for the train, I wanted nothing more than to go home. Home to 1970. Home to Patti and Hunter. Home where I would wait for two and a half years with a frightened but full heart, knowing Joe would be coming back to us. Back to *me*. He would need me. *Some of those guys were in pretty rough shape,* the ranger had said.

What had he gone through? What was he *still* going through in 1970? Were they torturing him? Was he injured? He was suffering greatly, of that I had no doubt.

It broke my heart to imagine. And yet . . . and yet he'd lived. He'd lived to come home.

I remembered that TV interview Joe and I had seen with a young soldier who'd been a prisoner of war in South Vietnam. He'd lived in a cage. Had been fed only rice. He'd alluded to torture so terrible he couldn't talk about it. I began to cry as I waited in line for the train, ignoring the glances of the people around me. Joe had turned off the interview, reassuring me that he'd be fine. He'd be nowhere near the fighting, he said.

A few weeks later, he was dead.

Only he wasn't.

I thought of Joanna. Our beautiful little girl. She was a self-confident child, far more so than I had been at twelve. Bright and cheerful. She was loved and treasured by her family. And she was loved and treasured by *me*, however quietly. However secretly.

But she didn't need me. Not the way Joe would.

How high, I wondered, was the tree house in Joanna's yard?

56

"I'm furious with you!" Myra said as soon as I identified myself on the phone. It was nearly eleven o'clock Monday night and I was back at the Sleeping Dog Inn, sitting cross-legged on my bed. "Beyond furious!" she shouted. "You abused my trust, Caroline, as well as Hunter's. You abused Temporal Solutions. Where the hell are you? What have you been doing?"

I wouldn't let her intimidate me. "I'm in New Jersey," I said. "I had to find my daughter. I had to know what had become of her."

She said nothing and I imagined her mind was reeling.

"Are you still there?" I asked. I was afraid of her hanging up on me. I needed her.

"I *told* you what became of your daughter," she said. "She was adopted. That was all you needed to know."

"Maybe that would have been all *you* needed, but I needed more," I said. "I needed to see for myself that she was fine."

"And?"

"She is. She's better than fine." I wondered if she heard the crack in my voice on the last word.

"Have you . . . you didn't interact with her, did you?"

"Yes."

Again that silence. I bit my lip, waiting.

"Mistake," she said.

"No, it's been all right," I assured her. "It's been good. Wonderful, actually."

"I should *never* have taken you on in the first place. Hunter should have known better than to send you to me. I should have sent you right back to 1970. Let nature take its course with your baby."

I sucked in my breath. "How can you say that?" I asked. "She's a beautiful, bright girl with a tremendous future ahead of her, and she only exists because you helped me."

She ignored my statement. "What do you want from me now?" She sounded suddenly tired.

"I want to go back to 1970."

"Well, finally!" Myra said. "That I will gladly help you do. That and only that. You need to go back to 1970 and stay there where you belong. Do you know of a stepping-off place?"

"Possibly," I said. "It's not over water, though, and—"

"Screw the water!" she snapped. "Where's the place?"

"It's a tree house."

"A tree house! Well, that's a first. How high is it?"

"I don't know exactly, but I think the second story is at least sixteen feet."

"Measure it to be sure."

"I will."

"I'll need the exact location," Myra said. "Where is it? I'll have to be able to find it on the satellite map for you to be able to use it."

I remembered seeing Joanna's yard on the satellite map when I was first looking for her house. I didn't remember seeing a tree house at that time, but I hadn't been looking for one, either.

"The address is 477 Rosewood Court in Summit, New Jersey," I said.

"How did you ever find her address?" she asked.

"It doesn't matter."

"Let me pull up the satellite while I have you."

I waited. I could hear the click of her computer keys.

"Hmm, I don't see . . . Ah, maybe that's it? In the southeast corner of the yard?"

"Yes," I said, relieved.

"All right," she said. "I'll work out the coordinates and look for portals. You want to go to Nags Head, correct?"

"Yes. Jockey's Ridge."

"When can you measure the height of the tree house?"

"Tomorrow night," I said. I would find a way to do it while I babysat. "And if you could make it—the travel—in a couple of weeks, that would be ideal." I wasn't ready to walk away from my daughter. Not yet.

She paid no attention to my request. "If you discover it's not at least sixteen feet above the ground," she said, "let me know right away."

"All right," I said. "And thank you."

She hung up without another word.

57

I bought a yardstick at a downtown hardware store the following morning. I thought Joanna and I could use it as
some sort of training tool with the dogs when I babysat
tonight and that would give me an excuse for bringing it
along with me. The Van Dykes surely had a tape measure
somewhere, but I didn't want to have to dig around for
one. I would wait until Joanna was asleep, then slip outside
and measure the height of the tree house as accurately as
I could with the yardstick. I played the plan out over and
over in my mind.

At two o'clock, though, my plan fell apart when Michelle
called to tell me they'd decided to go to a "family friendly"
movie, so they wouldn't need a sitter.

"I'm so sorry to call you at the last minute like this," she
apologized. "We didn't realize this movie was still playing,
and Joanna's been dying to see it."

I waited a couple of seconds, hoping she'd invite me to
join them, but it was clear that was not her intention. *You
are not a part of this family,* I reminded myself.

"I'll still pay you, of course," she said.

"No, no," I said quickly. "It's no problem. Enjoy the

movie." I was disappointed I wouldn't be able to see Joanna tonight, but the change of plans would make measuring the height of the tree house easier, since no one would be home.

Figuring the movie would start around seven o'clock, I left the inn at six forty-five, Poppy at my side. It was still light enough—barely—for me to see where I was going, but that would quickly change and I carried a flashlight in my purse and the yardstick over my shoulder. By the time I reached 477 Rosewood Court, I needed the flashlight to illuminate my path up the driveway. Opening the gate to the dark backyard, I winced when it let out a squeak, hoping no neighbors would see my light and wonder who was snooping around the Van Dykes' house.

I let Poppy off the leash and she immediately sped to the back door, barking her head off, looking for Jobs, I supposed. I probably should have left her at the inn; she was only going to be in my way here. I called her to my side and to my surprise, she fell into a heel next to me. I'd trained her better than I thought in my short time in Summit. Illuminating my way across the yard with the flashlight, I reached the tree house where I put Poppy on a down-stay. I set the yardstick against the tree and measured the height from the ground to the first story as carefully as I could, then I climbed the stairs and measured the height from the floor of the first story to the ceiling before ascending the circular stairway. On the deck of the second story, I measured the height of the railing. Nineteen feet, almost exactly. Pulling my phone from my jeans pocket, I texted *19'1"* to Myra.

Almost instantly, my phone chirped. *Excellent,* she wrote.

I put away my phone, then shined the flashlight toward the ground where Poppy was now standing. She looked up at me, tail spinning through the air in crazy circles, tongue hanging out. I gulped at how small she seemed. How far away. It was a long way down there, with no water below to catch me if something went wrong. Maybe this was a mistake. Maybe I should search for a bridge over water somewhere.

I was halfway down the stairs when Poppy suddenly swung her head toward the house and I heard the slamming of car doors. *Damn.* It had never occurred to me that they might have gone to an earlier movie. Quickly I descended the rest of the stairs, stumbling down them, wrenching my shoulder as I caught myself on the railing.

"Poppy," I called as softly as I could. I held out her leash, but she ignored me, running toward the back of the house and up the deck steps. I followed her across the yard and onto the deck quickly, but I was too late. Lights came on, illuminating the deck and the yard close to the house. Illuminating *me.* The back door opened and Jobs leaped onto the deck and the dogs began chasing each other, sailing off the deck and spinning like whirligigs across the yard.

Brandon stepped onto the deck.

"Carly!" He stopped short when he spotted me. "What are you doing here?"

I trembled all over, guilt and nerves getting the best of me. I offered him a sheepish smile, keenly aware of his gaze on the yardstick I held at my side. "I'm so sorry to trespass," I said, my mind racing. "I was talking to my cousin this afternoon and told him about your tree house and he asked if I could get some measurements for him. He wants to build one." I had no idea where that ridiculous story came from. It poured out of my mouth of its own accord.

Brandon simply stared at me. "Where does your cousin live?" he asked finally.

"North Carolina," I said.

"Did you get your measurements?"

"I did," I said. "I'm all set. How was the movie?" I added, hoping to get the conversation off me.

"Joanna and I liked it," he said. "Michelle nearly fell asleep. We dropped Jo over at a friend's to work on a project."

"Oh," I said, then added weakly, "Well, I'm glad you and Joanna enjoyed it." I called Poppy to my side and clipped her leash to her collar, feeling Brandon's eyes on me the whole time. "I'm sorry for just barging into your yard," I said, starting for the gate.

"Where did you write down the measurements?" Brandon asked.

I stopped walking. "All up here." I smiled, tapping my head. *Ridiculous answer*, I told myself, and Brandon stared at me with narrowed eyes. He didn't believe a word I'd said. In the last few minutes, I was quite certain I'd ruined the fragile relationship I'd created with him.

"Hold on a sec and I'll drive you back to the inn," he offered.

"Oh, no, thanks," I said, heading for the gate again. He'd

be full of questions I didn't want to answer. "I love walking this time of night. So peaceful." I waved as I neared the gate. "Tell Joanna I said 'hi,'" I said, and I escaped before he could say another word.

58

My phone rang as I was making one of the guest beds the
following morning, and I pulled it from my pocket to
check the display. Myra. I'd texted her earlier, telling her
I was going to look for a different stepping-off point. I
couldn't do it without water below me. She hadn't texted
me back. I quietly closed the door of the bedroom and
lifted the phone to my ear.

"Hello?" I said.

"You're leaving tonight," she said as greeting.

"What? No!" I said. "Didn't you get my text? I can't use
the tree house, and tonight is way too soon. I have to . . . I
have to give notice at my job." *And spend more time with my
daughter.* "I'll look for a bridge this after—"

"You'll leave tonight," she said, as though I hadn't
spoken. "Ten twelve, off the center of the top railing on
that tree house. You'll arrive in Nags Head in the early
morning hours. It's a perfect portal."

Panic rose in my chest. "Please, Myra," I pleaded.
"Could you give me another week at least?"

She let out a ragged-sounding sigh. "First of all, the tree
house turns out to be ideal. You know you're not going to

splat on the ground, Caroline. You need to stop being a baby. Second of all, you're not sticking around any longer. You've already caused me enough grief. You're leaving tonight."

I sat down on the edge of the half-made bed. My hunger to see Patti and Hunter and Joe was matched only by my need to have more time with Joanna, but I knew this portal would have to do. Myra held all the cards.

"All right," I said, my heart heavy. "All right," I repeated. "I'll go."

I had a lifetime of memories crammed into a few months and they were all I could think about as I did my chores in the inn. I remembered the fetal surgery and all the hope I'd poured into it. All that hope for a healthy baby I could take home with me to North Carolina. I remembered those months in New York when I'd been on bed rest. The kindness of Raoul and Ira and Angela. Then taking care of my sick baby in the CICU, pouring every ounce of my love into that little fighter, watching her reach milestone after milestone until she was nearly ready to leave. Then losing her through a slip in time. Did I go through all of that for my sake or hers? I wondered. The answer was easy. I did all I could for her. Now I had to give her to the future where I knew she truly belonged.

I wished I could see her one last time, yet I knew it was impossible. She stayed late at school on Wednesday afternoons, and after my weird behavior in the Van Dykes' yard last night, I couldn't imagine facing Michelle or Brandon again. Besides, seeing her one more time would only bring me pain.

Instead, once I was back in my attic room, I wrote her a note on a sheet of Sleeping Dog Inn stationery.

Dear Joanna,

I'm afraid I have to leave Summit unexpectedly. Getting to know you has been such a pleasure. You're a wonderful girl and I know you have an amazing future ahead of you.

I'll miss you very much.

Love, Carly

I sat on my narrow bed, reading and rereading the dry, vague little note, knowing that the truth lay between the lines. In my mind, I rewrote it:

You are my child, Joanna. My baby. I'll always remember how you and I fought the battle for your survival together. I'll remember all you endured when you were just a little thing. The way you'd look into my eyes when I held you in my arms. The way you wrapped your tiny hand around my finger while you were tethered to the machines that kept you alive. I'll never forget the surprise of your first smile, how despite all you were enduring, you felt happiness. I would have done anything to save you, Joanna. Anything to give you the joy-filled life you deserve. And that's why I'm leaving you here, my darling daughter, giving you a future I can never be a part of. But I promise

you this: I'll think about you every minute of every day
and carry you in my heart always.

I shut my eyes, tears slipping down my cheeks. When I opened my eyes again, I reached for the envelope on the top of my dresser. I looked at my blue and green rubber band bracelet as I slipped the trivial little note into an envelope and wrote Joanna's name and address on the front. I would wear that bracelet every day for the rest of my life.

59

I hated leaving Winnie in the lurch. I couldn't handle a conversation with her about why I was going; I would only get tangled up in lies. As I did with Joanna, I wrote her a note, leaving it on the table in the kitchen where she would see it first thing in the morning. I apologized for leaving so abruptly and thanked her for the job and for her kindness. *I need to leave quickly,* I wrote, *but I'm fine. You don't have to worry about me.* There was simply no way to give her more of an explanation. I told her I'd miss her and Poppy, and I would.

I hugged Poppy good-bye. She'd been "my dog" for only a few weeks, but I'd come to love her. I hoped Winnie would hire a housekeeper who would also take on Poppy's care. Someone like me, only . . . less encumbered. Someone fully rooted in the here and now.

I packed my few belongings, including the framed picture of Joanna and me, into Hunter's backpack, then set out to walk the mile to Joanna's house. Between the streetlights and faint moonlight, I didn't need to use my flashlight. I had almost an hour before I needed to step off and I carried more pain in my heart than I thought it could bear. *Joanna's fine,* I told myself. *She doesn't need me. Joe will.*

I stood on the sidewalk in front of Joanna's house. None of the downstairs lights were on, at least not in the front of the house, but as I felt my way toward the backyard, I could see that the windows of Joanna's room were filled with a dim light, more than her princess night-light would have produced. She was supposed to be well asleep by now, but I had the feeling she was either reading in bed or on her computer. I hoped she was deeply engrossed in whatever she was doing. The only lights burning other than Joanna's were faint, somewhere in the interior of the house. I was safe.

The hazy moonlight reached the yard in irregularly shaped patches and I took small steps, remembering the shrubs and flower beds dotting the perimeter that I didn't want to trip over or crash into. I scanned the distance ahead of me for the tree house, but couldn't make it out at all. I dared to turn on the flashlight for a moment, just long enough to see that I was still quite a distance from it. Turning out my light, I continued picking my way across the lawn. When I thought I was near the tree house, I turned on the light again to cover the last few yards and locate the steps, then I quickly turned it off again. I stumbled a bit climbing the stairs without the light . . . or maybe it was my fear that made me lose my footing. Or the deep, deep sadness I was trying to hold at bay.

I reached the second-story deck and shined the light briefly at the hard ground far below. Sweat broke out across my back beneath my light jacket and the backpack.

If only there was water down there! How was I going to get the courage to step off? I had to do it, though. There was no alternative. I glanced at my chronometer. I had ten minutes to stew about this. That was all.

I turned on my flashlight to quickly locate one of the deck chairs and turned it off again, setting it carefully on the deck as I moved the chair into place below the railing.

"Carly?"

I jumped at the sound of Joanna's voice from the yard below. *Damn it.* "Joanna?" I asked, even though I knew perfectly well that was Joanna down there. I found the flashlight on the deck and shone it toward the ground. She put up an arm to cover her eyes.

"What are you doing up there?" she asked.

"I . . ." I couldn't think of a thing to say to explain why I was in the tree house. All I knew was that I had to get her back in the house, someway, somehow, and I needed to do it quickly.

"Why are you here?" She left the circle of my flashlight and I heard her on the tree house stairs.

"Don't come up here, honey," I said, as her footsteps grew closer. "Please," I pleaded. "Just go back in the house."

"Dad said you were here last night, too," she said as she reached the deck where I was standing. I could see a glint of moonlight in her eyes. "What's going on?"

"I really need to be alone right now, Joanna," I said. "I'm sorry. I know it seems odd that I'm up here, but I thought it would be a good place to come and think. Do you mind going back into the house?"

She didn't budge. Her pale hair shimmered in the

moonlight and I fought the urge to reach out and smooth my hand over it.

"You're acting weird," she said. She was close enough that I could smell that shampoo scent she always carried with her, and my heart began to break. I reached for her, unable to stop myself. Pulling her to me, I buried my face in her hair.

"I love you," I said.

She stiffened beneath my arms, squirming away from my embrace. "I love you, too," she said, "but I don't get what's going on."

I looked at my chronometer.

Five minutes.

I was about to disappear right before my daughter's eyes. I had to tell her something. Give her some sort of explanation.

I had to tell her the truth.

"Listen to me, Joanna," I said, pressing my hands together. "This will be very hard for you to believe, but please try. Please just listen and try to understand what I tell you."

"Tell me *what*?" She was growing frustrated.

"I'm your birth mother, sweetheart." I reached out to touch her arm. "But it's very compli—"

"What?" She said the word so quietly I barely heard her. She jerked her arm away from my touch. "My birth mother is dead."

"Listen to me," I pleaded again. "I only have a few minutes to explain. I'm your mother. I promise you that. But I came here from 1970. I'm time-traveling, which I know sounds impossible, but I really am. I was pregnant with you in 1970, but you had that problem with your heart when you were inside me and I—"

"Stop it!" She took a step away from me. She put her hands over her ears. "Stop saying—"

"*Listen* to me," I said again. "Just listen. I found out I could have fetal surgery if I came to 2001 and that's what I did. And then . . . it's so complicated!" I blew out my breath in frustration. "I had to go back to 1970 for a few days and when I tried to return to 2001, I accidentally landed in 2013. I didn't realize it at first. I thought it was still 2001 and I tried to find you in the hospital where I'd left you, but then I discovered it was 2013 and . . ." I choked up. "I was devastated," I managed to say.

"Mom!" Joanna shouted toward the house.

"No, don't call!" I grabbed her arm, but quickly let go. "I had to try to find you and finally I did," I said, hurrying on. "And Joanna? You know how I went to Washington to look for the name of my uncle on the Vietnam Memorial Wall? That wasn't my uncle I was looking for. It was your *father* Joe Sears."

Joanna's eyes glistened with tears and I knew they had nothing to do with "Joe Sears" or even with me. They had everything to do with the terror I was creating in her. Still, I had to continue.

"I thought he—your father, Joe—was killed in Vietnam, but at the wall I discovered that he'd lived. That he was a prisoner of war and would be coming home . . . and I realized I have to be there to help him. I have to go back to 1970 and wait for him to come home."

"Oh my God!" She grabbed the deck railing. "You are insane!"

"I needed to find you to know you were all right, and you are," I said. "You're so much better than all right, and much as I love you and want to be in your life, I think Joe is going to—"

"Mom!" Joanna shouted again toward the house, her voice frantic. "Mom! Dad! Help!"

Oh, God. I was terrifying her. I looked toward the house. In one of the upstairs rooms, a light flashed on. "Shh, honey!" I said, glancing at the chronometer. Less than a minute. "I'm sorry, I'm sorry. I know this is overwhelming. Just believe me when I say I love you. I'll always love you."

"Daddy, help!" she shouted again.

"Listen to me. I have to step off the deck—the railing— of the tree house. It's—"

"What?"

I climbed onto the chair, squatting on the seat, holding on to the railing in front of me. "Don't be afraid," I said. "I know it sounds scary but it's not. It's all right. I've done this before." *Over water,* I thought. *I've done it before over water.*

"Are you drunk?" Joanna asked. "Did you take some kind of drug? Please get off the chair!"

She reached for my arm and I shook it off. Someone turned on the rear deck light. I was crying now, barely able to see the time on the chronometer. Rising to my feet on the chair, I leaned over to clutch the railing as I lifted one foot, then the other, onto the narrow length of wood.

"Stop!" Joanna shouted. She was crying hard, terrified.

"I'm sorry I said you're insane. I'm sorry, I'm sorry! Just come down, Carly! Please!"

"I love you," I said, one more time, and as I stepped off I heard her scream.

"Mom!" she wailed.

But I knew I was not the mother she was calling for.

60

NAGS HEAD

Cold. My body trembled with it and I couldn't seem to move. Water filled my mouth. *Salty.* I swallowed, then began choking. I lay on my stomach, gasping for breath. Fighting for the strength to raise my head from the ground. No, not the ground. *Sand. Water.* The ocean? Yes! It roared in my ears. It washed over my body, pushing me forward a few inches, pulling me back. I coughed, struggling in the dark to get to my hands and knees. I crawled forward, away from the water, the straps of the backpack cutting into my shoulders. Winded after a few feet, I turned around and sat down, lowering myself to my elbows, my backpack the only thing keeping me from sinking onto my back with exhaustion. In front of me, moonlight speckled the sea and the white crown of the waves rushed toward me. What time was it? I lifted my hand to look at the chronometer. Four twenty-seven, but I could see that the second hand had stopped.

Myra! Had she put me in the water on purpose? My thinking began to clear. I'd asked her to let me land on the dunes. Instead, she'd nearly drowned me on the beach. I looked at the chronometer again. It had definitely stopped. I had no idea of the exact time.

Worse, I had no idea of the exact *year*.

I struggled to my feet. To my left, perhaps a quarter mile away, the familiar Nags Head pier caught the moonlight. I was less than a mile from home. I turned around, kicked off my soggy sneakers, then began walking on the cold damp sand toward the Unpainted Aristocracy.

And toward, I prayed, 1970.

61

Hunter

John Paul had one of those stuffy fall colds that wouldn't let him sleep. Patti had been up with him at ten and again at midnight, so now it was my turn to take care of him. Poor little guy. I sat with him in the bathroom, holding him on my knee as I ran a hot shower to fill the room with steam. Sitting up, he could breathe a little easier. I pressed my cheek to his head.

"How're you doin', big fella?" I asked.

He leaned tiredly against me in response, his breathing noisy as he tried to pull air into his stuffed little nose.

Sitting there in that weird space between awake and asleep, I had too much time to think. Tomorrow night would be the fourth portal I'd given Carly. The fourth of five. If she didn't return then, she would have to wait until the final portal, nearly ten months from now. It would mean that her baby was still too sick to leave the hospital.

Or it would mean something had gone terribly, irrevocably wrong. That was the worry that kept me awake at night.

John Paul was finally asleep in my arms. Getting quietly to my feet, I left the sticky, hot bathroom and carried him down the hallway into his room, where I lowered him gently into the crib.

"Hunter?"

I turned at the whisper of my name from John Paul's dark doorway. Carly stood there, barely visible, and I shut my eyes, offering a silent word of thanks to the universe. She was a day early, which made no sense, but at that moment, I didn't care. She was home.

Walking across the room to the hall, I pressed my finger to my lips to keep her quiet. I shut the door behind me, then wrapped my arms around her. She was damp, her hair sticky with salt, her clothes cold beneath my arms. Had I messed up her landing site?

"I'm so relieved," I said, and only then realized she had no baby with her. Maybe she'd already put her in the crib that had been waiting for her for weeks. I stepped back. "Where is she?" I asked, worried. "Where's your baby?"

She pressed her hand to her mouth as if holding in a cry. "It's a long, long story," she said. "Just tell me the date, Hunter. Tell me what year it is."

"Nineteen seventy."

"Thank God," she said, her body sagging with relief. "Let's wake Patti up and I'll tell you everything."

62

Carly

"This is simply unbelievable," Patti said, when I'd told them about my time in 2013. We sat in the living room, talking by lamplight. I'd changed into dry clothes—old jeans and a sweatshirt I hadn't seen in months—and I sat curled up on the sofa, hugging my knees against my chest. I couldn't get warm. I felt shredded in a million pieces, happy to be home with my family, but aching with the knowledge that I would never see my daughter again. Her framed picture rested on the coffee table in front of me. Patti and Hunter hadn't reacted to it quite the way I'd expected. Patti simply said that Joanna looked like pictures of our mother at that age, and Hunter barely glanced at the photograph. He was too upset with himself that he'd "screwed up," as he said, and I'd been unable to return to my infant Joanna. He was horrified at the position he'd put me in, although I tried to reassure him that I didn't blame him. I knew I hadn't quite eased his guilt. Time travel was, if anything, an inexact science.

"Let's focus on the fact that Joe's coming home," Patti said, trying to lift Hunter's and my somber moods. "It's such a miracle! We have to figure out how to tell the government to change his status, don't we? They have him as dead. We have to tell them to—"

I shook my head.

"Don't tamper," Hunter and I said at the same time.

"I've done enough tampering already," I said wearily. "Now we just have to wait. He'll be home, and he's going to need our help." We had to get through two and a half years before Joe would be free. It was agonizing to think about what he was going through right now while the three of us sat, safe and secure, in the house. "I should go back to work," I said, without enthusiasm. "I should move back to Raleigh to see if I can get my old PT job back." I closed my eyes, suddenly exhausted. It was too much to think about right now.

Patti moved from her seat near the fireplace to the sofa. She sat next to me, her arm around my shoulders. "I know it must have killed you to leave her," she said, nodding toward the photograph. "To leave Joanna. But I'm so glad you didn't stay there." She pressed her temple to mine. "I know that's really selfish of me, but I couldn't stand it if you never came back and we had no idea what happened to you."

I looked at the photograph on the coffee table. "She printed that picture for me." I smiled to myself, remembering how I'd had to coerce Joanna into making the print. I studied her twelve-year-old face, trying to accept the fact that she would not even exist for another thirty-one years.

"You're home," Patti said. "That's all that matters."

I gave her a weak smile, the best I could manage. Patti would never be able to understand that yes, I was home, but I wasn't the same Carly I'd been before. I would never be that woman again. The new Carly came with a huge hole in her heart. I would most likely go on to be a good physical therapist, a loving wife, a supportive sister and sister-in-law. Perhaps I'd even have more children down the road. But no matter what the decades held for me, I knew this one truth: I would grieve my daughter for the rest of my life.

63

FEBRUARY 1973

TRAVIS AIR FORCE BASE, CALIFORNIA

I waited on the tarmac with a thousand other people. Some of them waved small American flags and WELCOME HOME and GOD BLESS YOU! signs, and on the roof of the building behind us, several men held an enormous sign that read THANKS! WELCOME HOME! Most of the people were simply proud and excited Americans, overjoyed that our POWs were finally coming home. But some of them were like me: family members who couldn't wait to wrap their arms around their husbands and fathers. We had our own small roped-off area as we waited excitedly for the plane to arrive from the Philippines. I stood with my hands folded in front of me, biting my lip, my entire body shivering with anticipation in the still, gray air.

I heard chatter from some of the other family members around me. Many of them had gotten to know each other during the years their men had been imprisoned. They'd supported one another. Become friends. Had regular calls from the army or air force or navy with reports on the efforts to release the prisoners.

I didn't know the other families, though. I never received those calls from the army. My case was unique. My husband had been dead to everyone, and I'd lived the last few years in a state of suspended animation, knowing what no one else knew: Joe Sears was alive. Occasionally I'd worry, wondering if that park ranger had been wrong and Joe really *had* been killed in Pleiku. Maybe his name really *did* belong on the wall that had yet to be dreamed up, much less built. But I believed she was right. I felt a connection to Joe; he was alive. Some might have said I was fantasizing, but who was to say what was possible? I'd traveled through time. To me now, everything seemed possible.

I'd been in the kitchen of our Nags Head house alone when the call finally came, and I managed to walk three steps to a chair before my knees gave out. I faked shock and surprise when the caller told me about the clerical error that had labeled Joe as "deceased." I faked surprise, but I didn't have to fake my joyful tears.

As we waited those long two and a half years for the war to end, though, we *did* have a genuine shock: Myra Poole appeared at our door one evening in 1971. John Paul was asleep and Patti, Hunter, and I were watching TV. Hunter answered her knock and there she stood, sixty-eight years old and on her fifth trip—the trip she knew would be her last.

Hunter yelped with joy, wrapping his arms around her, nearly lifting her off the floor. He brought her into the living room and she sat next to him on the couch, holding his hand in both of hers as she told us her reason for taking that final fifth trip.

"I've done everything I ever wanted to do professionally," she said. "I knew my Temporal Solutions staff could carry on without me." She looked at Hunter with more affection than I'd ever seen in her face. "I realized I just didn't want to live the rest of my life without my son."

"Here they come!" The man next to me interrupted my thoughts as he pointed toward the huge air force medevac plane taxiing toward us across the tarmac. I joined in the cheering, my heart pounding in my throat. Near me, I saw a teenaged boy twist a silver POW bracelet anxiously around and around on his wrist. I looked down at my own silver bracelet, Joe's name engraved on the surface. I couldn't wait to take it off. On my right wrist, I wore the bracelet of rubber bands Joanna had made for me. Reminders of two beloved people who had been lost to me for the past three years.

Until today.

The plane came to a stop and the roar of the crowd intensified around me as the door opened. A few men attached a long ramp to the doorway, and after a few minutes, a soldier stepped from the plane and waved to the crowd. I joined in the wild applause as he walked down the ramp. He shook hands with a couple of officers and then greeted his family—his wife and three children, who wrapped their arms around his waist and legs, nearly toppling him over.

I pressed my lips together, my eyes already beginning to fill.

Then a second soldier exited the door. He saluted before jogging down the ramp as if to demonstrate he was perfectly fine, not a care in the world. I didn't see who greeted him because Joe's name was announced next—*Captain Joseph Michael Sears*—and I leaned forward, trying to peer into the dark interior of the plane. He stood at the top of the ramp and for a disorienting moment, I didn't recognize him. His dress uniform couldn't mask his skeletal thinness. I watched him blink against the daylight, but then he smiled his wide Joey smile at the cheering crowd, holding the railing as he descended the ramp. I broke free from the other families to run across the tarmac toward the plane, my arms outstretched, tears flying from my cheeks, and I knew the moment he spotted me because his smile turned into a grin and his pace quickened on the ramp. He shook the hands of the waiting officers, then walked toward me, arms wide, his blue eyes glassy with tears.

Hands on my shoulders, he pulled me close. "Hey, girl," he said softly into my hair.

I wrapped my arms around him, feeling the sharp line of his jaw against my cheek, the bones of his shoulder blades beneath my hands. He held me in a tight, breath-stealing embrace, and I knew in that moment that I'd made the right choice. I would always be there for him. I'd help him heal. No matter how difficult the story he had to tell, I'd be strong enough to listen.

And when he was ready to hear it, I would have a story to tell him as well.

EPILOGUE

Carly

JUNE 2022
NAGS HEAD

I sweep the sand off the old wooden floor of the wrap-around porch. We had a good storm last night and I think the wind blew half the beach onto the porch and steps. Today, though, is glorious. Clear Carolina blue sky. Water the color of jade. The waves are smooth as glass as they make their unhurried way toward shore, and the storm seems to have cleared the humidity from the air.

Although it is not quite nine, a few sunbathers already dot the beach along with a handful of striped umbrellas and one of those cabana things. I don't like the cabanas. I think they mess up the view. One of my sons put a cabana up when he and his family visited last year and I bit my tongue. I realize it's just one more change I have to get used to. Time marches on.

I'm nearly done sweeping when I notice a girl walking on the beach near the water's edge. She holds the leashes of two dogs, one gold, the other brown. I stand still for a moment to watch her, a sweet wistfulness filling my chest. So long ago, I think. A lifetime ago.

The girl turns away from the water and slowly begins crossing the sand in the direction of the house. I watch her, suddenly breathless. As she grows closer, I see that she's more woman than girl. She's barefoot and wears a straw hat and sunglasses. A long, gauzy white shirt covers a two-piece bathing suit. The dogs are a golden retriever and a chocolate Lab.

For a second, my heart literally stops beating. "Oh my God," I whisper. I lean the broom against the porch railing.

The young woman is closer now. Close enough that I can see her hesitant smile as she stops walking. She speaks as I rush barefoot down the porch steps.

"Carly?" she calls, a hand pressed to her mouth. "Is that really you?"

I hurry across the sand to reach her, unable to speak myself. Poppy and Jobs snake around my legs as I pull my daughter into my arms. I feel her hesitate before her own arms lock across my back. Then I'm not sure which of us is holding the other tighter. As I finally pull away, my head knocks her hat askew and we both laugh. She takes the hat off to reveal long, platinum hair and she slips her sunglasses from her dark eyes to the top of her head. I hold her by her shoulders to study her beautiful face. For her, it's been nine years. For me, it's been half a century. I begin to cry.

"Oh, Joanna," I say. They seem to be the only words I can get out.

"I was afraid you wouldn't still be here," she says. "I was afraid I'd be too late."

I smile through my tears. "You thought I'd be dead, you mean."

Her expression sobers. Slowly, she reaches out to touch my cheek with a tenderness that nearly undoes me. "I just didn't want to be too late," she says.

I dry my cheeks with my fingertips. Take her hand. "Come sit with me," I say.

We walk together toward the porch, the dogs—they must be about ten years old by now—are calm at her side. Joanna and I are the same height, despite the fact that I've lost an inch or so over the years. We sit down on the broad porch steps, so close our bare arms touch. Jobs immediately lies down at the foot of the steps but Poppy rests her big head on my knees.

There's so much I want to say to this girl. This woman. I've talked to her often in my mind over the years. I never thought I'd have the chance to say it all out loud.

"Do your parents know you're here?" I ask.

She shakes her head. A strand of her pale blond hair catches on my bare shoulder. "I'm with some friends from school," she says. "I go to Rutgers. My parents know I'm in the Outer Banks, but they don't know—they have no idea—*you're* here." She picks at the rim of the straw hat on her lap. "They never really believed everything I told them about you. I wasn't sure *I* believed you, either." She offers me a small smile. "All these years, I couldn't wait to come to Nags Head to see if you'd really be here. I'm so glad you showed me where you live."

I showed her where I lived? I had no memory of that, but it didn't matter. I rest my hand on Poppy's big head, trying to think of how to begin. How to say what I've long wanted to say to my daughter. "I'm so sorry, Joanna," I tell her. "I should never have shown up in your life the way I did, with all the lies and the—"

She raises a hand in the air to stop me. "I'm so glad you did," she says. "And if everything you told me is true, I think I would have done the same thing." She slips her sunglasses on again. "I've thought about it a lot," she says. "You couldn't tell us—Mom and Dad and me—the truth, so I don't think you had a choice. And you wanted to get to know me. How else could you have done it? I'm glad you wanted to get to know me." Her voice suddenly sounds small and young. My little girl.

I dig my hands into the thick fur of Poppy's neck. Her muzzle is white. I can't believe I'm touching this dog. This child. It doesn't seem possible. Yet very little from that period of my life seems possible.

"You're very understanding, Joanna," I say. How I love saying her name aloud!

She sighs. "I admit I was mad at you at first," she says. "Mad and confused . . . I'm still pretty confused, actually," she says. "I mean . . . how did you do it? Travel through time? When you jumped off the tree house railing . . . Oh my God!" She presses her hands to the sides of her head. "I almost had a heart attack! But you didn't end up splattered on the ground. That's when I knew you must have been telling me the truth, as crazy as it sounded." She looks down at our hands, mine on Poppy's head, hers on the rim of her hat. Her hands are smooth, her nails pink. My hands are those of a seventy-nine-year-old woman who has spent too much time in the sun.

"My parents thought I had a bad dream or was sleep-walking or something." She digs her bare feet deep into the sand at the bottom of the steps. "We turned on the floodlights in the yard and of course you weren't there. I looked everywhere. Behind the bushes and—everywhere—but you'd really, truly disappeared into thin air. And then I knew you had to be telling the truth. I wouldn't shut up about it. I told my parents everything you said, about my father being in Vietnam and they said that was impossible, that Vietnam was way too long ago, and I told them how you never meant to leave me in the hospital and . . ." She shakes her head. "They said they were going to take me to a shrink, so I stopped talking about it. I never even told my friends because I was afraid . . . I knew no one would believe me. And I missed you." She glanced at me. "I'd just found out you were my birth mother and then all of a sudden you were gone."

"I felt so terrible that night, putting you through that," I say. "But I had to step off the railing at a certain time and I couldn't help that you were right there." I touch her bare arm. "I hated that I had to lie to you and your family so much."

She looks away from me toward the ocean, her sun-glasses reflecting the waves and sky. "If you'd told us the truth," she says, "my father would have had you locked up. He thought there was something really off about you from the beginning." She smiles at me. "You came into my life just when I needed a . . . a friend. I was at a new school and everything. I missed you when you . . . disappeared. But I felt . . . I *still* feel . . . lucky I had the chance to know you." She puts her arm around my shoulders, very gently, and I can tell she thinks of me as an old lady who needs to be handled with care. She should see me do the shoulder stand in my yoga class. Suddenly, I laugh.

"What's so funny?" she asks.

"I remember your mother's downward dog tattoo," I say. "I had no idea what it was. Now I do it every Monday, Wednesday, and Friday. I think of your mom every single time."

She leans away to study my face, a smile on her lips. "You do yoga?" she asks.

I nod. It's the gentle class with other septuagenarians, but I don't need to mention that.

Joanna sobers. "It must have been hard for you, being around my mother," she says. "Knowing I was . . . I guess you must have felt like I was really yours and you had to watch her . . . I don't know, take your place."

"It *was* hard," I agree, "but it was also reassuring to me to know how much you were loved."

Joanna seems to take this in as she looks toward the water. "You *were* a little strange," she says with a smile. "Kind of out of it . . . like you'd been living under a rock or something."

I chuckle. "Everything was so different from 1970," I say. "I was a little lost." I look down at Poppy's beautiful huge brown eyes. "How did you end up with Poppy?" I ask.

"Oh, after you left, Mrs. Corman from the Sleeping Dog Inn called my mother," she says. "She said she couldn't manage having a dog right then and was there a chance we'd take her. Mom said yes." Joanna bends over to hug Poppy, who licks her ear. "I was going to change her name to Stevie after you-know-who, but decided that would confuse her." She grins, then adds, "I was such a nerdy kid."

"A brilliant kid," I correct her.

She smiles at me. It's a radiant smile; there's no other word for it. I feel a sort of serenity coming from her. I feel forgiveness. I feel love.

"Thank you for finding me," I say.

She digs her feet even deeper into the sand and lets out a sigh. "It's not the sort of 'birth mother story' I can ever tell my friends . . . needless to say," she says, "but I'm glad I experienced it." She looks down at my wrist and I watch her eyes widen when she sees the blue and green bracelet I still wear. "Is that   Did *I* make that?"

I touch the bracelet. "I wear it nearly every day," I say, "though I'm very careful with it. I started having problems with some of the bands breaking a few years after you made it for me. So I put it away and waited until that loom became popular and then I found a young girl in the middle school here to repair it for me." I hold up my wrist to admire the bracelet. "She's grown now, but every time a band breaks, I ship it off to her and she fixes it for me."

She looks at me openmouthed. "That's incredible," she says.

I look toward the beach again. The jade-colored water. There is so much I still want to say to her. I want to tell her about her two brothers. Her three cousins. Her aunt Patti. And of course her late Uncle Hunter, without whom she would not even exist. Now is not the time to weigh her down with all of that, though. Instead, I get to my feet and reach for her hand.

"Come on, sweet girl," I say, giving her fingers a gentle squeeze as I lead her and the dogs up the stairs to the porch. "It's time for you to meet your father."

Acknowledgments

The story of *The Dream Daughter* has been in my mind in one form or another for many years, but I needed the stars to align perfectly before I was ready to write it. It was unnerving to write something so different from my previous twenty-five books, yet I was confident all along that I was still writing a story that was—as my UK editor, Wayne Brookes, describes it—"vintage Diane Chamberlain." I don't ever recall having more fun writing a book. I loved the mind-twistiness of it. The puzzle and the challenge. Occasionally my head hurt as I juggled calendars from different eras. At other times, I laughed out loud with the sheer joy of creating a story so complex.

I have many people to thank for their help in bringing *The Dream Daughter* to life. First is my partner, John Pagliuca, who helped me think through plot and structure over many months and who provided encouragement when I was afraid I might be going off the deep end with my story.

My brainstorming friends have had to listen to some version of this book for years. For their help, I'm grateful to fellow authors Mary Kay Andrews, Katy Munger, Sarah Shaber, Alexandra Sokoloff, Brenda Witchger, and especially

Margaret Maron, who read a draft of the book and spurred me on with her enthusiastic response to the story. Similarly, my sister, Joann Scanlon, read the story with her usual eye to detail. Their encouragement was just what I needed.

Special thanks to fellow author Therese Fowler, for her careful and thoughtful reading of a late draft of the book. Therese's input was invaluable.

Sharon Miglarese contributed her knowledge and expertise as a NICU nurse by helping me understand what Carly and Joanna would experience during their months in the hospital. My own former career as a perinatal social worker helped in that regard as well, but so much has changed in the decades since I worked in a hospital that I could never have written those scenes without Sharon's help.

It's been many years since I lived in the Northeast, so I'm grateful to David and Tricia Tait, Adele Stavis, and my agent, Susan Ginsburg, for sharing their knowledge of New York City with me. I'm also grateful to Tyler and David Farrand for inviting John and me to stay in their beautiful home in Summit, New Jersey, thus giving me a clear picture of Joanna's lovely neighborhood.

A few other people shared their thoughts, suggestions, and experiences with me as I wrote *The Dream Daughter*. I'm particularly indebted to my neighbor and dear friend David Samuels for sharing so much of his experience and knowledge as a Vietnam veteran. His wife, Elizabeth, was also a great support. My stepdaughter, Caitlin Campbell, contributed the name "Stir Crazy Mamas" for Carly's online support group, and Gary Fuller and Buzzy Porter helped me think through some elements of time travel. Readers on my "Diane Chamberlain Readers Page" on Facebook helped by contributing character names, sharing memories of the various eras in the story, and best of all, sending me baby pictures so I could really imagine Baby Joanna.

As usual, my assistant and research aide, Kathy Williamson, was a huge help throughout the writing of *The Dream Daughter*. Kathy's a whiz at finding any information I need to create my story, and she willingly takes on any task I need help with, from the sophisticated to the mundane. I'm grateful for her help and expertise.

My agent, the awesome Susan Ginsburg, not only supported the writing of *The Dream Daughter* but she also read an early draft and offered suggestions to make the story richer. I'm honored to call Susan both agent and friend. Thanks also to the rest of the staff at Writers House for their hard work on behalf of my books. Special thanks to Stacy Testa, Peggy Boulos Smith, Natalie Medina, and Maja Nikolic.

Thank you to my editor, Jen Enderlin, for taking a chance on *The Dream Daughter*. Jen barely batted an eye when I said I wanted to write a story that contained time travel and her unbridled enthusiasm for the finished manuscript was a welcome relief. Jen can see things in my work that I'm too close to see. Her perspective and suggestions are always right on and I'm lucky I get to work with her.

My publicist at St. Martin's, Katie Bassel, once again deserves special thanks. Katie's a master at setting up events and book tours and I'd be lost—quite literally—without her.

I'm also grateful to the rest of the folks at St. Martin's who get my books into the hands of my readers. Thank you to Sally Richardson, Brant Janeway, Erica Martirano, Jeff Dodes, Lisa Senz, Kim Ludlam, Nancy Sheppard, Malati Chavali, Jonathan Hollingsworth, Nancy Sheppard, Anne Marie Tallberg, Tracey Guest, Olga Grlic, Lisa Davis, Rachel Diebel, and everyone in the Broadway and Fifth Avenue sales department.

My UK editor, Wayne Brookes at Pan Macmillan, is always a joy to work with. I'm grateful for his constant support and all the behind-the-scenes work he—and everyone else at Pan Macmillan—do to get my books into the hands of my UK readers.

Finally, thank you to my readers around the world. Through your kind words and enthusiasm, you always encourage me to write the story that entices me. I hope you've enjoyed this trip through time with *The Dream Daughter*.

OUT NOW

Pretending to Dance

Diane Chamberlain

When the pretending ends, the lying begins . . .

It's the summer of 1990 and fourteen-year-old Molly Arnette lives with her extended family on one hundred acres in the Blue Ridge Mountains. The summer seems idyllic at first. The mountains are Molly's playground and she's well loved by her father, a therapist famous for books he's written about a method called 'Pretend Therapy'; her adoptive mother, who has raised Molly as her own; and Amalia, her birth mother who also lives on the family land. The adults in Molly's life have created a safe and secure world for her to grow up in. But Molly's security begins to crumble as she becomes aware of a plan taking shape in her extended family – a plan she can't stop and that threatens to turn her idyllic summer into a nightmare.

Pretending to Dance is a fascinating and deftly woven novel that reveals the devastating power of secrets.

OUT NOW

The Silent Sister

Diane Chamberlain

What if everything you believed turned out to be a lie?

Riley MacPherson is returning to her childhood home in North Carolina, a place that holds cherished memories. While clearing out the house she finds a box of old newspaper articles – and a shocking family secret begins to unravel.

Riley has spent her whole life believing that her older sister Lisa died tragically as a teenager. But now she's starting to uncover the truth: her life has been built on a foundation of lies, told by everyone she loved. Lisa is alive. Alive and living under a new identity. But why exactly was she on the run all those years ago, and what secrets are being kept now?

As Riley tries to separate reality from fiction, her discoveries call into question everything she thought she knew about her family. Can she find the strength inside herself to decide her future?

Incredibly gripping and emotionally powerful,
The Silent Sister is perfect for fans of Jodi Picoult
and Liane Moriarty.

A companion short story featuring Riley,
The Broken String, is available in ebook.

OUT NOW

Necessary Lies

Diane Chamberlain

The best intentions expose the darkest secrets . . .

North Carolina, 1960. Newly-wed Jane Forrester, fresh
out of university, is seeking what most other women have
shunned: a career.

But life as a social worker is far from what she expected.
Out amongst the rural tobacco fields of Grace County, Jane
encounters a world of extreme poverty that is far removed
from the middle-class life she has grown up with.

But worse is still to come. Working with the Hart family
and their fifteen-year-old daughter Ivy, it's not long before
Jane uncovers a shocking secret, and is thrust into a moral
dilemma that puts her career on the line, threatens to dis-
solve her marriage, and ultimately, determines the fate of
Ivy and her family forever.

Soon Jane is forced to take drastic action, and before
long, there is no turning back.

A companion short story,
The First Lie, is available in ebook.